"This is a story to which all Marines can easily relate. The bonds of friendship and their shared loyalty to Corps and country link the lives of Manny and Kenny in ways very familiar to Marines, and indeed, all members of the Armed Force."

—*Col Christopher J. Gunther, USMC (Ret)*

"Brad Gates belongs to that class of strictly upright, honest, and true men, of whom Marines afford so many noble examples. A personal mentor and role model since serving under him at the Basic School, I am a better man for my association with Brad Gates. *Two Good Men* captures the essence of what is truly great about our nation—young men and their families honorably and quietly bearing the heavy burden of service in defense of our nation's values and democratic principles."

—*The Honorable James M. Byrne, 8th Deputy Secretary of Veterans Affairs Veteran Marine*

"The personal stories of four friends and their families are rendered epic by the skilled prose of Mr. Gates, who intertwines the families' real-life events with scenes from Marine Corps' recruits training, Vietnam battles, captivity and hospital stay, and finally, graduation. Love rules above all. A pleasure to read also for those who have no prior direct experience of the Marine Corps."

—*Maria Francesca Nespoli Carlberg, Congressional Liaison, Embassy of Italy in Washington, DC*

Two Good Men

by Bradley Gates

© Copyright 2022 Bradley Gates

ISBN 978-1-64663-702-7

Published by

 köehlerbooks™

3705 Shore Drive
Virginia Beach, VA 23455
800-435-4811
www.koehlerbooks.com

Two *Good* Men

★——— BRAD GATES ———★

VIRGINIA BEACH
CAPE CHARLES

This book is dedicated to my wife and children, and all the good men and women with whom I was honored to serve.

TABLE OF CONTENTS

CHAPTER ONE

THE FRIENDSHIP BEGINS

Oceanside, California

ROY SMITH WAS NOT easily intimidated. The retired Marine Corps first sergeant had been in more than his share of tough situations, but today would be the beginning of the toughest challenge of his life. Today the old Marine was arriving in Oceanside, California, to pick up his two grandchildren, Manny and Cindy, and his daughter-in-law, Maria. Tomorrow the three of them would accompany him back to Colorado to live with him. It was a move that no one was very comfortable with, but Roy and Maria believed it was necessary.

Seven-year-old Manny picked the baseball out of the pocket of his glove and threw it back in. He picked it out and threw it back again and again as he mindlessly gazed out the window.

Maria Smith well understood the nervousness of her children. She, too, was concerned over the move they were about to make, but deep in her heart Maria knew that staying in Oceanside would only sustain her family's anguish; they must start healing soon. It had been almost four months since that fateful day when the green sedan arrived in front of her house.

For just an instant, her heart had pounded with joy as she saw the green-uniformed man get out of the car. Maria hoped that it was her husband, Sergeant Charles Smith, a Marine serving in Korea, coming home unexpectedly. But her moment of hope was soon shattered when the unfamiliar Marine approached the house to deliver the devastating news that Sergeant Smith had been killed in action.

"I don't want to go away," said five-year-old Cindy. "How will Daddy know where we are when he comes home?"

Even at his young age, Manny saw the look on his mother's face and recognized her pain and frustration that Cindy was not yet able to understand that her daddy was never coming home. Manny stepped beside his little sister and put his arm around her. "You don't have to worry about that, Cindy. Daddy will always know where the three of us are. Besides, we will be at Pappy Smith's, and Daddy knows where that is."

"I don't want to go live with Pappy Smith. I don't like Pappy Smith."

Maria was quick to respond this time. "Cindy, you should not say that. You just don't know him very well. Pappy Smith is your daddy's daddy, and Pappy Smith loves you very much. That's the reason we're going to live with him in Colorado."

After reassuring her daughter, Maria took a deep breath to reassure herself. There was a time when Maria had been uncertain about her feelings toward her father-in-law. But after Charlie was killed in Korea, his father showed up again without warning. He embraced Maria and cried unashamedly over the loss of his only son. Any uncertain feelings vanished as Maria and her father-in-law grieved the loss of their Charlie. Before returning to Colorado a couple days later, Roy told Maria that he would love to have her and the children come live with him. At first Maria said she could not; her family had already lost enough without being forced to leave everything and everyone they knew behind. But as time went on and she and her children grieved, Maria realized that it might be best for them all to get away.

"I think he's here," Manny said.

Little Cindy ran to the window beside her brother. "Here he comes," she said with delight, caught up in her brother's enthusiasm and forgetting what she had just said.

Walking up the sidewalk, Pappy Smith saw his only grandchildren waving at him through the window. He had been a career Marine and, like most Marines, liked to think he was still pretty tough; but now the old Marine could not hide the emotion, and tears rolled down his cheeks.

Meeting his grandfather on the porch, Manny asked, "What's the matter, Pappy Smith? Why are you crying?"

But their grandfather could say nothing as he went to one knee to hug the kids.

"Pappy is crying because he's so happy to see you," Maria explained.

With that, Pappy stood. "I'm very happy to see you also, Maria."

Maria went to her father-in-law and embraced him, both thinking of Charlie.

"I know I told you this on the phone, Maria, but I just have to tell you again how happy I am that you and the kids are coming to Colorado with me. I know it's a big decision, but in the long run, I think it will be best."

"I know, Dad. It will take some adjusting, but I wouldn't do it if I didn't think it would be better for Manny and Cindy as they grow up. I'm going to miss being near my family in San Diego, but we'll return for visits every year."

"How are your aunt and uncle?"

"They're well, thank you. They're coming over later and bringing dinner from the restaurant."

As the kids chattered at their grandfather, Maria thought of her aunt and uncle, Manuel and Carmella Rivera, who had raised her. Carmella's sister died of complications during Maria's birth. Her father was unable to maintain his job and care for Maria, so Carmella and Manuel took over. The sorrow Maria felt at not having a mother and father was more than balanced by the love and care she received from her aunt and uncle. Maria had been working in the Riveras' restaurant in San Diego when she first met Charlie.

"Maria, may the kids and I go for an ice cream cone?"

He had not said anything to the kids before mentioning it to their mother, but their loud cheers of support made it very obvious how much they liked the idea.

"You really don't have to do that, Dad."

"I know I don't have to, but I want some myself, and we'll only get one scoop each. I'm looking forward to the feast I know Manuel and Carmella will bring over for supper."

Maria started to say that she would go along but then decided it would be best if the trio went without her. They needed time to bond. Besides, she still had some packing to do before they left for Colorado the next morning. She had been at it all week, but so many people stopped to say goodbye that she hadn't gotten to everything she wanted to do.

Her most frequent visitor had been Aunt Carmella, who was devastated when Maria announced she was thinking of going to Colorado. Although Carmella totally understood the rationale behind Maria's decision, that did not make it any less painful.

There was a knock at the door, and Maria greeted her aunt and uncle with a warm smile and hug.

"Where are the little ones?" were Uncle Manuel's first words.

"Grandfather Smith arrived and took them for an ice cream cone. They should be back any minute now."

"I hope they don't eat too much ice cream and don't want any of the food we brought for dinner."

Maria nodded. "Well, I thought of that but decided I was most concerned about them getting to know their grandfather. It will be a long trip to Colorado, and I want them to be comfortable around him. Besides, I don't ever remember Manny having trouble with his appetite when it comes to your enchiladas."

Manuel laughed out loud as a smile came over his wife's face. It pleased Manuel also, that his namesake had a healthy appetite. Young boys did not grow up big and strong without one.

"I'll go to the car and bring the food in while you ladies set the table."

"It won't seem right not coming here each week to visit you and the kids."

"Aunt Carmella, please don't speak like that when the kids are around," Maria murmured, touching her aunt's arm gently. "I want them to be excited and looking forward to the move to Colorado."

Carmella turned and took a few steps away, her face in her hands. She could not help herself. Even after a month of mental preparation, she could not bear the thought of Maria and the children living so far away. She was still struggling to cope with Charlie's death.

"You're right, dear, and I will do my best to keep a stiff upper lip."

Manuel had his arms full of food as the kids and their grandfather pulled up in his car.

"Hey, Uncle Manny," yelled his seven-year-old namesake. "Did you bring any food for anyone else? I can eat all that myself."

Manuel put the two boxes down as the kids scampered over for their traditional hug. Behind them came their grandfather, swinging a bag with a half gallon of ice cream. They had decided on this compromise to ensure that little Manny could fully enjoy the goodbye feast.

"It's good to see you, Manuel. You're looking good."

"Thank you. It's good to see you too, First Sergeant."

Pappy had been called that so many times in the past that he didn't even notice. However, the greeting didn't elude the tuned-in little ears of Manny.

"Uncle Manuel, what did you call Pappy Smith?"

"Your grandfather was a Marine, just like your father."

Pappy Smith stepped in before the conversation could get too involved. "We have lots of time to talk all about it, Manny. But right now, let's go chow down on some of your uncle Manuel and aunt Carmella's good cooking."

"What is 'chow down'?" Cindy asked.

Manny was not sure what to think as the two old men laughed in unison, leaving Cindy's query unanswered. Pappy Smith swept her up in his arms and said to Manny, "If you're hoping to eat some of that feast, young man, you should help your uncle carry those boxes."

Without a peep, Manny did as he was told, and they all joined the ladies inside.

Pappy put Cindy down so she could run to Aunt Carmella, then followed to shake Carmella's extended hand.

"How have you been, Roy?"

"I'm fine, Carmella. It's good to see you."

He knew she held no personal animosity toward him, but she was clearly not happy to see this day arrive.

After they completed their courteous handshake, Pappy Smith said to his grandson, "When you meet a lady, Manny, wait for her to extend her hand to you. The lady should initiate the handshake if she cares to do so."

"What if she doesn't want to shake hands?" Manny asked, eager to soak in his grandfather's wisdom.

"Then you just smile and nod your head politely."

"We should be able to eat in just a few minutes. You kids take Pappy Smith and wash up with him," Maria directed them.

After they'd all sat down and the blessing was completed, Pappy Smith again expressed his enthusiasm for the bountiful meal before them. "Okay, kids, finally we get to stop waiting and chow down!"

"I get it. 'Chow down' means eat," Manny said. Cindy's mouth opened in a round O of realization.

"That's right, Manny, but it means a little more than just eat. It means to eat a lot of food with a lot of enthusiasm because it is so good."

"Well, I always chow down when Aunt Carmella and Uncle Manuel make the food. Especially enchiladas."

Carmella was overwhelmed with happiness that soon gave way to despair because this precious little man was leaving town in the morning. To avoid showing any sign of her sorrow, Carmella found herself saying what Maria hoped she would say. "It's going to be so exciting going to Colorado to live. I've always wanted to go to Colorado."

"Why don't you come with us?" asked Cindy.

Uncle Manuel entered the conversation to relieve his wife; it was obvious that she was having a bad time. "Don't you worry, Cindy. Aunt Carmella and I are already making plans to come and visit you in Lower Vale."

"And you'll bring lots of food, won't you?" chirped Manny.

"Of course we will" came the reply in unison.

Most of the conversation at the supper table that evening was about Colorado in general, and Lower Vale in particular, as the four adults attempted to discreetly prepare the children for the long trip ahead.

Pappy Smith asked Maria if she thought it would be okay to drive north along the coast of California before they headed east to Colorado.

"That will make the trip a little longer, but I know the kids and I would love to see the northern part of California," Maria said.

"That's great. I thought we could go as far as San Francisco and then head east to the Yosemite area. I hear it's really beautiful there."

"Oh my! You children are so lucky to have an opportunity to make this trip and see all the beautiful sights along the way. It will be wonderful!" Carmella enthused. Uncle Manny nodded and added, "When you cross the Rockies, I expect that there will be snow."

"I guarantee we will see snow on the mountaintops," Pappy Smith confirmed. "And before much longer we may see a lot of frost, and then snow, in Lower Vale. By next year this time, Maria, I bet that you and the kids will all be great skiers."

"Well, I'm looking forward to learning to ski, as long as the snow is not too cold." Maria grinned as if she were joking, but she wasn't.

"Daddy told me a couple times that he liked the snow, so I bet I'll like it too."

"Me too!"

"I'm sure you will," Maria said.

"I saw that your grandfather brought home some ice cream from the store. Would anyone like some ice cream for dessert?" Carmella asked the room.

Uncle Manuel responded, "I'm too full, but I bet Manny will have some."

"Manny, you really ate a lot for supper. Maybe you're too full for ice cream," Maria said.

"No, I'm not. I could eat a big bowl."

"Try to never let your ego determine your actions," his grandfather cautioned. "Let your brain tell you what is best."

Manny was not sure what Pappy Smith meant, but he did detect the firmness in his grandfather's voice and hung his head a little.

"Manny, I'm not scolding you. I just want you to learn that your ego doesn't always give the best advice."

"Your pappy is right, Manny," added Uncle Manuel. "If you want some ice cream, you may have some. But you shouldn't eat the ice cream only because you think that we expect you to eat it."

"I guess I'm not that hungry." He leaned back and patted his stomach, a little relieved.

"Well, I don't know about anyone else, but I'm really tired and ready for a little shut-eye," said Pappy Smith. He knew that it would be a hard night for Maria, the children, and her aunt and uncle as they said their goodbyes. Before he went up the stairs, he went to the Riveras and added, "I think you know that I will take good care of them. And I fully expect to see your car pull in our driveway in Lower Vale one day next summer."

Carmella could say nothing, but her husband replied, "You can count on it, First Sergeant."

The tough old retired Marine was glad to avoid the tearful goodbye. Not much later, he heard the kids thunder upstairs to get ready for bed. However, Pappy Smith had not slept much the past couple of days in anticipation of seeing Maria and the kids, so he was beat and fell sound asleep soon after.

The floodgates opened as Aunt Carmella held little Cindy close to her and cried out loud. However, she quickly regained her composure and told both of the children how much she loved them.

After Cindy and Manny were up in their beds, Manuel asked Maria, "What do you think you'll do about Manny's schooling in the fall?"

The young boy had not gone back to school after the third week in April when they'd learned about his father's death.

"I think I'll have him repeat second grade. He was one of the youngest in his class, so maybe it would be good to have him start again. And I want to find out what the lady living next to us is going to do with her son."

"Did your father-in-law say anything about the boy?"

"We really didn't get a chance to talk about him."

The boy they were talking about was seven-year-old Kenny Reynolds, who lived with his mother in the house next to Pappy Smith in Lower Vale. It was a tragic coincidence that Kenny was the same age as Manny and his father had been killed two weeks earlier than Charlie. Everybody was hoping that the two boys would become friends and help each other get through this terrible ordeal.

"I hope and pray that Manny and that little boy will be good for each other."

"I do too, Aunt Carmella. That's one of the main reasons we're going to Colorado. You know I'm not going for the snow."

Her aunt and uncle smiled as they finished cleaning up. Then the moment they all dreaded was finally at hand. Even Uncle Manuel cried as the three of them said their goodbyes.

"I love you," whispered Maria after the Riveras as their car rolled down the street, into the night.

She took a pill to help her sleep, but it did little good. Sound sleep had eluded Maria since Charlie's death. Many nights she cursed the Marine Corps for taking her beloved husband away from her, but often times she found herself sorry for her anger. She loved Charlie, and Charlie was so proud to be a Marine. He loved the Marine Corps. Maria wondered what it would be like living with her father-in-law, whose Marine Corps heritage was very obvious.

Maria woke again and looked at the clock. It was 6:30, although it certainly didn't feel that way to her. She decided to get up and do a few things before she woke the kids for the start of their long trip. As she reached the bottom step, Maria was startled by the sudden opening of the front door.

"Good morning, Maria. Sorry if I scared you! I was trying to be quiet, but I am so pumped up for the trip that I got up about an hour ago to do a maintenance check on the old car."

"That's okay, Dad. I just never heard you get up, and I usually hear things like that. Light sleeper. Do you always get up so early?"

"Nah, I used to get up with the roosters, but anymore I enjoy sleeping in until six."

"That late?" Maria responded, rolling her eyes good-naturedly.

"Hey, look on the good side. My face will be shaved and my teeth will be brushed before you even think about the bathroom in the morning."

"You have a good point there."

"What time should we wake the kids?"

"They can get up on their own. Let's get some breakfast ourselves before we feed them."

"If you're having some coffee, that's all I need. I'm still full from supper."

Sitting at the table, Maria ate a bowl of cereal as her father-in-law drank his coffee. She decided to bring up something that had been on her mind since Aunt Carmella mentioned it the night before.

"Dad, how are the lady and little boy next door doing?"

Pappy had expected the question. "Kathy Reynolds is much like you, Maria. She's having a hard time coping with the loss of her husband, but of greater concern to her is the terrible effect on her little boy. Kenny has become very withdrawn. Before, he would come over to my house with his dad and talk with me. Sometimes he would see me outside and come over on his own. But he hasn't spoken a word to me since the fire."

"Were you and Mr. Reynolds very close?"

"Considering our age difference, I think we got along very well. He was a fine young man and a superior athlete. He played professional football before an injury sidelined him. The whole town loved him, and I miss him still."

"What a terrible thing—for you to lose two people you cared for very much in such a short period of time."

"It was terrible, Maria. I will always love our Charlie, and I will always miss Ted Reynolds, but I'm trying to look ahead. That's why I hope and pray that things will work out between Manny and Kenny, as well as you and Cindy and Kathy."

"Has Mrs. Reynolds told her son we're moving in with you, and that Manny lost his father too?"

"Kathy said she was going to tell Kenny about it while I'm gone. She was very nervous about it. She's worried about Kenny's reaction. Have you said anything to Manny about what happened to the Reynolds family?"

"No, I have not. I hope you don't mind, Dad, but I was hoping that you would tell him. You know the boy, and you could better answer any questions that Manny may have. To tell you the truth, I wasn't sure that I could handle the situation if it creates a bad scene because Manny is upset by the similarity with his father's death."

"I think I understand very well. As soon as a good opportunity presents itself, I'll tell Manny about Kenny."

Maria was surprised that the kids showed little sorrow about leaving. As they headed north and passed Camp Pendleton, the kids prattling excitedly in the back seat, Maria felt the pangs of heartache. She thought of Charlie and all his stories about the training, and the men he served with, and the Marine Corps he loved. Maria turned her head west to gaze out over the vast, blue Pacific Ocean. She and Charlie and the kids had spent many happy hours on the white sandy beaches. She was going to miss the ocean and the beach, but she would return for visits as often as she could.

For the next hour, the four Smiths made small talk about everything and nothing. As they passed Los Angeles, Pappy suggested stopping for lunch north of the city.

"I don't know where my mind was; I could have packed a lunch for us."

"Please don't worry about that, Maria. I like to stop for a short break every now and then when I take a long drive. We'll get a bite to eat and get back on the road in no time."

After some sandwiches and Cokes, they strolled out of the diner, and Pappy said, "Manny, how about you sit up front with me? Maybe we can talk to make the time go faster." He glanced at Maria to get her nod of approval.

"That's a good idea. I was hoping to sleep a while."

"Sure, Pappy, I'll sit up front with you!" Manny beamed. He saw this as a big step up in stature. When there were two adults in the car, he was always relegated to the back seat. But today his mom and sister were in the back and he was up front. The trouble was that he was not tall enough to see over the dashboard.

His grandfather fixed that problem with a suitcase from the trunk.

"How is that?"

"Great!"

They drove on for almost an hour as Pappy Smith braced himself for the topic ahead. He and Manny discussed the sights along the highway while Maria and Cindy slept in the back seat. After a long silence, Manny turned and stared at his mother for about fifteen seconds to be sure that she was asleep, then looked at his grandfather.

"You were a Marine, Pappy, but you didn't die. Why did my dad have to die?"

The older Smith had known that one day he would have to answer that question, but that didn't make the conversation any easier. He found himself also glancing to the back seat to make sure the two girls were asleep.

"Manny, I wish I could give you a good answer. I've asked myself that same question a thousand times. I've asked God to please take my life and let my son return to his wife and children, but that will never happen. I don't know why your dad died. Life is not fair. It never has been and it never will be, but we have to go on with our lives and make the most of our precious time on this earth."

"I believe with all my heart that your dad wants you and your sister and your mom to go on with your lives and live them to the fullest. Your mom knows that also. That's why she and I agreed that it would be a good idea if the three of you came to live with me in Lower Vale."

"But I'll never forget my dad," Manny insisted.

"Of course not, Manny. You will always live with the wonderful memories of a father who loved you very much."

Maria hoped her father-in-law and son couldn't see her quietly wipe her eyes.

"This might be a good time to talk about another subject I've been wanting to bring up."

Manny looked attentively at his grandfather.

"I just told you that life is not always fair, and that applies to others as well." He cleared his throat. "Sometimes men die, leaving a young son without his father. In fact, Manny, there will be a boy living next to us whose father was killed in an accident about the same time your father was killed in Korea. He's seven years old as well."

The silence that followed was almost more than Maria could bear. She wanted so much to see her son's expression.

Manny just gazed straight ahead and said nothing. Pappy tried desperately to think of what to say, but his mind was blank as he worried about Manny's reaction.

"What's his name?"

"His name is Kenny Reynolds. Kenny and his mom and dad lived right next door to me. Mr. Reynolds was killed in a fire just ten days before your dad was killed. Mr. Reynolds was not a Marine, but he was a hero who died saving the lives of people in Lower Vale. Since his dad died, Kenny has not been back to school, and he doesn't speak much. He used to come over to my house and talk to me, but now he hardly responds whenever I speak to him. For his sake and for yours, I hope you and Kenny will be friends."

"What if he doesn't want to be friends with me?"

"Well, that's one of those things that you just can't force. You'll just have to offer your friendship and wait until he's ready to accept it."

"Aren't there other boys around that are his friends?"

Pappy Smith wasn't sure how to answer that question but decided to be direct with Manny. "Kenny stopped talking to his friends from school because he was so upset. His friends could not understand what Kenny was going through, and they got mad at Kenny because he didn't want to play with them, or even talk with them. The other boys could not understand how much it hurts inside when your father dies."

"I know how much it hurts. Do you think Kenny will talk to me?"

"As I said, Manny, we can only be patient and see."

After a few minutes of silence, the young boy asked his grandfather, "Does Kenny know that we're coming to live next to him? Does he know about my dad?"

"Mrs. Reynolds was going to tell Kenny about you and Cindy and your mother while I was away. So, by the time we get home, he will know about the three new Smiths living next door. His mother is very excited about getting three new neighbors. Her name is Kathy, and besides being a wonderful person, she is also a nurse."

The two were startled when Maria asked, "What are you fellows talking about?"

Maria decided that the conversation in the front was now safe enough to participate in. She was elated that Manny was handling the news about their next-door neighbors very well. Instead of taking the information as salt in his wounds, her son was showing concern for others. She got a little choked up. *Like father, like son*, she thought.

"I thought I should tell Manny about Mrs. Reynolds and Kenny, and the trouble that Kenny is having with the death of his father."

"Mom, did you know about Kenny and his mom?"

"Yes, I did."

"Why didn't you tell me?"

"Because I was worried about how it might affect you. Remember how upset we all were when we learned about your dad's death?"

Manny said nothing, so Maria spoke again. "What did you think when your pappy told you how Kenny lost his father?"

"It made me very sad for all of us. It's like Pappy said. It's not fair."

"No, it's not fair, Manny, but we have to go on with our lives."

Remembering what his grandfather said, the astute young boy added, "That is what Dad would want us to do."

"Yes, it is. We're all hoping that our family can help the Reynolds family learn to be happy again; and that they can help us cope with our loss as well."

"What does 'cope' mean?"

"Cope means to adjust to something, or to get used to something," said Maria.

"But how do you get used to someone you love dying?"

His grandfather wondered how a boy so young could be so incisive.

"You never get used to it, but you accept it a little better as time goes on," said Pappy Smith.

Without warning, a soft voice asked, "Are we there yet?"

Pappy and Maria smiled at each other in the rearview mirror. Cindy had good timing. They'd talked enough for now about the tragedies that had befallen the Smith and the Reynolds families. The subject would come up again and again as they adjusted to their new lives.

"No, sweetie. We still have a lot more driving to do and lots of things to see before we get to Lower Vale."

"I could use a short break to stretch this tired old back, if you don't mind?" Pappy Smith suggested.

"And I'm thirsty," added Manny.

"It's probably time for a short break, but after we go again, I would be happy to drive, Dad."

"I can drive too," said Manny, grinning at his little joke.

"You can't drive, Manny. You don't know how" was Cindy's quick comment.

Not taking any guff from his little sister, Manny shot back, "I can drive. I'm just not old enough!"

"What makes you think you can drive, hard charger?" Pappy interrupted the burgeoning argument between siblings.

"Dad let me drive one time at Camp Pendleton. I sat on his lap and drove while he worked the pedals on the floor."

"Manny, someday when you are much older, I am confident you will be a very good driver; but until you are old enough to drive and have your mother's permission, you must never attempt to drive a car. You could hurt yourself or others. Do you understand?"

"Yes, sir."

Cindy grinned because her usually confident big brother was now subdued. He always said "sir" when he was in trouble. Manny glanced at his little sister, resentful of how she was enjoying the moment, but quickly realized that he was better off keeping quiet.

"And what do you think is so funny, Cindy?" asked Maria.

"Nothing."

During the rest of the trip, the four Smiths spent much of the time talking about the scenery. It was totally different from Southern California. In San Francisco, Maria was very excited to see the city, as well as eat in a Chinese restaurant.

When they were back on the road, Manny said, "Pappy, can I ask you about something else?"

"Of course, Manny, that's what I'm here for."

"Well, I was wondering how you liked that Chinese food so much, and how did you learn to speak Chinese?"

"To answer your first question, I like many different kinds of food. Actually, there aren't too many types of cooking that I don't like. The size of the belly I'm starting to grow is proof that I like everything from your aunt Carmella's refried beans to Boston's baked beans. And to answer your second question, I picked up a few Chinese expressions when I was in China."

"Were you really in China?"

"Yes, I was. One of these days you and Kenny and I can sit down and talk about my travels in the Marine Corps."

Manny thought of his dad and of the fact that he still had his dad's garrison cover hidden in his clothes. Manny wasn't sure what happened to the rest of his father's uniforms, but he had the long thin hat that he took from the closet the day after they learned his dad was killed in Korea. Again Manny had the urge to talk about his dad, but he bided his time for now.

"Does Kenny know that you were a Marine in China?"

"He doesn't know that I was in China, but he knows I was in the Marines. His dad used to ask me about the Marine Corps."

"What did Kenny's father do before he was killed?" was the next question.

"Mr. Reynolds was a history teacher and the head football coach at the high school. They still say he was the best athlete to ever come out of Lower Vale High School. I know that Kenny has his dad's love of sports."

That pleased Manny because he really liked to play baseball, and football too.

"Maybe Kenny and I can play baseball for the same team."

"I hope you can."

Manny was a very friendly young boy, and he looked forward to arriving in Lower Vale, Colorado, to meet his new neighbors. But a part of Manny worried about Kenny's attitude, and that Kenny might not be anxious to meet him. Little did Manny know that as the Smith's car rolled closer and closer to Lower Vale, Kenny was having the same thoughts about meeting Manny.

Lower Vale, Colorado

Kenny Reynolds threw his basketball into the air, then caught it and instantly dribbled to his left a few steps where he quickly stopped and shot the ball.

Through the kitchen window, Kathy Reynolds watched her son go through his routine as she spoke to her friend and fellow nurse Jill, who sat at the kitchen table. "Mr. Smith called me earlier today. He said they should be home any time now."

"You sound a bit apprehensive about things, Kathy."

"I guess I am. It's been four months since Ted's death, and Kenny is still as withdrawn as he was the day after it happened. I just want, so much, for this thing with Mr. Smith's grandson to work out. I don't know what I'll do if it doesn't."

Kathy buried her face in her hands; it hurt her to see Kenny shooting baskets by himself. He and his dad had spent many hours together shooting baskets on the driveway, but now Kenny spent all that time out there by himself—almost as if he were waiting for Ted to return.

"It's going to work out. I just know it is! Kenny and the Smith boy will be the best of friends," Jill stated. "Does Kenny know that Mr. Smith is bringing his son's family to live with him?"

"Yes."

"And the similarity in circumstances?"

"We sat down the day Mr. Smith left for California, and I told Kenny everything I know about the Smith family, and about our similar tragedies."

"How was his reaction?"

"That's one of the things that bothers me. He didn't say anything. He just sat there and looked at the floor."

Kenny continued shooting and dribbling as three boys rode down the street on their bikes. One was older than Kenny, and the other two were Kenny's age and had been in his class in school. Kenny hadn't played with them often even before he lost his father, but now he showed absolutely no interest. The other kids could not understand how much Mr. Reynolds's death hurt Kenny, or how long the healing process was taking. And because the boys did not understand, they wrongly assumed that Kenny did not like them, so hard feelings had developed, along with some name-calling.

"Hey, Kenny, have you ever made a basket?" one boy said loudly.

Kenny had already ignored their remarks for a couple weeks before his mother first heard how they taunted him and told him to pay no attention to them. He didn't like them much anyway, so it was easy to ignore them. Most of the time, anyway.

A little later, Kenny was in the kitchen getting a drink when his mother exclaimed, "The Smiths are here!"

He quickly put down his glass and shuffled to the window to see. Kenny was a little surprised at the excitement he felt. He grinned when Mr. Smith waved at the Reynolds house and the little girl did the same. Then he saw a lady walk around from the other side of the car.

"There is Mrs. Smith," said his mom.

His mother didn't see the look he gave her—obviously that woman was Mrs. Smith, seeing as she was the only woman in the car—because she was so excited about the arrival of their new neighbors. She wanted to rush over and welcome them but decided it would be more polite to wait for them to settle. She would go over later with the cookies she'd made.

"I'm anxious to meet our newest additions to Lower Vale, but I'm afraid it will have to be another day. I have to get home," said Jill as she picked up her bag and headed for the door.

"Thanks for coming over, Jill. See you tomorrow."

Jill was about to step outside but stopped and said, "Goodbye, Kenny."

Kenny didn't respond. He was peering out the window at the young, dark-haired boy dragging suitcases from the trunk of the car. Kenny had the urge to go over and offer to help; that was what he and his dad would have done if his dad were there. But he was reluctant to go over himself, so he just stood in the kitchen and watched, grateful when his mom decided, "I think we should wait a little while before we go over to welcome our new friends and neighbors."

Maria and the kids followed Pappy Smith into their new home. Cindy clutched at her mother's skirt, so Maria reached down and held her hand as they entered.

The kitchen was very big, and very nice. She was expecting the worst, so this was more than she had hoped for. Although Maria did not care for her father-in-law's former wife, the kitchen had obviously been done over and modernized, much to Maria's pleasure. The living room was also a nice size, and it had a big fireplace.

"Hey, Pappy, let's build a fire!"

"Don't worry, hard charger, we will be building more fires than you care to build."

"What do you mean? I love fires."

"Well, I'm counting on you to help me chop wood for us to burn."

"That's good, Pappy. You can count on me," said the little tough guy.

The upstairs had three bedrooms and a large bathroom that also had a definite lady's touch. The plan was for Manny and Cindy to share a bedroom, and when Manny got older, Pappy would build a bedroom for him in the basement. Then Cindy would get the upstairs room all to herself.

"Maria, I hope this is going to be okay."

Maria hugged her father-in-law. "It's wonderful, Dad. I know we're going to love it here."

After a moment of silence, Manny spoke up with a common Manny concern: "I'm hungry. Are we going to eat the stuff we got at the store?"

"If it's okay with you, Maria, why don't we have a bite to eat now? Then we can spend the rest of the evening getting settled in."

"That sounds good to me."

"Me too," added the youngest of the Smith foursome.

While eating their sandwiches and bean salad, Pappy commented, "Please feel free to dig into this kitchen and reorganize it any way you want. Also, Kathy Reynolds said she wanted to get some time with you soon after you got here so she could show you around and help you get settled in."

"That will be great. The kids and I are anxious to meet the Reynolds family and the rest of our neighbors."

"Are there any other kids?" Manny asked.

"Sure, you'll make lots of friends—and I think the first friend you're going to make is heading this way with his mother right now."

Pappy Smith had expected Kathy and Kenny to stop over sooner, but glancing toward the Reynolds house as they ate, he saw them now on their way. The long-anticipated moment of introductions had come.

"Knock, knock."

Pappy walked to the back door and opened it. "Hi, Kathy. Kenny. Come on in. I want you to meet my family."

Before the elder Smith could say anything else, Maria stood and walked to Kathy. Nothing was said, but the two women embraced tightly.

Finally, Kathy said, "It's so good to meet you at last."

"It's wonderful to be here and meet you too, Kathy." Looking at the young boy at Kathy's side, Maria extended her hand and said, "I'm also glad to meet you, Kenny."

"Hello, Mrs. Smith. Nice to meet you." Just as he had rehearsed.

Manny and Cindy were still sitting at the table as Kathy approached them.

"Stand up when you're going to meet an adult, kids," Pappy Smith admonished.

The two kids stood quickly as Kathy reached to shake Manny's hand first. "Hello, Manny. I am Mrs. Reynolds."

After a quick "Hello" from Manny, Kathy turned to Cindy and said, "And this beautiful little girl would be Cindy."

Cindy smiled and peeked at her mother as Mrs. Reynolds gave her a warm hug.

Finally, the moment was at hand. "Manny, I want you to shake hands with Kenny Reynolds, the best seven-year-old basketball player you will ever meet. And, Kenny, you'll be shaking hands with my grandson, Manny. He can eat almost as much as me."

Pappy's comments seem to do the trick of breaking the ice. The two boys stepped forward and gently shook hands.

"Wait a minute. Wait a minute. When men shake hands, they do it with firmness and gusto. Now, you two shake hands again like you mean it."

The second handshake was done to Pappy's satisfaction, although not a word was spoken with either handshake.

Kathy held out the pan she was holding. "I hope you like these cookies I made for you."

"Thank you, Kathy. That was very kind of you."

"I've had your cookies before, Kathy, so I know they'll be good," declared Pappy, snagging one off the plate.

For the next hour or so, they sat around and made small talk about the trip from Oceanside, and about the community of Lower Vale. Maria was not surprised that her son was eating plenty of cookies, but she was surprised to see Cindy reach for a third one. "It seems that you really like the cookies that Mrs. Reynolds was kind enough to make and bring over for us."

Cindy confirmed this with a shy smile and a nod.

"Maybe when I bake more cookies next week, you can come over and help, Cindy."

Cindy looked at her mother for approval, then told Kathy, "Thank you."

Maria was anxious to learn what Kathy planned to do when school started next week. She darted her eyes back and forth to the door to indicate to Pappy that she would like him to take the boys out of the kitchen so she and Kathy could talk.

"Hey, while I have two strong boys here, I could use your help adjusting the front-porch swing."

As if they both thought there might not be any cookies left when they returned, both the boys reached for the cookie pan at the same time and bumped hands. They grinned as they each pulled back to let the other go first, and after a moment's hesitation they both reached again at the same instant. This time the coincidence brought a chuckle from both boys, and a comment from Pappy. "Come on, you two. There will be cookies when you get back. And if not, Cindy will make some more—right, honey?"

"Right, Pappy."

Cindy's apparent confidence pleased Maria, so she seized the moment. "Cindy, maybe you could go with Pappy and the boys to make sure they do a good job?"

"Good idea. You can try it out to make sure it works okay after we adjust it."

Cindy eagerly hopped off her chair, ready to go. After Pappy and the three kids left the kitchen, Maria spoke to her new friend. "Kathy, I understand that Kenny did not finish second grade either, and I was wondering what you expect to do this year. My father-in-law said that he thought school started next week."

Kathy had given the subject some serious consideration. "Because Ted was a teacher himself, I know many of the faculty at all three schools, and the elementary school principal was kind enough to sit down with me and talk at length about our sons' situation. I am confident that he will allow us to do whatever we ask regarding placement of the boys. Do you know what you want to do?"

"Manny was not a poor student, but he was not a good student either. And because he missed the last month and a half, I really wanted to have him repeat second grade."

"That would probably be best for him in the long run, and I have no hesitation about Kenny going through second grade again. He was a good student academically, but maybe a little slow socially. And there were some boys in his class last year that I would be happy to see not in Kenny and Manny's class."

"So, what do we do next?"

"Tomorrow we'll go to the school and sign our boys up for Mrs. Legarski's second grade. She is a wonderful teacher. Manny will like her just fine."

"That sounds good. Thank you so much, but please don't let us be a burden to you and Kenny."

"Don't be silly. I am so happy to have you and the kids here. I know it may take some time, but things will work out well for the boys. And I hope you'll let me have Cindy over to my house sometimes. I always wanted a little girl, and she is so sweet," Kathy answered with a wistful smile.

Pappy and the three kids returned. The trip to the front porch had obviously been a good one for Cindy. "The porch swing is really fun, Mama."

"I also have a swing on my front porch, and Kenny has a swing set in our backyard. You're welcome to play on either of them any time your mother says it's okay with her."

The smile on the little girl's face said it all.

"Well, Kenny, I think it's time we head home. It's been a long day for the Smiths, and I expect they're tired."

As the goodbyes and good nights were said, Kathy and Kenny were halfway out the door when suddenly Kenny stopped and said, "See you tomorrow, Manny."

"Okay!"

Kathy Reynolds looked at her son, then at Manny, then at Maria and Mr. Smith. Nothing was said, but the adults could read each other's thoughts.

The late-summer Colorado wind blew coolly on Kathy and Kenny as they walked across the grass, but neither minded. Kathy said, "How would you feel if we registered you to attend second grade again this year? I think there will be some nicer kids in your class."

"What grade is Manny going to be in?"

Kathy was surprised and pleased. "Manny will be in your second-grade class."

Though Kenny fell silent, Kathy could tell that her answer met with her son's approval.

The next morning, Maria primped to go with Kathy to the elementary school to speak with the principal and register Manny. She found the kids sitting on their newfound toy, the porch swing. "Are you ready to go with Mrs. Reynolds and me, Cindy?"

"Ready, Mama."

"What are you going to do to keep out of trouble, son?"

"I don't know."

"You could come with us and see the school. Maybe you can even meet your new teacher."

The look she got was the look she expected, so Maria suggested, "Why don't you go over to Kenny's house and see what he's doing?"

That was Manny's plan all along, so it was easy for him to respond, "Okay."

As he watched his mother, sister, and Mrs. Reynolds drive down the street, Manny heard Pappy talking in the house. Following his grandfather's voice, he found him on the telephone. After Pappy hung up, Manny asked, "What's going on, Pappy?"

"I was just talking to the lumberyard where I work. Today is my last day of vacation, so I have to go back tomorrow."

"What do you do at work?"

"I am the yard supervisor, son. I keep track of all the logs in the yard and make sure they're ready to go in the mill as needed."

"Can I see where you work sometime?"

"You can count on it. This weekend, the lumberyard will be closed and we can all go there. And someday I'll take you when the mill is operating so you can see the big saw cutting the logs, if that's something you think you want to see."

But Manny didn't hear the last part. He glanced out the window and noticed that Kenny had just come out of his house and was bouncing a basketball on the driveway.

"Why don't you go over and shoot a few baskets with Kenny? He's really good."

Kenny had been watching the Smith house and was pleased to see Manny come out and head his way.

"Hey, Manny. You want to shoot some baskets?"

"Sure, but I'm not a good shot. And Pappy says you're really good."

Kenny was pleased by the compliment. "My dad always said that being a good shot just takes practice. You'll be good in no time." Kenny surprised himself with the mention of his father, but then he decided it was not awkward at all.

As the two boys took turns shooting the basketball, Manny asked, "Do you like to play baseball?"

"Yeah, and football too. What about you?"

"Yeah!"

Just as all seemed right with the world, down the street came the three kids who liked to say mean things to Kenny. The older one always said something first, and the younger ones followed his lead. The two younger boys were the ones Kathy wanted to get Kenny away from.

"Hey, Kenny, who's dumb enough to play with a jerk like you?"

It had not been too difficult to ignore them when he was by himself, but now Kenny was embarrassed in front of his new friend. In anger and frustration, he shouted, "Shut up!"

Manny was not sure how to react, but he knew it wasn't good when the three boys abruptly slowed down and swerved into Kenny's driveway. They jumped off their bikes, and the older one got in Kenny's face. "What did you say to me?"

Kenny was cornered and he knew it. He was also scared, but he didn't want to back down and show his fear, so he repeated, "Shut up."

The force of the bully's push nearly caused Kenny to fall, but he backstepped quickly and retained his balance. Then the older boy came at him again; he never made it. A blur whooshed past Kenny and rammed into the older boy with enough force to topple him. Not content to just knock the older boy down, the angry Manny jumped on the boy and hit him once, then grabbed his shirt and yelled, "What are you trying to do?"

One of the other boys tried to pull Manny off, and Kenny surprised himself by shoving the second boy. The third bike rider, the little brother of the older boy, yelled at Manny and Kenny to get off. He then quickly rode his bike away, saying something about ". . . telling on you!"

Manny had scared the older boy so much that he started to cry, so Manny immediately released him. Seeing this, Kenny let his foe up as well. As quickly as they could, the two former bullies got their bikes and pedaled furiously down the street.

The new friends collected themselves.

"Thanks, Manny. I was afraid that he was going to cream me."

Manny eyeballed Kenny for a couple seconds and then said, "My dad used to tell me that good friends always take care of each other."

Nothing else needed to be said.

CHAPTER TWO

SENIOR YEAR OF HIGH SCHOOL

Lower Vale

"HEY, KEN. LET'S GO! School starts in twenty minutes."

"I'm comin'. Watch this shot."

"Pretty close. But I think you better reserve that shot for the driveway. Coach Marcus may get a little excited if you use a twenty-foot hook shot in a game," commented Manny.

"Aw, he gets excited too easy."

In the school cafeteria later that day, the discussion among Manny, Kenny, and their friends was about college. Graduation and college seemed like a long time away for students just three months into their senior year, but that morning their guidance counselor had spoken to all the seniors to remind them it was not too early to be thinking about their futures.

"Do you guys still plan to go to the same college?" asked Diane Holsinger.

"Sure, who will take care of Kenny if I'm not around?"

"And who will keep Manny out of trouble if I'm not there? We're a package deal."

Although Manny and Kenny used a lighthearted tone, they were serious. Their high school football team had an undefeated season, and each boy was a stellar player. Manny and Kenny were not shy about their desire to remain football teammates at the college level, and word had gotten out to the college coaches. For the smaller schools, the package deal was great because they would love to get Kenny and Manny. However, the bigger schools felt that Manny was too small to play major college football at 180 pounds.

"What do you think of going to State, Manny?" Ken asked.

"I would love to go, but that's the big leagues, buddy. I'm not the athlete you are."

"Where I play is not that important to me. Continuing to play on the same team with you is," said Kenny.

"I can't understand how an honor student like you thinks I can play at a major school. Those college guards weigh 220 to 250 pounds."

"But they aren't good lookin' like you, amigo," Kenny replied with a grin.

Only a few weeks later, the head coach at State visited Lower Vale.

Although Kenny was honored that Coach Taylor wanted him to accept a full scholarship to play football at State, Kenny made it clear that he was not inclined to attend any college that did not offer one to Manny as well.

"I'll have to study those game films again," replied Coach Taylor before saying goodbye to Kenny and Coach Gunn, the high school football coach.

"Why would you turn down a free ride to play football at State?" Manny demanded when Kenny told him about the interview.

Kenny got a little upset. "I thought we were going to college together."

"If possible, I hope so too. But there's no way I'll hold you back, Ken. You have tremendous potential to make it big, and nothing would please me more."

They let the subject drop as they headed home from school with Cindy. Going separate ways wasn't something they liked to think about.

"Hit the brakes, Ken!"

"What is it?"

"There's the new Marine Corps recruiting poster. I want to see it up close." Manny exited the car. "Wow, those guys really look sharp!"

"You still have thoughts about being a Marine?"

"Does Mama know about this? She's counting on you going to college," said Cindy in the back seat.

"I know. But the recruiter said with a college degree that I could be an officer. Pap said it takes a lot of work but it's well worth it."

Manny's fascination with the Marine Corps seemed only natural to Kenny. Manny's dad had been a Marine, and he grew up in the same house with Pappy Smith, who acted like he was still on active duty.

A couple weeks passed before Kenny received a phone call from Coach Taylor. State was offering scholarships to Kenny and Manny. The best friends would still be teammates.

Manny and Kenny were ecstatic that State was in their future, but as the second half of the school year quickly rolled past and summer began, eight-hour workdays in the hot sun at the lumberyard were their immediate future.

At the end of one long day, the two boys were walking toward their car when Pappy intercepted them in the parking lot. He had a paper bag under his arm and a somber look on his face. He told the boys, "I called your mothers and said we were eating out for supper. I have a dozen cheeseburgers and six Cokes. Let's go over there under the tree and talk."

The boys glanced at each other, not knowing what to expect.

"In case you don't know it, I'm going to have a tough time when you guys go off to college in a few months. But you will call home each week, right?"

"Sure, Pap," Ken said. Both boys nodded.

"College will be a lot different than Lower Vale High. Not everybody at the university will care about you like they do at home. Promise me you'll maintain your high standards of character. Try to get along with everyone, but don't trust anyone until you feel confident you really know what they're made of."

Again, the boys confirmed that they understood.

"I'm going to miss you, and I can't help worrying about you, even though you are both fine young men. You've been brought up right, and I know for a fact that you both come from good stock, but anyone can slip now and then, so you guys stick together."

"We've stuck together for the past ten years, Pap. We'll continue to stick together. You know that," stated Kenny.

When Pappy gave the boys their sandwiches and drinks, Manny stayed silent, staring at the ground.

Kenny met Manny's concerned eyes and asked, "What's wrong, Manny?"

With a sigh, Manny looked up. "Pap, you said we come from good stock, but the fact is that I don't know much about the stock I came from. All these years, when I asked about my dad, my mom would say that I must wait until I'm older. Well, now I'm older."

Pappy Smith dropped his chin in his hand as he wrestled with the problem. Manny deserved to know about his father, but his mother still couldn't talk about it. Though reluctant to talk with Manny about his father without Maria's consent, Pappy knew it had to be done. And now was as good a time as any.

After taking a big breath, the older man began, "Manny, in the Korean War, your dad was a sergeant and a howitzer section chief with Able Battery, First Battalion, Eleventh Marines. During a lull in the firing one day, the battery found itself under a heavy ground attack. There was no time to figure out where the North Korean infantry troops came from, but the battery position was very vulnerable. Witnesses reported that during the firefight, Sergeant Smith observed the Koreans moving onto higher ground on the battery's right flank.

"Realizing the imminent threat, your dad braved enemy fire and quickly moved to the area the Koreans were attempting to occupy. From that position, he was able to hold them off. This prevented the battery from being caught in a deadly crossfire, but Sergeant Smith was in a vulnerable position. Although hit twice in the leg, your dad continued to protect the right flank of the artillerymen, allowing them to move to a more defendable position. As he attempted to fall back himself, your dad was hit in the torso by multiple rounds. He gave his life to save his fellow Marines."

Kenny watched Manny, not sure if the story was harder on Manny or his grandfather.

"Pap, why has Mom been so reluctant to tell me the truth?"

"Your mother knows that you keep your father's Marine Corps cover hidden away."

Manny was surprised. He'd thought that Kenny was the only person who knew about the old hat.

Kenny defended himself. "I never said anything to anyone!"

"I know, Ken."

"Your mom has always recognized your interest in the Marine Corps, Manny. But she hopes that you won't join. She's afraid to lose you like she lost your father. She asked me to discourage you, and got upset when I said I couldn't do that. However, I did agree to not encourage you to be a Marine. I have tried to be supportive and help you as you've grown, and you too, Kenny. But what you and Kenny do with your lives is up to you, not your mother or me."

"Mom was afraid that the story of my dad would inspire me to be a Marine. Isn't that about what it comes down to?"

"That's about it."

"You can't be mad at her, Manny. She's just trying to protect what she loves. That's a mother's basic instinct," Kenny added.

"Manny, you have a wonderful opportunity to go to college and get an education. I think you should follow through with that plan. The Marine Corps will be there after college if you still want to be a Marine," Pappy advised his grandson.

"I have always, deep inside me, wanted to be a Marine. And someday I'm going to make that happen."

It was a quiet ride home for the boys. Kenny knew that his buddy was deep in thought. As they parted, Kenny said, "Let me know if you want to talk."

As days turned into weeks, Manny never brought the subject up again, and the time to leave for State arrived.

The night before, in the Reynolds kitchen, the six of them had dinner as they discussed driving the boys to college the next day. Instead of packing into one car, they would all go in two cars. In a prearranged conversation, as they sat at the table, Pappy asked the boys, "What are you boys going to do with your car while you're away at college?"

Kenny looked at Manny and nodded, so Manny said, "We already talked about that, and we're hoping that Cindy wouldn't mind taking care of it."

The sixteen-year-old screamed with glee and jumped up and down. She hugged her big brother, then her other big brother. Pappy, Maria, and Kathy laughed at Cindy's delight.

"Be sure to follow Pap's instructions, Cindy," Kenny told her.

"I will! I will! I will!"

About eighteen hours later, Cindy had tears in her eyes as the Reynolds and Smith families drove away from the university. She had often thought she would be pleased when Manny and Kenny went off to college, but now that they were gone, it was not as enjoyable as she imagined.

State University

The freshman football players were told via letter they should report to the south side of the stadium at 9 AM on September 3. Manny and Kenny saw several guys they'd played against in football, and

Manny spotted two heavyweight wrestlers he knew. *They are big,* Manny thought.

"I hope you're all happy to be here at State," stated Coach Carper, head coach of the freshman team at State. "We have a proud tradition, and we expect one hundred percent out of you guys to keep it going. Coach Taylor will talk to you right here, this afternoon at four, while varsity is practicing. See me later if you have any problems. If not, be sure you're settled in the dorm."

Later that day, as four o'clock approached, the freshman football players sat in the stands, watching varsity go through calisthenics. Freshmen were not allowed to practice until they started classes, which would be the next day.

Eventually, Coach Taylor came into the stands and spoke to the assembled players.

"I expect you've all settled into your dorms and had a chance to look around the campus. Make it a point to find out what buildings your classes will be in. I have high expectations of you men, and you have every right to have high expectations of my staff and me. With a lot of good effort and dedication, you will find yourself proud to be in one of the finest football programs in the nation. Be at the locker room tomorrow at four to get your gear, and be ready to become a State football player."

The freshmen were all sky high as Coach Taylor walked away. Most of them stayed to watch the varsity practice for a while, but little by little they drifted away. Many headed to the dining hall to have dinner. After dinner, Manny and Kenny left the dining hall to check their campus mailboxes. They both received some junk mail, but Manny also received a copy of a bill from the university.

He showed it to Kenny, who assured him, "This bill is some kind of mistake. When we go to the locker room tomorrow, just show it to the coach. He'll know what to do."

Later that night Kenny said, "I'm so nervous that I don't know how well I'll be able to sleep."

"Yeah, I know. I honestly had some reservations about coming here, but now I'm so excited that I doubt I'll get much sleep."

When they arrived at the locker room the next day, some of the other players greeted them. Kenny joined the group as Manny slipped away and headed for the coach's office. The door was open, but several coaches were sitting and chatting with the freshmen coach, so Manny knocked.

"What can I do for you?" said Coach Carper.

"I'm Manny Smith, Coach. I received this bill from the university and was hoping you could tell me why."

Manny got a bad feeling from the expressions in the office. Coach Carper asked his assistants to step out so he could talk to Manny. The bad feeling turned scary as Manny accepted the offer to sit down.

"I'm really upset that you received that paper before I had a chance to talk to you, Manny. The truth of the matter is that we had a few changes that we did not expect. One of the changes was a player we expected to drop out of school decided to stay and keep his scholarship," the coach told Manny.

"How does that affect me?"

"We only have so many scholarships to give out, and the one we were giving to you was the one that we expected the other guy to give up."

Manny said nothing as his stomach dropped.

"We know you're a fine football player, so we hope that you'll stay with the team, but we don't have that scholarship available anymore."

After a minute, Manny stood and said, "I'm not sure what to think, Coach. I thought I was getting a scholarship. Without the scholarship, I'll have to work to pay for school."

The coach did not indicate any sense of regret. Manny was not sure what to think of the look in the coach's eyes. He turned to leave, then heard the freshmen coach say, "Think about what you want to do and let us know."

Manny exited the office and started down the hall. As the assistant coach passed him on the way to the head coach's office, Manny thought of a question about the school bill and abruptly turned and headed back. The assistant coach clearly did not realize Manny was about ten feet behind because just as Manny went through the door, the assistant coach said, "Do you think he bought it?"

Stunned, Manny quickly left the office and the building.

While getting his equipment stowed in his assigned locker, Kenny scanned the room for Manny, wondering where his buddy was.

Manny went nowhere near the locker room as he paced, deep in thought. He was confident that the freshman coach had lied to him. Based on what the assistant coach said, State had offered him a scholarship they had no intention of giving him. And they did it in order to get Kenny to play for them. Manny knew that he was not going to stay at State, but he had a serious dilemma; he did not want to ruin his best friend's future with the team.

By the time the football players were released from their meeting, Kenny was very concerned that Manny was still nowhere to be seen. He was relieved to see Manny sitting on a bench outside the dorm, but Manny's posture and the look on his face alarmed him.

"What's going on?"

"I have a problem, Ken."

"What kind of problem? Is it about that bill in the mail?"

"I'm afraid so."

"Manny, what's going on? Tell me what's wrong!" implored Kenny.

Manny reluctantly explained, "There was a mix-up with the scholarships. They thought they had one to give me because one of the fellows told them he wasn't returning to State this year. But he decided to return, and so he keeps his scholarship. That means there are none left for me."

Lying to Kenny felt awkward, but Manny repeated what he had been told by the freshmen coach so Kenny would not throw away his own opportunity.

"This is not right. They told you that you had a scholarship, and let you come the whole way here to find out you don't. And you found out through a letter in the mail."

"They were going to tell me today."

"This is crazy. What do they think they're trying to pull? I don't care how big this school or football program is," Kenny said, growing more agitated.

Manny stood and yelled, "*KENNY!* Sit down and listen to me."

Kenny bit his tongue, then sat down.

"I have to admit something to you: I wasn't that crazy about attending State. The main reason I wanted to come here was because we've always said we would go to the same college. I doubt that I'm good enough to play football here, and I'm not sure I'm college material, academically."

"You've never been one to lack confidence. Why are you selling yourself short?"

"Because I'm just not sure this is what I really want."

"What do you want, Manny?"

Manny met Kenny's gaze. "The Marine Corps. You know that."

Yes, Kenny knew that, but he wasn't prepared to lose his best buddy yet. "But what about your mother? She'll be really upset."

"She'll realize that college will be very difficult without the scholarship."

The scholarship. The mention of the word made Kenny see red.

"I'm going to see Coach Taylor."

"Kenny, wait a minute. You want to be here. Please don't hurt your opportunity because of me."

"This university is not the only place to play football and get an education, Manny. But you are my only best friend."

Kenny headed to the football office to speak to Coach Taylor, not knowing that at that very moment Coach Taylor was speaking with the freshmen coach and his assistant. Coach Carper was confident that Manny had realized there was never really a scholarship for him.

"You goddamned *morons*!" Coach Taylor snapped. "How could you be so stupid? If we lose Reynolds because of this, you two can pack your bags."

The head coach had spoken face-to-face with Kenny Reynolds and knew his reputation as a young man of high principles. Coach Taylor was not sure how Kenny would react after he talked to Manny.

Only a few minutes later, Kenny arrived at the football office.

"Excuse me, Coach," said one of the assistants. "Kenny Reynolds would like to talk to you. Do you have a minute?"

"I was planning on calling you, Kenny. We have to talk about Manny."

Kenny had always been taught to be polite to his elders, so even though he was very upset, he said to the coach in a respectful voice, "Coach, I don't understand why there's no scholarship for Manny. You said there was."

"In this business, Kenny, I have a lot of hard decisions to make. The NCAA only allows us to give a limited number of scholarships, and there are so many good players out there. I give them to the players I feel are the best, players like yourself, who I know will be an asset to our program here at State. You have to realize the opportunity you have here at State. You need to leave high school behind. I know that Manny is your best friend, and you can continue to be best friends."

Kenny leaned forward in his chair but said nothing as he listened to the coach's roundabout excuse.

"You have reached a time in your life when you must look ahead. This is an opportunity to look to the future, and to do something about it."

Finally, Kenny calmly said, "Sir, I came to ask you about Manny and his scholarship."

The coach lost his composure. "Didn't you hear me, Kenny? I only have so many scholarships, and I can't give them out based on friendship."

Kenny suddenly felt ill as the realization hit him. Coach Taylor never had any intention of giving Manny a scholarship. He simply said that to get Kenny to play football for State. Just as suddenly, Kenny realized that Manny had lied because he didn't want Kenny to get upset over Coach Taylor's deceit.

As Kenny glared his resentment toward the head coach, Taylor lost his temper and raised his voice. "Damn it, Kenny! You need to wake up and realize that what I did was not only best for the university; it was best for you too."

Kenny dropped his eyes to the floor.

More softly, Coach Taylor continued, "I wish Manny was good enough to get a scholarship; he is not. But you are, and you need to be out there playing football."

"I will be out there playing football, Coach Taylor, but it won't be on your team."

Kenny stood abruptly and walked out of the football office. He heard the coach say something but didn't care what it was.

Walking back to the dorm, Kenny thought of what Pappy Smith had said that day at the lumberyard a few months prior. There really were some shitheads in the world, but he never expected Coach Taylor to be one of them. That the coach didn't think Manny was good enough to play at State wasn't so bad, but to lie about it was unconscionable. It didn't make Kenny feel any better when he considered his influence on the whole thing. Manny hadn't been much in favor of going to State in the first place. He only did so because he was such a good friend who always put others ahead of himself.

The dorm was just ahead, and Manny was still sitting on the bench. Kenny was confident that Manny knew they had been deliberately deceived. As Kenny approached his best friend, Manny stood and asked, "Am I correct in assuming that neither of us is attending State?"

"You are correct."

"I'm really sorry, Ken."

"That's okay, Manny. I told you before, your friendship is ten times more important to me than any college."

Manny was unable to reply.

The two friends started to meander. Kenny did not know what he was going to do. He and his mother had always planned on him going to college, but this first attempt was a real bust.

Suddenly, Manny proclaimed, "To hell with State, Ken. We both know many other schools would love to have you."

"What about you, amigo?"

"Really, Kenny? You really need to ask what I plan to do?"

Kenny grinned from ear to ear with embarrassment. He knew Manny would soon fulfill his dream of joining the Marine Corps. "Oorah!"

"OORAAAAAH!" Manny repeated, twice as long and twice as loud.

Kenny considered his earliest memory of the Marine Corps. He was just a squirt, but he remembered his dad asking Pappy Smith about Pappy's years in the service. His dad had probably been a big admirer of the Marines. He definitely admired Pappy Smith.

The more Kenny thought about it, the more excited he got. Why not join the Marines with Manny? They'd always said they would be on the same team.

"What are you thinking about?" Manny asked.

"Just enjoying a great idea."

"Thinking about another college?" asked Manny.

"Nope."

"Am I going to be forced to squeeze it out of you, or are you going to tell me what you're grinning about?" Manny asked the smug-looking Kenny.

"The way I see it, if the Marine Corps is good enough for you, it's good enough for me."

"You're going to join the Marine Corps?" Manny demanded.

"Yep. The Marines have long advertised that they are looking for a 'a few good men.' I think they will be happy to get *two good men*!"

CHAPTER THREE

MARINE CORPS RECRUIT DEPOT, SAN DIEGO

Lower Vale

IT WAS A TOUGH phone call for Manny. He knew his mother would be disappointed. She had been so pleased that her boy was going to college.

Pappy was at the school to pick up the boys the next morning. On the ride back to Lower Vale, he told the boys, "It was tough on your moms, but they'll be okay."

Walking into the kitchen, Manny found his mother sitting at the table. She tried to smile at him, but it wasn't the big natural smile he liked to see on her face. As she stood to greet him, Manny wanted to cry. He hated causing the pain he knew his mother felt.

"Manny, it's okay. I understand what you're feeling. It's okay."

"I'm so sorry that I've hurt you, Mom."

"You haven't hurt me. I just cannot help worrying about you. I love you so much."

Standing in the kitchen, holding her little boy who was not so

little anymore, Maria felt responsible for her son's remorse. She knew
his heart was not in going to college, but she'd hoped that he would
grow to like it. However, it was not to be, so now she needed to be
supportive of Manny's dream to follow his dad's footsteps into the
Marine Corps.

"I know you're upset about me not going to college."

"I just want you to be happy, Manny. You are your father's son,
and Pappy's grandson. You don't see it like I do, but in many ways,
you are just like them. It's only natural that you want to follow in their
footsteps." She put her hand to his cheek, tears in her eyes.

"Mom, please try to not be upset."

"I will, Manny, but you're wasting your time if you ask me to not
worry."

While Manny and his mother embraced again, he thought of
Kenny and Kathy Reynolds.

Totally disgusted by the State coaches' deceit, Kathy was not
extremely upset that Kenny left State. But she forgot all about the
previous day's incident when she heard her son's tone.

"There's something I have to tell you, Mom."

"What is it, Kenny?"

"Well, I guess you know that Manny wants to join the Marine
Corps."

"Yes, we all expected that," Kathy answered in a cautious tone.

"Mom, I'm also going to join the Marine Corps."

After a minute or so of agonizing silence, he said, "Mom, please
talk to me. I need to know what you're thinking."

"I guess I shouldn't be surprised, but are you sure that being a
Marine is what you want for yourself, or is it because your best friend
wants it?"

"I can honestly say that I've thought about it before on my own. I
haven't talked about it like Manny, but when I hear Pappy Smith talk

about the Marine Corps, I'm fascinated by what he says."

"You never said anything about this before."

"I know, but it's not because I wasn't thinking about it."

After a short minute of reflection, Kathy beat her son to the punch when she said, "Your dad always enjoyed talking to Mr. Smith about the Marine Corps."

"I know. I was just a young boy, but I remember Dad and Pappy talking. Pappy told me that he thought Dad would have made a great Marine."

"I think Pappy Smith was right about your father. I also think that you will make a great Marine."

Kenny hugged his mother and said, "Mom, after I get out of the Marines, I promise I'm going to college."

"I genuinely hope so, Kenny. College has so much to offer, and it's the key to any number of wonderful careers you may choose to pursue in life."

The boys felt as if a heavy weight had been lifted from their shoulders. Although it was hard to say that they had their mothers' total support, at least both women were reconciled to the boys' wishes to enlist in the Marine Corps. Manny and Kenny saw the recruiter the next day.

Maria was now very supportive of the boys talking to Pappy Smith about the Marine Corps. She wanted them to be as prepared as possible because she knew a few things about recruit training. Manny's father had been a drill instructor at MCRD-San Diego when Manny was born.

Thinking back, it seemed like only yesterday that Charlie had walked into her aunt and uncle's restaurant in San Diego. Although the Mexican food was very good, the young Marine returned often for other reasons. Charlie was assigned to the naval hospital in San Diego while he recovered from wounds received in the war against the Japanese. Upon his release from the hospital, Charlie asked Maria to marry him. She would have said yes anyway, but Maria was extremely happy when she learned that Charlie had been assigned to duty there in San Diego.

The day finally arrived when Manny and Kenny would depart for the Marine Corps Recruit Depot, San Diego, California.

"Promise me that you will take care of yourself," cried Kathy as she hugged Kenny.

"I promise, Mom."

Sending the boys off to the Marine Corps was a lot more traumatic than sending them off to college. At least Manny and Kenny would be near Uncle Manuel and Aunt Carmella. Although Maria knew the boys would not be allowed any visitors during their three months of recruit training, it was still some relief knowing that family was nearby.

"Don't worry, the Marine Corps will take good care of them," assured Pappy.

Both mothers gave Pappy a dirty look. "That 'care' you are referring to is what has us worried," Kathy said.

Cindy snickered, which did not go over well with her mother.

"That's enough out of you."

When he was younger, Manny enjoyed when Cindy got in trouble. But now he felt the need to bail her out.

"Cindy, Kenny and I are counting on you to let us know how the team does this year."

"And take good care of the car," added Kenny.

"I will. I promise."

San Diego, California

The bus ride was a long one, but the bus was never crowded, so neither boy had to sit beside anyone. They expected to see Manuel and Carmella at the bus station for a short visit, but the Marines found Manny and Kenny before the Riveras.

"Are you two reporting in to the Marine Corps Recruit Depot today?"

"Yes, we are."

"Get on that green bus; it's ready to go," one Marine instructed the boys.

The instructions were direct and civil, but as the newly reporting Marine recruits soon learned, the civil part quickly went away.

"Sergeant, how soon will they give us something to eat?" asked one of the older-looking boys as the Marine Corps bus pulled away from the San Diego bus station.

"NOBODY GAVE YOU PERMISSION TO SPEAK, DIPSHIT! AND DON'T YOU EVER CHALLENGE THE FEEDING SCHEDULE OF THE MARINE CORPS! DO YOU UNDERSTAND ME, WORMBRAIN?!" screamed the sergeant.

Startled by the unexpected outburst, the young man meekly said, "No."

"WHAT DID YOU SAY TO ME?" the sergeant shot back at the confused young man.

Not really sure what he'd said, the recruit stuttered, "Yes . . . No . . . I don't know!"

"FROM THIS MOMENT ON, THE FIRST AND LAST WORDS OUT OF YOUR MOUTH WILL BE 'SIR'! THAT'S TWICE YOU HAVE FAILED TO ADDRESS ME AS SIR OR 'DRILL INSTRUCTOR'! DO YOU UNDERSTAND ME?"

"Yes, drill sir," the tongue-tied boy replied.

Manny and Kenny glanced at each other quickly. Manny was sure that the sergeant was going to be all over the terrified boy, but the unfortunate victim was saved by another recruit, who thought the improper reply was funny.

"WHAT DO YOU THINK IS SO FUNNY, ASS-WIPE?"

"Sir, nothing is funny, sir."

"Well, maybe something is wrong with my hearing because I thought I heard you laugh at your fellow recruit."

Then he turned his attention away and spoke to all the recruits. "YOU CLOWNS BETTER LEARN RIGHT HERE AND NOW THAT IF ANY OF YOU ARE GOING TO MAKE IT THROUGH YOUR RECRUIT TRAINING, YOU ARE GOING TO HAVE TO LEARN TO WORK TOGETHER! THROUGHOUT YOUR TIME IN THE MARINE CORPS, YOU WILL LEARN THAT TEAMWORK IS ONE OF THE STRENGTHS OF OUR CORPS."

There was silence for a few seconds.

"DO YOU HEAR ME?"

Without thinking, Kenny heard himself responding with a hesitant, "Sir, yes, sir."

"Do you have a pair of balls between your legs, recruit? If you do, I expect you to use them when you answer me. DO YOU HEAR ME?"

"Sir, yes, sir!" yelled Kenny.

"I was talking to all of you! The *s* on the end of *clowns* makes it plural. *Do you hear me?*"

"Sir, yes, sir," most of the recruits said.

"I CAN'T HEAR YOU, LADIES!"

"SIR, YES, SIR!" they shouted in unison.

When the drill instructor walked toward the front of the bus, Kenny glanced at Manny. Manny only moved his eyes, giving Kenny a quick sideways smile and a wink. Kenny could not help but think that Manny would do well at boot camp; he seemed to be enjoying himself.

When the bus pulled to a stop, the drill instructors debarked but were quickly replaced by another mean-looking, red-faced sergeant, who screamed, "I'M ONLY GOING TO TELL YOU THIS ONE TIME, SO YOU BETTER GET IT RIGHT! GET OFF THIS BUS AND GET ON A SET OF YELLOW FOOTPRINTS. *DO IT NOW!*"

The young men scrambled off the bus and onto the yellow footprints painted on the blacktop surface. When a befuddled recruit made the mistake of looking around to determine if he was doing what he should be doing, a drill instructor was in his face instantly to remind him that he should be at attention, with eyes straight ahead.

Manny suddenly realized that all the drill instructors had departed from the formation, and they'd said nothing as they left. Standing alone and facing the formation was a lone staff sergeant. Without shouting, but in a loud, booming voice, he said to the young men, "My name is Staff Sergeant Joseph. I am your senior drill instructor. Life as you once knew it has ceased to exist. From this moment on, my fellow drill instructors and I will dedicate our lives to turning you young men into United States Marines.

"Recruit training is extremely challenging. Some of you will not make it. For those of you who do make it, you will experience a feeling of pride and accomplishment like you cannot imagine at this time. Good luck to you, and hang tough. Sergeant Barnes, let's see how many of these young men have what it takes to earn the title of United States Marine."

From out of nowhere came another loud voice: "When I say 'left,' you will pivot on the heel of your left foot and the ball of your right foot until you are facing ninety degrees to the left of the direction you are currently facing. When I say 'face,' you will sharply bring the inside of your right heel to the inside of your left heel. You will do this while maintaining a rigid upright position with your hands along the seam of your trousers. DO YOU UNDERSTAND ME?"

"SIR, YES, SIR!"

"Very good. Maybe this platoon has some potential," said the sergeant. "LEFT—"

But Sergeant Barnes never had the opportunity to finish his drill command as the formation of young men turned into a twisted mass of clumsy, uncoordinated human bodies. Some of them turned to the right, some turned too hard and were facing to the rear, some even tripped over their own feet and fell to the pavement.

"WHAT CIRCUS DID YOU CLOWNS COME FROM! MAYBE LEARNING HOW TO DO SOME MARINE CORPS PUSH-UPS WILL HELP YOU TO LEARN A BASIC FACING MOVEMENT!"

After twenty push-ups, the men were again directed to the yellow footprints where they once again were told the steps in executing a "left face." The second time, they were also told which direction was their left. After three more tries, and the accompanying sixty push-ups, the platoon finally executed the movement properly.

"We are going to march to your uniform issue. The key word is *march*, which means we will all be in step. My command will be 'Forward, march.' On the execution command of 'march,' you will step off with your left foot to a thirty-inch march step."

After putting on their first uniforms, the new recruits looked nothing like the drill instructors who wore the same sateen green utility uniform. The DIs wore a sharp-looking "Smokie" hat, had their sleeves rolled up, and the bottoms of their trousers were bloused up to the tops of their spit-shined boots. The recruits had to keep their trousers hanging out and their sleeves rolled down with their top buttons always buttoned. Their matching green utility cover had to be worn pulled down to their ears. They were told they would have to earn the right to wear their uniforms properly.

One foolish young man made the mistake of saying a little too loudly, "We shouldn't have to wear our hats down to our ears. I think it makes us look stupid."

"DON'T THINK, PRIVATE! JUST DO AS I TELL YOU. AND SPEAKING OUT LIKE THAT PROVES YOU ARE STUPID."

"Sir, yes, sir!"

The time spent with Pappy Smith helped Manny and Kenny understand much of the instruction they received. Some of the other young men responded just as quickly, but quite a few others seemed to have trouble grasping what was expected of them.

"Private, are you naturally stupid, or do you just practice a lot?"

"Sir, no, sir."

"Did you attend high school?"

"Sir, yes, sir."

"Did the teachers ever teach you difficult things to remember, like which is your left and which is your right?"

The private hesitated to answer because he knew he would be in trouble for any answer he gave; however, his silence did not sit well with the DI either.

"Let me guess, recruit. You think that if you ignore me, maybe I will go away. Is that about what your strained little brain is thinking?"

"Sir, no, sir."

"Well, that's good thinking because for the next ten weeks, I own you."

"Sir, yes, sir."

"I and my fellow drill instructors will never leave you. Long after you have completed your training here, you will remember us. It is our job to make sure that you never forget us or the things we teach you. Do you believe me, recruit?"

"Sir, yes, sir."

Manny thought back to conversations with his grandfather. Pappy Smith had mentioned the name of his drill instructor several times, and Manny wondered how many Marines still remembered his dad from when he was a drill instructor at this very place almost twenty years earlier. It would be difficult to forget someone who made such a big impact on your life, and the DIs were good at making an impact.

Outside the uniform-issue building, the recruits stood in formation with their initial issued clothing items in seabags slung over their right shoulders. Manny was pleased to hear they were going to the chow hall but rolled his eyes in despair when the drill instructor said, "We are going to march to the chow hall. If we don't march properly, we may never make it to the chow hall. RIGHT . . . FACE!"

Manny couldn't believe it when he found himself face-to-face with the confused recruit to his right. Although the young man quickly turned to face the proper direction, the mistake did not go unnoticed.

"I realize it has been almost an hour since we did any facing movements, so I shouldn't be surprised that some of us have forgotten our left from our right. GET ON THE DECK AND WE'LL SEE IF SOME PUSH-UPS HELP YOU REMEMBER."

"Sir, yes, sir!" responded the recruits.

After the push-ups, they again stood in formation with seabags over their shoulders. This time the drill commands were carried out properly, and they marched off toward the chow hall. The cadence of the drill instructor was interrupted as another DI shouted at one of the recruits, "WHEN YOU MARCH IN A MARINE CORPS FORMATION, YOU MARCH AT ATTENTION, DIRTBAG! THAT MEANS YOU KEEP YOUR EYES LOOKING STRAIGHT AHEAD."

At the chow hall, the recruits dropped their seabags and moved inside by a column of files. It had been about five hours and five hundred push-ups since most of the recruits had eaten, so the food put before them went down with no problem. Manny was disappointed at the quantity; he would surely lose weight if this continued.

As they stood in formation outside the chow hall, the recruits heard one drill instructor say to another, "Let's get 'em to the barn."

The barn was the building where they would live for the duration of their boot camp training. The building was more formally known as a barracks, and the large open room where they would sleep was called the squad bay. However, there were enough bunks to sleep more than just a squad; the whole platoon would be berthed there.

"I will show you just once the proper way to make a Marine Corps rack. You will do it this way the rest of your Marine Corps career. Don't ever screw it up, or I will take it as a personal insult."

As the recruits started to make their beds, or racks as the sergeant called it, they were instructed, "Stand at the foot of your rack as soon as it is made. Top rack on the right, bottom rack on the left, and get it done quickly."

The first attempt was a failure. "TOO DAMN SLOW! EVERYBODY TEAR UP YOUR RACKS AND SHOW ME A PILE OF SHEETS AND A BLANKET ON THE CENTER OF YOUR MATTRESS. IF YOU HAVE THOUGHTS OF GETTING ANY SLEEP TONIGHT, I SUGGEST YOU MOVE MUCH FASTER THIS TIME!"

The recruits scrambled to get their bunks made up much quicker the second time. Although it was much better than the first time, the recruits heard loud and clear, "TOO SLOW. TEAR THEM UP AND WE'LL TRY AGAIN!"

Making their racks was the last evolution of the evening, and the recruits were all very happy to finally crawl into their bunks. Kenny said his prayers and had started to think of his mother when suddenly he heard a loud crash, followed by the continuous banging of metal on metal. On top of all this was the thunder of drill instructors screaming something about getting up and standing at the feet of their racks.

"Why are they making us get back up?" Kenny mumbled, disoriented.

He got a hot blast of breath in the ear. "IT'S TIME FOR REVEILLE, SLEEPING BEAUTY! GET YOUR LAZY ASS IN GEAR BEFORE I HAVE TO TEAR OUT YOUR TRANSMISSION!"

Kenny could not believe it. He'd just put his head to his pillow a few seconds ago. He could not imagine that he had slept for six hours, but it was true.

The yelling sergeant moved on to break someone else's eardrum. As Kenny watched the bedlam in the squad bay, he questioned the sanity of giving up college for this. Then he thought of the recruiter back in Lower Vale, who warned them that it would be crazy.

"You recruits have been here for less than twenty-four hours, but I expect most of you are already wondering why you joined the Marine Corps," the officer on the platform said.

Kenny wondered if anyone noticed the stupid look he was sure he had on his face.

"Let me tell each of you a little about yourselves. Some of you joined the Marine Corps because you thought you were tough, and you wanted to be in a tough unit because of the reputation that goes with it. Others joined because you knew the Marine Corps was tough, and you wanted the Corps to make you tough also."

After a deliberate pause he continued, "Well, those of you who think you are tough will learn that you are not so tough after all. And those of you who want to be tough will have the opportunity to be tougher than you ever imagined. But nothing will happen if you quit on yourself. It's easy to want to quit this place, but it will be hard to live with yourself if you do. Recruit training is very demanding, but completing your training here may be the best thing you ever do for yourself. Hang in there!"

As the officer departed, a sergeant yelled, "ATTENTION ON DECK!"

The recruits all stood and snapped to attention. Kenny was inspired by the officer's encouragement, which sounded like a Pappy speech all the way.

"Take your seats," they were told.

The next couple of hours were occupied by paperwork, supplemented frequently by a healthy dose of insults from the DIs, who were patrolling the area and looking over the recruits' shoulders. To his dismay, Kenny found that he had trouble remembering simple things with a sergeant standing behind him, waiting for Kenny to make a mistake.

After all the paperwork was completed, the recruits received their first formal classroom presentation, on the history and traditions of the Marine Corps. Even though Pappy Smith had already told some stories to Manny and Kenny, the class was interesting.

Kenny glanced around the classroom to observe the other recruits as they learned the legends of the Marine Corps. Suddenly, the instructor changed the pitch of his voice and yelled, "What are you looking around at, recruit?"

Oh, no. I'm in big trouble now, Kenny thought. But the instructor was not looking at him. While Kenny had luckily escaped the wrath of the instructor, someone else had not.

"STAND UP, SHIT FOR BRAINS!"

Slowly the young man stood up.

"AM I BORING YOU? MAYBE YOU ALREADY KNOW THIS MATERIAL AND YOU CAN GIVE THE CLASS?"

"Sir, no, sir," answered the recruit.

"WELL THEN, CAN I ASSUME THAT YOU JUST DON'T CARE ABOUT THE HISTORY AND TRADITIONS OF THE MARINE CORPS?"

"Sir, no, sir."

"YOU DON'T CARE ABOUT MY MARINE CORPS!" screamed the instructor.

"Sir, yes, sir. I mean, no, sir. I mean, I care, sir. I care about the Marine Corps," the terrified recruit answered.

"Then pay attention when I am giving a class, AND THAT GOES FOR THE REST OF YOU!"

Kenny took a few deep breaths to regain his composure.

"Are you okay?" Manny asked softly.

"Yeah, I'm okay," Kenny answered, shaky after his close call.

Although not as dedicated as Manny, Kenny was very excited to be issued his M-14 rifle. Just outside the armory, the platoon conducted an impromptu school circle for some instruction on their rifles.

While the platoon was aware of his constant presence, Staff Sergeant Joseph did not say a great deal to the recruits directly, but the moment he stepped into the center of the school circle, the privates eagerly awaited what he had to tell them.

"I hope you realize the significance of this event. You recruits have been given the honor to carry a Marine Corps M-14 rifle. One day you may be called on to use a rifle such as this to save your life, or the life of a fellow Marine. Pay close attention to the instruction you receive on the use and care of your rifle. It is an important step toward becoming a United States Marine."

Kenny and Manny were doing fairly well at boot camp and were in the top of their platoon. But the leading man was Rocky Perez. Like Manny, Rocky was half Mexican, and he was sharp at just about everything the recruits were required to do. He was not only very capable but also very motivated. Rocky's mentor was his father, a sergeant major still on active duty. Sergeant Major Perez had fought in the Pacific in World War II, like Manny's father, and he had been in Korea as well.

Rocky was not shy about letting people know that his goal in life was to be a Marine Corps sergeant major too. If Rocky had an Achilles heel, it was his lack of patience with his fellow recruits who were not as capable or motivated as he was.

During the fifth week of boot camp, the platoon was conducting a field day. This was the Marine Corps name for a thorough cleaning of the recruits' living area. During the course of the day, Rocky expressed his dissatisfaction with the performance of two recruits in the platoon.

"You guys need to get your shit together. If we're going to be honor platoon, we can't have anybody slacking off and not performing," Rocky pointedly told them.

"Screw you, Perez. Who the hell do you think you are?" replied one Marine.

"Yeah, fuck you, ya Mexican beaner," said the other.

The veins in Rocky's temples bulged as he went after the mouthy recruits, but Manny grabbed the smaller Rocky and restrained him in a bear hug.

"Let me go, Smith!"

"Rocky, calm down! What's wrong with you?"

"I'm going to kick their deadbeat asses. We have no room for non-hacking shitbirds in this platoon."

"Starting a fight in the squad bay is only going to make things worse, so calm down," Manny told the fiery Rocky.

By this time, more recruits had gathered to see what the commotion was about. As Manny loosened his grasp, Rocky glared at the two recruits he had chastised, then walked away.

"Thanks, Smith," said one of the slackers.

The other added, "Perez is such a gung-ho asshole."

Manny said in a firm voice, "Say what you will about Rocky's attitude, but his comments about you two are right on the money."

The two recruits gave him sour looks and went to occupy themselves somewhere else.

"What was that about?" Kenny whispered to Manny.

"Oh, Heckle and Jeckle were screwing around again, and Rocky took it upon himself to tell them to square themselves away. But they gave Rocky some lip and he got pissed off and went at them."

"Rocky is really wound up tight," Kenny said.

"I know, but he's also one dedicated and squared-away Marine," said Manny, with a definite tone of admiration.

That evening, the men sat on their footlockers in the squad bay as they cleaned their rifles. After Rocky finished assembling his weapon, he stood and went through the manual of arms, adding a little extra showmanship as he spun the rifle in his hands.

When Rocky finished, Manny approached him. "That was great. Would you teach me to do that?"

"Sure thing," Rocky said. Then he added, "You know, Smith, I never thanked you for stopping that fight. If anyone had gotten hurt, it would have been my ass. So, thanks for the help."

"Forget it. Besides, we beaners have to stick together."

Rocky was caught unprepared by the beaner comment, but he saw the smile on Manny's face and grinned. "You're half Mexican too, right?"

Manny looked Rocky in the eye and said, "My heritage is fifty percent English American, fifty percent Mexican American, but my future is one-hundred-percent United States Marine Corps."

"Damn straight! Semper fidelis, amigo."

Manny and Rocky were so caught up in the moment that they failed to see the drill instructor enter the squad bay. One of the other recruits called the platoon to attention, but not before Rocky and Manny caught the DI's attention.

"You big mouths are to be cleaning your weapons, not flapping your lips," the sergeant said to them.

"Sir, yes, sir," Manny answered.

For ten minutes the sergeant made Rocky and Manny go through the manual of arms outside, using their footlockers as rifles. After he was confident that he'd made an impression on them, the sergeant left them to their own devices. The two exhausted recruits trudged back to the squad bay entrance.

Manny said, "I don't think I could lift my arms over my head."

"I know what you mean. I'm one tired beaner."

Manny grinned at the hard-charging Rocky.

Reveille came too early the next morning. But getting out of bed was only the beginning of Manny's problem; physical training was the rest of it.

"GET THE LEAD OUT OF YOUR ASS AND GET OVER THOSE LOGS! THIS IS A TIMED EVENT, AND SLOW TIMES WILL NOT BE ACCEPTED, SO PUSH YOURSELF!"

"What's the matter, Smith? Having a little trouble getting up the rope today?"

"Sir, no, sir."

Even on a good day, Manny was not as fast over the obstacle course as Kenny. Not only did Kenny seem to overcome the obstacles effortlessly, but his speed between the obstacles was very incredible. Kenny seemed a sure bet to have the fastest time for the O-course.

Physical training wasn't the only preparation Marine recruits had to deal with. The following week, the recruits left their base at San Diego to train at Camp Pendleton for a few weeks. As the bus rolled out of the gate at the recruit depot, Kenny whispered to Manny, "I wonder if this is what it feels like to get out of prison?"

"I don't know. I just hope I don't get homesick while we're away." Manny almost broke out laughing at Kenny's grimace.

The trip north up the coastal highway to Camp Pendleton only took about an hour. The recruits would spend the next couple weeks at the rifle range where they would undergo their rifle qualification. This was a big step toward becoming a Marine. It was one thing to be able to drill with a rifle, but the ultimate use of a rifle was in shooting it. Every Marine was a rifleman, they were told, and total proficiency with a rifle was demanded. Manny and Kenny had shot with a .22 caliber rifle, but now they would be expected to fire the .30 caliber M-14 at distances of up to five hundred yards.

"Your first week will consist of instruction and snap-in. Pay close attention to everything you are told and everything you do. Carelessness during your time here can cause someone to not qualify— or kill someone."

"Attention on deck!" someone commanded, and the recruits jumped to their feet.

Walking to the front of the assembled Marines was a tall, slender officer. "I am Chief Warrant Officer Dickins. I am your range officer, which makes me a little like God. Safety is the most important thing you will observe or execute while you are on my range. If anyone is observed doing anything unsafe, he will be kicked off the range, and you don't want that to happen. Pay close attention to the instruction you receive. Work hard, and good luck."

A week later Staff Sergeant Joseph gave one of his infrequent talks to the recruits, and the young men strained their ears to hear every word he said.

"This is your qual' week. If you are nervous, that's good. It means you are conscientious and want to do well and your juices are pumping. Do not get upset and choke. Each and every one of you can do well. Just concentrate on what you have been taught to do and do it. I'm starting to think that we may have the makings of a lot of real fine Marines here. Good luck. Hold 'em and squeeze 'em."

Manny received his ammo to qualify with a sharp sense of excitement.

"Here we go, Kenny. Good luck."

Kenny smiled at his best friend's eagerness. Minutes later, their relay moved to the two-hundred-yard firing line to begin their rifle qualification.

While positioning himself to shoot, Manny heard, "Hey, Mex." He looked over his shoulder and Rocky continued, "Hold 'em and squeeze 'em."

Manny nodded in acknowledgment. He had been improving a little more each day, but today was the day they fired for record. Today was the day that counted.

"Good job, Smith. You just keep concentrating on what you're doing and you'll do well," said Manny's range coach as they moved back off the two-hundred-yard line.

That evening at chow, there was a mood of celebration. The platoon had done very well. Everybody qualified, which was the most important thing, and Manny and Kenny both shot expert. To no one's surprise, Rocky was high man for the whole range with 241 out of 250.

On the bus ride back to the recruit depot, the two friends discussed their rifle training and their upcoming graduation.

"I'm anxious to tell Pappy that we both shot expert."

"How many times do you think he'll have to explain it to our moms before they'll understand it?"

"I don't know," laughed Manny. "But I wonder if our moms will come with Pappy to graduation."

"Is Pap coming?"

"He hasn't said that he was, but I wouldn't be surprised."

Manny was right. A few days before graduation, they were excited to learn that Pappy would be there, along with Aunt Carmella and Uncle Manuel.

The day before, the platoon was thrilled to see their senior drill instructor, Staff Sergeant Joseph, be promoted to Gunnery Sergeant Joseph.

When the long-awaited graduation day finally arrived, the platoon stood tall and proudly waited for their newly promoted instructor to lead them onto the parade deck. They looked sharp in their tropical service uniforms, but what really stood out was the gleam in their eyes.

Just as it was about time to go, Gunnery Sergeant Joseph stood in front of the platoon. After a moment of silence, he said, "I want you all to know that I have enjoyed the opportunity to work with all of you, and I would be willing to serve with any of you, wherever it may be. I am proud of you all. Good luck to you, Marines."

Manny wanted to burst wide open. He was so proud and happy that it was tough to contain himself. Boot camp was over, and he was no longer a recruit. He was a Marine. As Manny looked to his left rear to find Kenny, he suddenly heard, "Platoon! Atten . . . *tion!*"

Instinctively, his head jerked straight to the front as his body snapped to attention. The graduation march-on was beginning, and after what felt like minutes, graduation was over, and the new Marines were dismissed.

"Easy, Pap. You're breaking my hand," said Kenny as Pappy Smith congratulated him after the ceremony was over.

Once Pappy released him, Aunt Carmella gave Kenny a big hug. Kenny whispered to Manny, "Hope I get all these hugs when we get home for Christmas."

CHAPTER FOUR

CAMP PENDLETON, CALIFORNIA

Lower Vale

THE BOYS WENT HOME with Aunt Carmella and Uncle Manuel, who would spend the holidays with them at the Smith house in Lower Vale and then bring the boys back after the new year.

Even driving nonstop, the trip seemed to take forever. Once they arrived home, though, it was worth it.

The boys spent the first couple of days with their families, but there were lots of visitors. Christmas Eve and Christmas day were the best Manny could remember. The fireplace in the Smith house burned continuously.

It was almost suppertime on Christmas day when Kathy Reynolds said to her son, "Kenny, I have to tell you something."

"What is it, Mom?"

"Dr. Wheeler is coming over for supper in a little while. I've been seeing him the past few months."

After a moment's silence, Kenny said, "Does Dr. Wheeler make you happy?"

"Yes, son. Ron Wheeler is a very nice man."

"Then I'm glad you're seeing him. I want you to be happy," said Kenny, hugging his mother.

"Thank you, dear."

"Do you think you'll marry him? 'Cause it's okay if you do."

"That's not in the near future for us. He lost his wife only about ten months ago, and I don't want to rush into anything."

Knock, knock, knock went the back door.

"That must be the doctor. I'll let him in after I lay down some ground rules about dating my mother."

Kathy just grinned at her clever son.

"What the heck?" Kenny exclaimed as he opened the back door. There stood Manny, Larry Sheehan, and . . . Sarah Dilling?

"Me Tarzan, this Jane," said Larry, with a smile from ear to ear.

"Can you believe these two are dating?" exclaimed Manny.

"Who would have ever thought?" said Kenny.

"Not me, that's for sure," said Sarah.

As the four friends stood talking in the kitchen, Manny had a major flashback to their sophomore year in high school. A bunch of the guys had been walking home one evening after seeing a Tarzan movie when they passed Sarah Dilling, a quiet classmate of theirs. Larry Sheehan startled everyone by suddenly screaming at Sarah, "Me Tarzan, you Jane!" The boys guffawed, but a very intimidated Sarah ran away from them.

Ever since that night, Larry was better known as Tarzan, and much to her dismay, Sarah was given the nickname of Jane. The Reynolds's front doorbell rang, startling Manny from his reverie.

"That must be Dr. Wheeler," said Kenny.

"Who?" asked Manny.

"Come on, we need to go. I'll explain it to him, Kenny," Sarah said.

As the threesome left the Reynolds home, Manny asked, "Explain what?"

"Kenny's mom has been dating Dr. Wheeler for a few months," Sarah told Manny.

"The doctor who sold us the car?"

"He's the one."

"My dad said the doctor sold you and Kenny his old car because his wife couldn't drive with her health failing," Tarzan added.

"Now that you say it, I do remember Kenny's mom mentioning that to us." Manny considered this new information. "I wonder how Kenny feels about his mom dating Dr. Wheeler."

"It sounded like Kenny was expecting the doctor, and he seemed okay. How would you feel?" asked Sarah.

"What do you mean?"

"Oh, come on, Manny. Your mother is a very attractive lady, and I'll bet there are plenty of men who would like to take her out. How would you feel about her dating?"

There was a moment of silence before Tarzan said, "Let's go, Sarah. It isn't any of our business."

"Wait, you're right, Sarah. But what do I say to my mom?"

"If you're okay with her dating, you might tell her that you're happy for Mrs. Reynolds. Then tell her that if she ever wants to go out with a man, it's fine by you."

"I think I will. Thanks, Sarah."

"Sarah? Don't you mean Jane?" she demanded with a smirk.

"We'll see you again before you go," Tarzan said.

"I'm counting on it."

Manny took Sarah's advice that very night. While Maria's response was vague, she was touched by her son's concern. Manny had truly become a man.

The next day, Manny and Pappy finally got some time alone.

Pappy asked, "Well, Marine, how is it going?"

"It's going good, Pap."

For the next hour the two Smith Marines talked about MCRD and ITR. Pappy enthusiastically listened to his grandson relate his experience at boot camp. As expected, the older Marine was thrilled to learn that both boys shot expert on the rifle range.

It was a wonderful two weeks of leave, but as always, the days passed too quickly, and it was soon time for the trip back to California.

"I love you, Mom. Try not to cry."

"How about me?"

"I love you too, Cindy," Manny told his little sister.

They were on the road for a while before Aunt Carmella finally said, "Manny, I'm very proud of what you said to your mother. It was very mature of you. Your Uncle Manuel and I have asked her in the past if she was dating anyone, but she always avoided discussing the subject."

"Thank you, Aunt Carmella. It was a little awkward at first, but Kenny and I want our mothers to be happy."

Most of the conversation on the trip back to Camp Pendleton centered on the previous two weeks at Lower Vale. Being home for the holidays had been wonderful, but now it was back to the Marine Corps.

Camp Pendleton, California

The gate to Camp Pendleton was just off the main highway, but then it was several miles to the area referred to as "main side" where the boys would check in. After waving goodbye to Uncle Manuel, the boys picked up their seabags and headed toward the single-story white wooden building designated as the reception center.

"You men might as well get your orders out before you go in there because they'll ask for them right away," said a voice from behind them.

"Thanks . . . uh, thank you, sir," said Kenny, quickly saluting the captain going past them.

Manny also snapped to attention and saluted the officer. "Good morning, sir."

"You men carry on, and good luck to you."

"Thank you, sir," Private Smith and Private Reynolds replied simultaneously.

Pappy had told them that their chances of being in the same battalion were about one in three. They did not expect to beat those odds but were still pleased to learn in boot camp that they would be together in the artillery regiment. Manny was eager to be a Marine artilleryman, just like his father had been.

While the admin chief was contemplating where Manny and Kenny would be assigned, a sergeant major walked in and said something to the staff sergeant. The senior enlisted Marine then looked at the two young privates and said, "Grab your seabags. You Marines are going to Golf Battery, 3-11."

Manny and Kenny were still together after all.

"Golf Battery needs some good men, and I'm counting on you."

"Yes, Sergeant Major."

"Your first sergeant and battery gunny are top notch. Your gun platoon sergeant, Richwine, is a mean son of a bitch, but he knows howitzers inside and out. Pay attention to what he says, and you'll be okay. I don't know who each of you will get for a section chief, but most of them are really good and will help you as much as they can."

"May I ask a question, Sergeant Major?" said Kenny.

"Of course, Private. What's on your mind?"

"The staff sergeant at regiment said we're just in time to begin the next gun bunny class. I'm not sure what he meant."

"The Marine Corps decided that you two will be howitzer cannoneers. In official terms, you will be trained to qualify for a military occupational specialty of 0811. You will get your technical and qualifying training here at the 11th Marines in our Basic Cannoneers School. The next course starts in about a week."

"What will we do until then?"

"Whatever your battery needs you to do. But I do know that we are all going on a battalion hump on Friday. The battalion commander, Lieutenant Colonel Wolf, likes to go on conditioning hikes about once a month. Keeps us in shape and builds morale."

Friday came quickly.

"Close it up, Reynolds!" the platoon sergeant yelled.

Kenny had been looking around too much and left an interval of about eight feet between himself and the man in front of him. With a few extended strides, he easily caught up. Soon after that the battalion took a short break to get a drink and check feet. From the first day of boot camp, Marines were told the importance of taking good care of their feet.

"Everybody knows the drill," shouted Staff Sergeant Richwine. "Face outboard and keep your eyes open. Get those boots off and check each other out. Let the doc know if you got any problems when he comes by you."

"Anybody here having any problems?" yelled Doc. Doc was the name given to any US Navy corpsman serving with the Marine Corps. They were an invaluable asset.

"Yeah, Doc. I could use a cold beer."

"Do you think that if I had a cold beer, I would give it to you?"

"How are your feet, Private?" the corpsman asked when he got to Kenny.

"Just fine, Doc. Thanks."

"Let me know if they get tender."

"I will, thanks."

The break only lasted a few minutes.

"All right, guns platoon. Saddle up; were moving out."

No other unit in the battalion was getting ready to continue their march, but Staff Sergeant Richwine was always ready ahead of time.

"What's his hurry?" asked one corporal.

"That's the way he is," another Marine answered.

"Yeah, and he always has a burr under his saddle," the corporal replied.

Kenny was content to listen to the other men's comments about Staff Sergeant Richwine. Although he had been in the platoon just a few days, he agreed that the old platoon sergeant seemed to have a chip on his shoulder.

After completing their hike that morning, the battalion stood in formation on the softball field in front of the headquarters.

"Good effort today, men," said Lieutenant Colonel Wolf. "Battery commanders, it's Friday and it's payday. Get your gear cleaned and stowed and sound liberty call."

A soft roar of approval sounded in response—especially at the part about payday and liberty.

That evening, the boys decided to hang around the barracks rather than go into Oceanside. However, they had a good evening with a bunch of other Marines in the battery.

11th Marines, Basic Cannoneer School

"Marines, this is the M101A1 105-millimeter howitzer. It has been the primary weapon of direct support artillery since World War II. It saw extensive use in Korea, and you can bet your sweet ass it will see plenty of use in future combat operations. It is most definitely an oldie, but a goodie. Learn it well; your skill with this weapon can save the lives of many of your fellow Marines," the sergeant told the younger Marines.

It was the first day of the Basic Cannoneers School. Manny and Kenny were part of a class of sixteen Marines going through the BCS to qualify for the MOS of 0811. The 0811s, or cannoneers, operated the big howitzers along the battery gun line. A battery consisted of six howitzers, with each howitzer manned by eight Marines, often referred to as a gun section.

"Private, I'm not standing here talking to you for my health. I'm trying to teach you to be the best cannon cocker you can be. Pay attention to what I say."

"Yes, Sergeant," the Marine said half-heartedly as he rolled his eyes.

"This is the first day of your training, and you have an attitude problem already?"

"I already know how to use the howitzer. We've been going to the field every week for the past couple months," answered the Marine.

"You listen to me, wise-ass. You only think you know about the howitzer. The time you spent getting on-the-job training was good, but it was nothing compared to what you'll learn here at BCS. We will teach you what to do, why to do it, and how it works. If you think you're ready to take and pass our final exam, you really are one stupid private," the sergeant said sternly.

Kenny was amazed that a young private would show such apathy. He raised an eyebrow at Manny, who returned the look with a shake of his head.

Both boys enjoyed the four weeks of BCS. Kenny finished highest in the class on the written exams, but Manny's higher average on the practical exams put him first. As a result of being the class honor man, at the graduation ceremony Manny was meritoriously promoted to the rank of private first class.

"Congratulations, PFC Smith," said Captain Tanner, the commanding officer of Golf Battery.

"Thank you, sir."

"Good job, Smith," said the battery first sergeant, who accompanied the captain.

"Thank you, First Sergeant."

Then Manny heard, "Way to go, hard-charger." He turned to see Sergeant Major Chambers giving him a thumbs-up as he strolled by with the battalion commander. Manny could not have appreciated a hundred-dollar bill more than that gesture of approval.

Disneyland

Entering the gate to Disneyland the next day, Kenny asked, "Well, Manny, what do you think?"

"It's not as nice as the Fourth of July carnival back home, but since we're here, we might as well stay and try to enjoy ourselves."

Kenny just grinned as he shook his head.

"I need to use the head," Manny said.

"Okay, I'll wait here and look at this map," replied Ken.

Within a couple minutes, Manny exited the restroom to find Kenny talking to two pretty girls in front of the large map.

"Manny, I would like to introduce you to these ladies, but I'm afraid I can't because I have not met them myself."

"I'm Suzy," said the blond girl. She gazed admiringly at Kenny for a moment, then looked away before he could notice her interest.

"And I'm Lori," said the other girl, a pretty brunette.

"It's nice to meet you. I'm Kenny, and this is Manny."

"Is this your first time here?" asked Manny.

After a short laugh, Lori said, "No, we work here. But from the way Kenny was studying the map, we figured it was your first visit." Lori had also known immediately from their haircuts that Manny and Kenny were Marines, but their demeanor seemed different from other Marines she'd met—different enough to be intriguing to the two cousins.

"Where do you work?" asked Manny.

"See that concession stand on the corner?" Suzy said, pointing.

"Yeah, I see it," Manny answered.

"Well, we don't work there," Suzy said, followed by a quick giggle.

"Yes, we do," Lori said as she smacked Suzy on the arm.

His eyes glued to Suzy, Kenny said, "Well, maybe later we won't stop by there so we won't see you because you don't work there."

"Okay, I guess we won't see you later," said Suzy. The two girls sauntered back through the crowds toward the concession stand.

"What do you think, Kenny?"

"I think this is the 'too good to be true' your uncle was warning us about," Kenny said.

"I wonder why they stopped to help you?" Manny pondered.

"Probably my good looks."

"Maybe, but if they work here, they probably already know the original Goofy."

The rest of the morning, the boys rode all the rides they could get on. Around noon, Kenny asked, "You want to get something to eat?"

"Sure, what are you hungry for?"

"Whatever Suzy and Lori sell."

"How did I guess that's what you would say?" Manny responded.

Lori was cleaning off tables as the boys entered the concession area. She smiled and held up one finger to indicate she would be a minute or so. The boys got in line to order lunch.

"We got in the wrong line. Suzy is working the other one," Kenny said.

"There are too many people in that line. Let's stay put. We'll talk to them if they can get a free minute," Manny replied, more focused on obtaining food.

Both boys were surprised to hear Lori behind them. "This is a really bad time. Can you stop by around two?"

"Not a problem," answered Ken.

The two o'clock rendezvous with Suzy and Lori was short but sweet. The boys learned that the two beautiful girls were seniors in high school, and their moms were sisters. Lori Baker was a local girl, born and raised in Anaheim. Suzy Miller was from Vista, which was just south of Camp Pendleton. Suzy stayed with her cousin in the summer and on weekends when they worked at Disneyland. Much to Kenny's disappointment, both girls were coy on the subject of boyfriends and politely declined offers to go out on a date. Manny suspected the difficulties of military life were more than they wanted to deeply consider at this point.

On the way back to Camp Pendleton later that night, Kenny told his best friend that he was going to keep in touch with the girls even if they did have boyfriends. Manny was not surprised at all.

★

The following Tuesday found Golf Battery going to the field for a shoot. It would be their first live fire training since completing BCS, and both boys were excited. After a couple hours, the battery commander called a cease fire for the men to have some lunch.

"I like the field training better than the garrison training, but the chow hall food sure is better than this stuff," Manny announced.

"What did you get?" someone asked.

"Dog meat, again," answered Manny.

"SMITH!" Manny heard. Manny unhappily recognized the voice as that of Staff Sergeant Richwine, which usually meant trouble.

"Yes, Staff Sergeant."

"Are you bitchin' about the food?"

"Maybe just a little."

"Well, knock it off!"

"Yes, Staff Sergeant."

Later that day, after the equipment was loaded, the battery convoy started back to the 11th Marines camp at Las Pulgas. With the battery in the gun park and cleaning up the howitzers, Manny approached his best friend.

"How did it go today on your section?"

"There wasn't much to it. For the whole shoot I served as powder man, so subtracting the difference between seven and the announced powder charge was all I did. It was kind of a no-brainer and no-challenge job."

Kenny did not realize that the battery gunny was within earshot, nor did the boys notice the gunny stride away and speak briefly to Sergeant Cartwright.

"DO WE HAVE ANY MARINES IN THIS BATTERY WHO ARE NOT COMBAT PICK QUALIFIED?" shouted Gunnery Sergeant Chandler.

"I have one on my gun," replied Kenny's section chief, Sergeant Cartwright.

"Marines have to be ready at all times. Send him to me," said the gunny.

"Private Reynolds, let's see if you're coordinated enough to handle a combat pick," the sergeant said.

Sergeant Cartwright handed the section pick to Kenny with instructions to report to the battery gunny, who stood near the center of the gun park.

"What must I do, Gunny?" Kenny asked as he approached the second most senior enlisted man in the battery.

"Being good at firing the howitzer is important, Reynolds, but if our position ever gets overrun by the enemy, it will be hand-to-hand fighting that saves our lives. In the artillery, we use these picks to dig in the trails of our howitzers, but we also use them for close-in fighting. Do you follow what I am saying?"

"Yes, Gunny."

"Does it make sense to you? Are you smart enough to realize that sometimes all the fancy equipment in the world won't work to kill the enemy as well as a combat pick?"

"Yes, Gunny."

The battery gunny had a big rag and a piece of cardboard in his hand. As he dropped the cardboard on the ground in front of Kenny, he said, "This will be your target. Now, turn around and face away from your target."

Kenny did as he was told.

"Get a good grip on the pick, and when I say the word *kill*, you turn as fast as you can with the pick, swinging as you turn, and strike the target."

Kenny thought it was a simple task, but he gripped the pick and stood ready.

"Kill," shouted the gunny.

In one quick motion, Kenny spun around and swung the pick, striking the cardboard right in the middle.

"Yeah, good kill," said Sergeant Cartwright.

"See if he can do a night kill," yelled another Marine.

"Okay, Reynolds, that was fast and accurate. But let's see how good you are when you can't see so well," challenged the gunny. "Put the target back on the ground."

The battery gunny stepped toward Kenny and held up the rag. "Tie this around your eyes so you can't see."

As Kenny applied the blindfold, his field cover got in the way.

The gunny said, "I'll hold your cover for you so you can put that blindfold on real tight. You weren't planning on cheating were you, Marine?"

"No, Gunny," Kenny said.

"I hope not," emphasized the gunny.

However, as Kenny put on the blindfold, he was careful to note the location of the cardboard on the ground in front of him. Then he said, "I guess I'm ready."

"It's not that easy, Reynolds. Now you have to turn around."

Even turned, he still felt confident that he could locate the cardboard on the ground behind him. Then he felt the gunny's hands on his shoulders as the gunny said, "Now, let's turn you around a little faster and a few more times."

"Sounds good, Gunny."

Kenny heard the other Marines laughing as he spun; it was obvious that he would have no idea where the target was. When the gunny stopped turning him, Kenny heard, "What you are trying to kill is on the ground directly behind you."

"Okay, Gunny."

"You ready, Marine?"

"Ready."

"KILL," shouted the gunny.

Kenny spun around, swinging the pick as he had before. As he drove the pick into the ground, he heard a loud roar from the rest of the battery, which had been watching closely from the beginning.

"I DON'T BELIEVE IT, REYNOLDS! A perfect kill on your first try. You are either really good, or one lucky son of a bitch."

As he smiled from ear to ear and then reached to take off the blindfold, Kenny heard the gunny say, "It usually takes most guys at least three or four tries to kill their cover."

The other Marines cackled like crazy as Kenny ripped off the blindfold. There on the ground, with the pick head stuck through it, was Kenny's field cover. Kenny yelled out in dismay.

To make matters worse, during the excitement, the captain and the first sergeant had arrived at the gun park and seen the whole thing. Now they were watching Kenny with big smiles as they clapped their approval.

"That was great, Reynolds," said one Marine.

"Yeah, it took me four tries," said another.

After receiving congratulatory barbs from much of the battery, a familiar voice drawled, "I think I'll have to write an article and send it to Lower Vale. It'll make probably make the front page of the paper."

"Yeah, well, if you do, you better include some facts about yourself. The paper will want them for your obituary," Kenny told Manny.

Kenny glanced up to see Gunny Chandler staring at him.

"Reynolds, I expect you're feeling a little stupid about now, but the embarrassment you feel is nothing to what you would feel if you cut the wrong charge. That could cause your gun to shoot where it wasn't meant to shoot. How would you feel if we killed some friendlies because you were bored with your job and cut the wrong charge?"

"Pretty bad, I'm sure," answered Kenny.

"You're damn right. You may think that being the powder man is boring, but it is every bit as important as the other responsibilities required for a good shooting howitzer section. Don't ever let yourself become apathetic. Okay, Marine?"

"Okay, Gunny. And thanks."

"Just doing my job."

After a few moments, Kenny mused, "You know, Manny, it's becoming very obvious that a guy doesn't have to go to college to get a good education. There's a lot to learn around here as well."

Back at the barracks, the Marines heard, "MAIL CALL!"

By the look on Kenny's face when "Reynolds!" was called, Manny was confident that the letter was from Suzy.

"How's Suzy?"

"Ask me on Sunday. I'm going to see her Saturday night."

Manny was very happy for his best friend, who was crazy about the pretty blonde from Disneyland.

Over the next couple of months, the training with machine guns and rifles intensified. No longer was anybody denying that the increased schedule was a result of national concerns about the deteriorating situation in Vietnam.

Because of the rigorous training during the week, the Marines enjoyed their weekends all the more, and the weekend coming up would be especially good. Suzy had invited Kenny and Manny to spend the weekend with her and her parents in Vista. Lori would be there also, and Kenny was told that the girls had something special planned.

"Ken, I don't know what you're expecting this weekend to be, but let's not get carried away," Manny warned as their bus rolled closer to Vista.

"What are you talking about? I'm not getting carried away."

"Then try to stop drooling."

Kenny acted like he hadn't heard Manny's comment. Still, he would play it cool.

After stepping off at the bus stop, he heard his name.

"Kenny! Kenny, over here." Suzy climbed out of a car parked at the curb.

Kenny could not contain the big smile that crossed his face as he strode toward Suzy. For a brief moment he was concerned about how to greet her, but his concern vanished in an instant as Suzy threw her arms around him in a big hug, overjoyed at their reunion.

"It's good to see you. You look great."

"It's good to see you too. Hi, Manny."

"Suzy," replied Manny as he glanced around for Lori. Suzy noticed and smiled.

"Lori isn't with me. My mom took her to the doctor. She may have broken her ankle."

"What happened?" asked Kenny.

"We were jumping on the trampoline, and as she hopped off, she landed wrong."

"That's too bad. Will that affect our plans for the day?"

"It will slow her down a little at the beach tonight. Of course, if she had a big strong guy to carry her, that would be a big help," Suzy said.

"At your service. Happy to help." Manny grinned.

"Maybe I should break your ankle so I can carry you on the beach tonight," Kenny said to Suzy.

"Kenny Reynolds, you're such a romantic devil."

"Well, you got half of it right," laughed Manny.

"I'm calling Ed Sullivan. He's always looking for great comedians," said Kenny.

"Try to not act weird in front of my parents. I told them you guys were really nice."

"Us, weird?"

It didn't take long to get from the bus stop to Suzy's house. As they pulled in the driveway, Suzy said, "Looks like my mom and Lori aren't back from the doctor yet."

The garage door opened as they climbed out of the car.

"Daddy, these are our house guests for tonight, Kenny Reynolds and Manny Smith."

"Welcome, fellas, it's nice to finally meet you."

"It's nice to meet you, Mr. Miller. Thanks for having us," said Kenny.

"Yes, sir," added Manny. "We really appreciate a night away from the barracks."

"We're glad to have you. Just don't break any ankles like my niece."

The Miller house was very nice. Pat Miller had his own real estate business, and by the looks of their home, business was going very well. The swimming pool in the backyard was the nicest private pool the boys had ever seen. They stood in the backyard, gazing at it.

Mr. Miller told them, "I have a bunch of extra swim trunks. Why don't you guys put some on and go in for a dip? I'll get lunch ready."

The boys looked at Suzy, who smiled indulgently and nodded in approval as she padded back into her house.

"I can't believe we're going swimming outdoors in early April. I wonder if the water will be very cold," Kenny said.

"I hope it's cold. You're going to need something to cool you off after you turn around."

Kenny turned to see Suzy emerge in her bathing suit.

"Daddy says all Marines can swim. You two aren't the exception, are you?"

Manny wasn't paying any attention to what Suzy said. He was focusing on Kenny's reaction to Suzy.

As Kenny tried to answer, he discovered that he could not speak. Suzy was a very attractive girl in everyday clothes, but in the bright-red bathing suit showing off all her curves, she was a drop-dead knockout.

At Manny's laughter, Kenny regained his composure. "Of course we can swim. But one of us may end up drowning before the day is over," Kenny said, glaring at his best friend.

The weather was pretty nice, but the pool heating unit made the water feel great. The three of them shot a plastic ball through a floating basketball hoop. The boys got competitive with each other, and Suzy soon found herself out of the game and decided to leave them to it.

Kenny noticed her getting out of the pool. "Where are you going?"

"To see my dad. He won't ignore me like some guys I know."

"Way to go, knucklehead," snapped Kenny.

"Me? You were trying to beat me too," replied Manny.

When Suzy returned, Kenny said, "I'm really sorry, Suzy. I wasn't ignoring you, honest."

"That's okay. My mom always says that boys will be boys. Maybe

I can hold your attention with some lunch."

"I assure you that lunch always gets my attention," Manny replied.

On the kitchen table was a big plate of cold cut luncheon meats and cheeses. Another plate contained lettuce, tomatoes, and pickles, as well as multiple bowls of condiments.

"Go ahead and help yourself," Suzy told the boys.

Before the boys could dive in, Mr. Miller stated, "I think your mom and Lori are home."

The four of them headed through the kitchen door into the garage to see Mrs. Miller opening the car door and handing a pair of crutches to Lori.

"What did the doctor say?" asked Suzy.

"Nothing broken, just a bad sprain. Hi, guys," said Lori.

"Mom, I would like you to meet Kenny Reynolds and Manny Smith," Suzy said.

"Nice to meet you boys. I've heard a lot about you," Louise Miller replied. "Let's talk as we eat. I'm starved. You did save a little food for us, I hope, Manny?"

Manny was caught totally off guard. Everyone burst out laughing.

"I'm sorry, Manny. Lori put me up to that trick," explained Mrs. Miller.

"Good job, Lori!" exclaimed Kenny. "I'm going to mention your name to Ed Sullivan too."

"I'll explain later," Suzy said when a puzzled Lori shot her a glance.

While they ate lunch, Mr. Miller asked, "Have you boys ever caught grunion before?"

"Daddy!" was Suzy's quick comment.

The sharp, loud response from his daughter made Mr. Miller realize that he'd spoken out of turn, so he just said, "Sorry." The boys tried pressing for details, but the girls kept their mouths shut behind secretive grins.

After lunch, the four went for a drive in Mr. Miller's car. They told each other about growing up in Colorado and California. Around three, Lori said, "It's been over two hours since we fed Manny. Maybe we should stop and get something."

Kenny laughed at Manny's obvious embarrassment, and Manny growled, "We can turn that sprain into a compound fracture, you know."

"Oh, take me home, Suzy. I'm so afraid of this tough Marine."

Manny's embarrassment increased, and the other three laughed with delight.

"You know, Ken, suddenly I think I would prefer the company of Staff Sergeant Richwine."

"Oh, hit him, Lori. You don't realize how much you've just been insulted."

"Later. I like surprise attacks."

The doctor had said Lori could go swimming with the cloth ankle wrap she had on, so for an hour before dinner, they all splashed around in the pool. They also shot a few more baskets, but the boys were careful to include Suzy and Lori in the games.

"We're almost ready to eat," Mr. Miller yelled from the grill.

Pat and Louise Miller always enjoyed entertaining friends with a cookout, and barbeque ribs was a favorite menu item.

Manny was determined to not overindulge at supper, but after his first bite of the barbequed ribs, he knew that would be impossible.

"These ribs are great, Mr. Miller."

"Thanks, Kenny. What do you think, Manny?"

The nod and ear-to-ear smile told everybody what Manny thought of the food he was eating.

That evening, the four kids went to the beach. As Lori hobbled out of the car with her crutches, Suzy said to her cousin, "You won't need those."

"What do you mean?"

"She means you won't need them," said Manny as he swept Lori off her feet and into his arms.

"Manny will carry you, and Kenny will carry the rest of the stuff, and I will lead the way."

"Something tells me I should be worried."

"Why, Lori, what could you possibly be worried about?"

After settling on a large blanket laid on the sandy beach, the girls told the boys how they would go about catching the little grunion fish. According to the girls, the fish came onto the beach to spawn during the full moon. Manny and Kenny exchanged disbelieving looks, suspecting they were going on a snipe hunt at the seashore, but the girls insisted that they were not fooling the boys.

"You'll see. Just wait 'til the sun goes down."

"How about a sunset walk on the beach, Suzy?" Kenny asked hopefully.

"The cripple and I will stay here to hold down the fort," said Manny.

"Just don't be gone too long. We didn't bring any food with us, and I don't want to be eaten while you're away."

"I'm telling you, Kenny. She is a female version of the platoon sergeant."

Kenny and Suzy passed several other blankets with people sitting and watching the sunset. One couple was lying in full embrace, kissing. Suzy observed Kenny shake his head slightly, so she asked him, "What are you thinking?"

"Nothing."

Suzy decided to drop it, but eventually she spoke again to break the silence. "Think you'll be fast enough to catch some grunion tonight?"

"I don't care."

"What do mean, you don't care?"

"Catching or not catching the fish is no big deal to me. I'm just happy to be here with you this evening."

"Me too."

Sometimes doing things for the first time can be a little awkward, but there was nothing the least bit awkward as Kenny put his arms around Suzy and kissed her. He was in another dimension as Suzy pressed her lips, and then her full body, against him. It may have been for ten seconds or ten minutes, but when their lips finally parted, Kenny's knees felt weak.

"Do all boys from Colorado kiss like that?"

"Only when they're crazy about the girl they're kissing."

Kenny was thrilled that Suzy held his arm as they walked back.

Soon after dark, a man stopped by their blanket to ask if they were after the grunion. "Make sure you don't catch the scouts," he advised them.

"What are the scouts?"

"They're the first ones in. They come in to check out the beach. If you catch them, they can't return to the school, so the others won't come in."

"Thanks for the advice, sir," Manny said.

"You're welcome, Marine. Good luck."

"You girls never told us to leave the scouts alone."

"I never knew the first ones were scouts," confessed Suzy.

"Darn, my first chance to catch some grunion, and I get a second-rate guide," said Manny.

"That guy could be a nut that doesn't know what he's talking about," Lori said.

"On the other hand, it does kind of make sense," added Kenny.

"We can let the first ones get away. If it's a big run tonight, there will be more than enough for you guys to catch, cook, and eat," Suzy said.

Soon they heard a commotion further up the beach.

Lori suddenly yelled, "Look, there they are!"

Wiggling in the sand, wet from the receding wave, were several small fish. Manny and Kenny jumped up to get a better look, but another wave came in and covered the fish. As the water hurried back down the slope of the sandy beach, the fish were gone.

"They don't stay around very long," Manny said.

"We'll have to be quick," noted Kenny.

Soon, another wave splashed onto the beach. As it receded, it left dozens of the little fish squirming in the sand.

"Let's get them!" Kenny yelled excitedly.

"Are they the scouts?" laughed Manny.

"There are too many of them," Kenny answered. "This is the main attack."

The boys scrambled to grab the silver little fish squirming in the sand. They were so concerned with scooping the grunion into their bag that they never noticed the big wave rolling in on them. Manny spotted it just in time to stand and was hit at the waist, but Kenny was bent over and off balance. The force of the wave hit Kenny in the butt, splashed up over him, and knocked him to his knees.

"*Aaah!*"

It was bad enough to hear Manny laughing at him, but to see Suzy and Lori cackling on the blanket was really embarrassing. While the boys shuffled back to the blanket, Suzy stood and said, "Did we forget to mention that you have to watch out for the next wave? Maybe you Colorado boys thought the waves would stop while you picked up the grunion?"

Suzy giggled again, and the boys looked at each with big grins on their faces. There was no denying they looked pretty silly. After deciding they really weren't interested in cooking and eating the little fish they caught, Kenny stepped back into the water to release the grunion—the source of so much fun that evening.

After church and lunch the next day, the four friends went back to the beach for the afternoon. Then the girls drove Kenny and Manny to Camp Pendleton. Back in their battery area, the boys hopped out, and Suzy exited and opened the trunk for them to get their things. Manny went to the front passenger window to say goodbye to Lori as Kenny and Suzy stood by the trunk.

"I can't tell you what a wonderful time I had with you."

"I had a wonderful time, too," Suzy told Kenny.

"I would like to kiss you, but I'm afraid I wouldn't be able to stop."

"That wouldn't be so bad."

"It might be around here," Kenny said, glancing toward the barracks.

"Okay," Suzy said. She gave Kenny a quick peck on the cheek and added, "But you owe me a serious kiss."

"It's a debt I look forward to paying."

As the girls drove away, the guys waved farewell. Manny turned to say something to his buddy but then saw the look on Kenny's face and didn't say anything.

CHAPTER FIVE

VIETNAM

Camp Pendleton/Oceanside, California

"I KNOW YOU'RE NOT going to like hearing this, but I've been told that orders to Vietnam could come any day."

Manny was right. Kenny was not at all pleased with the prospect of leaving Camp Pendleton to go anywhere. Things could not be better between him and Suzy. After Lori hurt her ankle, both girls had decided to quit their jobs at Disneyland, so Kenny was able to see Suzy on most weekends. Sometimes Lori came down from Anaheim and went out with Manny. Manny wasn't obsessed with Lori the way Kenny was Suzy, but the four of them always had a lot of fun together.

"I know it's probably going to happen, but I hope it doesn't happen soon."

"A lot of guys are anxious to get over there. They want to see some action."

"I like the action in Vista."

"I know you do, Ken. What do you want to do this weekend since Suzy is away with her parents? How about if we go into Oceanside for a movie?" Manny suggested.

"That sounds good."

On Saturday night, as they walked down the main drag in Oceanside, Kenny asked, "So, what do you think of Bond, James Bond?"

"He's okay, but I think I like Wayne, John Wayne, better."

"I should have guessed you would say that."

"So, why did you ask? You want to get a burger?" Manny asked, changing the subject to one he liked much better.

Just then, the boys heard a muffled scream.

"Did you hear that?" asked Manny.

"Yeah, listen."

They heard another scream, followed by a growling voice and the sound of a slap. The sounds came from around the corner, just down the small side street the boys were crossing.

"Come on!"

"Wait a second, Manny."

But Manny dashed down the street to determine what was going on, so Kenny followed. To their surprise and horror, around the corner they found five guys wearing motorcycle jackets, clearly part of a gang. Two of them held a terrified girl, and all five were not happy at the intrusion.

The man standing in front of the girl spoke first.

"Get the fuck out of here."

Manny and Kenny said nothing as they surveyed the situation, which wasn't good.

Then another gang member said, "If you assholes think the Marine Corps is going to save the day, you're fuckin' wrong. Now get out of here, or we'll kick the shit out of the both of you."

The girl cried sharply, "Please help me."

"Shut up!" yelled the gang leader, slapping the girl across the mouth.

"*HEY!*" Manny bellowed.

The gang members were startled by the sudden outburst, but then the leader demanded, "What's your problem?"

"You have the problem. What the hell are you doing? Five of you picking on one girl?" Manny snarled.

"She owes us money, so mind your own fucking business unless you want us to pick on you."

"We just want you to quit hitting her," Kenny said.

"I've had enough of you assholes," the apparent gang leader said.

Everyone was surprised by the sudden roar of "SMITH, REYNOLDS!"

Manny and Kenny gasped as Staff Sergeant Richwine ambled calmly into their midst. "I can't believe you two are having an ass-kicking party and didn't invite your old platoon sergeant."

"Who the fuck are you?" asked the gang leader.

But Staff Sergeant Richwine acted like he hadn't heard the angry thug. "Well, no hard feelings. But why waste more time? Let's get this party started."

In the blink of an eye, the platoon sergeant had doubled over the tough-talking leader with a hard punch to the diaphragm. Then he took down a second gang member with a karate-type kick, with a simultaneous punch to the face of a third. Kenny couldn't believe what he was seeing. Richwine was a madman.

As two others went at Richwine, Manny threw a cross-body block at their knees, and the three of them tumbled to the ground. Suddenly, Kenny's nose exploded with pain as a gang member knocked him to the ground with a punch to the face. Kenny rolled to get away from his attacker and heard several loud, excited yells. Snapping his gaze up to see what was going on, a kick to the chin knocked him out.

Holding one gang member in a scissors lock with his legs and another in a full nelson with his arms, Manny looked up to see two more Marines come flying around the corner to ram into the gang members. Richwine leveled one of the gang and spotted Manny struggling with the two on the ground.

"Great party, huh, Smith!"

Manny couldn't believe his ears.

The gang member in the leg lock managed to twist around and punched Manny in the mouth. Manny lost the full nelson on his other foe in response, but as it turned out, both gang members were more anxious to get out of the area than to continue the fight. As they scrambled to get away, some other Marines went after them, but Staff Sergeant Richwine yelled, "At ease!" The criminals were allowed to flee.

Two of the newcomers helped Kenny to his feet.

"Are you okay, Ken?" Manny asked.

"Yeah, I think so. But I gotta say, a night on the town with Suzy is a lot more fun than a night on the town with you."

The boys' platoon sergeant ambled up to them and said, "Hell of a good party. I'd like to buy you men a beer."

"Thanks, Staff Sergeant. Then we'll buy you one," said Manny.

"That's the spirit, Marine. OOOORAAAAAH!" replied Richwine.

"*OOORAAAAAAH!*" responded Manny.

As they departed the area, Kenny said to Manny, "Wonder where the girl is?"

"I didn't see where she went."

"Maybe she used the distraction to get out of there. Oh well, hope we helped a little."

"You okay, Reynolds?" Staff Sergeant Richwine asked.

"I'll be okay. Where did you come from?"

"I was coming up the other side of the street. I had just noticed you two when I saw you run down this alley. I had a bad feeling, so I sent Red to get a couple more guys, and I followed you. Hope you don't mind me being a little curious?"

"Not at all. I was glad to see you," said Kenny.

"Smith, next time you attend a party like tonight, leave your wrestling moves in the school gym. These parties require lots of hard and fast fists. Understand?"

"Yes, I do, Staff Sergeant Richwine. And thanks!"

The next day, word of the fight was all over the battalion. Manny and Kenny received "attaboys" from everyone. Kenny was a little embarrassed, but he had to admit that it was fun getting all the attention. But everyone forgot the Saturday-night fight after the news broke on Monday morning.

They were deploying to Vietnam.

A few days later, Manny called Pappy Smith. "They're giving us two weeks of leave, so we'll be flying into Denver."

"Let me know the flight number and arrival time, and I'll be there."

"Okay, Pap. How do you think we should tell our moms?"

After a moment of silence, Pappy said, "I'll tell them if you want me to. Maybe that will be best."

"We were hoping you would tell them," Manny confessed.

"There will be some advantages to hearing it from me before you two get home. By the way, I think you should know that your mom is dating someone you know," said Pappy.

"Who?"

"She's been going out with Coach Gunn for about six weeks."

"Wow, I don't believe it. That's great!"

"She's enjoying her time with him, but she and Kathy will be unhappy when they learn of your orders. When she read about the landing at Da Nang in March, she was in a bad mood for a few days—"

"Da Nang! That's where we think we're headed."

"I'm not surprised."

"I better go now, Pap. I'll call again with the airplane information. Bye for now, and good luck with Mom and Mrs. Reynolds."

The next day on the phone, Manny told his grandfather, "We'll be arriving in Denver at 2:30 on Tuesday, Pap."

"Okay, I'll be there."

"How is Mom taking it?"

"I haven't told her yet, Manny. It's tougher than I thought."

"What do you think we should do?"

"I'll tell her and Kathy tomorrow evening, so she'll know by the time you get home. Try to be strong. It'll be tough on your mom; she'll need your help," said Pap.

Lower Vale

The next evening, after a cheerful dinner with Pappy Smith, Kathy, Dr. Wheeler, and Mr. Gunn, Maria asked Pappy, "Are you feeling okay?"

"As a matter of fact, I haven't felt good for several days."

"What is it? Are you sick?" asked Maria. Kathy and the two other men broke off from their conversation and turned their attention to Pappy, concerned.

"Maria, Kathy, I'm sick in my heart for what I have to tell you." After a moment of silence, the old man took a breath and said, "The boys have orders to Vietnam."

"Oh no!" Kathy gasped.

Maria put her face in her hands and cried, "Manny, oh Manny!"

It was a terrible moment for all. Maria cried out loud, and Kathy sobbed softly at the news. The three men sat helplessly. There was nothing they could do.

Kathy spoke first. "What else can you tell us?"

"I can tell you that I'm picking them up at the airport in Denver at 2:30 tomorrow. They have two weeks of leave before they have to be back at Camp Pendleton for departure overseas."

The tears started to flow again, but some were tears of joy in the knowledge that their sons would be home the next day.

"Maybe the coach and I should leave?" suggested Dr. Wheeler.

"No, Ron. It's okay. Please stay."

"Yes, there is no need to leave—unless you don't like chocolate cream pie," Maria said, managing a slight smile.

Pappy's lower lip quivered a little as he almost lost his composure. He was relieved to see Maria handle the situation so well. He really had been heartsick for the past several days as he worried about how his daughter-in-law would react.

Picking up on Maria's lighthearted comment, Coach Gunn said, "I, for one, love chocolate cream pie. And I know that if I want a piece, I better get it today."

Conversation at the table centered around the next two weeks, but in the back of everyone's mind was what loomed after that.

"If you'll excuse me, folks, I think I'll take a little walk," said Pappy to the two couples.

"Good chicken, Roy," said the coach.

"Yes, it was," added Dr. Wheeler.

"Glad you enjoyed it." Pappy left the group with heavy shoulders.

The visit was one of mixed emotions. Everyone was glad to have the boys home, but as always, the time passed quickly, and all too soon, the day to return to Camp Pendleton arrived.

"I'm sorry for crying," Kathy apologized to Kenny.

"It's okay, Mom."

"Good luck, Kenny. Take care of yourself," said Dr. Wheeler, who also had a tear in his eye.

"Thank you, sir. Please take good care of my mother."

"I promise."

Camp Pendleton

The boys each caught a little sleep on the flight back to San Diego. As expected, Uncle Manuel and Aunt Carmella were there to greet them. Kenny wasted no time in getting to a phone. He talked with Suzy for a long time, and plans were made for the coming weekend— their last before Kenny departed. After hanging up, Kenny found Manny and said, "Lori can't come down, but she's hoping you'll call her to say goodbye before we go."

"Yeah, I will. Thanks for the message."

The weekend was sweet sorrow for Kenny. He and Suzy had a wonderful time, but his liberty would soon be over. Kenny knew

Suzy must soon leave, so he gazed at her and said, "I was wondering about something."

"What are you wondering?" Suzy asked.

"I was wondering if you know that I love you."

"Yes, Kenny, I know that. Are you aware of the fact that it takes love to know love?"

This time Kenny didn't care who saw. He grabbed Suzy and kissed her passionately.

"Hey, I hope you save a little part of that kiss for me," Manny interrupted.

Kenny and Suzy jerked back and then grinned at each other. Kenny said, "I guess you can have a little kiss."

"Sorry, Kenny. This guy gets a big hug and kiss," Suzy said. She gave Manny a big smack on the cheek and hugged him tightly.

"Bye, Suzy."

"Goodbye, Manny. Take care of my guy, and take care of yourself."

"I love you," Kenny said to Suzy as she drove away.

"Love you, too," she called back.

Vietnam

Compared to the trip from San Diego to Denver, the plane ride from Southern California to Hawaii took forever. The Marines were allowed to get off the plane for a short while as it was fueled and checked, but they were soon back on the plane and on the way to Okinawa.

"Holy shit," said Kenny as he stepped out of the plane and the heat of the day smacked him in the face. The weather back in California had been nice, but it was very warm on the southern Japanese island where they had landed.

"This heat will be good for our acclimatization. It's going to be a lot warmer in Vietnam," the battery gunny said.

The battery commander heard the conversation and added,

"The gunny is right, but the body can adapt to that with a little time. One of the main reasons we're stopping over here on Okinawa is to get immunizations against lots of nasty things our bodies are very susceptible to acquiring."

"Like what, sir?" someone asked.

"Like typhoid, or yellow fever, or a whole lot of other stuff that none of us would ever be aware of getting."

The immunizations truly ran the gamut. Not since the footlocker drill at boot camp had Manny's arms been so sore. "I can hardly lift my arms," he said to Kenny. "I wonder if we have to get any more shots tomorrow."

"The doc said we're done, but there will still be some aftereffects to contend with."

"What aftereffects? Sore arms? I already got 'em," Manny moaned.

"No, the doc said some guys will get physically sick."

"Oh, great," Manny said. "That will take my mind off my arms."

The corpsman told the men which shots would likely have the worst effect on them, but no one really cared. Most of the Marines in the barracks that evening were feeling poorly.

"Let's go, Marines. We have briefings to attend," yelled the gunny the next day. "GET MOVING, GUNS PLATOON!"

There was a definite rumbling of dissatisfaction. One of the cannoneers made the mistake of saying a little too loudly, "This is bullshit."

The guns platoon sergeant was quick to tell the complainer, "If you have a problem, take it to the chaplain. If you want sympathy, check the dictionary. You'll find sympathy somewhere between shit and syphilis!!"

The complaining stopped, but there were still some hurting Marines.

Later that evening, as some of the Marines discussed the battery commander's speech, they all agreed that he had taken twenty minutes to give a five-minute talk.

"The captain meant well," Manny said.

"But he must think we're all stupid and never thought of what we were getting into," another man said.

"We all know that any of us could be killed," added Kenny, "but I think that's something we shouldn't dwell on."

"What does 'dwell on' mean, Reynolds?" asked another Marine.

"It means that you shouldn't think about it too much."

The mood was a little too somber for Manny, so he said in an upbeat tone, "Hey, the better we all do our jobs, the less chance we have to worry. As good as we are, I don't see us worrying a bit."

"You're damn right, Smith," interjected Staff Sergeant Richwine. "I know better than anyone how shit-hot this battery is, and I know that if called on to do so, we'll kick some ass."

"Oooraaaaaaah!" yelled Manny.

"*Ooooraaaaaaaah!*" the rest of the men responded.

"Staff Sergeant, you saw action in Korea, didn't you?"

"That's right."

"What was it like?"

"A lot of boredom, with occasional periods of chaos and terror. I don't know what Vietnam will be like, but I suspect it will be a lot of the same."

There was a moment of silence.

"Most of you are worried about whether or not you'll measure up and do the job required of you. Well, I'm telling you that you'll do just great. Remember your training, and don't forget, semper fi!" Then Richwine turned on his heel and marched away.

"He acts like a mean son of a bitch, but he cares about the Corps and his Marines," interjected Sergeant Cartwright.

The next afternoon, they were back on the planes and in the air.

"Next stop, Da Nang, South Vietnam."

Compared to the previous two legs of their flight, the trip from Okinawa to South Vietnam was a short one. Exiting the airplane, each man remembered what Gunny Chandler had told them about the heat.

"This place feels like the boiler room at the high school," Manny told Kenny.

"I know; this is going to take some getting used to."

For the longest time, the Marines just waited around. Then a few trucks showed up, and about half of the battery was off to their new home at Hill 55. Manny and Kenny were part of the second group to get shuttled. As they arrived, the battery was already positioning guns and distributing ammo.

"Wow, by the way things are going, you'd think we're going to be firing tonight," Kenny commented.

"I guess we have to be ready, just in case," Manny said.

"I just heard the gunny tell Richwine that there is no 'just in case' involved. I think we already have a mission for this evening," Sergeant Adams told them.

"What's the target? Did the gunny know what we're firing at tonight?" Kenny asked.

"He said it was most likely H&I of any enemy night activity," Adams said.

"H&I" meant harassment and interdiction, a fancy term for firing on suspected targets at random.

Around 1800, the gunny instructed everyone to stop for chow.

"My favorite," Kenny said, "ham and lima beans with a canteen of warm water."

"I heard that Captain Tanner is expecting food for our cooks to prepare for tomorrow evening's meal," Manny said.

"I'll believe it when I see it," added a cynical doubter.

As they bunked down for the night, the two best friends thought of their families back in Lower Vale. Kenny also thought of Suzy. He hoped to find something to send her as a graduation present.

It was only a matter of minutes before the boys were sound asleep.

BOOM, BOOM.

"What the hell?" said one man in confusion.

"INCOMING!" screamed another.

"Kenny, get your flak jacket and helmet on!" said Manny, flattening himself on the ground.

Then the young Marines heard laughing as a familiar voice said, "I told you this would be fun, First Sergeant." Manny looked up to see the battery first sergeant, battery gunny, and guns platoon sergeant chuckling among themselves.

"What's the matter with you men? You shouldn't be afraid of your own howitzers," said Staff Sergeant Richwine.

BOOM, BOOM, fired the two howitzers again.

"We told you men that we had an H&I mission tonight," the gunny said.

Some of the men grumbled at being scared and then laughed at by their seniors, but Manny thought it was funny. He fell for it hook, line, and sinker.

"Hey, Manny, I'll bet those guys at college think a panty raid at the girls' dorm is fun."

"Hell yes. Not only are we having all this fun, but we're getting paid for it. Ooorah!"

After lunch, Sergeant Cartwright approached Kenny and two other Marines. "You three, come with me. The plumbing has arrived, so we have to get our shitter into operation."

Plumbing? Kenny wondered.

"No more trips to the bushes outside our perimeter," the sergeant said, grabbing half of a fifty-five-gallon drum. "You men each grab one of these also."

As they carried the large metal containers toward the back of the position, Sergeant Cartwright yelled to the gunny, "Ten gallons of diesel per hole?"

"Yes, motor transport has eight cans sitting out," replied Chandler.

"There it is," the sergeant told Kenny and the others after a one-minute walk.

Lying on the ground was a piece of four-by-four plywood with four large holes cut in it. It suddenly became clear that beneath each hole in the plywood would be a half drum for the men to crap into.

"For now, we will elevate the seat on sandbags, then build something more permanent later on," Sergeant Cartwright told them.

As they finished setting in the four-holer seat, Kenny asked, "What were you and the gunny saying about diesel, Sergeant?"

"We put ten gallons of diesel in each can we'll shit in," he replied.

"Why not just use water?" another Marine asked.

"Because water doesn't burn," the sergeant said.

"What?" said Kenny.

"Reynolds, you're a smart guy. How do you propose we get rid of a hundred or more pounds of shit each day?" Cartwright continued, "We have to burn the shitters, or actually, we burn up the shit in the large half drums we shit into. Each day, one or two men will pull out the drums from under the seats and then mix the shit and diesel really well. Then you simply throw in a match and hope you're not downwind."

The three young Marines grimaced at each other for a moment and then cracked up laughing.

"You probably should warn your buddies that they all can expect to do lots of shitter duty. It's a daily requirement, if you know what I mean. It's also a rite of passage for a private in the Marine Corps," Sergeant Cartwright advised them. Then he said, "Get another man and grab the eight cans of diesel from the motor pool. I'll get the required paperwork."

As the three men went back into the battery area, Kenny said, "Would you mind getting two other guys to help? I want to trick Smith into volunteering for shitter duty."

The two other Marines readily agreed. They knew how motivated Manny was, so a trick like this would be good for a few laughs.

"Hey, Manny. I just volunteered us for a special assignment tomorrow."

"Yeah, what is it?"

"It's some burn detail. Sergeant Cartwright said he did it because it's a rite of passage as a Marine, so I thought you may want to do it too."

"Okay by me."

Kenny was worried about pulling off his trick after Manny used the new battery four-holer that evening, but apparently Manny did not make the connection.

The next morning after breakfast, Kenny said to Manny, "Did you confirm with the gunny that you want to volunteer for the burn detail?"

"I thought you said you already volunteered me."

"He wants to be sure you want to be the first burner in this position."

"Okay, guess I'll go tell him now," said Manny and went to find Gunny Chandler.

Less than thirty minutes later someone exclaimed, "What the hell is burning?"

Kenny turned to see a steady flow of thick black smoke rising from the area where the four-holer was located. As he started to laugh, another Marine asked, "What's so funny, Reynolds?"

Kenny could only stop laughing long enough to say, "I'm in big trouble."

The rest of the day, Manny took a lot of good-natured ribbing over the trick. But it was a good joke, and Manny remembered his grandfather's advice that it was good for everyone to be humbled now and then.

"Staff Sergeant Richwine was right about the boredom of combat," Kenny said.

"I know," Manny answered. "It seems like we've filled ten thousand sandbags for every round we've fired."

After being in Vietnam for over a month, the battery position was very well established. They even had a tarp suspended over the shitter so they could take dumps in the shade.

The exchange truck would come around now and then, selling toiletries, candy, cigarettes, and some other things that helped sustain morale. But nothing helped morale like mail from the States.

"I can tell from the smile on your face that you got a letter from Suzy."

"She just wrote to say thanks for the jade tiger necklace. Says she loves it."

"She would have loved anything you sent her."

"Maybe so, but thanks to you and the platoon sergeant, I was able to send her a nice graduation present."

Manny had asked Staff Sergeant Richwine if it was possible to get a nice gift for Kenny to send his girl. The crusty guns platoon sergeant only said that he would look into it, but the next day he produced a small green tiger with a gold clasp on a gold chain and asked, "Think this would be okay with Reynolds?"

"I'm sure it would be. How much?"

Kenny was ecstatic to pay the twenty dollars and send Suzy the necklace.

One afternoon, the peace and quiet of Marines reading their mail was suddenly interrupted by "INCOMING!"

Multiple rockets hit near Golf Battery.

"Gunny, check on post three. That thing hit somewhere in that area," said Captain Chandler.

"I'm on my way, Skipper," the gunny answered.

Arriving at the sandbagged position, the gunny called out, "Everybody in there okay?"

Manny stuck his head out the entrance and answered, "Yeah, Gunny, we're okay. But did you happen to bring a couple extra pair of underwear with you?"

"What's the matter, Smith? A little too close for comfort?"

"I don't think I want 'em any closer than that."

Manny and the other Marine occupying post three exited the small bunker and followed the gunny to the wire, where they peered at the crater on the other side.

"Nothing like a little incoming to get the heart pumping, huh, men."

Writing home that evening, Manny remembered telling Pappy in a previous letter that he hated guard duty because it was so boring.

He thought of telling his grandfather about how interesting his guard watch was that day but then decided against it.

"Listen up, gun two," said Sergeant Adams.

Something about the tone of the section chief's voice made Manny move closer.

"We just got word that we're leaving Da Nang tomorrow," Adams told them.

"Where are we going?" asked a couple Marines in unison.

"Looks like we're moving to occupy a position in support of ground operations to the west," was the sergeant's reply.

"What's going on? Some big offensive, or what?" Manny asked.

"Whenever I learn more details, I'll tell you right away. You all know that," Sergeant Adams told his men.

Private Vaughn said to Manny, "Wonder if the whole battalion is going?"

Adams overheard. "I don't think so. They sounded like it was just going to be Golf Battery."

"That's right," added Staff Sergeant Richwine as he passed the section.

"Have you heard anything other than what the gunny told us?" Adams asked Richwine.

"Gunny didn't say anything else, but I heard yesterday that 3/11 may be sending a battery to set up a firebase out in the bush. Looks like that scuttlebutt was accurate," Richwine replied.

"What is our mission if we operate from a firebase?" Manny asked.

"Nothing different," the platoon sergeant said. "It's just that we'll be located away from our battalion. Local security will be a much bigger factor than back here at Da Nang."

The battery did not have any fire missions that night, but there was an unmistakable sense of excitement in the air as the Marines talked of their pending move from Da Nang. Then the word came to maintain their ability to shoot but start making preparations to move out in the morning.

As the battery convoy was staged and awaiting orders to move out, Manny said to Corporal Patella, "I wonder how secure the area is between Da Nang and where we're going."

"It's my impression that around here, nothing is ever totally secure."

"I guess there's nothing to do but keep our guard up and be ready for anything."

"That's how I see it."

"FIRE 'EM UP, GOLF BATTERY!" came the yell from Gunny Chandler.

As the engines started, Manny felt the electricity in the air. He thought about home. Suddenly the truck lurched forward, and the battery was on the move.

Not long after they left the flat plain behind, the terrain started to get hilly. The hills didn't concern Kenny, but the heavy vegetation alongside the road made it impossible to see very far. As if he were reading Kenny's mind, Sergeant Cartwright yelled to his men, "Stay alert back there."

Fortunately, the battery arrived with no significant problems. They grabbed some chow after arriving on the hilltop that would be their new firing position, but the break was short lived.

"Let's go, gun platoon. Get these howitzers laid. We have missions to shoot!"

Just as the crusty old platoon sergeant had stated, the cry came early the next morning: "FIRE MISSION!"

"Here we go, men. Let's do it right," encouraged Richwine.

To everyone's surprise, the battery fired only two rounds per gun.

"That was a short fire mission," Corporal Patella stated.

"How many rounds did we fire, Lender?" Sergeant Cartwright asked the recorder.

"Twelve, Sergeant," replied Private Lender.

"How long do you figure we'll have to work with only five on a gun?" Vaughn asked.

"Until we get the perimeter a lot more secure, I'm sure the captain will keep three men at every post," answered Sergeant Cartwright.

"It's going to be tough firing for any long period with just five of us," Vaughn said.

"I know, Vaughn, but when we're firing, we are very vulnerable to a ground attack. We have to be able to shoot, but we have to protect ourselves so we can shoot. It's a double-edge sword, you might say, but out here, alone in a firebase like this, we have to make the best of it," the section chief said. Then he added, "We can handle it."

"OORAAAAAH!" yelled Manny.

Over the course of the next several months, the Marines continued to provide artillery support of one type or another on a daily basis. When they were not firing, the men spent their days improving their position. For the most part, they had taken only sniping fire and sporadic mortar fire, though they received word that some of the other firebases had caught hell.

However, one morning, the helicopter that brought in the supplies, mail, and other things had just released the large cargo net that hung below the aircraft when the first mortar exploded in the middle of the battery position.

"Incoming!" cried several men at once.

But it was too late. Kenny was hurrying toward the cargo net when the first mortar exploded to his left and knocked Kenny and two others to the ground.

"KENNY!" Manny screamed in terror as his best friend went down.

With no regard for the other mortar rounds exploding throughout the area, Manny sprinted to Kenny and the other wounded Marines.

"SMITH, TAKE COVER!" shouted Richwine.

Manny never heard him. Twenty feet away, Manny saw one of the injured men roll over and shake Kenny. Then another round hit behind Manny, and the concussion knocked him forward and to the ground. Getting to his feet quickly, he arrived at the three downed Marines.

"Henry is dead. Reynolds is still alive," said a radioman named Aungst.

"Hang in there," Manny said, grabbing Aungst and Kenny by the backs of their collars and looking for the closest cover. Manny dragged the two Marines toward the sandbagged wall around the mess tent. Not wanting to stop, and unable to jump, Manny ran into the sandbags and fell over them. Instantly he sprang up to pull the others over the low barricade.

"CORPSMAN!" yelled one of the messmen as he helped Manny drag the two wounded Marines over the sandbags.

The doc was already behind them. "Let me in here closer," the corpsman said.

After the corpsman removed Kenny's flak jacket, Kenny regained consciousness.

"Hey, Ken, that was a little too close."

"What happened?"

"Mortar attack."

Another round suddenly exploded close enough to send shrapnel through the canvas tent beside them. As Manny flattened himself on the ground beside Kenny, the doc fell sideways.

"Doc?" said Manny.

He called to the corpsman again before spotting the blood running from his left temple. The shrapnel had penetrated the doc's head just behind his right eye. He'd died instantly.

"Stay down. Everybody stay down," said Sergeant "Grits," the battery mess chief.

The next thing they heard was the mixed sound of helicopter rotors and machine-gun fire. The mail chopper had located the enemy mortars and was firing on them.

First Sergeant Richards was on the scene just as the firing stopped.

"What's the situation here?"

Manny answered, "The doc is dead. So is Henry. Reynolds and Aungst are wounded."

"So are you, Smith," Sergeant Grits added.

Only then did Manny realize blood was coming from the back of his legs. "It's not bad."

As another corpsman arrived at the mess tent, Kenny lost consciousness again.

"Kenny," said Manny.

"He'll be okay, Smith. The doc will take good care of him," the first sergeant said.

Later that day, a helicopter came in to evacuate the dead, as well as Aungst and Kenny. Manny refused any attention for his flesh wounds. Lying on the stretcher, Kenny said solemnly to his best friend, "You only have a couple months left. Promise me you'll be very careful."

"I will; you just get better, and I'll see you soon," said Manny with a forced smile.

Watching the chopper fly away, Manny felt empty. Although Kenny had been hit several times in the neck, shoulder, and arm, he would be okay. The empty feeling came from knowing that he wouldn't be close by to talk with.

The next day, Staff Sergeant Richwine told Manny, "When I saw you run out into the open during that mortar attack, I called you a stupid son of a bitch. But if you hadn't gone for those two, the round that got the doc would have killed Reynolds and Aungst for sure." After a short pause, the platoon sergeant said, "You're an outstanding Marine, Smith, and I'm proud to serve with you. Now, let's get back to work and get ready to shoot."

"Yes, Staff Sergeant," Manny answered.

The next day, Captain Tanner told Manny, "Lance Corporal Smith, you're a superior Marine, and long overdue to be promoted. I need a good corporal, and I think you can do the job. What do you say?"

Humbled, Manny couldn't speak for a second, then said, "I'll do my best, sir."

"I know you will," said the battery commander.

Just over a month later, during a small, short ceremony, the captain said, "Congratulations, Corporal Smith."

"Thank you, sir," Manny answered.

"A well-deserved promotion," added the first sergeant.

"Thank you, First Sergeant," said Manny.

Then, to Manny's surprise, Captain Tanner said, "First Sergeant Richards, read the citation."

"With pleasure, sir," said the Golf Battery senior enlisted Marine.

Manny was overwhelmed. Not only was he promoted to corporal, but he was also decorated with a Bronze Star for gallantry in action for saving the lives of Kenny and Aungst. Manny thought of his grandfather, his father, his mother, and his best friend. He wished they could have been with him to share his happiness, but he knew they were with him in spirit.

Manny would soon be ending his tour, and he was anxious to see everybody back home. When the day finally arrived, he experienced more mixed emotions. He was leaving some good friends behind to finish their tour.

While waiting at the exchange snack bar, PFC Vaughn said, "Sometimes I thought the days had about a hundred hours in them."

"We put in a lot of hours filling sandbags and digging holes in the ground," Manny agreed.

"And how many hours of guard duty do ya figure we stood?" asked Vaughn.

"And don't forget the hours of shitter duty."

Both Marines broke out laughing.

Then a loud voice interrupted. "What's so funny, you broke-dick Mexican beaner?"

Manny grinned ear to ear as he recognized the voice and turned to see his old boot camp buddy, Rocky. "Hey there, Rocky. It's good to see you."

"Same here. How ya been?" asked Rocky.

"I've been good. A bunch of us are heading stateside in a few hours," Manny answered.

"Why don't you stick around with me? We can kick some ass together," Rocky said with that unmistakable arrogance.

"I don't think so. Are you just getting here?"

"Yeah, they sent me to the Dominican Republic for a while to unfuck things down there. But now they want me to clean up this mess," Rocky told his old friend.

"If anybody can do it, I know it's you," Manny replied with a slight grin.

"Where's Reynolds these days?" Rocky asked.

"Back in San Diego, going through rehab treatment. He got hit pretty bad in a mortar attack and still has only limited use of his left arm," Manny said.

Rocky said something in response, but Manny didn't hear it. His best friend was in the same situation his father had been in just over twenty years earlier. Manny worried that the bad arm would prevent Kenny from ever playing football again.

Then Manny heard Rocky say, "Manny, you okay?"

"Yeah, Rocky. Sorry I drifted. I was just wondering how Kenny is doing with his rehabilitation program."

"You guys kind of grew up together, didn't you?"

"There's no 'kind of' to it."

"Tell Reynolds I said, 'Hi and get well,' and give my best to your grandfather and mom."

"I will, and the same goes from me to your family."

After a firm handshake, Manny went to relocate Vaughn.

Later that day, as the plane lifted off the ground, Manny was looking out the window when Staff Sergeant Richwine said, "Don't worry about looking too hard, Smith. You'll see it again."

CHAPTER SIX

SAN DIEGO, CALIFORNIA

Naval Hospital

"WHAT ARE YOU GRINNING about, Mr. Rivera?" Kenny asked Manny's great-uncle.

The older Mexican gentleman said nothing.

"What it is?" Kenny questioned, as Carmella joined her husband in smiling.

Within seconds, tears formed in their eyes, and Kenny stood and turned to see his best friend striding toward them across the hospital cafeteria. "Manny!"

"Hey, Kenny. How are you doing?"

"I'm much better now that I know you're back safe."

The two boys each extended their right hand to shake, but then Manny threw his arms around his best buddy and hugged him tightly.

"Easy, Manny. My shoulder is still tender."

"Sorry, Ken."

"You can hug me, you know," Carmella said.

"Aunt Carmella," Manny said, embracing his great-aunt.

"Oh, Manny. I prayed so hard that God would let you return safely to us," she said with tears rolling down her cheeks.

"Uncle Manuel, it's wonderful to see you," Manny said. He struggled to extend his hand with Aunt Carmella still hugging him.

"Carmella, let Manny breath."

After they all sat down again, Manny asked Kenny, "How is the arm?"

"I can tell the therapy is helping. The elbow is still a little stiff, and I have soreness in the shoulder, but I can feel it getting better."

Manny frowned at his buddy, wondering if Kenny was overstating his recovery.

Kenny added, "Hey, it's not my throwing arm anyway."

Uncle Manuel stood and said, "We're going to leave you boys alone to talk. Can we expect you at the restaurant for dinner?"

"Are you allowed out?" Manny asked Kenny in turn.

"Of course I'm allowed out. This isn't prison. I've been to the restaurant several times already."

"And here I was feeling sorry for you."

Aunt Carmella said to Manny, "One night he brought a very attractive young lady with him."

"How is Suzy?"

"She's good."

After walking the Riveras to their car, Manny asked Kenny, "Can we go back to the cafeteria? I'd like a Coke."

The two friends relaxed as they sat and talked. They had written each other a couple letters, but this was their first time talking face-to-face in months.

"How is your mom?" Manny asked.

"She's fine. She and Dr. Wheeler were here to see me two days after I arrived stateside. My mom was pleased to meet Suzy, and she was especially happy when I told her the Marine Corps expects to discharge me in time to start college in the fall."

"That's great, Ken. I mean, of course I'm sad for you. But you're back on the college track at least. Where are you going?"

"Well, my mom isn't too happy about it, but I've been accepted here at San Diego State University."

"I guess she would like you to be closer to Lower Vale."

"Yeah, but I want to be close to Suzy. In my favor for staying here is the need for continued therapy."

"Not to mention the fact that I'll be nearby at the recruit depot," Manny stated with a mile-wide grin on his face.

"You're kidding!"

"I'm going to be a drill instructor. What do you think of that?"

"That's great!" Kenny said, shaking his fist in excitement. He winced at a twinge of pain in his shoulder.

"No sports at San Diego State I assume."

"No, not this year for sure," Kenny replied. Then he asked, "Does your mom or Pappy know about your assignment to MCRD?"

"Not yet. I plan to tell them as soon as I get back to Lower Vale. Is there any chance of you going back for a visit?" Manny asked.

"The leave papers have been typed up for over a week. I've just been waiting for you to get here."

"How about if we try to get tickets for the day after tomorrow?"

"That's fine by me, but I've been told by your uncle Manuel that we are welcome to drive his car if we don't want to spend the money for plane tickets," Kenny informed Manny.

"Sounds like a good idea to me," Manny said.

After another Coke and lots of talking, the two best friends departed the hospital and went straight to dinner.

"Aunt Carmella, you'd think that after twenty years I would get tired of your enchiladas, but it hasn't happened yet, and I can't imagine that it ever will," Manny said to her.

"Do you think you want dessert right away, or can you wait a while?" she asked.

"Let's wait a little while," Manny answered.

"Do your mothers know of your plans yet?" Uncle Manuel asked.

"We need to call them and let them know what we're doing," Kenny said.

"Let's do it."

Maria Smith knew that Manny was back in the States and visiting Kenny, and Kathy Reynolds had been to San Diego to visit Kenny soon after he arrived at the Naval Hospital, but both mothers were now elated that their sons would soon be home in Lower Vale.

After his mother finally gave up the phone, Manny heard Pappy say, "I hope I can control your mother until you get home."

"I suspect controlling a herd of wild horses would be easier," laughed Manny.

"I'll keep the horses under control. You boys just make sure you have a safe trip," Pappy told his grandson.

"Okay, Pappy. We'll call when we're about an hour away, if we can."

"I'm anxious to hear from you, Corporal."

"Thanks, First Sergeant. See you soon."

As the boys headed north out of San Diego, Kenny remarked, "It sure feels good to be heading home."

"Well, if you like, we can skip our stop in Vista and keep driving to Colorado," Manny said with a smirk.

"I have to hand it to you, Manny. After a year in hell, you can still come up with the dumbest of jokes."

"So, how long will it take you to get from San Diego State to the University of Southern California?"

"Too long."

Suzy was attending USC, and their plan was to meet on the weekends at Suzy's home in Vista, where they were now headed.

"Have you seen Lori?" Manny inquired.

"Yeah, she's been to see me twice with Suzy."

"How is she doing?"

"Ask her yourself. She'll be here tonight."

"Great." Manny thought about the pretty girl who enjoyed verbally jousting with him.

When they arrived at the Millers, Pat said, "I just put the ribs on the barbeque a little bit ago. Are ribs okay with you, Manny?"

The smile on Manny's face said it all.

Mr. Miller started to speak, but Lori beat him to it. "Since when did you become particular about what you put in your stomach?"

"One of these days, Lori. One of these days . . ."

Satisfied with his reaction, Lori dropped it.

Suzy's mom asked, "Are you pleased with your assignment to MCRD?"

"Very much, Mrs. Miller. I've thought of being a drill instructor since I was a boy. My dad was a DI at San Diego, and my grandfather always speaks very highly of the responsibility they have."

"Manny will get them straightened out; right, Manny?" Kenny said.

Before Manny could answer, Mrs. Miller interjected, "Don't you wish you could get Lori into one of your training classes, Manny?"

"Heeeey," said Lori in protest as everyone laughed.

During the course of the evening meal, the conversation stayed light and comfortable. But that evening, as the four youngsters sat on the beach, watching the sun go down, the topic of Kenny's injury came up.

"It still scares me terribly when I think of how close the two of you came to being killed," Suzy said.

"It's one of those things a person can't dwell on. You have to put it behind you and move on," Kenny replied. "I think we should change the subject. Let's talk about something that isn't so depressing."

"Like what?" asked Suzy.

"We could talk about food. That always makes Manny happy," Lori stated.

Manny growled.

"Better watch it, Lori. I think you're making him mad," Suzy said.

"Either that or he wants a can of Alpo," giggled Lori.

Looking at Suzy as she spoke, Lori didn't see Manny's big arms reaching toward her. In an instant, he had picked Lori up and was carrying her toward the water.

"Put me down, you big bully."

"I wonder if the grunion are running tonight?"

"Why, are you hungry already?" said Lori, defiantly.

"Yes, I am, Lori. See if there are any fish in this big wave coming in."

"Manny, I'll *kill you*!"

But her threat did no good. Manny pitched Lori into the large wave rolling up the beach. Although the bottom of Manny's shorts also got a little wet, Lori went completely under and was drenched.

"You're dead, Smith! It may not be today, or tomorrow, but one of these days you are going to pay dearly for that," Lori said as she stalked out of the water.

"Hey, I owed you that."

"Now I owe you."

"That was funny, but I wouldn't want to be in your shoes," Suzy told Manny as they returned to the blanket.

"Better watch your six, Manny," added Kenny.

"Maybe I better," Manny confessed.

The next morning in the kitchen, Mr. Miller said, "Manny, I'm surprised to see that you were allowed to live through the night."

"I just want him to have time to think about how I might kill him," Lori said.

Nothing more was said about the previous night until after breakfast as the boys readied to pull away for their trip to Colorado. The last words out of Lori's mouth were, "Goodbye. I'm anxious to see you again so I can make sure I never have to see you again."

"I love you too, sweetie," yelled Manny as he blew a kiss at Lori.

"Yuck!" she cried.

The three Millers looked at each other and smiled as the boys drove away.

A while later the conversation went back to Vietnam, and Manny suddenly said, "I forgot to mention it to you, but guess who I saw at Da Nang the day before I flew back to the States? Rocky Perez."

"No kidding, how's he doing?"

"He was fine, still the same cocky, gung-ho guy he was at boot camp."

"He went infantry, right?"

"Rocky is a grunt, through and through."

"He's the only guy I know who may be more motivated than you," Kenny stated.

"OORAAAAAAAAH!" Manny screamed.

Lower Vale

Kathy Reynolds was watching through her window and was across the driveway before the boys even came to a stop. Moments later the door to the Smiths' house burst open, and Maria Smith came running.

"Manny!" she said, embracing him.

Manny quickly freed his left arm from his mother's hug as Cindy came to his side. Hugging his mother and sister, Manny saw his grandfather coming down the steps of the porch.

"Hi, Pap," said Manny.

"Welcome home, hard charger," responded the elder Smith.

Maria released Manny to go hug her other son, but Kathy Reynolds did not approach Manny just yet, allowing the moment between grandfather and grandson. After Manny finally turned, Kathy hugged him and said, "It's so good to have you home, safe and sound."

"Thanks, Mrs. Reynolds. It's good to be home."

The six of them stood talking for a few minutes until they were startled by the sound of car horn. The front passenger window of the car rolled down and someone yelled out, "Welcome home, you guys."

"Who was that, Mom?" Kenny asked.

"I don't think I know."

"Lower Vale is not a big city, so most people know you boys were on your way home. I suspect that car just had some folks happy to discover that you boys arrived safely," Pappy said.

"I happen to know several girls who were very interested in when you two were coming home," Cindy added.

"Maybe we should go inside to avoid more potential distractions," Maria said.

"Good idea," Manny commented. "Is there anything to eat?"

"As if you didn't already know that your mom would have the refrigerator and pantry filled," Pappy said.

They sat in the kitchen and talked as they ate. Kenny told the story they'd all waited so long to hear, about Manny's heroism in saving Kenny's life. Everybody was very proud and grateful for Manny's courage, but Manny was happy that it created a somber attitude in the Smith house. It allowed for a great entry into a not-so-somber tale.

"The truth of the matter is that I hesitated to go get Kenny after he was hit because of what he did to me earlier at Da Nang," Manny told everyone.

As all eyes turned toward Kenny, he broke out laughing and said, "I've been waiting for this moment for months."

"Go ahead and get it out of your system," Manny said. "Tell the story."

Kenny told the story of the burning shitters, and how he tricked Manny into volunteering for the job. The women cringed at the process but laughed at the trick. Kenny was enjoying the moment; but then Pappy said, "Kenny, I'm not sure the three ladies know that you are combat pick qualified."

Everyone looked at Kenny, who looked at Manny, who burst out laughing and said, "Now I get to tell the story."

Kathy, Maria, and Cindy enjoyed the story of the combat pick.

"What did you do with the hat, Kenny?" Cindy asked.

"I still have it," he replied.

"Seems you two enjoy keeping old hats," Maria said, gazing at her son.

"I actually kept it to remind me of a lesson learned. Now I'm especially glad that I kept it to help me remember the teacher of that lesson," Kenny said as he and Manny exchanged an understanding look.

When Kathy and Kenny rose to leave, each mother gave her other son another big hug.

Their time home in Lower Vale was wonderful. Being with their families and talking about old times was great. The boys visited all their old haunts and spent hours rehashing high school memories with their friends.

As always, the leave period ended much too quickly, and the boys prepared to head back to California. After Maria hugged Manny for the fourth time, Pappy said, "Maria, he'll be home for Christmas. You need to let the boys get going."

"Shut up, Dad. If I thought they would take you, I would send you back to the Marine Corps instead."

The comment provoked laughter from everyone, including Pappy. He made a token retreat by saying nothing in response. The old man was smart enough to back off.

"That was some leave," Manny remarked as they drove out of town.

"Boy, it sure was," Kenny said.

For the next few hours, the boys made small talk about the previous three weeks. It had been a very enjoyable, though chaotic, time for them. Then they fell silent for a while.

"There's something I want to ask you about, Ken."

"Go ahead, shoot."

"Captain Tanner talked to me before we left Vietnam, and he wants me to go to college so I can be an officer."

"Alright, that's an outstanding idea."

"But I want to be a drill instructor, Ken. Like my dad, and Gunny Joseph."

"What about doing a couple years as a drill instructor, and then going to school?"

"That's what Pappy said. I think he wants me to be an officer, too."

"Pappy wants what's best for you, Man."

"I know. Think I can get into San Diego State?" Manny asked.

"You can do anything you set your mind to do, buddy—anything," Kenny emphasized.

MCRD, San Diego

About two years earlier, Manny had been a recruit entering the gate at MCRD, San Diego, with a little bit of motivation and a lot of fear. Now he was a corporal, going in with a lot of motivation and a little bit of fear. Going through DI school would not be a walk in the park, but Manny knew he would make it.

He not only made it through DI school; Manny was the top graduate. Immediately after the graduation ceremony, Manny heard someone say, "This is almost as exciting as graduating from boot camp, isn't it, Corporal Smith?"

Manny couldn't believe his eyes as he glanced over and saw Gunnery Sergeant Joseph standing in front of him.

"Gunny Joseph, how are you doing? They told me you checked out a few months ago."

"I did check out. I'm just passing through on my way to Vietnam. I've been at school, brushing up on my explosives procedures."

"I guess I didn't know you were an engineer."

"Well, I knew that one day you would be a drill instructor."

Manny was speechless.

"Good luck to you, Corporal Smith. Seeing Marines like you makes me proud to have been a small part of your training."

"Thank you, Gunny, but you were a big part of it."

That Saturday, Manny and Kenny waited with football tickets for the girls.

"Hi, ladies," Manny greeted them as they approached.

An irritable Lori immediately answered, "Just give me my ticket and don't speak to me. I came to see a football game, not speak to a liar like you."

Very much taken aback, Manny wasn't sure how to interpret Lori's remark.

"You better apologize, Manny Smith. You told Lori you would visit her at school, and a couple phone calls is an inadequate substitute," Suzy told Manny.

Lori was watching for Manny's reaction.

"I'm sorry, Lori."

"Okay, I'm putting you on probationary forgiveness."

Manny looked at Lori, then at Suzy, then back at Lori.

"I won't totally forgive you until you visit me in LA and take me to dinner," Lori said.

"I guess I'm getting off easy."

"A lot easier than you deserve," Suzy emphasized.

The tension passed, and as the game started, they all had fun cheering for San Diego. Watching and cheering was fun for Kenny, but deep inside he wished he were out on the field playing. Although he'd told no one, Kenny had every intension of playing football next year for San Diego State.

At the Marine Corps Recruit Depot, Drill Instructor Manny Smith was at the peak of his game, physically and mentally. To hear Manny yell at the recruits, one might think he hated his work and the young men he trained. But the fact of the matter was he truly loved working his heart out to train the young recruits and turn them into Marines.

"DO YOU THINK I'M OUT HERE AT ZERO DARK THIRTY BECAUSE I HAVE NOTHING BETTER TO DO WITH MY TIME, RECRUIT?" Manny screamed.

"Sir, no, sir" was the reply.

"THEN QUIT FEELING SORRY FOR YOURSELF AND GET YOUR ASS UP THIS ROPE."

As the young Marine used his newly acquired motivation to climb, Manny stepped away. Suddenly a scream came from high on the rope. Manny instinctively moved to the scream as the recruit lost his grip. Under the recruit in time to partially catch him, Manny paid a price.

"The doctor says the clavicle is broken."

"Tough luck, buddy," Kenny sympathized.

"Yeah, right before graduation, too."

"Hey, minor setback. This won't keep you down, right?"

"Right."

"Good thing you went to visit Lori last weekend."

"I'll say. She accepts fewer excuses than any DI here, so a broken bone just wouldn't cut it with her," Manny laughed.

The next weekend, Manny was telling Kenny, Suzy, and Lori how much he would miss working directly with the recruits.

"What are they going to have you do?" Lori asked.

"I'll be a classroom instructor."

She hesitated for a minute, then could clearly no longer resist the urge to ask Manny, "Do you think they'll want you to give classes on how to build and burn the poopers?"

Manny reached for Lori with his good arm, but she was edging away as she finished her dangerous remark and so escaped with only a threatening look.

"She likes to live on the edge," Kenny commented.

"She always has," added Suzy.

"It was bad enough to tell that story to all of Lower Vale, but you just had to tell Lori the Tormentor," Manny yelled at Kenny.

"Will this duty allow you to take a few more classes yourself?" Kenny asked, changing the subject.

"I already thought of that. When I mentioned to the first sergeant that I was considering taking an extra class at night, the captain overheard us talking and said he was glad to hear of my interest in continuing my education," Manny stated. "So now I feel like I better go to school or have the captain on my back."

"Not to mention the increased harassment you will get from me if you don't go to school," Lori said as she rejoined the three others.

"Oh no, where do I sign up?" mocked Manny.

★

Spending the Christmas holiday at home with their families was very enjoyable. The best Christmas gift Maria received was the news that Manny was going to enroll in college. The months passed quickly as Manny instructed by day and learned by night. The semester came to a finish with Manny getting a B in English and a very proud A in sociology. After informing the first sergeant of his grades for the semester, Manny told the older Marine, "I'm anxious to get a new platoon this summer."

"Not until the fall."

"What? Why not? My shoulder is all healed," Manny demanded.

"You did very well in school, Corporal Smith. You should continue," the first sergeant said.

"I don't want to go to school," Manny protested.

"Too bad. The captain wants you to go, and the colonel agrees. I would say that means you're going back to school," emphasized the first sergeant.

Manny argued with the first sergeant for a minute. Then the older Marine gave him an evil look, and Manny dropped the subject. The decision had been made. It wasn't that Manny didn't want to go to school, but he liked training recruits much more.

"Are you registered for the summer?" asked the first sergeant.

"No, First Sergeant," Manny replied.

"Then I suggest that you get registered," he was told.

Kenny and Suzy were spending the weekend doing a whole lot of nothing when Ken mentioned Manny.

"Speaking of Manny, why doesn't he call Lori more often?"

"I don't know, Suz. I know he really likes her."

"I think so too, but sometimes he acts kind of cold toward her."

"I know what you mean, and I have a crazy idea about why he acts that way."

After Kenny said nothing else for a few moments, Suzy demanded, "Well?"

"Big opposing linemen never intimidated Manny, and deadly mortar fire never made him afraid to do his duty, but he may be intimidated by Lori's beauty and intelligence."

"Oh, Kenny, that is crazy. My cousin may be very intelligent and very beautiful, but she is also a very down-to-earth person," Suzy remarked with frustration.

"I know, but everyone has their Achilles heel. For Manny it may be a sense of insecurity. He has never said it, but I think that he expects Lori will one day be a very successful and important doctor, and she may consider herself to be—"

"Stop right there, Kenny," Suzy said. "What Manny imagines is a long way from reality. I don't know if Lori and Manny will ever fall in love, but I know that if my cousin falls in love with a man, it will not matter if he is a United States Marine or a United States senator. She will love him unconditionally."

"Why are you getting angry with me? I'm just trying to help figure this out. You're the one who asked why Manny's not more interested in Lori."

"Kenny, you are Manny's best friend. You should tell him that he may lose the best thing that ever happened to him if he isn't careful."

"I'll tell him this week when he stops by after his class."

"I wonder if I can say anything to Lori? She's mentioned Manny's lack of romance with her."

"You might tell Lori that the better things in life are worth waiting for."

"I hope you're right about that, in more ways than one."

Kenny put his arms around Suzy, pulled her close to him, and said, "I am, baby, trust me."

★

Manny was daydreaming in psychology class one evening when his thoughts were interrupted by his professor.

"Mr. Smith, I would be especially interested in hearing your thoughts on heredity or environment as the greater influence on a person's life, considering what you do for a living."

In a low voice, someone said, "Does killing come naturally, or were you trained to destroy human life?"

Manny knew to ignore comments like that. It wasn't the first time he'd heard such a remark. However, the professor did not let it pass.

"Mr. Arnold, if I ever hear another comment like that out of you or anyone else in my class, you will no longer be in my class. If you don't believe me, just try me, and you will learn that I am very serious."

There was an air of tension in the room, but Manny responded to the professor's question. "Well, sir, I think that under normal circumstances, both heredity and environment influence a person. But a shock environment, like a recruit experience at boot camp, I believe has a greater influence than heredity."

"Shock environment," repeated the psychology professor, "is an interesting description. Do you think the effect is long lasting?"

"I believe it is," Manny answered.

"Especially if it motivates you, right, Mr. Smith?" said the professor.

"Oorah, sir," Manny said back.

Almost all of the other students gave Manny a funny look, and several even laughed at Manny's response, but the professor never blinked.

Later that evening, Kenny asked his best friend, "Have you talked to Lori recently?"

"I've been meaning to call her, but I'm always afraid that I'll disturb her studying or something," Manny explained.

"Manny, I have to get something straight between us."

"What's the matter?"

"Sometimes I think you really like Lori, but sometimes I'm not so sure. Would you tell me what you think about your feelings for her?"

After a second of reflection, Manny asked, "What brought this on?"

"Suzy really cares about her cousin and doesn't like to see her hurt," Kenny explained.

"How am I hurting Lori?" asked Manny.

"Suzy thinks that Lori is really crazy about you, but you don't seem to feel the same about her. Suzy thinks Lori is hurt by the inconsistent way you treat her."

"Kenny, when Lori and I are together and having a good time, I'm in heaven. But I know that it's just because she is a beautiful and wonderful person. I'm sure that every guy she goes out with at UCLA is in heaven when he's with her."

"The way Suzy tells it to me, Lori doesn't go out all that much because she's afraid of missing a call from you."

"Kenny, my currant long-range goal is to be a sergeant major in the Marine Corps. Lori is going to be one of the most beautiful doctors in the world. She and I are like mud and perfume."

"Manny, I can't believe what I'm hearing. You have never been one to lack confidence. Why are you intimidated by the possibility of being with a beautiful girl who aspires to be a doctor?"

Manny said nothing, so Kenny continued, "I can't tell you what to do, Manny, but I think that if you care about Lori, you need to let her know it. If you don't want to stay involved with her, you should tell her." After a short pause, Kenny added, "I really think you would be fortunate to have a great girl like Lori, and I also think that Lori would be fortunate to get a great guy like you."

"I don't know what to think," Manny said.

Kenny grinned. "You always think better on a full stomach. Let's go get some chow."

"Yeah, a couple burgers and some jalapeno chili would really hit the spot!" exclaimed Manny.

"Ooraah!" yelled Kenny as the two friends walked off laughing.

★

Time flew by for the four friends. They were all busy with their studies, and Manny was again a drill instructor. More importantly, Manny was to be meritoriously promoted to sergeant. Kenny surprised Manny by showing up to the ceremony with Lori and Suzy. Afterwards, there was a lot of handshaking and congratulations extended. With almost no one remaining in the conference room, they agreed to go celebrate, and the new sergeant could treat.

Later, when the foursome was about to leave the restaurant, Kenny asked, "What do we want to do now?"

"Let's go for a walk," Suzy recommended.

"Yeah, let's work up an appetite so we can eat some more," Lori said.

"Don't start with me, Tormentor," Manny warned Lori.

"If we are all going to walk together, you two better settle down. Otherwise, you're walking by yourselves," advised Suzy.

"Don't you just hate civilized people?" Lori said to Manny.

Soon after starting their walk up the street, Manny suddenly asked, "Is there a chance of you girls spending the holidays in Lower Vale?"

Everybody stopped in their tracks.

"Are you inviting me to Lower Vale for Christmas?" Lori asked Manny.

"Yes, I think you would enjoy it, and I know I would love to have you," Manny replied.

Lori burst into tears and wrapped her arms around Manny's neck.

Manny instinctively put his arms around Lori but darted his eyes to Kenny and Suzy with a perplexed expression. Suzy and Kenny smiled at Manny and then at each other before walking on.

"Are you okay, Lori? I'm sorry that I upset you," Manny told her.

"You can upset me like that any time you want to," Lori replied.

While catching up with Kenny and Suzy, Manny said, "Aunt Carmella has told my mom about you, so I know my mom would love to meet you. Pappy and Cindy also."

"I would love to go to Colorado with you, but we're having family come to our house. My parents would be upset if I spent Christmas somewhere else," Lori said.

"Of course. I understand," Manny replied.

Then Lori asked, "Could you come by my parents' house for a short visit before you head off to Lower Vale?"

"Sure, I would like that," Manny told her.

"Great!" she replied.

The next day, as the two girls got ready to head back to Los Angeles, Manny and Lori kissed goodbye. He said, "It's been a great weekend, and I thought I would end it by telling you that I'm sorry I am not as romantic or attentive as I should be." After a short pause to catch his breath, Manny continued, "But I want you to know that I do love you."

For the second time in less than twenty-four hours, the pretty young pre-med student burst into tears and threw her arms around Manny. This time Kenny and Suzy were on the other side of the car, so they did not hear what had caused the outburst.

"What's wrong?" asked Suzy as she quickly came around the car.

"I told her that I don't think we should see each other anymore," Manny said.

For a brief moment, a look of devastation came over Suzy's face, causing the boys to break out laughing. Suddenly Kenny had to defend himself as Suzy began to pound on him.

"Hey, take it easy!"

"Let him go, Suzy. I'm sorry."

Then Lori told her cousin, "He said he loved me."

"It's about time," Suzy said, giving Manny a dirty look.

Watching the girls drive off, Kenny said to his best pal, "That was a great weekend."

"It sure was, Kenny. It sure was."

CHAPTER SEVEN

CHRISTMAS IN LOWER VALE AND SAN DIEGO

Lower Vale

"I CAN'T IMAGINE THAT I will ever get tired of coming home," Manny confided to his best friend as they crossed the state line and entered Colorado.

"I know what you mean."

"It would have been nice to bring the girls to Lower Vale."

"One of these days we will."

After rolling to a stop on the street in front of their homes, Kenny said, "The snowplow just went by. Looks like the first thing we get to do this vacation is shovel out the driveways so we can park off the street."

Without letting anyone inside know that they were home, each boy retrieved a snow shovel and began digging away the wall of snow preventing them from pulling in either of their driveways. Manny mused, "Speaking of good times growing up, how many tons of snow do you figure we shoveled from these driveways and sidewalks?"

"More than I care to remember," Kenny replied.

Their snow shovels clanking on the front porch made enough noise to announce the boys' arrival. Going in to the fireplace was a welcome treat for the tired and cold travelers, and being home was wonderful. Kenny's mom and Dr. Wheeler joined the crowd for an impromptu late-night party. As usual, everyone had many questions and comments. Maria was thrilled to hear about Manny's classes, and all present were pleased to learn that Kenny made the dean's list at SDSU. Manny's mother awkwardly broke the news that she was no longer seeing the boys' old high school football coach, just in case he'd expected to see Coach Gunn during the holidays. Manny hoped that one day she would find someone who made her feel like his father had.

He was still tired when he woke up the next day, but he could not sleep, so he went to the kitchen and found his grandfather drinking coffee.

"I heard you say last night that your battalion commander supports you going to school. How do the other drill instructors feel about it?" Pappy asked.

It was obvious to Manny that Pappy was concerned about animosity from his peers, so Manny explained, "I really don't think that any of them resent me for attending college. They've all been offered the same opportunity, but none of them do so. Besides, I go out of my way to pull more than my share of the load when I'm at the depot."

"It sounds like you don't have a lot of time for a social life."

"What we miss in quantity, we make up for in quality," replied Manny with a grin.

Kenny popped out of his house and waved at Manny to come over. Approaching the Reynolds house, Manny saw Kenny on the phone through the window.

"What's going on?" Manny asked as he joined his friend in the kitchen.

Kenny took the phone away from his ear and asked, "Do you have any plans for the twenty-sixth?"

"I don't think so. What's up?" Manny said.

Kenny hung up the phone. "A bunch of our old crowd is getting together for a party."

"Tarzan's hunting camp?" Manny said.

"You got it," Kenny said with excitement.

Except for the party with their high school friends, the next few days were uneventful for Kenny and Manny, and that was fine with them. They were happy to be home with their families.

Just after breakfast on the twenty-ninth, the boys had their vehicle packed for the return trip to California. They weren't especially anxious to leave home, but they were anxious to see their girlfriends, and Suzy's parents had invited them to a New Year's Eve party. The plan was for Kenny to drop Manny in Anaheim late on the thirtieth, and then Manny would go to Vista with Lori on the thirty-first. The four of them were not crazy about spending New Year's Eve with friends of Suzy's parents, but the Millers were so nice to the boys that they couldn't say no when Mrs. Miller invited them.

"See you tomorrow," Kenny yelled as he drove away from the Bakers' house.

After dinner that evening, Manny was pleased to hear Lori's mother say to Mr. Baker, "Let's go to the furniture store to see if that sofa I liked is still available."

Manny didn't quite understand the reply Mr. Baker mumbled, but as Lori's folks pulled out of their driveway, Lori said, "I can't believe I finally have you to myself."

"Well, now that you have me, what are you going to do with me?"

"I have a few ideas. What do you want me to do with you?"

"Maybe we can play doctor. Do you think you're qualified to give me a physical?" Manny said with a big grin.

"I'll do my best. Let me start with your tonsils," replied Lori as she wrapped her arms around the big Marine and French-kissed him passionately.

The next evening at the Millers' New Year's Eve party, Suzy knew almost everyone and made all the introductions. Most people were very polite and exchanged courteous greetings.

However, one uncomfortable encounter occurred when a couple asked Lori and the guys what they did. The couple was thrilled to learn that Lori was going to school, and complimented Kenny on attending college. Then Manny said, "I'm a sergeant in the Marine Corps."

"Oohhh," the lady said with a bit of hesitation in her voice.

There was an awkward pause before the man asked, "How long will you have to serve before you can get out of the Marines?"

"I don't expect to get out. I hope to make a career of it, just like my grandfather did," Manny replied.

"Really?" the woman asked.

Before Manny could answer, the man said to his wife, "I think it's common for Mexicans and others like them to gravitate to the security of the military."

Suddenly Kenny was in the man's face, "Just what are you trying to say, mister?"

"Kenny, please," said Suzy.

"Let it go, Kenny," Manny said, pulling Kenny toward the door.

Lori was livid as the four of them moved away from the couple. She glared back at the them. "Assholes."

"I'm not surprised that you two are a couple," the man said indignantly.

Within moments after the kids walked out the door, they heard a commotion in the house. Suddenly Mr. Miller yelled, "That young man is twice the man you'll ever be."

They couldn't hear the reply, but everyone in the neighborhood heard Mr. Miller's next statement: "Get out of my house, you bigoted son of a bitch!"

As the man and woman exited the Miller's house, they saw Manny, Kenny, and the girls standing in the driveway and scurried across the lawn and into the cul-de-sac where their car was parked.

"Manny," said Mrs. Miller when the foursome ventured back inside, "I'm so sorry about that. We only recently met the Dillards, and we certainly have no interest in ever meeting them again."

"It's okay, Mrs. Miller. People like those give us something else to laugh about."

"Mom, your other friends are all very nice—" Suzy started to say.

"It's okay," her mother cut in. "You kids don't have to stay."

After a brief discussion of what they might do, Suzy went in to tell her folks that they were heading for the beach to watch the fireworks display at midnight. She took a little longer than Lori or the boys expected, then emerged carrying a box.

"My mom insisted that we take a bunch of food with us."

"I really love your mom, Suzy," Manny stated.

"Oh great, now he won't pay any attention to me. How can I compete with your parents' cooking?"

"Try spreading cheese and chili sauce all over yourself," laughed Kenny.

"Babe, you know you're my favorite little chili pepper."

"Oh, Manny, you say the sweetest things."

Sitting on their blanket at the beach, the four friends talked about Christmas. The girls had considered their holiday a big bore until Manny and Kenny returned to rescue them from their families. Most of the conversation revolved around the boys' time in Lower Vale. Both Suzy and Lori already knew the story of Larry and Sarah, better known as Tarzan and Jane. But when Manny informed the girls that Tarzan was hoping to ask Jane to marry him, Lori and Suzy were as happy as could be.

"Some girls have all the luck," Suzy said mockingly.

"I thought good things were worth waiting for," Kenny responded.

"Sometimes a good thing now is better than a great thing who-knows-when?" Lori added.

Manny quipped, "It sounds to me like you girls think you're funny enough to be a comedy act for Ed Sullivan."

Then Kenny added, "Maybe we'll all get to attend Tarzan and Jane's wedding, and maybe they will return the honor one day."

"That's a wonderful dream to hold on to," Lori said as she hugged Manny.

"I'll second that," Suzy said.

Manny knew that he loved Lori and that Lori loved him. And he fantasized a few times about marrying, but he never had the courage to mention it to her. But Lori's comment told Manny that she also had thoughts of spending their lives together. He could not find the right words, so he just tightened his arm around her and kissed her on the head.

Lori squeezed Manny's kneecap and said softly, "I know."

"I hate to be rude, so we should eat some of this chow that your mom fixed for us," Kenny said to Suzy.

"Hey, that's my line," Manny said.

"We should eat first, Suzy. That way we can be sure of getting something," Lori commented.

"It looks like my mom sent enough for breakfast as well," Suzy replied.

After removing several containers from the box, Lori said, "Hey, check it out!" She held up a bottle of champagne.

"Your mom is great," Kenny said.

The four of them ate and drank for the twenty minutes leading up to the new year.

"It's almost midnight," Manny said. "Let's fill our glasses with the rest of the champagne. I want to make a toast."

Kenny poured. "Go ahead, Manny."

After a few seconds of silence, Manny said, "I'm not sure that this is a proper toast, but I just want to say how grateful I am for the love and friendship we share, and I hope it will last forever."

After breakfast the next day, Kenny said, "We still have a couple days before we all go back to work and school. Any ideas on what we want to do?"

"We always spend most of our time in the San Diego area. How about if we do Los Angeles?" Manny suggested.

"On the way we can stop at my house for lunch. My mom would love that," Lori said.

Manny and Kenny looked at each other with stupid grins, but they said nothing.

"*Yes*, we can go to Disneyland for a while this afternoon," Lori said. She and Suzy exchanged smiles about the big kids they loved.

On the way to Anaheim, the boys planned their strategy to make the most of the time they would spend at their favorite playground. Suzy and Lori provided technical advice.

At the Bakers' house, Mrs. Baker came outside to greet them, her whole face beaming with happiness.

Entering the kitchen, Lori said, "Mom, there are only four of us. Who's going to eat all this food?"

"We have a refrigerator, young lady. What the boys don't eat, your father and I will eat tonight and tomorrow," Lori's mom answered.

"And a lot more tomorrows after that," Lori teased.

Mrs. Baker raised an eyebrow at Lori, then turned to Manny and said, "Manny, if she sasses me one more time, I'm going to ask you to paddle her for me."

All eyes were on him as he replied, "If you keep fixing all the great chow for me, I'll paddle her anytime you ask, Mrs. Baker."

"Thank you, Manny."

"My pleasure."

Lori started to speak, then stopped herself and just gave Manny a threatening look.

An hour later, as the four youngsters headed out of the Baker house, Mrs. Baker asked, "Can I expect you for supper?"

"No, Mom," Lori replied. "We'll grab a sandwich in Hollywood."

"But you will be back here to spend the night, won't you?"

"Yes, Mom."

"Have a good time, and be careful," Mrs. Baker said as she again beamed her happy smile.

"You're such a show-off, Manny Smith. I hope all that food you ate makes you throw up on Mr. Toad," Lori scolded him once they were on the road.

"Hey, I figured I needed to build up my strength in case you need paddling," Manny said with a giant grin.

Lori started to speak, but glancing at Kenny and Suzy, she again clammed up and said nothing. But the look in her eye was ominous.

Entering Disneyland, Suzy took out her camera and said, "I want to ask someone to take a picture of us in front of the big map where we met."

"Great idea, Suzy."

Although the girls went on some of the rides, they spent much of the day watching the boys and taking pictures. That evening, the girls attempted to serve as tour guides as they drove around Hollywood. The four of them had their picture taken again at the famous corner of Hollywood and Vine.

Manny then said, "Where do you think I should leave my picture and address in case John Wayne decides to retire?"

His serious tone delighted the others.

Later that evening, after having their fill of Hollywood at night, the four friends sat on rotating stools in a little restaurant that reminded the boys of the Soda Jerk back home. While they sipped on Cherry Cokes, someone behind Manny said, "I think I smell a warmonger. Yeah, I'm sure I do because it smells like shit."

Glancing quickly over his shoulder, Manny spotted two men, tall and slender in build. It was obvious by their comments and scowls that the two troublemakers were angling for a fight. Manny fully intended to ignore them, but Lori responded, "You're not impressing anybody. Why don't you two go play in traffic."

"Well, looks like we have a good-looking sassy bitch here," one stranger said as he stepped toward Lori.

Manny spun around to face the two men behind him. "She is definitely good looking, and if you make her angry, she can most definitely be sassy. But she is my girl, so I'm only telling you this one time to leave her alone," Manny warned them, remaining on the stool.

Both men moved closer, standing shoulder to shoulder and glaring down at Manny.

"Stand up, soldier shit," the first one said.

"Please go away," Lori said.

The two bullies both glanced at Lori; their big mistake was taking their eyes off Manny. As quick as a rattlesnake, each of Manny's hands shot out and landed on a neck. Before they knew what hit them, Manny was squeezing their larynxes between his thumbs and index fingers. In reflex, both bullies reached up to grab Manny's hands, but it was too late. The excruciating pain took away all of their strength.

As he brought both of them to their knees, Lori exclaimed, "Manny, they've had enough."

"Okay," he replied. He pushed them to the floor where they gasped for air.

While everyone in the restaurant gaped at the scene, a very white-faced restaurant manager approached the four friends and nervously said to them, "Please leave."

"Sorry about the trouble," Manny apologized to him.

"Where did you learn that?" Kenny asked as they left the restaurant.

"Yeah, that was scary," added Suzy.

"I never used it before, but one of the lieutenants in the company has a black belt, and he was showing us stuff about pressure points," Manny replied.

"You need to show me some of that," Lori told Manny.

"Not in a million years."

"Chicken."

"But not stupid."

Driving back to Lori's, the four friends made casual conversation, but after a short period of silence, Manny stated out of the blue, "Before I finish my tour on the drill field, I want to produce an honor platoon."

Manny's comment caught the other three off guard, but Kenny replied, "But you only have what they give you to work with, and it's not always honor platoon material."

"Honor platoon, honor roll—I just think we all have to do our best and let the cards fall where they may," Suzy said.

"Suzy's right. We just have to do our best," Lori added.

Nobody said anything for about a minute. Then Kenny said, "With no football games to attend this semester, I guess you girls won't have much reason to get to San Diego."

"I guess we won't," Suzy replied.

"Why don't you plan to attend an MCRD graduation parade? You might be surprised and really enjoy it," Manny said.

"I agree," added Kenny. "And you should bring the old swabby."

"Bring who?" asked Lori.

"Your dad," Manny laughed.

For the next hour the four friends talked of attending the parade and taking Lori and Suzy's parents. They stayed about fifteen minutes in Anaheim, but finally it was time to go.

"Thanks for having us, Mrs. Baker," Kenny said. Suzy thanked her aunt as well.

"You're welcome anytime. You know that," Mrs. Baker told them.

Kenny and Suzy walked to the car as Lori and Manny entered the kitchen. "Thank you for having me, Mrs. Baker. And please pass on my thanks to Popeye the sailor."

Mrs. Baker laughed. "I can't wait to tell him that," she said.

Manny lingered with Lori on the porch for a minute. "Will you call me to let me know you're back in San Diego?" she asked.

"I always do," he answered.

With a tear in her eye, Lori said, "I'll miss you."

Manny wrapped his arms around her and held her close. Then, to break the sadness he said, "I better not hear that you've sassed your mother. If I do, I'll have to drive up her and paddle your sassy bottom."

"Promise?" Lori asked with a coy smile.

Manny smiled back before guiding Lori's lips to meet his.

A few minutes later in the car, the engine running, Manny kissed Lori one more time as she leaned in through the window. "Study hard. I'll call you later," he told her.

"I love you," she said.

"Love you, too," Manny replied.

Pulling away, Suzy commented, "'Love you too.' You sure are getting mushy these days."

"What are you talking about?" said Manny defensively.

"Nothing. But I wonder what your recruits would think if they knew their big tough drill instructor was really a big teddy bear?"

"Suzy, those guys in the restaurant were not faking the pain you saw on their faces," Manny said.

"You may think you're real tough with your martial arts, but I can handle you anytime I want," Suzy countered.

"Is that right?" Manny asked.

Suzy fastened her gaze on Manny, and in a threatening voice she said, "If you lay one hand on me, Smith, you'll never again taste my father's barbeque ribs."

The surprise on Manny's face caused Kenny and Suzy to burst out laughing. The thought of Suzy carrying out her threat immediately gentled Manny.

"The man has two serious vulnerabilities," Kenny said. "Lori and your dad's ribs."

"I wonder if Lori knows that her biggest competition for Manny's affection is a side of beef," Suzy said.

"Come on, Suzy," Kenny said. "Manny prefers Lori to any side of beef. Especially if she's been covered with barbeque sauce."

Kenny and Suzy cackled with delight. Manny sat silently, plotting his revenge. But as the three of them continued south, Manny had to admit that Suzy and Kenny were right. He was crazy over Lori.

That evening, when it was about time to leave the Millers' house, Manny said to his host, "I sure would like to get your recipe for barbeque sauce, Mr. Miller."

"Then you would have no reason to ever come and visit me again," Pat Miller replied.

"You know that's not true," Manny countered.

"Well, maybe one of these days I'll pass on my secret recipe because I know it will always be appreciated," said Mr. Miller.

"Now, that is very true," Manny said with a grin.

Suddenly the car's horn sounded and Kenny yelled, "Manny, let's go."

Approaching the car, Suzy said, "We were late leaving Anaheim because you couldn't pull yourself away from Lori. And now you're late leaving Vista because you can't pull yourself away from my dad's barbeque ribs. I don't know what to think of you, Marine."

Manny could do little but grin and bear it.

With the car pulling away, Suzy yelled, "Bye, I love you."

"Love you, too" was Kenny's reply.

Manny said nothing. His mind was back in Anaheim.

MCRD, San Diego

Manny was extremely proud when his recruits were recognized as honor platoon at the graduation parade. They shared a special feeling of pride and accomplishment, from youngest recruit to the senior drill instructor. Manny wished Lori and her folks could have been there, but an ill family member prevented it.

After the parade, Manny heard a familiar voice. "Congratulations on the platoon. They looked sharp."

With an ear-to-ear smile, Manny turned to see his old friend Rocky.

"Thanks, Rock. Are you coming here or passing through?" asked Manny.

"Just passing through. I have orders to Quantico," Rocky told him.

The two friends talked a long time before Rocky mentioned the *V* word. "You've been here for a while. Am I correct to assume you'll probably get orders back to Vietnam soon?"

"Yeah, my sergeant major says my orders will be cut this week or next."

"You take care. That place is a real shithole."

"Thanks, Rocky, I will."

Within a couple weeks, Manny did receive his orders back to Vietnam. He thought he had prepared Lori for the inevitable, but she still took it very hard. He hated seeing her upset, but there was nothing he could do.

Spring was always a beautiful time of the year, but the day of Lori's graduation could not have been any more beautiful. There was not a cloud in the sky, and the temperature was just right. Manny sat with Lori's parents and beamed with pride. As the graduates marched to their seats, Manny said to Lori's father, "This graduation reminds me of a Navy ceremony I once saw. They weren't worried about being in step either."

"Okay, jarhead, I owe you one," Mr. Baker replied.

Mrs. Baker just smiled and rolled her eyes as she sat between the two men.

After the graduation, there was a big party at the Bakers' house. Kenny and Suzy and her parents had everything ready when the three Bakers and Manny returned. Manuel and Carmella drove up from San Diego with a load of food. Mr. Baker ate a couple of Carmella's enchiladas and then commented, "Get out the antacids, dear. I gotta have some more of these."

After a week of doing very little but relaxing and having fun, Lori drove Manny to the airport so he could spend a week in Lower Vale prior to going back to Vietnam. At the airport, Manny said, "Why don't you come to Lower Vale with me so you can meet my mom, my sister, and Pappy?"

"I can't wait to meet your family, Manny. You know that I hope someday they'll be my family too. But for now, you should be there without me. I don't want your mother to resent me for taking away some of her time with you."

"I love you," Manny said.

"I love you, too," Lori said softly as she blew him a goodbye kiss.

★

Lower Vale

Manny thought he would get some sleep during the flight to Colorado but found that not to be the case. His mind wouldn't quiet down. He only had two more weeks until he was to depart to Vietnam. He would spend a week in Lower Vale with his family and then a week in California with Lori.

As he expected, his grandfather awaited him in the arrival area of the Denver airport. After a good hearty handshake, they headed for the parking lot.

"You're looking good, Pap. Those ladies must be taking good care of you."

"At ease, Sergeant Smith. That information is classified."

It was a great week for the Smith family. Manny was especially surprised by how much he liked Cindy's boyfriend. Brian seemed to have a good head on his shoulders. Maria Smith was on vacation for the week, so she was in her glory waiting on her boy. Several days after Manny returned home, she looked at him with a strange smile.

"What?" Manny asked.

"Lori seems like a very nice girl."

"What do you mean?"

"Kenny called you, but since you weren't here, I talked to him. Then he was polite enough to introduce me to Lori over the phone. We had a nice conversation about you."

"Exactly what did you two talk about?"

"Oh, nothing you would be interested in. It was just girl talk."

"I may have to choke Kenny."

"I know you really love her, don't you, Manny?"

"Yes, I do. She's wonderful."

"Wonderful enough to spend the rest of your life with her?"

"Yes, Mom, she is that wonderful."

"I'm very happy for you, and I can't wait to meet this girl who owns my son's heart," Maria said as she wrapped her arms around

Manny and held him tightly.

That night, Manny called Lori and talked to her for about fifteen minutes. He wanted to tell her about the conversation with his mom but decided he would wait and do it in person. The last thing they did over the phone was confirm the time of Manny's flight into Los Angeles.

After putting his things in the car, Manny turned to see tears running down his mother's cheeks. His own eyes filled with tears as he hugged her firmly. It was so painful to see his mom upset. Cindy was also teary eyed, and Mrs. Reynolds. As Pappy and Manny drove away, Manny turned to see his mother bury her head in Kathy Reynolds's shoulder.

Manny discarded any thoughts of sleeping on the plane. He continued to think of his family, and how painful it was to leave them. To fight the depression of missing his mother, sister, and grandfather, Manny turned his thoughts to seeing Lori. He knew that the week would pass quickly. For that reason, he tried to think of ways to make the time seem to pass slowly.

"Sir, would you please fasten your seat belt? We are starting our descent to Los Angeles," the stewardess said to Manny.

Oh, wow, he thought. Just thinking about Lori made the time pass quicker. It would undoubtedly fly by when he was with her over the next six days.

Manny heard her voice before he saw her: "Manny, over here."

"Hey, babe!" He embraced Lori and kissed her like there was no tomorrow.

"Manny, you're squishing me."

"Sorry, I get carried away sometimes."

"I like it when you get carried away, but not too carried away."

During the next five days, they did everything they could to make each day a full one. For three days they spent time with Kenny and Suzy, but the other days were reserved for just the two of them. A trip to San Diego, a visit to the Millers in Vista, a short day at Disneyland, a lot of time on the beach just lying in the sun, and lots of long walks passed the time enjoyably—and, as Manny predicted, too quickly.

"I have to go say goodbye to Uncle Manuel and Aunt Carmella tonight."

"I know. Do you want to go alone?"

"No, I'm sure they'll expect you to be with me, and I know they want you to visit while I'm away."

"I definitely intend to."

After visiting for a couple hours, Manny looked at his great-aunt and uncle and said, "It's getting late. I'm afraid we have to be going."

On the way to the car, Lori seemed to be okay, but Manny found her crying as he got into the driver's seat. He scooted over to hold her and then said, "Does this mean you're going to miss me?"

She only cried harder. Manny tried to hide his slight smile.

They would spend their last night at Kenny's apartment. Manny knew that Kenny would not be home that night because that was the way the boys planned it.

"Do you want something to drink?" Manny asked his girl as they entered the apartment.

"Sure, does Kenny have any soft drinks?" she asked.

"Most likely. I'll get us something."

Lori went to the bathroom to check her makeup, and when she returned Manny was on the sofa with a couple drinks. She plopped herself down on his lap.

"I love you so much."

"Do you think you always will?" he asked.

"What a silly question. You know I will," she answered with slight indignation.

Manny slipped his hand between the cushions of the old sofa. With his hand still between the cushions, he asked Lori, "Does that mean you would be willing to wear this?"

As he said that, Manny revealed his hand; in it was a small ring box, which he deftly opened with his thumb. She gazed down at the diamond ring.

"Oh, Manny."

"I will love you forever, Lori Baker. Please do me the honor of being my wife."

"I love you. I love you, yes, yes, *yes!*"

"Your yes is not official until you put the ring on your finger. Don't you know that?"

"Then put it on."

Manny slid the ring onto Lori's finger, then looked up at the tears of joy in her eyes. They kissed again, and Manny put one of his arms around her back and the other under her legs, lifting Lori as he stood. He turned and started to drop to one knee to place her on the sofa.

"We have some good memories on this old sofa, but why don't you carry me into the bedroom so you have room to be beside me? Two of us don't fit very well on this thing, or don't you remember?" Lori asked with a smile.

Manny did not hesitate to carry his new fiancée to the bedroom. It would be their last night together for a long while, it was the night of their engagement, and he could not be happier.

With the bedspread pulled to the bottom of the bed, Manny watched Lori reach back to unzip her navy-blue dress.

"May I help you out of that pretty dress, pretty lady?" Manny asked her.

"Manny Smith, I'm worried about that tone in your voice and the look in your eyes. Should I be nervous about your intentions?" Lori asked coyly.

"I don't know, Lori. What intentions of mine would cause you to worry?" Manny replied as he stepped close and put his arms around her waist.

Lori breathed deeply and looked up at him, silent. Manny moved his hands from the small of her back to her shoulders and gently pulled the dress straps off her shoulders. With her dress on the floor, Lori gazed into his eyes.

"Well, Marine, are you going to answer my question? What are your intentions?" Lori murmured.

"Lori Baker, a few minutes ago you agreed to be my wife, and I want our marriage to be one of honesty. With that said, I have to confess that you should be very concerned over my intentions at this time."

With no warning, Lori pushed Manny onto the bed and exclaimed, "My parents can be concerned, but I am very excited about your intentions, Manny Smith!"

Lori jumped onto the bed and kissed him as she attempted to undo the buttons of his shirt. Simultaneously, Manny fumbled with the hooks of Lori's bra. With the last shirt button undone, Lori pushed herself up and straddled him. When she leaned down to kiss him, he again reached for her white lacy bra, and with a simple snap of his fingers, it came undone.

"Well done, lover boy," Lori said deliberately as she pulled the straps over her arms, tossed the bra onto her dress, and lay on top of Manny.

The passion he felt for her almost took his breath away. Lori breathed heavily as they embraced and kissed.

"I love you, so much, Manny," Lori whispered in his ear.

"I love you, too."

Never in his life could Manny have imagined the love and passion he felt this evening. He was also overcome with feelings of gratitude, contentment, and satisfaction. It was the greatest night of his life.

The next day, Manny and Lori turned the corner onto the Millers' street in Vista. Kenny and Suzy were leaning against the car in the driveway. "There they are," Lori said.

Before the car rolled to a stop, Lori was opening her door to jump out. She ran to her cousin and said, "What do you think?" as she held up her hand to show Suzy the ring.

The screaming of the two girls brought Mrs. Miller out of the house. Upon learning the good news, she hugged her niece tightly. "That's wonderful, Lori."

"Just like you planned?" Kenny asked his best friend.

"Just like I planned," Manny replied with a grin.

After saying goodbye to Mr. and Mrs. Miller, they were on their way to the airport. Suzy, Kenny, and Lori accompanied Manny as far as they could. Kenny shook his best friend's hand but could only force out a faint "Take care. No heroics, understand?"

"I understand. You take care of these two girls," Manny responded.

Kenny nodded. Then Suzy gave Manny a big hug before she and Kenny headed off to give Manny and Lori and minute alone.

"I'll tell you about the wedding plans in my letters," she said.

"Do I get any say in this wedding?" Manny asked.

"Maybe a little," Lori teased him.

When many of the other servicemen started to board the plane, Manny said, "Don't worry about me. Just remember that I love you. And good luck with your studies."

"I love you," she said as the tears rolled down her cheeks.

"I love you, too," he said. Then he turned and headed for the plane, pausing once to look back briefly at the woman who wanted to be his wife. They waved briefly; then he was gone.

It was early June in Southern California, but watching Manny disappear onto the plane gave Lori a chill.

CHAPTER EIGHT

COLLEGE GRADUATION AND VIETNAM AGAIN

MANNY TRIED NOT THINKING of the unpleasantness awaiting him in Vietnam. Instead, he dwelled on the wonderful memory of the past three weeks. His thoughts were interrupted when the young Marine beside him looked at the ribbons on Manny's chest and said, "I see you're heading back for another tour."

"Yeah, I'm afraid so," Manny said.

"What do you mean you're afraid?" the PFC demanded.

"It's a figure of speech. I'm not afraid of going back, but there are other things I would enjoy doing a lot more."

"Well, there's nothing I would rather be doing than killing gooks."

"Good luck to you," replied Manny. He looked away and hoped for no more discussion.

The drive back to Anaheim was a quiet one. Lori wiped an occasional tear from her eyes and turned down a suggestion to stop and get a drink. But then it was Lori who broke the silence when she said to Kenny, "I'm assuming you knew that Manny was going to propose last night."

"Hey, of course I knew. I tried to talk him out of it, but it was no use," Kenny replied with a big grin.

"Pay no attention to my idiot boyfriend."

"Aw, lighten up. If you two give me a bad time, I won't tell you what it was that sealed Manny's decision to propose," Kenny told the girls.

Later, as Kenny and Suzy got into their car to depart the Bakers, Lori said, "I hope you two will stop by every once in a while."

"Lori, what a crazy thing to say. You know we'll be here often."

"I expect you to come and visit me in San Diego. Friendship travels both ways, you know," Kenny told her.

"Lori, Manny's great-aunt and uncle will be expecting you to visit them now that you're joining the family. I wonder if they know the big news?"

"They know," Kenny confirmed.

Lori waved one more time as her cousin and Kenny drove off. She stood in the driveway for a minute, unmoving. A feeling of emptiness drained her strength. Lori knew she still had Suzy and Kenny for moral support, and she was very happy for that. But Suzy and Kenny were a part of her relationship with Manny, so as they drove away, the pain of missing him increased all the more.

"Come inside, sweetheart," Mr. Baker said, coming to stand alongside his daughter and put his arm around her.

"It hurts so much, Daddy."

Driving down the highway, Suzy said to Kenny, "Maybe we can have a double wedding. It would be kind of fitting since we're cousins and you guys are like brothers and we all met at the same time. Don't you think?"

"Yeah, that would be great," Kenny agreed absently, but his thoughts were with Manny.

A few days later, Kenny was at the San Diego Parks and Recreation office bright and early for his job interview. He hoped to earn money for a diamond ring so they could have that double wedding Suzy wanted. He was hired on the spot.

During the first month of his new job, Kenny found himself very busy. He was actually busier than he needed to be, but he enjoyed what he was doing. On the one evening—or sometimes two—a week that Kenny was free, Suzy usually drove down to be with him.

One particular evening was special because Lori was coming along, and they were all going to meet at the Riveras' restaurant.

"Carmella, your pacing won't bring the girls any faster," Manuel said.

"Mind your own business," Carmella replied.

Manuel shook his head at Kenny. Kenny only smiled.

Just as Carmella finally gave in and came to sit at the table where the two men waited, Manuel and Kenny stood quickly and said in unison, "They're here."

Carmella passed them in an instant to throw her arms around Lori. "I'm so glad to see you."

Kenny embraced Suzy and gave her a kiss but soon felt something tugging at his arm. "Let go of her," Carmella said huffily. "You get to hug her all the time. Now it's my turn."

Kenny released Suzy and stood back as Aunt Carmella and then Uncle Manuel hugged the girls.

Before they were even seated, Carmella asked Lori, "What's the latest from our Manny? Is he okay? Does he need anything?"

"He said he's fine."

"How often do you hear from him?" asked Kenny.

"I usually get two or three letters a week," Lori answered.

"What the heck," said Kenny. "I've only received four letters since he's been gone. I can't believe he writes you more than me."

After eating too much, Kenny and the girls decided to take a walk. They waved goodbye to the Riveras and started down the street. After a few comments about how much they all had eaten, Lori said, "I have some news about Manny that I didn't want to say in front of his aunt and uncle."

Kenny and Suzy stopped dead in their tracks.

"In a letter I received just yesterday, Manny said that his captain asked him about becoming an officer."

"An officer? How?" Kenny asked excitedly.

"Manny said that it's not likely, but because he has a bunch of college credits and a good record, and because they really need officers, he was asked if he was interested," Lori said.

"What did Manny say? Did he tell you what he said?" asked Suzy.

After taking a deep breath, Lori said, "Manny told his CO he was really flattered but doubted that he was qualified. Then the captain told Manny that the Marine Corps would be the judge of that."

After a moment of silence, Lori asked, "What do you think, Kenny?"

"Manny is already a better officer than many of the officers. I'm betting that someone is smart enough to take advantage of Manny's potential and he'll be a lieutenant soon," Kenny said.

Little did Lori, Kenny, and Suzy know that the recommendation to award Sergeant Manny Smith a battlefield commission was already being considered. The Marine Corps needed good, experienced officers, but before an enlisted Marine could be entrusted with the responsibility of a battlefield commission, he had to be exceptionally good.

It had been only five weeks since the captain spoke to Manny, but in early August a board of senior officers closely studied Manny's record and the endorsements he'd received. When the members of the board reviewed their findings, they were unanimous in approving Manny for promotion to the rank of first lieutenant. His Marine Corps school records, his college credits, and his combat record were all superior. The fact that his father and grandfather were Marines was just icing on the cake.

Manny was expecting to be promoted by his captain but learned that the battalion commander would exercise his privilege as senior officer.

"Congratulations, Lieutenant Smith," said his battalion commander. "I hate to lose a good sergeant from my battalion, but I am happy to see the Marine Corps gain a good officer."

"Thank you, sir," Manny responded as he saluted the departing lieutenant colonel.

"Pardon me, Lieutenant Smith. May I please have a word with you, sir?"

It was the battalion sergeant major asking to speak with Manny.

The silence was scary. All the Marines gathered there were taken aback by the significance. The sergeant major was never the one to do the asking; he did the telling. Yet here he was, asking Manny for permission to speak with him. Manny felt like a Little League baseball player being asked for an autograph by Stan Musial.

"Of course, Sergeant Major. Excuse me, men."

Manny was extremely grateful that his rubbery legs did not give out on him as he walked off with the battalion's senior enlisted Marine.

The sergeant major spoke first. "I'm sure you know there will be some trying moments for you as a new lieutenant. Some people will support you as much as I do, but we have some assholes in the Marine Corps who will test you every chance they get."

"I know, Sergeant Major. I've thought of very little else all day," Manny said.

"I wanted you to stay in this battalion because here you're already a proven commodity. By sending you to the 12th Marines, there will be more critics to put up with, but the decision has been made," lamented the older Marine.

"I can't tell you enough how much I appreciate your concern," Manny replied.

"Just do your best to take care of your men, and they will take care of you. And don't let them get away with any crap. Demand the best they can give you. You will slip up now and then, Lieutenant; we all do. And things will frequently go really shitty for you, but you just keep your chin up and your pride deep, and you'll be okay. Good luck, sir," the sergeant major said as he stuck out his hand.

Manny was genuinely touched by the sergeant major's gesture. As he turned to walk away after shaking hands, the older Marine said, "Lieutenant, you forgot something!"

The sergeant major stood at attention, saluting the new lieutenant. Manny returned the salute and with a little bit of embarrassment said, "Thank you, Sergeant Major. I won't forget again."

The next day, Manny joined his new unit.

"Welcome aboard, Smith. The colonel informed me that he talked with the CO of 2nd Battalion and you're going to Delta Battery. You'll be the assistant executive officer for a month or so before taking over as the XO," the adjutant informed Manny.

"How will I get to 2nd Battalion?"

"The colonel himself is taking you."

"What?"

"Have a seat, sir. The colonel's jeep will be here ASAP."

Manny heard people approaching and could not believe his eyes when Colonel Wolf walked in and said, "Welcome aboard, Lieutenant Smith. Looks like the Marine Corps has us serving together again."

Manny shook hands with his old battalion commander from Camp Pendleton and again marveled at how small the Marine Corps was.

On the way to the headquarters of the 2nd Battalion, the regimental commander and Manny talked briefly about the common acquaintances they had. When they arrived at their destination, Colonel Wolf was greeted by the battalion XO, who said the battalion CO had to go to Echo Battery for some reason. Manny sensed that Colonel Wolf was not happy about something, so he slipped away to find the battalion S-1 and wait for transportation to his new unit.

★

Vietnam as a Lieutenant

The heat in South Vietnam was seldom enjoyable, but on this particular day in August, it was just plain miserable. After growing up in the moderate climate of Colorado, Manny believed he had adjusted to the heat of Southern California quite well. But there was no getting used to Southeast Asia, especially in a helmet and flak jacket.

It had only been three weeks or so since Manny joined Delta Battery, but Lieutenant Cain left suddenly, and Manny was now the executive officer. His primary responsibility was running the gun line, and no one did it better. That was why Manny had been sent to Delta. Although he was the new guy, the Marines of Deadly Delta learned quickly that their new lieutenant had his shit wired.

"It looks like you took over the gun line just in time, XO," said Captain Honeywell.

"In time for what, sir?" Manny asked the battery CO.

"The colonel says he's sending us into the boonies to occupy a firebase," Honeywell explained.

"Damn, we're already down to four or five men to a howitzer. If we have to do a 360 security, it will degrade our ability to fire for extended periods of time," Manny said.

"I know, but orders are orders."

"Yes, sir. We can do it."

"Get the first sergeant and gunny so we can plan out this move."

"Your hooch in ten minutes?" Manny asked.

"Check."

In just under ten minutes, Manny strode into Captain Honeywell's bunker. With the CO was Lieutenant Stevens—the battery fire direction officer, or FDO. Manny liked Stevens and looked up to him because Stevens was extremely bright and easy to talk with. The FDO was even happy to take time to review details of fire direction procedures.

The captain started the brief with a surprise. "Helo support will be here tomorrow. We'll be airlifted to the firebase the morning after."

"Will the trucks follow us to the firing position?" Manny asked.

"Not a chance, XO. This hill is flat on top but high and steep."

"Son of a bitch!" the gunny exclaimed, glaring at the ground.

"Go ahead, Guns. Let's hear the rest of your thoughts."

"Me and Lieutenant Smith have both been to this kind of place before. They can be harder than a motherfucker to defend," the battery gunny bitched.

"First Sergeant, see if battalion has any idea when we might get some more cannoneers," the captain instructed.

"I'll check it out, Skipper."

"And ask for all the wire they'll give us, and more mines."

"And lots of hand grenades," said Manny.

"Damn straight, lots and lots of hand grenades," the gunny emphasized.

It was often difficult to shoot at an enemy as he was climbing a steep slope toward you, especially when you were on the level top of the hill. Lobbing grenades down the sides of the hill was often much more effective and did not expose men to the enemy.

"Sir, if there are no roads to this position, how was it prepared?" Manny asked.

"I get the impression that it was bombed so many times by the wing that it's relatively cleared out," the CO answered.

"They have to be kidding," grumbled the gunny.

The next day was hectic as the choppers arrived and picked up Delta for movement to the remote firebase. Captain Honeywell went on the first bird with an advance party of Marines to make sure the location was safe and secure.

Manny's responsibility was to make sure everything got out of the battery position in good order. He would board the last chopper to the new battery position. All the helicopters flew a different route to the site.

Ten minutes into the flight, Manny and the others were startled by a loud crash near the front of the aircraft. Although it was obvious to all on board, the crew chief screamed at Manny and the three other men from the battery, "BRACE YOURSELF! WE'RE GOING DOWN!"

Manny was knocked out by the impact of the crash.

As he regained consciousness, he realized that he was being dragged through the jungle by several men. His head and shoulder hurt terribly, but his hands and feet were bound, and he was in no condition to resist.

Manny had no idea how long he had been dragged through the jungle, but after the group stopped, he heard loud voices speaking Vietnamese. Lifting his head, Manny saw that he was at a small jungle village. Only minutes later, Manny was again being dragged along the ground, this time for less than a minute before he was roughly dropped into a hole in the ground.

Lower Vale

Kenny sat in his mom's kitchen, reflecting on the past few days. Earning his college degree in three years had not been easy, but the look on his mother's face at graduation made every hour of studying worthwhile. The only bad thing was that Suzy's graduation had been on the same day. But even though they couldn't attend each other's graduations, the joint celebration at the Millers' house was fantastic.

Suzy would be flying into Lower Vale that afternoon to spend a week with Kenny. And according to his plan, when she departed, Suzy would be Kenny's fiancée.

"A penny for your thoughts, graduate," Kathy Reynolds asked her son. She was still beaming with pride.

"I was just thinking about graduation, and Suzy." After a deliberate pause Kenny added, "and about asking her to marry me."

As his mother turned, Kenny held up the open ring box for his mother to see.

"Oh, Kenny, it's beautiful."

"I hope she says yes."

"Suzy is a very intelligent girl, and more importantly, she loves you very much. I am confident that she will say yes."

"Yeah, how could she pass up such a great catch?"

"By the way, Mr. Great Catch, when do plan to propose?"

"I was thinking I would ask her tonight after I take her to dinner."

There was a knock at the back door, and Cindy said, "Mrs. Reynolds, may I get a couple cups of sugar?"

"Of course, dear. Come here for a second to see what Kenny has," Kathy told Cindy.

Kenny held out the ring box and said, "What do you think?"

"It's really nice, Kenny, but I'm afraid I have to say no. It's bad enough living beside you; I could never handle living with you," Cindy said with a straight face.

Mrs. Reynolds broke out laughing.

"Manny Junior, that's what I ought to call you," scoffed Kenny as he walked away.

He thought about leaving for the airport a little early, but then picked up the basketball to work on his patented thirty-feet hook shot. After a couple misses, he made one shot, then missed two, and then made three in a row. *Yes!*

"Pretty good shooting," Kenny heard Pappy yell.

"Thanks, Pap," Kenny yelled back.

Cindy emerged from the house with the sugar and meandered across the driveway. "Sorry if I broke your heart, Kenny. I know you'll find someone else."

Kenny said, "It will take a lot more sugar to make you sweet, brat."

Later that day when Kenny and Suzy arrived home from the airport, Mrs. Reynolds and Cindy came out to greet them. Kenny was immediately concerned that Cindy would spill the beans.

"Welcome, Suzy," Kenny's mother said, glowing. "I'm so happy to have you here."

"Thank you, Mrs. Reynolds. I'm very happy to be here."

"Suzy, this is our neighbor, Cindy Smith," said Kathy.

Cindy quickly said, "Gee, Suzy, you're really pretty. You could have done much better in picking a boyfriend if you ask me."

Kenny gave Cindy the evil eye while the three women laughed. Then Suzy said, "There's no doubt in my mind that you are Manny's sister."

"You can say that again!" exclaimed Kenny.

"Suzy, I was just heading to the store. May I get you anything?" asked Kathy.

"I would like to come with you if I may," Suzy said in return.

"Glad to have you," Kathy said.

Less than an hour later, Kenny heard his mother's car pull in, stopping at the beginning of the driveway to leave plenty of room for shooting baskets. His mother and Suzy each carried a bag down toward the garage where Kenny was bouncing the basketball. He glanced up. Then he spotted something behind them.

As if someone had thrown a switch, Kenny froze in place. His body went numb, and his well-conditioned athletic heartbeat jumped from sixty to one hundred twenty beats a minute. His mind raced back through the years, and his silent subconscious screamed.

"Kenny, are you okay?" Kathy asked in alarm.

But he could not answer her. Even if he'd heard his mother, Kenny could not speak. His mouth was dry, and his eyes filled with tears as they fixed on the green-uniformed man now walking up the sidewalk toward the Smith house.

Kathy Reynolds turned to see the green sedan parked on the street. Then she caught a glimpse of the Marine as he stepped onto the front porch of the Smith house.

"Kenny?"

Suzy didn't seem to understand what was happening, but soon tears were running down Mrs. Reynolds's face as Kenny's mother realized the significance of the green sedan.

The very thing that Kathy Reynolds prayed would never happen to her was now happening to her good friend Maria.

They heard Maria's cry of anguish, and Kenny dashed toward the Smith house. As Kenny entered the front door, he saw Maria and Cindy holding each other and crying on the sofa. Maria held out her arms to him. He dropped to his knees and gathered Maria and Cindy to him, then let go as his mother arrived. Kathy embraced the Smith women as they all cried.

"What can you tell me?" Kenny asked the Marine.

"Lieutenant Smith is missing in action," the staff sergeant told Kenny. "I will try to get more details as soon as I can. I'm very sorry. I'm just following my orders."

"I understand, Staff Sergeant. It's okay. You can leave now, but please let us know when you learn more," Kenny said.

Going back to Maria, Cindy, and his mother, Kenny found that Suzy had joined them, her face also wet with tears. She knew Manny too well to not be affected by the terrible news.

Kenny said to Maria, "I'll go to the lumberyard and get Pappy."

Maria nodded her consent.

In the car, Kenny grabbed Suzy's hand and held it tightly. "He's still alive. I can feel it. He'll be okay."

As Kenny approached Pappy at the lumberyard, the old man saw the look on the younger man's face. Pappy's lower lip began to quiver.

"He's MIA, Pap. We don't have any details yet," said Kenny.

Even during one of the worst moments of his life, Pappy was polite to the young lady in the car. He sank into the back seat and nodded cordially. "It's nice to finally meet you, Suzy. I wish it were under better circumstances."

"I'm glad to finally meet you too, Mr. Smith," Suzy replied.

Then Pappy said to Kenny, "Let's go by the recruiting office. I want to see the notification and use the phone."

"Maybe we ought to go home first, Pap. I told Mrs. Smith I would get you."

"You're right, Kenny. I don't know what I'm thinking."

Arriving back at the Smith house, Pappy, Maria, and Cindy clutched each other for a minute as Suzy and the Reynoldses held hands nearby. Kathy had called Ron Wheeler after Kenny and Suzy left to get Pappy. The mental anguish they all shared was insufferable alone. Minutes later, Dr. Wheeler arrived and was greeted by all. He tried to say something to Maria, but his voice broke, and he could not finish.

Pappy broke the silence. "The fact that he's listed as MIA is positive. Because Manny is now an officer, he was likely taken prisoner. Manny is tough. If we keep the faith, I believe it will help him get through this and return safely home."

Kenny retreated from the scene as tears once again filled his eyes. He couldn't stand being in the house. Wandering blindly for quite some time, he found himself at the post office, looking at the recruiting posters. He remembered how much Manny enjoyed looking at them.

Kenny was caught by surprise when he heard Dr. Wheeler say, "Your mother and your girlfriend are very worried about you, and they don't need anything else to worry about."

"They don't need to know I was here," Kenny replied.

"I agree, Kenny. Come on, let me give you a ride home," Dr. Wheeler said.

On the way home, Kenny asked, "How long did you have to look for me?"

"As long as it took to drive to the post office," the doctor answered.

"How did you know I would be there?"

"Pappy Smith said you might be," the doctor said.

Kenny shook his head. "He is amazing."

"I think wise with experience is a more accurate description," Dr. Wheeler added.

Shortly after he returned to the house, Kenny's mother cornered him and said, "When I first asked Dr. Wheeler where he found you, I knew he wasn't telling the truth by the way he looked away from me when he answered."

Kenny said nothing.

"Do you think you're going to go back to that horrid place and rescue Manny?" his mother asked in frustration.

With tears in his eyes, Kenny said, "I may not be able to affect what happens to Manny, but I know deep in my heart that if I were a POW, my best friend would come after me."

He turned away from her, unable to argue the point, and rejoined the others in the living room.

Suzy felt very awkward because she knew there was nothing she could do for Kenny to ease his pain. Then a thought occurred to her. "Do you know if Mrs. Smith talked to her aunt and uncle in San Diego? And what about Lori? Did the Marine Corps notify her?"

A strong sense of guilt swept over Kenny when he realized he did not know if Aunt Carmella and Uncle Manuel knew the terrible news. And he was sure the Marine Corps had not notified Lori. "Oh, Suzy, I'm so ashamed. I've been so upset that I haven't thought about the people in California."

"How do we find out?" she asked.

Pappy told them, "I asked Maria about calling the Riveras, but she said she wasn't up to it. I'll talk to them in the morning. Regarding Lori, the Marine Corps doesn't notify fiancées, so I doubt seriously that she knows what's going on."

"Maybe you should call your mom and dad," Kenny suggested to Suzy.

After a short pause, and with a faint and fearful voice, she said, "Maybe I should fly back to be with Lori?"

Kenny hesitated, then said, "I don't want you to go, but things around here are not good, and Lori will need you. Maybe you should."

Tears again welled in her eyes, and Suzy lowered her head as she started to cry. Kenny encircled her in his arms and held her tightly. He'd never dreamed he could feel so miserable, but to make matters worse, he must now inform Suzy of his intentions to go back into the Marine Corps.

With all the strength and courage he could muster, Kenny said, "Suzy, I'm going back into the Marine Corps."

For just a moment, she said nothing. Then as Suzy seemed to

realize the situation and what he was saying, she pleaded, "Kenny, you can't. Please don't!"

"I have to. Don't you understand?"

"I understand that you love Manny, and that you are very upset. But what about me? I thought you loved me too," Suzy said with great pain in her voice.

"I do love you, Suzy. I've loved you from the first day I met you at Disneyland. And I want to be with you forever. But I have to know that I have done everything I can possibly do for Manny, or I could not live with myself," Kenny tried to explain.

Unable to bear the moment, she fled from the Smith house and down the street.

Cindy followed.

"Do you mind if I walk with you, and maybe talk a little?" Cindy asked.

Suzy shook her head and said, "But I don't know what there is for us to talk about."

Cindy acted as if she didn't hear Suzy. "I love Kenny like he's my own flesh-and-blood big brother. And it's obvious that you love Kenny and want to marry him. I happen to know that he feels the same about you, but you have to realize that Kenny and Manny are more than best friends, or even brothers. They share a common soul. Neither had a father growing up. They had Pappy, but more importantly they had each other. Kenny was Manny's father, and Manny was Kenny's father. Kenny is doing what is in his heart. It's the same heart that he loves you with, but you are not in trouble like Manny."

The two young women walked a little further, both silent.

Then Suzy said, "But you know the odds are that if Kenny goes back to the Marine Corps, it will only make things worse."

"I think we all realize that, but when love and devotion are involved, the odds go out the window," Cindy responded.

"Oh, God. Why did this have to happen? Yesterday everything was so wonderful, and today everything is so terrible. I can't believe it," Suzy lamented.

"Suzy, stop for a moment and listen to yourself. Your boyfriend may go away for a while, but at this time he is here and he loves you very much. My brother is not here, and for all we know, he may never be here again!" Cindy said, bursting into tears. She hurried away.

Suzy immediately sank down on the sidewalk, too weak to stand as a wave of guilt and shame came over her. She loved Manny very much, but all she had thought about the past hour was herself. She wasn't even thinking about Lori. As Suzy sat on the concrete, she began to cry again. She thought about all the wonderful times the four of them had together. She thought about Manny and said a short, silent prayer for his safety. Then she thought of Lori and started to think of how she must break the news to her cousin.

After Suzy returned to the Reynolds house a little later, Kenny's mother was there to greet her. "You must be exhausted, Suzy. Why don't you go to bed and we'll see what the morning brings?"

Suzy nodded in agreement.

The next morning, Suzy entered the kitchen, looking for Kenny.

"Kenny and I had words a little earlier," Kathy told her, "as I suspect you may have heard. Anyway, he went out to get breakfast elsewhere. May I get you something to eat?"

"If you have any cereal, that would be fine," Suzy replied.

The two women sat at the kitchen table.

"Suzy, I wish I knew what to tell you to make this easier, but I am afraid I don't. Kenny has never been the stubborn type, but this thing about returning to the Marine Corps has him possessed."

"I know, Mrs. Reynolds. I can't understand it either," Suzy replied.

"However, I do know that my son loves you very much. It seems to me that he hopes you two will marry in the not-too-distant future," Kathy said.

"Those were my hopes, too. But I can't stand the thought of him going back to Vietnam. And in light of what happened to Manny, how can he expect me to accept it so lightly?" Suzy said, frustrated.

"I understand your fears, Suzy. I share them."

"I have my bags packed. Will someone please take me to the airport so I can be with Lori?"

"What about Dr. Wheeler? He is a wonderful man; I'm sure he'll volunteer."

Ten minutes later, as the two ladies stood by the car, Suzy said, "Thank you for having me, Mrs. Reynolds."

"I expect you back one day soon" was Kathy's response.

"I hope so," Suzy said.

California

Under most circumstances, Suzy would be anxious for a plane ride to end. But as the captain announced that they were about to make their descent to Los Angeles, Suzy dreaded what lay ahead. Her parents would be waiting for her as she arrived. She told them only that she and Kenny had a fight but did not inform them of the other reason for her early return.

After being so upset for so long, the sight of her parents caused Suzy to break down as she came off the airplane. Sitting in the airport with her parents, Suzy explained that the three of them had to go to the Bakers' house to inform Lori of the Marine Corps' notification that Manny was missing in action.

When the Millers' car pulled into the driveway, Mr. Baker came around the house to greet them. "Hey, this is a nice surprise," he said. But the smile on his face disappeared quickly.

"We have some very bad news, Max. Please get Lori," Mr. Miller said.

Mr. Miller immediately knew the subject of the news. "How bad is it?"

"Manny is missing in action," Pat Miller replied.

Just as Mr. Baker turned to get his wife and daughter, they came around the corner. Lori immediately spotted the look on her cousin's face. "Suzy, what's wrong?"

Suzy could not speak, but she rushed to Lori and put her arms around her cousin as more tears erupted.

Lori jerked her head toward her aunt and saw the tears running down Mrs. Miller's face.

"*What's wrong*?" she demanded.

Mr. Baker settled a comforting hand on his daughter's shoulder and said, "Lori, yesterday the Smith family was notified that Manny is missing in action."

"*No*, oh God. Please, no!" Lori cried out.

Mrs. Baker put her arms around her daughter, and Lori pulled away from Suzy to embrace her mother, crying out in anguish, "Manny, Manny, Manny!"

For several minutes the six of them stood in the driveway, terrified by the news. Then Mr. Baker said, "Come on, dear. Let's go inside."

When her parents tried to nudge Lori toward the house, she took one step and collapsed to the ground. Her face was pale white as they rushed to her side.

"Somebody call the ambulance," pleaded Mrs. Baker.

Pat Miller dashed into the house to make the call.

"Do you really think we need the hospital?" asked Lori's father.

"Yes, I do," said Mrs. Baker. Then she met her husband's eyes and continued, "I'm worried about more than just Lori; I'm also worried about Manny's baby."

They weren't at the hospital very long before the doctor came out to say, "News like that in her condition can be extremely stressful, but I'm happy to report that Lori and her baby are both fine."

Up until this point, Mr. Baker had been fairly strong, but learning the news that his baby and her baby were going to be okay seemed to be more than he could take. He sat back down on the chair and cried openly. Mrs. Baker moved to her husband and settled on the arm of the chair, putting her arm around him. The three Millers hugged each other as well.

"She could go home, but it might be better if she stayed here tonight so we can keep a close eye on her. We all think your daughter is very special," the doctor said.

"Can I stay with her?" asked her mother.

"Of course, Mrs. Baker. The mother of our favorite lab assistant is always welcome," the doctor replied.

"I'll need some things," said Mrs. Baker, looking at her husband.

Before Mr. Baker could answer, the doctor offered, "Mrs. Baker, we have a wide selection of nightgowns here. Of course, they are all white and open in the rear, but they are quite comfortable. One size fits all."

Mrs. Baker smiled politely. It would take a lot more than hospital-gown humor to take her mind off her worries about her daughter and grandchild.

Kenny called Suzy the day after she went back to California. He was still sick with grief and frustration over the situation with Manny and the situation with Suzy. Kenny was anxious to hear how Lori took the news about Manny, and he was anxious to let Suzy know how much he loved her.

"Hello," Suzy's mother answered.

"Mrs. Miller, it's Kenny. Is Suzy there?" he asked.

"I'm sorry, Kenny. Suzy is at Anaheim with Lori," she answered.

Kenny mentally kicked himself. He knew Suzy was with Lori.

"Do you know how soon she will return?" Kenny asked without thinking.

"It's hard to say. She may be gone for a couple days or a couple weeks," Mrs. Miller explained.

"I was hoping to ask her about Lori. Can you tell me how she is?"

After a moment of silence, Mrs. Miller asked, "Is your mother there, Kenny? I think it's best that I speak with her."

"She's next door with Manny's mom. What's wrong, Mrs. Miller?

Why can't you tell me how Lori is doing?" Kenny asked fearfully.

"Lori is obviously upset about Manny. Suzy is there to help her in any way she can. Kenny, I want to talk to your mother. Please ask her to be home in about thirty minutes so I can speak with her," Mrs. Miller requested.

"Okay, I'll get her back here shortly, but before you hang up, will you please tell me how Suzy is?"

"Suzy is obviously upset about Manny, and she's upset about the problem between you two."

"Please believe me, Mrs. Miller. I love Suzy very much," Kenny stated.

"I know you do, Kenny. Again, I will call your house in thirty minutes. Please ask your mother to be there. Goodbye, Kenny."

His mother saw Kenny approaching the Smith house and went out to greet him.

"Mom, I called Suzy's house and she wasn't there. I tried to talk to her mom, but Mrs. Miller insisted that she wanted to talk to you, and said she'll call you in thirty minutes," Kenny told her.

Kathy Reynolds said nothing but was very curious.

The next thirty minutes passed slowly for Kenny. When the phone rang, he pounced.

"Hello," he said. His mother approached, and Kenny held out the phone and said, "It's Suzy's mom."

Without covering the phone, Kathy said, "Kenny, please go outside so I can speak with Mrs. Miller privately."

"Mom?"

"Kenny, please do as I ask," his mom stated firmly.

He wasn't sure how long his mom was on the phone. Kenny shot baskets with little or no concentration, continuously watching the door. Finally, his mom appeared in the doorway and said, "Come inside, Kenny. We need to talk."

Her voice had that worried tone she had when there was a problem. They sat across from each other at the kitchen table.

"Sit down, son. Let me tell you few things, and then we'll talk about them," Kathy said. "Regarding Suzy, as expected, she is still upset that you want to go back to the Marine Corps. That's something that time will take care of. Lori is naturally devastated about the bad news." After a short pause, Kathy continued, "That news is complicated because Lori is pregnant with Manny's baby. Maria does not yet know that Lori is expecting her grandchild. Mrs. Miller and I discussed our thoughts on how to tell Maria about the baby, and we decided that I should tell Maria the good news." Kathy clasped her hands together on the table. "So, what do you think?"

Kenny could not speak. He found it difficult to breathe. This was all happening too fast.

Kathy added, "We thought that if Sergeant Smith isn't there when I talk to Maria and Cindy, then Cindy can talk to her grandfather."

"I'll talk to Pappy here," Kenny replied. "What about the Riveras?"

"The Millers will take Suzy to San Diego to inform them, if Maria approves," Kathy said.

Kathy Reynolds was very nervous yet very excited about speaking to Maria. On the way over, Kathy noticed Pappy looking out the window. *Great-Grandpappy Smith*, Kathy thought, smiling openly. She suddenly felt relaxed about the news she was about to deliver.

"Come in, Kathy." Pappy held the front door open.

"Mr. Smith, would you have a minute to talk to Kenny at my house?"

"Of course, Kathy," he replied, heading directly over.

Seeing Maria and Cindy sitting on the sofa, Kathy did not hesitate for a minute. "I received a phone call from California a few minutes ago."

Maria quickly asked, "Is Lori okay?"

"Lori is much better than okay. In fact, the doctor confirmed a little while ago that Lori and Manny's baby are both doing very well."

After a couple seconds of shock, followed by screams of surprise and joy, Maria settled down with a joyous expression. She commented,

"I never knew my mother or grandmother, and I was so happy when I became a mother. Even after Manny told me he wanted to marry Lori, I honestly did not think about becoming a grandmother." After a brief silence, Maria said, "I better start thinking about this because I really like the idea."

Cindy cut in. "What is there to think about? You're a wonderful mother, and you will be a wonderful grandmother."

"Maria, Suzy loves Manuel and Carmella, and I think she would like to break the news to Carmella and Manuel in person," Kathy said. "Are you okay with Suzy visiting to share the good news about the baby? I think Suzy wants to spend time with them as well."

After a brief discussion, Maria concluded that it was a good idea.

Then Maria surprised everybody when she told them, "I want to call Lori and talk to her. She needs to know I am very happy about my coming grandchild."

CHAPTER NINE

OFFICER CANDIDATE SCHOOL AND RESCUE

Quantico, Virginia

KENNY WAS NOT GOING to change his mind about going back to the Marine Corps. In several ways, he was very excited about it. The truth was, Kenny had been a little jealous when Manny became an officer. As a young enlisted Marine, he had not had a great deal of direct contact with the officers in his unit, but he greatly admired some of them.

As he recalled, many of the officers were married. With that in mind, Kenny decided to call Suzy again in an attempt to have a good conversation. His two previous calls had ended abruptly as Suzy hung up crying, once because she loved him and missed him, and the last time because she hated him for leaving her.

After exchanging polite greetings with Suzy's mom, Kenny asked, "How is Lori?"

"She's a little better. The calls from Manny's mother are a big help."

"That's good. I know that Mrs. Smith likes talking to Lori."

"Kenny, can I put Suzy on the phone for you?"

"Please, Mrs. Miller. But before you do, could you tell me how she's doing?"

"She's okay, Kenny. Here she is now," Mrs. Miller replied,

"Kenny, you know I don't hate you. I just hate the thought of not being with you."

"I know, Suz. I love you so much."

"Oh, Kenny, I love you too."

After several minutes of loving small talk, Suzy broke the ice and asked, "Are you still going back to the Marines?"

"Yes, Suzy, I am. It's what I have to do. Please try to understand," he replied.

"I'm trying," she said.

It was 6:15 AM as Kenny placed his things into Pappy's car for the trip to the airport, but the early hour didn't reduce the number of well-wishers. Kenny spent at least ten minutes shaking hands and giving hugs as people came by to wish him well. He wanted so much for Suzy to be there, but they'd said their goodbyes the evening before on the phone. The final hug from his mother was the hardest one to deal with. Kenny knew how upset she was about him leaving.

"Promise me you'll take care and not do anything stupid," Kathy told her son.

"But the stupid stuff seems to come so easily to me," Kenny replied.

"Exactly my point," she shot back.

"Please keep reminding her that this is only OCS, would you, Dr. Wheeler?" Kenny asked.

"I will, Kenny. Best of luck to you," the doctor replied.

Although he'd hoped to say goodbye to Manny's mother, Cindy walked toward the car without her. "Mom says goodbye, Kenny. I'm afraid she didn't have a good night, and she's upset about you leaving. She asked me to kiss you goodbye for her," Cindy said softly.

"Don't I get a goodbye hug from you, also?" Kenny asked.

"It's not nice to take advantage of a girl when her guard is down," Cindy said with a slight smile.

"All aboard for Quantico," everybody heard Pappy yell. Kenny had a plane to catch.

While Kenny stood in the Washington, DC, bus terminal, peering around at the hustle and bustle, he heard a man behind him say, "I didn't know Washington combined their bus station and zoo in the same building."

Kenny glanced back to see another fellow about his age. "Yeah, this place is really something."

The man asked, "You wouldn't be heading for The Basic School, would you?"

"Not yet, but if things go well, I'll be heading there in a few months."

"OCS, huh?"

"Yep, and The Basic School for you?"

"Oorah!"

"How did you guess I was heading for Quantico?"

"Hey, you have Marine Corps written all over you," said the stranger as he stuck out his hand and said, "I'm Mark Richards."

"Lieutenant Mark Richards, I assume. I'm Kenny Reynolds, sir."

"Hey, Ken, for the next twelve weeks at OCS, they are going to treat you like shit, but I'm not on the OCS staff, so stay loose around me. I'm on your side," Mark assured him.

"Thanks, I appreciate it," Kenny said.

Vietnam

After many days of captivity, Manny realized his underground location might be more permanent than he'd hoped. During the first few days, he expected to be moved to a bamboo cage or other restraining structure aboveground. That was not to be, and he remained in his dirt prison. The worst part of his underground life was the stagnant darkness. The highlight of each day was the short period of time when the entrance cover to his literal hole in the ground was removed and he was given something to eat. The fresh air and light were appreciated as much as the food.

Manny hoped and prayed that others survived the crash, and worried that they also were being held captive. He gritted his teeth that first day and shored up his reserves of courage, determined that he would never provide any information to his captors if he were interrogated—but at no time was Manny beaten, or even questioned. Like many servicemen in Vietnam, Manny knew a few basic Vietnamese expressions, but when he addressed his captors he received no response. He suspected they didn't know what to do with him.

At times Manny considered how he would describe his condition and decided that "enduring" was fairly accurate. Although he had lost track of time, Manny felt his strength and general health waning under meager rations of rice and water and no exercise. It was easy to start feeling sorry for himself. When Manny felt depression rising and his morale dipping low, he turned his thoughts back to the world and all he loved back home.

He thought of Lori and when they would be together again; but he also worried how Lori was taking the news of his situation. He thought of his mother and sister and Pappy and his friends at Lower Vale. His mom would be out of her mind with worry, and Manny felt terrible knowing the anguish his current situation was causing his family and friends.

Manny also thought of his best friend. He knew that Kenny would be suffering mentally, but Manny didn't know that he had also served as an inspiration to his best friend.

Triangle, VA

Driving south through Virginia on US Route 1, the bus pulled into a small parking lot in front of a yellow brick building.

The bus driver announced, "This is Triangle, Virginia, also the bus stop for the Quantico Marine Base."

"Guess this is it, Ken. Good luck to you, and I'll see you at TBS in a few months," his new friend Mark said.

"Thanks, Lieutenant. Good luck to you," Kenny replied.

Getting off the bus, Kenny observed several young men coming out of the building. Close behind them was a Marine staff sergeant, who announced, "If any of you are on orders to OCS, get on the van."

It was not a long drive through the base before they were ordered back off the van.

"This is it, gentlemen. The headquarters for the United States Marine Corps' Officer Candidate School. While you are here, you will be referred to and you will refer to yourself as 'candidate.' Get your things and go inside for processing. I expect I will have the pleasure of seeing many of you quite often over the next ten weeks, or at least for as long as you are here," the staff sergeant told them with a sneer as he walked away.

It was late afternoon as the new arrivals entered the building to the greeting of "Let's go, candidates. Daylight is a-passing quickly, and we have much to do."

The rest of the day and into the evening, Kenny had numerous flashbacks to boot camp. The way he reasoned, a candidate was just a recruit with a college degree. Over and over again, the candidates were made to hurry from one place to another so they could wait in line to do something, just like at MCRD San Diego about five years earlier. Later that evening, after processing, chow, and uniforms issue, the candidates headed to the barracks that would be their home.

When a Marine learned to march, he was taught to always keep his eyes straight ahead while in formation. But as Kenny's platoon marched toward their barracks, a train went steaming down the nearby tracks, and well over half the candidates turned their heads to the right to see the train.

"Platoon, halt!" the staff sergeant screamed.

The platoon's clumsy response was almost comical, and Kenny knew exactly what to expect as a result of their poor performance. Push-ups were a way of life in Marine Corps indoctrination.

On the next trip to their barracks, Kenny thought the platoon did a fairly good job, especially considering how little time they had marched together. However, Kenny was not surprised when they were turned around and marched back to the headquarters. As they arrived back at their starting point, the sergeant announced, "Maybe we will march better on the way to your barracks if we have a little practice here on the grinder first."

After a half hour of drilling, the platoon was in formation, listening to the staff sergeant berate them for how poorly they performed. Kenny was in the second squad of the platoon and heard a low soft voice behind him say, "This is bullshit."

Without warning, a voice from behind the third squad exploded, "THAT'S RIGHT, CANDIDATE, THIS IS BULLSHIT! BUT IT'S ONLY A SMALL SAMPLING OF THE BULLSHIT YOU ARE GOING TO HAVE PILED ON YOU WHILE YOU ARE HERE. OCS EXISTS TO SEE IF YOU ARE TOUGH ENOUGH TO HANDLE THE BULLSHIT WE HIT YOU WITH! IF YOU ARE NOT, THE MARINE CORPS DOES NOT WANT YOU. ARE YOU SMART ENOUGH TO UNDERSTAND THAT, CANDIDATE?"

Kenny could not believe his ears. Even after five years, he knew that voice.

Staff Sergeant Perez continued, "Staff Sergeant Calder, I appreciate the extra help you're giving these candidates, but I need to get them to the barracks. We have things for them to do there."

"They're all yours, Staff Sergeant Perez. I was afraid I was never going to get rid of them" was the reply.

"I will only say this once, so listen up, candidates. My name is Staff Sergeant Perez. You will address me as 'sergeant instructor.' Your platoon sergeant is Gunnery Sergeant Adams, and you will address him as 'platoon sergeant.' Your platoon commander is First

Lieutenant Fabizi; you will address him as 'sir.' Any time any member of the staff enters your squad bay, you will immediately call the squad bay to attention.

"At this time, we will march to the barracks for rack assignments and barracks rules. We will return here to the grinder later tonight for more drill practice if I see that it is needed."

Marching back across the tracks, Kenny was sure that Rocky got a good look at him. Yet the hard sergeant never batted an eye to indicate recognition. Later that evening with the lights on in the barracks, Kenny angled his head to see Rocky looking at him. The sergeant instructor just turned and marched out of the bay without acknowledgment.

Late that evening, the candidates of 4th Platoon, Company G were finally able to hit the rack after the traditional Marine roar, of "Good night, Chesty Puller!"

A candidate's scream woke Kenny, but as he came to his senses, he realized what was causing all the commotion. Another train was roaring down the track. It sounded as if it were right outside the barracks, and it continued to pass for several minutes.

"Son of a bitch, how are we supposed to sleep if that fuckin' train passes by here every night?" exclaimed the candidate in the top bunk to Kenny's right.

"What's the matter, college boy? Didn't you have any trains on campus?" Gunny Adams stood in the doorway, laughing at the candidates' reactions to the unexpected train. Kenny figured the old platoon sergeant had been looking forward to this event all day.

A bit of low-key bitching and grumbling could be heard as the train finally passed.

"I *seriously* suggest you candidates get back to sleep. If you don't, you will regret it tomorrow," Adams stated as he left the squad bay.

Within ten to fifteen seconds, and with a little bit of grumbling, the squad bay became quiet again as all the candidates heeded the platoon sergeant's advice and tried to fall asleep again.

The next morning, it only took a moment for Kenny to recognize the sound of a steel object being vigorously beaten against a steel trash can.

"WHERE DID YOU GO TO SCHOOL, CANDIDATE, THE COLLEGE OF CLUMSY CLOWNS?" screamed Staff Sergeant Perez. "EVERYBODY GET BACK IN YOUR RACK! *MOVE!*"

The young men scrambled back into their beds.

"We are going to try this again. My recruits at Parris Island were able to get it right on the second try. Let's see if you're as smart as they are," Perez said.

Oh, no, Kenny thought.

"What the hell?" yelled a candidate as another candidate from the top rack landed on him.

Both candidates ended up in a pile, although neither was seriously hurt as they scrambled to their respective positions for formation. However, their mishap did not escape the eyes of the sergeant instructor.

"IF YOU TWO ARE TRYING TO PISS ME OFF, YOU'RE DOING A GOOD JOB!" Perez yelled at them. "BACK IN THE RACK, MORONS!"

As the candidates waited for the sign to get out of the rack again, Staff Sergeant Perez said, "I will tell you ladies one more time: the candidate on top gets out of bed on the right side, and the candidate on the bottom gets out of bed on the left side. If I see two candidates getting out of the same side of the rack again, I might think you two secretly want to sleep in the same rack. And although you might do that shit in college, you don't do it in my Marine Corps."

The first PT session was little more than short exercises and a slow jog around the perimeter of the grinder a couple times. Kenny was surprised to see several of the candidates laboring to complete their morning workout. He was also surprised at how much he enjoyed the chants Staff Sergeant Perez sang out as they ran.

"My Ma-rine Corps color is green," the sergeant sang.

"My Ma-rine Corps color is green," repeated the candidates.

"Shows the world I'm tough and mean," Perez led.

"Shows the world I'm tough and mean," echoed the candidates.

Suddenly the chanting made Kenny sad. Nobody liked Marine Corps motivation chants more than Manny. It was not uncommon for Manny to chant to himself when riding in the car. Kenny remembered Lori making fun of Manny for his Marine Corps singing. He was sure that Lori would happily endure nonstop Marine Corps chants and songs if the father of her baby came home safely.

California

Lori read everything she could about prenatal nutrition and ate only those things which would be good for the baby. However, as Lori prepared to go grocery shopping on this particular day, she was concerned about more than good things for her and the baby. Maria was coming to visit.

Later, at the airport, Lori's heart pounded when Maria entered the luggage area. On the one hand, she wanted to run to Maria to embrace her, but on the other hand, she was afraid to make such a gesture—until the moment Maria smiled and held open her arms to Lori. Maria and Lori hugged for several moments before they let go of each other.

"Mrs. Smith, these are my parents."

"I'm so happy to see you," Maria said, extending her hand.

During the drive to the Bakers' house, Lori assured Manny's mother that she was feeling well. After supper that evening, they finally had the chance to be alone together, so they went on a stroll. They only mentioned Manny briefly because the topic upset them. Maria surprised Lori when she told her that one day she would like to return to Southern California to live.

After a brief period of silence, Maria said, "When I first met you at Kenny and Suzy's graduation party, I worried that something was wrong."

"What made you think that?" Lori asked with concern.

"It's hard to describe. I was afraid you were not genuinely happy to see me," Maria answered.

"I was very happy to finally meet you. I must admit that I was worried about the circumstances because I was afraid I might be pregnant," Lori confessed.

"I guess it was my mother's intuition. I can't explain it," Maria said softly.

"Oh, Mrs. Smith. Please don't worry. I love Manny with all my heart and soul. Please don't ever doubt my love for Manny. After he returns and I have our baby, I will be the happiest girl on God's green earth," Lori exclaimed.

"We are going to have a wedding, aren't we?" Maria asked with a smile.

"Of course," Maria confirmed, laughing in embarrassment. She couldn't believe she'd forgotten to mention the wedding to Manny's mother.

For almost an hour, the two women walked and talked. Maria told Lori that she had not wanted Manny to reenlist but was not surprised when he did. Then she added, "I was married to a Marine for almost ten years, I have lived in the same house with my Marine father-in-law for almost twenty years, and my son has been a Marine for over five years. You would think that after all that time, I would understand the Marine Corps."

Left hanging, Lori finally asked, "Well, do you?"

"No, and it drives me crazy. I don't understand their deep sense of loyalty and commitment. They call it pride, but I call it crazy," Maria stated.

Quantico, VA

Kenny was impressed with the enthusiasm most of the candidates displayed in their training, and disappointed at the lack of effort by others. Kenny wondered why they even applied to be a Marine officer if they were not willing to make the sacrifice. Kenny was reminded of the boot camp incident when Rocky took it upon himself to let slackers know that their poor effort would not be tolerated. But here at OCS, as a platoon sergeant instructor, Staff Sergeant Perez had the authority and responsibility to weed out those who did not perform to standards.

Today, the candidates were being interviewed by their platoon commanders, and the platoon sergeant and sergeant instructor were in attendance. Lieutenant Fabizi didn't mind if his sergeants asked an occasional question.

As required, Candidate Reynolds pounded on the doorframe of the platoon commander's office.

"Enter" was the command.

Kenny did so and positioned himself in front of Lieutenant Fabizi's desk.

"Candidate Reynolds reporting as ordered, sir."

"It's amazing how small the world is. Don't you think, Candidate Reynolds?" asked the lieutenant.

Obviously Rocky had told the platoon commander of their prior acquaintance, so Kenny answered, "Yes, sir."

"It's clear you were a very good Marine, so we have high hopes that you will be a good Marine officer," the lieutenant stated.

"The candidate will do his best, sir," Kenny responded.

"What made you decide to come back, Candidate Reynolds?" asked Gunny Adams.

After a brief moment, Kenny responded, "A sense of obligation to my best friend, Platoon Sergeant."

Then Rocky spoke up and asked with a big smile, "How is that hard-chargin' Mexican beaner, Sergeant Manny Smith?"

Unable to look at Rocky, Kenny managed to say, "The Marine Corps was smart enough to make him a lieutenant—"

"No shit. Battlefield commission. That's great!" Rocky interrupted.

But Fabizi waved his hand at the staff sergeant to be quiet.

"What else, candidate?"

Taking a deep breath, Kenny said, "Lieutenant Smith is currently MIA."

Nobody said a word, but the atmosphere in the room was very intense. Finally, the lieutenant said, "We are all very sorry to hear that, Candidate Reynolds."

"Thank you, sir," Kenny replied.

"What happened?" Rocky demanded.

Kenny told the three Marines what Pappy had been able to learn through his network. Rocky started to ask another question, but Gunny Adams cut him off and said, "This isn't the best time to get into it."

Rocky looked angry but said nothing. The lieutenant ended the interview by concluding, "Candidate Reynolds, you have a lot of potential. I hope you will use good judgment and work hard to live up to that potential. You are dismissed."

"Good morning, sir," Kenny replied as he stepped back, did an about-face, and departed the office. Before he'd reached the double doors into the squad bay, Kenny heard shouting from the office. The platoon sergeant and sergeant instructor seemed to be in strong disagreement about something. Just a minute or so later, the double doors burst open, and Staff Sergeant Perez stormed into the squad bay.

"ATTENTION ON DECK!" screamed a candidate.

On most occasions, even if he was just passing through the squad bay, the sergeant instructor would glance left and right as he walked through. But on this trip, he was looking straight ahead with an expression that would scare a rattlesnake.

At 5 AM the next day, Staff Sergeant Perez was his old self again as he conducted reveille on the platoon.

"RISE AND SHINE, CANDIDATES! IT'S ANOTHER BEAUTIFUL MARINE CORPS MORNING!" Rocky shouted.

Kenny grinned, thinking that if only OCS were on the West Coast, he could get another three hours of sleep each morning.

"What's so funny?" asked Candidate Mussleman.

"I think the sleep deprivation is making me goofy," Kenny responded.

"EARLY CHOW THIS MORNING, LADIES! FORMATION IN TWENTY MINUTES," screamed the sergeant instructor. As Perez began the movement of the platoon toward the chow hall, he called out, "CANDIDATE WILLIAMS, THE CADENCE IS YOURS."

"Now yo' left, with yo' left, step your left, right, left, now yo' left," sang Williams on their way to the chow hall.

"This isn't a social hour, girls; eat your chow and be ready to roll. We don't want to keep the O-course waiting," stated Perez.

Although he knew he was not in great shape, Kenny enjoyed the challenge of the logs and bars and rope of the O-course. He had not run the thing since boot camp, but he was looking forward to it.

Arriving back at the squad bay, the candidates scrambled to change out of the green utility uniform and into their physical training uniform of shorts, T-shirt, and running shoes. Once in formation, they were surprised to see Staff Sergeant Perez leave the barracks in PT clothing.

When the platoon neared the obstacle course and came to a halt, a Marine approached them and gave instructions for the candidates to fall out and gather around the beginning of the course. Then he added, "For most of you, today will be a great day in your lives, because today is your introduction to the Marine Corps obstacle course. OOOORAAH!"

"OOOOORAAAAAAH," responded many of the candidates.

"Marine Corps motivation. There's nothing like it," he said. Then he continued, "We are going to walk down the length of the course, and as I describe the requirement for each obstacle on the course, my partner will demonstrate how it is done. Then each of you will have the opportunity to do the course at your own pace. From then on, you will be expected to run the course each time as fast as you can.

"This first time is for technique, candidates. Get your technique down so you don't hurt yourself when you go for speed," the instructor emphasized.

Kenny felt his adrenaline pumping.

"For those of you having trouble, continue to work on your technique. If you think you are able, go full bore and get a good workout. Before completing OCS, you will be timed on a double running of the O-course," the instructor said.

Then Rocky instructed the candidates to get into two lines. "I want those of you who need to work on technique to get in the right line, and those of you who think you can kick it in the ass, get in the left line."

When it was almost Kenny's turn in the left line, Staff Sergeant Perez got into the right line and held back the candidates to clear the path on the right side. Suddenly, Kenny realized that his old friend and current sergeant instructor at OCS was going to race him. As Kenny stepped up to the line to start, he glanced over to see a slight grin on Rocky's face.

"GO!" came the command.

Going through the course, Kenny's speed and height gave him a slight lead. When he arrived at the rope climb, the last obstacle, the sergeant instructor was just behind him. Kenny jumped up to grab the rope and heard Rocky growl. About halfway up the rope, Kenny's arms burned as he spotted Rocky moving up the other rope, passing him.

Rocky reached the top and gave out a triumphant "MARINE CORPS!"

When Kenny made it to the top, Rocky said, "You're still damn good at this."

Breathing heavily, Kenny replied, "Give me a few weeks. I'll get you next time."

Rocky laughed and said, "Sorry, Reynolds. There won't be a next time." Then Rocky slid down the rope.

The next day, the candidates were surprised when Gunny Adams walked in the squad bay. After they came to attention at the foot of the racks, the gunny said, "At ease, candidates. Some of you have mail. If I call your name, come here and get it."

After six or seven letters were passed out, Adams said, "I hope this letter is from a girl, Reynolds, because if it isn't, I'm going to stay away from you in the shower."

Kenny went to retrieve the letter, very excited that it might be from Suzy. The platoon sergeant handed him a pink envelope carrying a very strong smell of perfume. Returning to his bunk spread the strong fragrance throughout the squad bay. He opened the letter and read:

Dear Kenny,

Pappy told me he got in trouble one time for receiving a perfumedletter in the barracks. So, I quickly got out this paper and perfume to send this letter to you.

LOVE,
Cindy

As Kenny explained the letter to the other guys bunking near him, the door opened and Staff Sergeant Perez entered.

"ATTENTION ON DECK!" came the warning.

As the sergeant instructor walked in, there was no way to hide the smell.

"Which one of you sweeties spilled her perfume?" Perez asked. Then he saw the letter in Kenny's hand and walked over to him.

Before the staff sergeant could say anything, Kenny explained, "The candidate received a gag letter from a friend's little sister." He offered the letter to Rocky to examine.

As Rocky read, a big smile came over his face. Then he said, "I like Cindy." Then he added, "How is the first sergeant?"

Kenny replied, "The first sergeant is fine, Sergeant Instructor."

Rocky nodded his approval and walked away.

For the most part, Officers Candidate School flew by for Kenny. The academic instruction was easy for him, and the physical training and field training were fun. For Candidate Kenny Reynolds, the hardest part of OCS was thinking about Manny and missing Suzy.

At the halfway mark in the program, the platoon had lost ten candidates for various reasons. But now was the opportunity for the candidates to DOR, or drop on request. There were several surprises in both the drop and no-drop category. Two candidates who were constantly bitching about the program did not elect to drop, but one of the better men in the platoon decided it was not what he wanted and departed OCS.

After returning to the barracks following their evening meal that day, the outside door swung open with a bang, and in walked Staff Sergeant Perez.

"ATTENTION ON DECK!" a candidate yelled.

Like every other candidate, Kenny responded automatically and snapped to attention.

On most occasions, the staff passed on through the squad bay on their way to the offices, and the candidates would quickly go back to what they were doing. But this time Staff Sergeant Perez went directly to Kenny and stood in front of him. Kenny was three to four inches taller than the sergeant instructor, so he was staring out over the top of Rocky's short hair. After several seconds of avoiding eye contact, Kenny could stand it no more and glanced down to see a strange look on the face of the tough sergeant instructor.

For about ten seconds, Rocky continued standing silently as Kenny's heart pounded and his knees weakened. Finally, Rocky took a deep breath and said, "Manny is alive. That hard-charging, gung-ho, Mexican beaner Marine is okay. They found him and rescued him this morning. He's going to be okay."

Kenny could not speak. But he didn't need to speak out loud; he closed his eyes and thanked God that his prayers had been answered. As he opened his eyes, tears streamed down his cheeks. Rocky also had trouble with his composure as the two old friends rejoiced in the good news.

By now the heads of the other candidates in the platoon were turned, watching the scene between Kenny and Rocky, but the two of them were oblivious to the inquisitive candidates. Finally, the deep, mellow voice of Candidate Williams suggested, "Sergeant Instructor, request some time alone for Candidate Reynolds."

Rocky said nothing. He looked at Williams, then at Kenny and said, "Let's go make a phone call. Follow me."

The two walked out the hatch and into the darkness outside.

Kenny asked, "How did you find out?"

"The colonel called me," Rocky said.

"What colonel?" Kenny inquired.

"Our colonel."

"The CO of OCS called you with information about Manny?" Kenny challenged.

"My old man and the colonel go back a long way. The colonel knows about you and Manny and me. He has made a few periodic calls about Manny, but tonight one of his old friends called the colonel from Vietnam as soon as they got confirmation," Rocky explained.

Walking through the darkness of the cool Quantico air, Kenny asked, "Where are we going?"

"To use the colonel's phone. I think you ought to make a couple calls and let First Sergeant Smith and the rest of the family know that Manny is okay," Rocky explained.

"We don't have to use the CO's phone," Kenny remarked.

"You do if he tells you to," Rocky replied with a grin.

Kenny never had a more rewarding phone call in his life. Talking to Pappy, Kenny learned that everybody had already received the good news. A little earlier in the day, Manny had been able to call home, and Lori, from Vietnam.

Walking back to the barracks, Rocky asked, "Now that Manny is safe, are you sorry you're here at OCS?"

"I was thinking of that, and I'm not sorry. I know how proud I feel to be a part of the Marine Corps again," Kenny said.

With a grin, Rocky asked, "You won't order me to race you on the O-course again, will you?"

"I might," Kenny said, chuckling. "Do we know any details of what happened?"

"Not details, but the short story is that a local village we thought was friendly was not really friendly. He was being held in a tunnel near the village. It seems a snitch told our guys about Manny, and as they were there asking the village leader about him, they heard Manny yelling from somewhere. There was a brief firefight, but they found Manny and brought him in safely," Rocky said.

Arriving back at the barracks, Kenny stuck out his hand and said, "Thank you, Sergeant Instructor."

"You're welcome, candidate," Rocky replied.

Kenny entered a darkened squad bay, but it seemed like the whole platoon was still awake as Candidate Mussleman asked, "Kenny, you don't have to tell us if you don't want to, but we're on your side. It sounded like your buddy Manny was rescued. Is that right? What happened?"

Another man said, "Does Perez know your friend?"

Kenny and the other candidates had shared a lot of adversity over the past weeks, and he felt close to most of them. Kenny decided it was time to come clean and tell his friends the whole story, to include today's development.

"Are you going to try and DOR now that your buddy is safe?" someone asked.

Kenny scoffed and gestured around the squad bay. "And miss out on all this fun? You have to be joking."

Vietnam

On Manny's side of the world, it was morning, and he woke up in a bed with clean sheets and a pillow. He was in the hospital of the Marines' Force Logistics Command, located at Red Beach near Da Nang. Manny wasn't too happy to be there. It was generally assumed that only men in bad shape were given a bed in this hospital, and Manny did not think his injuries were that serious.

Although he was very hungry, Manny lay there for a while, reflecting on the events of the past twelve hours. It was all like a bad dream, but the two bullet holes in his leg and the large sores on his body were not the result of a dream. And neither was losing thirty-plus pounds. But all things considered, the doctors were amazed that he was in such good shape physically. They wanted to make sure there were no hidden mental wounds, though.

"Good morning, Lieutenant. How about a big breakfast?" the nurse asked.

"That would be great. What's for breakfast?" Manny replied.

"Just about anything. But try to not make yourself sick," the nurse added.

It was a little past 1030 when several doctors approached Manny and said they would like to speak with him regarding his experience as a prisoner. One doctor asked most of the questions as the others listened and took notes. Manny answered the best he could. Some of the questions were directly relevant to Manny's feelings about being captured and held prisoner, but others seemed less relevant.

Later in the morning, after the doctor's Q&A session, Manny decided to wander around a little. As he entered the area designated as the patient lounge, he heard a familiar voice.

"Well, well, you just can't seem to stay out of trouble."

With a grin, Manny turned to see his old gun platoon sergeant, Staff Sergeant Richwine, sitting in a wheelchair. Approaching his old friend, Manny said, "How are you doing, Staff Sergeant?"

"It's Gunny Richwine to you, Smith, and what are you doing here?" the former platoon sergeant demanded as if scolding Manny.

"I took a couple rounds in the leg, but they're just flesh wounds," Manny answered. "What are you here for?"

Gunny Richwine pulled the sheet from his lap and displayed a left leg with no foot attached. "Some gook put a mine right where I needed to step."

"I'm really sorry, Gunny," Manny said.

Richwine countered, "You're just sorry because I won't be able to get down the alley fast to pull your sorry ass out of trouble again."

The two Marines sat and talked for a while about old times and old friends. *Still the same old sourpuss,* Manny thought as a nurse came to roll the gunny away for treatment.

Leaving the area, the gruff old gunnery sergeant turned his head and grinned. "Good luck to you, Lieutenant. We're all real proud of you."

Manny could only smile and shake his head.

That evening, a captain came to get Manny's account of the rescue, but Manny first wanted to know what actions preceded the event. He distinctly remembered the Marines saying that they were looking for him, but he had no idea what the circumstances were.

The captain from the division civil affairs office told Manny, "The village that captured you had us fooled completely. We thought they were very supportive of us, and against the NVA. We are still not sure why they kept you in their village. We passed through or very close to that village almost every day."

"Maybe they thought that it was safer to keep me than move me."

"That was one of our theories," the captain said.

"If you didn't suspect that village, how did you know to look for me there?" he asked.

"Your name never showed on a Red Cross list, so we guessed that you never made it to the North. Because of that, we harassed a couple villages we suspected to be NVA sympathetic. Apparently, someone in one of those villages said something that aroused suspicion about the village that had you," the captain explained.

"And that's when they came to that village," Manny stated.

"That's correct," said the captain. After a short pause, and with a big smile on his face, the captain said, "Lieutenant Smith, if you don't already know it, I'm happy to be the first to tell you that you only have another couple of days in Vietnam. You're going home."

Manny attempted to call Lori later that day, but there was no answer. However, he was able to complete a radio-telephone call to Lower Vale using the Marine Affiliated Radio Station. His mother giggled every time she was required to say, "Over." Maria was so happy that her boy was safe and coming home that just about anything remotely humorous made her laugh.

"I couldn't get through to Lori, Mom. Please call her for me, over," Manny said.

"Okay, Manny, over," Maria replied.

"Hey, hard charger! We're anxious to see you, over," Pappy said after getting the phone from Maria.

"Me too, Pap. How's Kenny? Over," asked Manny.

"He is doing just fine, over," Pappy responded.

No one had yet told Manny that Kenny had rejoined the Marine Corps; nor was he told of Lori's pregnancy.

"I have to go now. I'll call you from Los Angeles. My love to all, and goodbye, over," Manny said.

When their call ended, Pappy turned to Maria and said, "Manny is going to be overwhelmed with big news when he arrives in LA."

"Yes, but I know my son, and the news of his baby and about Kenny will both be good news to Manny," Maria stated, beaming with happiness.

"Yes, I'm sure you're right." Pappy's thoughts drifted to Anaheim.

Lori had called Suzy immediately after she got the phone call from Pappy telling her that Manny was safe. Suzy was so excited that she drove to the Bakers' house that night. The visit also allowed Suzy to go with Lori to her doctor's appointment the next morning, which was why Lori was not home when Manny tried to call her. Returning home from the doctor's office, Suzy asked, "How are you going to tell Manny about the baby?"

"I'm not sure yet. I've rehearsed it about a hundred different ways," Lori confided to her cousin.

"It won't matter how you tell him; he is going to be overjoyed," Suzy assured her.

Lori smiled as she pictured telling Manny the news. Many nights she'd cried herself to sleep, afraid that Manny might never know she was having his baby.

Suzy added, "I heard you tell the doctor that you hope to breastfeed the baby."

"That's right, why?"

"I was just thinking that if it's a boy, and he eats like his father, you're in big trouble!"

After the two girls shared a laugh, Lori asked about Kenny and his training.

"It's going well. I can tell from his phone calls and letters that he loves it," Suzy said.

Lori wasn't sure how to interpret Suzy's tone of voice, so she said nothing.

Then Suzy continued, "They breathe tear gas until they choke and snot comes out their noses. They crawl in the mud and eat food that was canned ten years ago and get treated like prisoners, but he loves it. How in God's name can you explain it?"

Lori grinned. "You sound like Manny's mom."

"Speaking of moms, I guess I can tell you now about a phone call I got from Kenny's mom," Suzy told Lori.

"Go on," Lori said with curiosity.

"Several weeks ago, Mrs. Reynolds called me to talk. She asked how I was doing, then she told me she knew Kenny really loved me. She confided in me that Kenny was going to propose while I was in Lower Vale, but we got the news about Manny before he had a chance to do so," Suzy said.

"And after that, things fell apart and he never asked you. I'm sorry, Suzy," Lori said.

"It's okay. He can ask me over Christmas," Suzy said, smirking.

Lori looked at her cousin for a moment. "What aren't you telling me?"

"In several letters, Kenny has said how he wished I was with him in Washington. Well, for Christmas my parents are giving me a round-trip plane ticket to Washington. I'm going to surprise him and be there to see Kenny graduate from OCS," Suzy said excitedly.

"Suzy, you are clever. He will be so surprised. Have you told Mrs. Reynolds?"

"Not yet, but I will soon. Do you think she'll mind?"

"She'll be happy because she knows how happy it will make Kenny. However, she will probably also be a little jealous."

"I'm worried that he'll get a plane ticket to fly home the same day he graduates," Suzy stated.

"Yeah, that could be a problem."

"My dad said I should just tell Kenny, but I want to surprise him."

As the girls pulled into the Bakers' driveway and came to a stop, Suzy said, "I think I hear your telephone."

The girls looked at each other for a fraction of a second before Suzy said, "I'm closer; I'll get it."

Lori entered the door to the kitchen to see Suzy frantically waving her hand. "Hurry, it's Manny's mom."

"Hello," Lori answered eagerly.

Suzy was dying with anticipation as she watched the expression on Lori's face. Suzy knew it was good news but awaited the details beyond Lori's short responses. As Lori hung up, Suzy screamed, "What? What? Tell me!"

With joy in her heart and tears in her eyes, Lori said, "Manny is flying into Los Angeles in two days."

CHAPTER TEN

HOMECOMING AND COMMISSIONING

LAX, Los Angeles

THE BAKERS DECIDED ON the way to the airport that Mr. and Mrs. Baker would greet Manny first as he entered the terminal. Then they would direct him to where Lori would be sitting and waiting for him. That way, she could break the big news privately. Lori was so nervous that she felt sick.

Manny was a little nervous himself as he departed the airplane. He wasn't sure what to expect. He didn't even know if his family ever got through to Lori or her folks. It was entirely possible no one would be at the airport to greet him.

When he entered the arrival terminal, Manny spotted Mr. and Mrs. Baker waving at him and felt instant relief, but his stomach dropped in disappointment. *Where is Lori?*

"Oh, Manny, we're so happy to have you safely home," said Mrs. Baker.

"You've lost quite a bit of weight, son. How are you doing otherwise?" Mr. Baker asked.

"All things considered, I'm just fine. But I would be much better if Lori was here," Manny said as he hugged Lori's mom and shook hands with her dad.

"She's here, Manny. She hasn't slept a wink since finding out that you were coming in today, so she's over there sitting down and resting," Mrs. Baker told Manny.

"Is something wrong?"

"No, Manny. Nothing is wrong. Just go over to talk with Lori."

All the way home, Manny had imagined seeing Lori and how they would run into each other's arms to embrace and kiss passionately. But now he was walking to Lori as she just sat waiting for him. Manny felt sick and worried that his knees would buckle, but he made it to Lori.

"Lori, is something wrong?"

"Oh, Manny, I wanted to jump up and run to you, but running is beginning to be a little bit of a problem, so I sat here as I planned to do."

"I don't understand."

"There's something you don't know about us, Manny. When you left to go to Vietnam, you never left me entirely. A part of you has stayed with me."

Finishing her statement, Lori brushed her coat away from her stomach and stood, holding her blouse tight to display the bump of her pregnancy.

Manny looked at her stomach, then at Lori's face, then at her stomach, then at her face and said, "We're going to have a baby?"

Lori could only nod yes, and Manny embraced her with all the love and affection a man could ever experience.

"I love you, Manny Smith."

"Oh, Lori, I love you. And I love our baby!"

Seeing Manny and their daughter embrace, the Bakers hurried over to the loving couple. As the four of them headed for the luggage area to get Manny's seabag, he said, "Do you mind if we get something to eat? I'm starved."

"That's my Manny," Lori laughed.

"As far as I'm concerned, you can eat nonstop. I don't like to see you so thin," said Mrs. Baker.

"How much weight do you think you lost, Manny?"

"Between thirty and thirty-five pounds."

Then Lori said to Manny, "I have some other big news to tell you."

"Let me guess, you have the wedding all planned."

"No, Smith, you're not getting off that easy. And it's not about us. Kenny is currently at Quantico, Virginia, where he is enrolled in the Marine Corps Officer Candidate School."

"You're kidding!"

"It's true, Manny," confirmed Mr. Baker.

As Lori told him all she knew about Kenny and OCS, Manny was genuinely touched by his best friend's reaction and loyalty. However, when Lori told him that Rocky Perez was Kenny's sergeant instructor, Manny howled with delight.

"Of all the sergeants in the Marine Corps, Kenny had to get Rocky," Manny laughed.

Sitting in the airport snack bar, Lori brought Manny up to date on the developments of the past few months. He seemed most concerned that Lori was not attending medical school.

"I can begin next fall," Lori told him.

"And I will keep the baby during the day," Mrs. Baker added.

"What will happen to you now? What are your orders?" asked Mr. Baker.

"Just like my dad and Kenny were, I'm being assigned to the naval hospital in San Diego for a period of convalescence."

"How long will that be, and where to after that?"

"I'm sorry, babe, but I don't know yet."

After a moment of silence, Mrs. Baker said, "Manny, I think you should call your family to let them know you've arrived safely."

"You're right, Mrs. Baker. Thank you."

The three Bakers were anxious to get Manny back to their house where they knew some people were waiting, but they also enjoyed seeing the happiness on Manny's face as he talked on the phone.

Finally, he said, "Okay, Mom, I'll call you as soon as I know. Bye, I love you."

"When are you going to Colorado?" asked Lori.

"Tomorrow, I hope," Manny said, "and I was also hoping you could come with me."

As Lori and Manny looked at her parents, Mr. Baker smiled and said with great satisfaction, "I'm way ahead of you." He pulled out airplane tickets from the pocket of his sport jacket.

"Daddy, you're the greatest," said Lori, giving her dad a big hug.

The drive from the airport to the Baker house was not long, and as they pulled in the driveway, Mr. Baker had to slam on the brakes to avoid running over Aunt Carmella as she ran toward her great-nephew.

Manny was out of the car in a flash and picked up his great-aunt to hug her. Right behind her was Uncle Manuel and the Millers. Friends and neighbors stood back a ways, all wearing smiles.

"God has answered my prayers and brought you home to us."

"Yes, he has, Aunt Carmella."

"You are so thin, Manny."

"Do you have any ideas how we can correct that?"

The elderly lady smiled with pleasure at his love of her cooking.

"Uncle Manuel," Manny said, hugging his great-uncle.

Uncle Manuel said nothing as he hugged his namesake for dear life. Then Suzy took her turn and gave Manny a big hug. As she did, she whispered in his ear, "If you ever give us a scare like that again, I will beat the shit out of you, Smith."

Manny released Suzy and replied, "What a nice thing to say, Suzy. I missed you, too."

Mrs. Miller made the mistake of hesitating for a second, and Mr. Miller stepped in to hug Manny first. "I went out yesterday and bought a huge rack of ribs for you. I hope I can do them soon."

"You can count on it, Mr. Miller," Manny responded.

Then Mrs. Miller pushed her way between her husband and Manny. As she embraced the Marine, she said, "He hasn't made his ribs for anyone the whole time you were in trouble."

"I guess we have some catching up to do," Manny told the Millers.

Mr. Miller grinned from ear to ear.

After everyone greeted Manny, Carmella said, "You must be exhausted, Manny. You need to get some rest."

"I have his room all prepared."

"A little nap would do you some good," added Mr. Baker.

Lori said nothing but wore a slight smile.

A minute or so after the Riveras and Millers and others pulled away, Manny was escorted to his room. "I guess I'm tired, but I think I'm too excited to sleep."

"Just lie down a while and rest," Mrs. Baker suggested.

When her parents left the room, Lori picked up a stool from a makeup dresser and placed it close to the bed. Manny smiled and said, "I bet this soft bed is more comfortable than that stool."

Lori smiled and sat on the bed beside the reclined Manny. He placed his right hand on her stomach, and she placed her hand on his.

"I love you so much," he said softly.

"And I love you, too," Lori replied.

She leaned over to gently kiss him, but Manny pulled her down to him and kissed her passionately, holding her tightly against him.

As their lips parted, Lori said, "You better enjoy holding me close while you can, because as each week passes and I get bigger and bigger, that'll be more difficult."

"I like a challenge," Manny countered.

Lori rolled over so her back was to Manny and pressed herself against him. Manny wrapped his arm around her, touching her stomach again. His life had been a living hell these past months, but as he held Lori and their child-to-be, Manny was in heaven on earth.

At breakfast the next morning, Lori told Manny and her parents of Suzy's secret plan to go to Quantico for Kenny's graduation from

OCS and then spend a couple days visiting Washington, DC. She added, "But Suzy is worried that Kenny already has plans to come home the same day he graduates."

"We can tell Kenny to plan on staying in the area for a few days because Pappy is coming to see Kenny get commissioned," Manny said.

"Good idea," said Lori.

"Maybe not," replied Manny. "It's very likely that Pappy really is going to see Kenny."

"Oh boy," Lori said in frustration. "Now we're back to square one."

"Not really. If Suzy can share Kenny for just a day or so, I know Pappy won't hang around too long. He's a pretty sharp old guy."

"I have a feeling she's hoping Kenny will propose," Lori confessed.

"What about the ring? He wrote that he was going to buy one, but I doubt he carried it with him to OCS," Manny said.

"Pappy can take it to him," Lori suggested.

Mr. Baker spoke up. "Be careful to not manipulate this too much. We know Kenny loves Suzy, but maybe we should let him propose on his own terms."

"But, dear," said Mrs. Baker, "if we women did not do a little manipulating, you men would seldom do anything right."

The four of them had a good laugh over Mrs. Baker's little jab, but she continued, "Seriously, we have to find out what Mr. Smith intends to do before we can do any manipulating."

"I expect I can talk to him tomorrow," Manny offered.

"And I will talk to Suzy and Kenny's mom," Lori said.

Lori's dad said, "While you're at it, you better manipulate a plan to get yourselves to Colorado if we miss your plane."

"I'm all packed," Lori responded.

"And I never unpacked," Manny added.

Mr. and Mrs. Baker were driving Lori and Manny to the airport when Manny suddenly said, "This sounds kind of goofy, but I've only been in Lower Vale once when Kenny wasn't there."

"Well, I'll be there. Doesn't that mean anything?" Lori asked, hurt.

Manny was embarrassed and did not say anything for a moment, which gave Mr. Baker a chance to say, "Sure it does, dear, but you can't throw the football or shoot the basketball as good as Kenny."

Mr. Baker's comment made everyone smile, but Manny felt bad for hurting Lori's feelings. While he loved her more than he could say, his bond with Kenny was also too strong to describe. He wondered what Candidate Reynolds was doing at that moment.

Quantico, VA
Anaheim, CA
Lower Vale, CO

As week eight ended, Kenny reflected on how the training had progressed. He had been a little bored by the early history and traditions classes, having heard most of them before, but at this point came more classes on leadership and the problems of leadership. He enjoyed these very much. The uniform vendors' visit really brought home to Kenny that there was light at the other end of the OCS tunnel. The candidates would graduate in their Winter Service "Alpha" uniform. He wished Suzy could be there to see his commissioning.

That evening, Kenny had an opportunity to call her.

"Hello, Miller residence," Kenny heard over the phone.

"Is this the beautiful and sexy Suzy Miller?" Kenny asked.

"No, but it is her beautiful and sexy mother," Mrs. Miller said.

Kenny was dumbfounded with embarrassment. Suzy's mother had sounded exactly like Suzy when she answered the phone.

"Kenny, are you there?" Suzy asked.

After a moment of hesitation, Kenny realized that this, the voice that first answered the phone and said hello, was Suzy's voice. In a flash, Kenny realized that he had been set up.

"You and your mom may be beautiful and sexy, but the two of you are also goofy," Kenny commented.

Kenny distinctly heard two ladies laughing.

"We had you going for just a moment."

"Yes, I admit it. For just a second, you had me in a panic."

"I just love it when two women can cause a big tough Marine to panic."

"Hey, you. I get all the harassment I need from the staff here at OCS."

"I thought you said the harassment was tapering off a little."

"It is. We've even had a little free time in the evenings."

"Well, the next time I get to be with you, I won't give you any free time at all," Suzy told him.

"Is that a threat or a promise?" he asked.

"Both," she replied.

After a moment's hesitation, Kenny asked, "Speaking of us being together, is it possible for you to come to graduation to see me be commissioned?"

"Kenny, do you mean that I would have been allowed to come to Quantico for your graduation if I wanted to?" Suzy asked with disdain in her voice.

"Yes, is there a problem?" Kenny asked.

"Well, I wasn't sure that the Marine Corps would allow girlfriends, and Manny said that Pappy Smith would probably be going to your commissioning, so I told my mom to go ahead and schedule her surgery that day," Suzi lied to Kenny.

"What's wrong with your mom?" Kenny asked.

"Just female stuff that some women need," Suzy answered. "I'm so sorry, Kenny. I would really love to be there. I can't wait to see you."

"It's my fault. I should have told you sooner," Kenny said in a somber tone.

"Maybe I can fly to Lower Vale and meet you there," Suzy suggested.

Kenny's spirits lifted. "That would be great. We have some unfinished business there."

That night, an OCS graduation meeting took place in the Smith house that rivaled the detailed planning of the Secret Service. Kenny's mom and Dr. Wheeler joined Lori and the Smiths as the seven of them went over the arrangements for Mrs. Reynolds, Dr. Wheeler, Pappy, and Suzy to fly to Washington. Suzy would fly from San Diego and meet the other three in DC. Dr. Wheeler would then rent a car, and they would all drive south to the Quantico Marine Corps Base. Lori informed the others that Suzy was so intent on surprising Kenny that she was going to purchase a cheap wig and wear a big hat and sunglasses.

Just a few minutes later, as people finished their cake and coffee, the phone rang. Manny was seated next to the phone but made no motion to answer it as it rang a second time. Cindy got up instead. Manny allowed her to get within a couple steps before he plucked it off the receiver and said, "It's probably for you, but I'll get it." Smiling at the aggravation he had just caused his sister, Manny said into the phone, "Hello, Cindy's answering service. May I help you?"

Years earlier, Manny would have triggered a much livelier response from his little sister, but all she did this evening was act bored with his antics.

However, no one could act bored when Manny said, "*Kenny!*"

"Hey, Lieutenant. How are you doing, sir?" Kenny laughed.

"I'm just fine. How's everything at OCS?" Manny asked.

"It's going well. Staff Sergeant Perez gave us on-base liberty tonight," Kenny replied.

"That Rocky must be getting soft."

"Not a chance. He's still as tough as nails," Kenny told his best friend.

After a few minutes of personal inquiries, Manny said, "Your mom and Dr. Wheeler are here at the house with us."

Kathy came to the phone. After a minute or so of small talk, she said, "Kenny, Dr. Wheeler is probably more excited about you becoming a lieutenant than I am. He wants to take me to Quantico to see you graduate next week. Would it be okay if we came with Pappy Smith?"

"Are you kidding? That would be great!" Kenny responded.

Then Mrs. Reynolds said, "Lori told us that Suzy is very disappointed that you two got your wires crossed and she can't be there because of her mother's operation."

"Yeah. I could just kick myself for not asking her six weeks ago," Kenny replied. He quickly added, "But she is coming to Lower Vale as soon as she can."

"Oh, that will be wonderful," Kathy told her son.

A minute later, as Kathy hung up the phone, Lori asked, "Do you think he suspects anything?"

"No, I don't think so. You could tell by his tone that he is very disappointed Suzy can't be there. If we don't give it away this week, I think we'll fool him completely," Kathy said.

"We need to have our cameras ready for when he sees her," Pappy said with a smirk.

Manny added, "Kenny and I have played some great tricks on each other, but this may be the best one of all."

Everybody in the room smiled, basking in the relief of having such joyful concerns after the horror of Manny's capture.

That evening, Manny and Lori went for a walk.

She shivered. "I can tell we're not in Southern California."

"If you're too cold, we can go back to the house," Manny offered.

"No, I'm okay. Let's keep walking," Lori said.

As they meandered the neighborhood, Manny reminisced about growing up in Lower Vale. Lori had heard many of the stories before, but she loved listening to Manny talk.

"Sometime when we are here in the summer, I want to take you up into the mountains. There are beautiful meadows and crystal-clear streams that are ice cold in midsummer," Manny told Lori.

"I can't wait to see them," she answered. After a brief silence, Lori asked, "Do you think we should get married soon?"

"The sooner the better. I can't wait to make you my bride."

Manny was awake early the next morning, thinking about a few of his old friends as he got out of bed. He glanced out his bedroom window and saw a new accumulation of snow on the ground, so he prepared to shovel the sidewalk and driveway.

Over an hour later, after he had eaten breakfast and cleared the snow, Manny knocked on Lori's door and heard a faint "Come in."

"Hey, sleepyhead. Wake up. It's almost nine," Manny told her, leaning around the open door.

"Which is still sleepy time for me," Lori replied.

Manny's mother confronted him in the hall and scolded him. "Manny Smith, you let Lori sleep as long as she wants. She needs her rest."

As Manny backed out of the doorway, Lori waved goodbye and flashed a big smile of satisfaction.

Later that morning, Lori asked him, "What are we going to do today?"

"Well, I thought I would drive you around and show you what Lower Vale looks like in the daytime," Manny answered.

"You get to ride in style today, Lori," Pappy said with a big grin. "Manny's going to drive you around in my old snowplow."

After a speechless moment, Lori replied, "This will be a first for me. We don't have many snowplows back in Southern California."

"We can do better than just ride. I'll teach you how to use it so you'll be the only girl in Southern Cal who knows how to plow snow," Manny told her.

"Oh, Manny, what a thrill. All the other girls will be so jealous," Lori said mockingly.

Driving around town in the old snowplow truck was actually kind of fun for Lori. It seemed that every other person they passed would wave and yell at Manny. He was always quick to wave back, and most of the time, Manny would call people by name.

While they were driving down Main Street, an excited Manny suddenly said, "There he is."

"Who?" Lori asked.

But instead of answering her, Manny rolled down the window and stuck his head out to yell, "*Aaaaah-eeaaaaah-eeaaaaaah.*"

Lori started laughing as he quickly pulled the truck to the curb in front of the Sheehans' store.

"Manny!" yelled his old friend Tarzan.

Manny jumped out of the truck, and the two old friends embraced. Within seconds, Sarah exited the store, and Manny picked her up and swung her around. Shortly after Sarah came Mr. Sheehan with a big smile and his right hand extended. Lori always thought Manny was a fairly big man, but she noticed that he wasn't so big standing between the two Sheehans. Lori saw Sarah peering into the truck, then walking toward it. Lori climbed out.

"You must be Lori. I'm Sarah, and I am so pleased to meet you."

Lori knew instantly that she and Sarah would be good friends. "It's a pleasure to finally meet you, Sarah. Manny has told me so much about you that I feel as if I already know you and Tarzan." Suddenly Lori was embarrassed, afraid Sarah might be offended by Lori's familiarity.

Sarah gave her an understanding smile and a warm hug as she said, "If you're going to be his friend, you are expected to call him Tarzan. And don't worry about me either way. I answer to both Sarah and Jane."

"Hey, Lori, save some of that hugging for me," said Tarzan.

"Come and get it, Ape Man," Lori replied.

After the hugs ended, Tarzan said, "Hey, if you guys can get away tonight, there's a new restaurant you probably don't know about. What about the four of us going out?"

"A great idea, and Larry can treat us all to dinner," Sarah said.

Before Tarzan could protest, Manny said, "Gee, thanks, Tarzan. That would be great."

Driving away, Lori said to Manny, "They seem like two wonderful people."

"Yes, they are. Sarah used to be kind of shy, but she has come out of her shell and is a real sweetheart. I loved the way she set up Tarzan to pay for dinner."

Quantico, VA
Washington, DC

The day finally arrived for Mrs. Reynolds, Dr. Wheeler, and Pappy to depart for Quantico. Final coordination was made with Suzy the previous evening regarding when and where they would meet at the airport. Pappy asked Manny to drive the three of them to catch their flight in Denver, then told him to park so Manny could walk them to the departure terminal.

After opening the trunk of the car and unloading the suitcases, Manny said, "I'll carry your suitcase to baggage check-in, Mrs. Reynolds."

"Thank you, Manny," she responded.

"Here, hard charger. You ought to carry this one too," Pappy said.

Manny was happy to carry his grandfather's suitcase, but something about Pappy's tone puzzled Manny.

"You don't want me to carry that suitcase, do you?" Pappy asked.

"No, Pap, I have it," Manny replied.

With a twinkle in his eye, Pappy then said, "Well, you should. It has your clothes in it."

For a moment Manny was dumbfounded. Then he saw the large smiles and suddenly realized he had been tricked by everyone. He was going to Quantico instead of Pappy.

"Judging by the look on your face, it's obvious you didn't have a clue," Pappy said.

Manny could not speak. Finally, he said, "I feel badly, Pap. You should be going. Kenny is expecting you."

"No, he isn't," Mrs. Reynolds said.

"I don't believe this. What did Lori say?" Manny asked.

"She likes the idea. Over the next few days while we're in Washington, Lori can spend time with your mother and sister and grandfather," Mrs. Reynolds replied.

Less than an hour later, Manny waved goodbye to his grandfather and headed down the tunnel to the plane. After he and Kenny's mom and the doctor found their seats, Manny said, "This is really exciting, but I still feel guilty about going in Pappy's place. I wonder why he insisted I go instead."

"Because he loves you, Manny," Kathy Reynolds said simply.

The flight to DC was long but very smooth. Manny awoke when the captain announced the landing to his passengers. After the plane stopped, Dr. Wheeler advised Kathy and Manny, "We might as well stay seated. We have some time to kill before Suzy's plane arrives."

As they proceeded to the baggage area, Mrs. Reynolds pressed a hand to her stomach. "I'm a little queasy. I think I need to eat something."

"Let's pick up our bags and find a restaurant to eat and relax while we wait for Suzy's plane," Dr. Wheeler suggested.

"Sounds good to me," Manny said. "I relax much better when I'm eating."

Manny was excited to see Suzy. Although he'd seen her only a week earlier in California, this time they were in DC and on their way to see Kenny.

It was a very happy reunion for Mrs. Reynolds and Suzy. The conditions under which they'd last seen each other were less than happy, but now that was all behind them, and they looked forward to seeing Kenny and having a little time in the capital.

"I'm so excited, Mrs. Reynolds. Do you think Kenny suspects anything?" Suzy asked.

"I'm confident he doesn't suspect a thing. Men are so easily tricked," Kathy said, winking at Manny.

Before Manny could respond, Suzy added, "Setting you up this time was easier than having you chase grunion, but watching you get your butts wet was funnier."

"All it takes is one little phone call to my friend Rocky, and suddenly there is no big surprise," Manny told her.

He would never do such a thing, and Suzy knew it also, but the look on her face made Manny chuckle a little, pleased to have put Suzy under his thumb.

The next morning, they left bright and early for the trip to Quantico. The sentries stopped their car at the gate, and Manny presented his military ID card. "We're here for the OCS graduation."

"Just stay on this road and look for the signs. Have a good day, sir," one sentry said as they both came to attention and saluted.

As the car drove on, Suzy told Manny, "I'm impressed, Lieutenant Smith, but don't ever expect me to salute you."

"You'll never have to salute me; however, after we're married it is proper military etiquette for Lori to salute me. And now that he will be an officer, you should salute Kenny after you two get married," Manny told Suzy.

"Really?" Suzy asked in a moment of uncertainty.

Manny did not even attempt to contain his ear-to-ear grin. Fortunately, the wild flurry of slaps and punches did not interfere with Dr. Wheeler's driving. He and Kathy just smiled at the shenanigans in the back seat.

Approaching an area congested with cars, Suzy reached into her large handbag and pulled out a black wig and sunglasses. As she did, she gave Manny a threatening look, which erased the smile forming on his face. "This is to be a surprise, or did your pea brain forget, Smith?"

Manny started to comment but then decided against it.

"It's not as cold as I was afraid it would be," Kathy Reynolds said while she, Dr. Wheeler, and Manny made their way toward the bleachers. Manny turned his head to look back at the disguised Suzy, following them by about thirty feet.

The graduation began as Manny expected it would. The music started right on time, and the candidates began marching onto the large asphalt drill area to the front of the bleachers. As each platoon stopped and faced the guests in the bleachers, Manny noticed a proud Kathy Reynolds pressing her lips together to minimize the smile on her face.

"What do you think, Mrs. Reynolds?" Manny asked.

"I'm very impressed. They're even better than the Lower Vale High School marching band," she replied.

He and Dr. Wheeler smiled at each other. Manny glanced around for Suzy, but she was nowhere to be found. However, Manny quickly located Kenny in the ranks and pointed him out to his mother and the doctor.

"They all keep their heads directly to the front. I assume they're required to do that?" Kathy asked.

"If they don't want their heads knocked off," Manny answered.

"I have to say that I am very impressed," Dr. Wheeler said.

"The march on isn't too difficult. Let's see how they handle their rifles," Manny said.

Manny was pleased as the candidates conducted their manual of arms with their rifles. He thought of Rocky. *They obviously had a good teacher*, he thought. Then the commanding officer of OCS spoke to the guests and the candidates.

The colonel's remarks were very short as he praised the young men for their tenacity. "It is almost impossible to make it through this school without it," he said.

Soon they were marching away. "Where are they going?" Kathy asked.

"They have to put their rifles away, Mrs. Reynolds," Manny told her. "I suspect they will be back very soon."

While the guests milled about, Manny was surprised and thrilled to see Rocky's father approaching with his hand outstretched.

"Sergeant Major, it's great to see you," Manny said, shaking his hand.

"It's good to see you, young man," the retired Marine said.

After Rocky Sr. met Kenny's mother and Dr. Wheeler, the four of them chatted for a while until they were interrupted by a dark-haired girl wearing sunglasses.

"Where are they?" Suzy demanded.

"Here he comes!" Manny said excitedly.

Suzy ducked her head and started to scurry away before realizing she had been the victim of Manny's deceit once again.

"Don't expect me to feel bad if you accidentally fall off the Washington Monument," Suzy said, giving Manny a dirty look.

Not much later, they really did see some of the young men jogging toward the graduation area. Kenny wasn't jogging, but Manny soon spotted him heading their way at a brisk pace. Kathy Reynolds enfolded her son in her arms. Offering his congratulations, the sergeant major departed, and the foursome chatted happily.

While they were speaking, Kenny noticed growing smiles.

"What's so funny?"

His mother answered, "Turn around and see for yourself."

The surprise behind him almost buckled his knees. "Suzy!"

In an instant the cute little blonde was in his arms as they embraced.

"Gotcha!" Suzy said after Kenny released her.

"I can't believe you lied to me."

"I didn't lie. I fooled you," she replied.

"It's called affection deception," Kenny's mother interjected.

"So, I can safely assume you were in on it," Kenny said.

Manny clapped a hand on his shoulder. "We all were, Kenny. So just relax."

A new voice intruded. "Begging the lieutenant's pardon, but QUE PASO, AMIGO?"

"*Rocky!*" Manny yelled.

As the two friends exchanged a long, firm handshake, Rocky said, "You had us worried for a while there."

"I was a little concerned myself," Manny replied. "I saw your dad a little bit ago, but where is he now?"

"He and the colonel got to chewing the fat, so I decided to come find you," the squared-away staff sergeant said.

Kenny cut in and introduced his mother, Dr. Wheeler, and Suzy. After a short exchange of pleasantries, Rocky reminded everyone to get to the commissioning ceremony early if they wanted a good seat. Then he snapped to attention and saluted Manny. "Have a good day, sir."

Manny automatically came to attention himself. "Thank you, Staff Sergeant. You have a good day, too."

By force of habit, Kenny also snapped to attention during the exchange. After Rocky left and the two boys relaxed, Suzy asked, "Is that formality required between old friends?"

Manny answered, "It's kind of hard to explain, Suzy."

"Try me," she challenged him.

Kenny cut in and said, "There are rules and regulations, and there is also a strong measure of pride and respect."

Suzy was not sure she was satisfied with that answer but decided to let it go. She doubted she'd ever understand life in the Marine Corps.

Later that day, Manny watched with great satisfaction as Suzy and Mrs. Reynolds pinned the gold second lieutenant bars on Kenny's shoulders. Dr. Wheeler snapped several pictures of the event and then several more of Kenny posing with his mother, then his girlfriend, then both ladies together. Finally, Kenny said, "Come on, Manny. Get over here and get your picture taken with me. You have a lot to do with this happening."

"Actually, Smith, you are ninety-nine percent responsible," Suzy stated.

In the hotel dining room that evening, everyone had their fill of the large buffet—the hotel's specialty. After dinner, as they sat in the lounge, Dr. Wheeler said, "Raise your glasses, everyone. I want to propose a toast." The doctor continued, "It's been a long, hard ten weeks, and although we never had any doubts he would make it, raise your glasses and drink to the man of the hour, Lieutenant Kenny Reynolds, United States Marine Corps."

After the clinking of glass and the loud "Ooooraaaah!" from Manny, they all drank.

"And another toast," Kenny said. "To family and friends and the love we all share."

After the second drink, they placed their glasses on the table. Manny stood and said, "Please excuse me while I visit the little boys' room."

Manny returned to the table just two minutes later to find several strangers standing there. Kenny suddenly stood up, and Mrs. Reynolds looked scared.

Arriving at the table, Manny said, "You weren't going to have a party and not invite me, were you, Kenny?"

Ten seconds earlier, Kenny had been furious at the comments the three long-haired men made in front of his mother and Suzy. But at his best friend's reference to Staff Sergeant Richwine's comments several years earlier in Oceanside, Kenny suddenly laughed. Manny was pleased that his impromptu comment tickled Kenny's funny bone and started to laugh also. One of the three uninvited guests made the mistake of stepping toward Manny, and in a fraction of a second, Manny's laughing eyes turned to a cold-steel stare.

Suzy remembered a similar situation with Manny and jumped in front of him to defuse the encounter. "Manny, no, *stop!*" She turned to the three strangers and said, "I don't know what your problem is, but you have no idea what will happen to you if don't leave us alone."

Before anybody could say or do anything, two men in suits and the bartender approached the table and asked what the trouble seemed to be.

Dr. Wheeler announced, "My friends and I are guests of the hotel. We were just having a drink after enjoying your excellent buffet when these three fellows approached our table and made offensive remarks about this young man's decision to serve in the Marine Corps."

Realizing they were now on the defensive, one antagonist said, "We are customers of this bar and took offense at their toast to a warmonger."

"Warmonger? My son is not a warmonger," Kathy scoffed.

One of the men in a suit turned to the bartender. "Hope these three weren't good customers, Mike, because they are leaving now."

One young bearded man started to protest but realized it would be to no avail, so he said to the other two, "Let's get out of here."

After discussing the intrusion, Kenny and Manny were forced to explain the origin of Manny's remark about the party. Suzy had heard the story before, but Kenny's mother was shocked to hear of her son's involvement in an alley brawl with a motorcycle gang. Dr. Wheeler could not condone the event, but it was obvious he enjoyed the story.

It was only about 9:30, but Kathy was done in. "It's been a busy day, and I want to enjoy seeing DC tomorrow, so I'm going to bed."

They all stood, and Kenny said to Suzy, "I'm still keyed up from all the excitement of the day. Want to go for a walk?"

"I would love to go for a walk. It's only 6:30 by my body clock," Suzy replied.

"Well, Lieutenant, are you allowed to give your mother a good night hug and kiss?" Kathy asked.

"I don't think there's anything in Marine Corps regulations that prohibits kissing a mother good night. Is there, Manny?" Kenny asked his buddy.

"Mom kisses are okay, but girlfriend kisses are forbidden," Manny replied, grinning at the contempt on Suzy's face. He just couldn't help himself.

When Kenny wrapped his arms around his mother's shoulders, he felt her reach around his waist and realized she was putting something in the front left pocket of his trousers. When the embrace ended, Kenny dropped his hand to his pocket. Immediately, Kenny realized the object was the box containing the diamond engagement ring for Suzy—the one he never gave her three months earlier.

"I love you, Mom."

"And I love you," she replied with a big smile.

Later that night, Suzy slipped into the room as quietly as she could but was surprised when Kathy said, "Congratulations."

"Thank you, Mrs. Reynolds. In more ways than one," Suzy replied.

"You're quite welcome, dear," Kathy said to her future daughter-in-law.

CHAPTER ELEVEN

MANNY AND LORI'S WEDDING

Washington, DC

SUNNY AND UNSEASONABLY WARM, the next couple of days could not have been better as they toured the nation's capital.

"It must be nice to live in a place with so much culture," Kathy commented as they departed an art museum. The plane back to Colorado would be leaving in a few hours, so they strolled toward the street to hail a taxi.

"Not to mention all of the history," added Dr. Wheeler.

"What's the one thing that you enjoyed most?" Kenny asked him.

After a moment of reflection, the doctor replied, "I would have to say that seeing the original Constitution was very moving for me. Sometimes we think people who lived a long time ago could not have been as smart as people today, but the men who wrote that document were brilliant."

"Well, are we all ready to leave this history behind and head back west?" Manny asked, clapping his hands.

"Ron and I are enjoying our visit very much, so we actually decided to extend our stay in the area by going south to Fredericksburg. We called to change our tickets last night."

"That's great, Mom. You're going to love it."

"We're very anxious to visit some of the Civil War battle sites."

Dr. Wheeler was all smiles as he nodded in agreement.

The five of them bid each other farewell at the curb. Waving to his mom and her boyfriend, Kenny climbed into the taxi after Suzy and Manny. "Well, let's head to Colorado. I suspect someone there is very anxious to see one of us."

Denver, CO

The three friends searched for Pappy upon entering the Denver airport terminal, but to their delight they were greeted by Lori, Tarzan, and Jane.

"Hey, beautiful," Manny said as Lori ran to his outstretched arms.

"Hi there, Marine. Looking for a good time?" she asked.

Kenny and Larry each grabbed the other's outstretched hand to shake but then continued into a strong hug with multiple slaps on the back.

Sarah said, "Hi, Suzy. I'm Sarah Dilling, also known as Jane."

"Hi, Sarah. I'm so glad to finally meet you." She and Sarah shared a hug like two old friends.

After several minutes of greetings and smiles, Kenny stated, "We're really glad to see you guys, but how did you convince Pappy to let you come instead of him?"

"Your grandfather hurt his back at the lumberyard, but that's not the only change of plans," Lori said.

"What do you mean?" asked Kenny.

"Lori and Sarah drove here together in your car, and I followed in ours," Larry told them.

When none of the three new arrivals said anything, Lori continued, "The four of us are going to spend a day or so in Denver and go back to Lower Vale tomorrow."

"That's great!" exclaimed Suzy.

"Hey, can't you two stay with us?" Manny asked.

"I'm afraid I have to get back," Larry answered.

"But we are counting on going to dinner one night soon. Larry still wants to takes us out, don't you, sweetie?" Sarah stated, grinning at her special guy.

"Yeah, yeah. Whether I like it or not" was the glum reply.

"Well, thank you, sweetie," Kenny said.

After getting their luggage and walking to the cars, the other four waved goodbye as Tarzan and Jane drove away.

Getting into their car, Lori asked, "How was the plane ride?"

"Don't ask," said Kenny.

"Are you sure you want to marry this guy, Lori? You could do so much better," Suzy said.

"Your cousin is such a big baby," Manny told Lori.

"And to think the plane didn't crash," Lori replied.

They all decided a nap before supper was needed. To satisfy the hotel and their own conscience, the boys got one room and the girls another. Even though they were engaged and Lori was pregnant, they were still not married. And that was the center of conversation for the evening.

While they ate, Lori confirmed that she would like to get married very soon.

Manny replied, "You name a date and location, and I'll say okay."

Kenny interjected, "I have to confess that I've also been thinking about your wedding, and I was hoping it would be in early January before I have to return to Quantico to attend The Basic School."

"Let's plan on the first Saturday in January," Lori replied. "It would be the third."

"Sounds good to me," Manny said, giving her a smooch.

"This is so exciting," Suzy replied.

"Did you tell your mother about your engagement?" Lori asked her cousin.

"I didn't have any choice. She asked me directly if Kenny proposed yet," Suzy replied.

"So, the second time was a charm, huh, Kenny?" said Lori.

"Yeah, and it was easier this time since one of us was good enough to not get shot down and captured," Kenny replied, glancing at Manny.

"I just didn't want you to rush into something I figured might be bad for you, Ken," Manny said with a big grin.

"Manny, please let us enjoy the evening," Lori begged.

After more conversation about the pending weddings, the topic changed to Kenny's return to Quantico.

"Manny told me a little about The Basic School, but what can you tell us?" Lori asked Kenny.

"I guess the best way to describe TBS is to first describe OCS as a type of screening process. OCS is very difficult, and the Marine Corps figures that if you want to be a Marine officer badly enough to put up with all the rigors of OCS, then you have what the Marine Corps requires of a lieutenant," Kenny stated. "After completing college and Officer's Candidate School and passing a physical exam, the Marine Corps will give you a commission as a second lieutenant. But the Corps requires about six months of intensive professional training before it will allow a young officer to assume the responsibility of leading Marines."

"So, TBS is an intensive course in professional training to prepare young men and women to carry out their leadership responsibilities," Lori summarized.

"That's very well stated," answered Kenny.

"But what about Manny?" Suzy asked.

"The Marine Corps often has enlisted Marines, just like Manny, who have continued to demonstrate their outstanding leadership ability. And like they did with Manny, many are given a commission so they can maximize their leadership ability," Kenny stated with pride as he looked at his best friend.

"Will you go to OCS and TBS?" Lori asked Manny.

"I don't think so," Manny answered.

"What do you think they'll do with you?" Kenny asked.

"I'm not sure. I expect they'll send me orders soon," Manny said.

After their dishes were cleared from the table and they were waiting for their dessert, Lori started discussing the plans for the wedding. Except for an occasional yes or no from the boys, with a few nods for emphasis, it was very much a conversation between Lori and Suzy.

"Have you decided what you'll wear?" Suzy asked.

"My mother has a friend who asked if she could make a wedding gown for me. This lady said she can make a gown to accommodate my big belly, and it will still look sexy, even though there is no way I can feel sexy in this condition," Lori answered.

"Hey," Manny interrupted. "You look sexy to me."

Lori looked at Suzy and then at Manny. "The bigger boobs are for the baby, not the father."

Manny and Kenny cracked up.

After the boys settled down, Suzy asked Manny, "Are you going to wear your uniform?"

"I hate to admit it, but I hadn't thought about it."

"Manny, you should get married in dress blues," Kenny declared.

"Yeah, they might even make you look handsome," Suzy added.

Manny ignored her. "I don't have a set of officer's dress blues."

"When we get to Lower Vale, we'll get on the phone and call Pendleton and San Diego. I bet we can find a set of blues somewhere," Kenny said.

"It would be nice if the best man also had his dress blues," Lori hinted.

"We'll have to work on that too," Manny agreed.

Long after the four friends had finished their dessert, they sat at the table and talked of old memories and future plans. Although they had a waitress throughout the evening, they were interrupted by a gentleman in his mid-fifties who asked them if they would like anything else.

Realizing how late it was, Lori said, "We've been here too long. We should be going."

But the gentleman raised his hands and said, "On the contrary, you are welcome to stay as long as you like. And besides that, the owner has said your meal is on the house."

"Gee, that's great!" said Manny.

"Yes, sir. Is the owner here so we can thank him?" Kenny asked.

"There's no need to thank me. I'm pleased to have a couple of young devil dogs and their beautiful ladies in my restaurant," the gentleman said.

"I guess their stylish haircuts gave them away," Suzy said.

"That was my first clue, but your waitress heard a few comments as she waited on you and told me she thought you were Marines," the owner said.

Manny rose from his seat and extended his hand. "I'm Manny Smith, and this is my fiancée, Lori Baker."

"It's a pleasure to meet you. My name is Jack Robinson," he replied.

After greetings were exchanged, Lori thanked him despite his protestations. "It was very nice of you to pay for our dinner. You really did not have to do that."

"Please, it was my pleasure to pick up the tab for a couple of fellow Marines," Jack said.

"You were once a Marine?" Suzy asked.

Jack directed a big smile at the boys and said, "Do you want to tell her, or should I let her in on the secret?"

Manny sat back down and rested his arm on the back of Lori's chair. "The saying is 'Once a Marine, always a Marine.' So Mr. Robinson is entitled to refer to himself as a fellow Marine."

Mr. Robinson gladly accepted the offer to join Manny and Kenny and the ladies. He told them he served in World War II and was medically discharged for severe wounds to his lower leg. After chatting about the Marine Corps for nearly thirty minutes, the waitress approached.

"Dad, there's a phone call for you in the office."

"You will have to excuse me, but feel free to order anything you like," said Jack as he rose.

"Thank you," the four said in unison.

As he walked away, they noticed a definite limp.

"Mr. Robinson really loves the Marine Corps," Lori said.

"I think you'll find that there are a lot of Mr. Robinsons in the world today," Manny said contentedly.

"I know she may not want to admit it, but I think our future mother needs to get to bed. I know I'm tired and will sleep well tonight," Suzy stated.

"That's probably a good idea," Kenny said. "Let's hit the rack."

Lower Vale

The arrival at the Smith house was jubilant. Maria rushed out the door and straight at Kenny. "Congratulations, Kenny. We are so proud of you," she said. She hugged Suzy. "Congratulations to you as well. It's wonderful to see you again, Suzy."

The house door opened, and onto the porch walked a hunched Pappy. "Hey, Lieutenant. Welcome home."

"Hey, Pappy. How's the back?" asked Kenny.

"I'm fine," the elder Smith responded.

"Then why are you carrying the cane?" asked Manny with a sour tone.

"I carry it to thump young smart-ass kids like you."

"Same old Pap," Manny said to Kenny with a smile.

Maria looked lovingly at Lori. "How is my grandbaby treating you today, Lori?"

"Much better than the other day, thank you," Lori responded.

"Anything decided in Denver?" Pappy asked in reference to the wedding. "We need to get these plans finalized to make travel and lodging arrangements."

Lori felt a little embarrassed that she had not given much thought to the complications facing people coming in from out of town. She looked at Manny and replied, "I'm going to call my mother tonight and ask her to find out if our church is available the first Saturday in January. That will be January 3."

"Oh my, this is all so soon and so exciting," said Maria.

"Don't worry, Maria. It will all be just fine," said Pappy.

"How can you be so calm? The wedding will be here soon, and we don't have plane tickets, and I have to get off work, and I don't have a new dress yet," exclaimed Maria.

"What, no new dress!? Stop everything, Manny. You can't expect to get married when your mother hasn't got a new dress yet," Pappy mocked.

"Oh, shut up, Dad," said Maria as she marched away in a huff.

Shortly after supper, Lori called her parents and learned that her mother already knew the schedule for the church and the church social hall. And it would be available for a January 3 wedding.

"So, that's it. You are soon going to be Mrs. Manny Smith," Manny said.

"And sooner than we realize, you are going to be Daddy Smith," Lori replied as she placed Manny's hand on her stomach to feel the kick.

"What about your wedding dress?" Maria asked Lori.

"My mother's friend said she can make it in no time at all. She's a wonderful seamstress," Lori replied.

"That's good," Maria said nervously.

"Mom, try to not worry. Mr. and Mrs. Baker will have everything under control. We just have to show up and enjoy it," Manny told his mother.

"What about plane tickets?" Maria asked, looking at Pappy.

"I'm calling the airport now," Pappy answered.

"Don't forget Dr. Wheeler and Mom and me," Kenny reminded Pappy.

To the relief of all, everyone from Lower Vale was able to get a ticket to Los Angeles on the same flight. With that concern alleviated, things were more relaxed as preparations got underway for the Christmas season. However, there was a small problem when the topic of where people would spend Christmas surfaced. The decision was finally made that everybody would spend Christmas at their own homes, but Manny and Kenny would join the girls for New Years in California.

On December 23, the boys took Lori and Suzy to the airport.

"Do you think you can live without me for a few days?" Kenny asked Suzy at the gate.

"It will be tough, but I'll try," she said with a protruding lower lip.

Manny and Lori were standing only a short distance away, their thoughts also on the few days they would be apart.

"Don't do anything too strenuous while you're at home," Manny instructed.

"Yes, sir," Lori responded with a mock salute.

Manny pulled her close for one last kiss. "I love you."

The girls stopped momentarily for a final wave goodbye and then disappeared down the walkway to their plane.

"What do think?" asked Manny. "Lunch at Robinson's?"

"Sounds good to me," replied Kenny.

Anaheim, CA

The boys' flight to Los Angeles was a little bumpy at first but then smoothed out, and they landed to clear and cool weather. Waiting at the arrival gate were Lori and Suzy.

After the initial hugs and kisses, Manny said, "As we were leaving Denver, Pap said there was a surprise waiting for us in California."

"I don't know what he's talking about," Lori said with a big grin that meant she knew exactly what Pappy was talking about.

Suzy smiled at the boys' puzzled faces.

Manny and Kenny didn't want to give the girls the satisfaction of pleading for information, so the subject was not brought up again. On the drive to the Baker house in Anaheim, the boys told Suzy and Lori about Tarzan's announcement: he and Jane would have their wedding in early June.

"That works. I was hoping to have our wedding in May," Suzy stated.

"Sounds good to me," Kenny said with a nod. "What a year for weddings."

"I don't think I like the idea of a May wedding," Manny sniffed.

"Good, you don't have to come," Suzy shot back.

Kenny and Lori just looked at each other and rolled their eyes.

When they arrived at the Baker house, the girls' parents came out to greet them. After a few minutes of pleasantries, Mr. Baker said, "I can't wait any longer. Let's get these two jarheads inside and get it over with."

Manny and Kenny looked at each other in bewilderment as they followed everyone into the Baker house. Suzy stopped the boys in the kitchen and said, "Before you go any further, you should know that this surprise took the effort and coordination of a bunch of people here in California. And not only were these gifts Dr. Wheeler's idea, but he insisted on paying the bill himself."

With that said, the boys were required to close their eyes as the girls led them into the living room. When they opened their eyes, Manny and Kenny were overwhelmed.

There on the sofa before them were two sets of Marine Corps officer dress blues. The boys stared, mouths wide open, at the sharp-looking uniforms. The girls each hugged their guy. Moments later, Manny and Kenny hugged and whooped and slapped each other on the back.

"I can't believe it! This is so great!" Manny cried.

"That Dr. Wheeler is really something," Kenny said.

"Why don't you call him to say thank you," Lori suggested.

"I'll dial the number. Your hands are shaking too much," said Suzy in jest.

Kenny took the phone from Suzy and waited as the phone rang. "Mom, this is so great. Is Dr. Wheeler there?" asked Kenny.

Kenny heard his mother say, "It's for you. I think it's a couple of Marine lieutenants that are all excited about something."

After Dr. Wheeler took the phone, Manny and Kenny poured out their hearts in gratitude. Finally, the generous doctor said to Kenny, "You are both very welcome, but I have to confess that Pappy came up with the idea because I didn't know what to get you. Just consider your dress blues as a commissioning gift and Manny's wedding gift. I'm very proud of the two of you."

Later that evening, Kenny managed to get Mr. Baker alone. "Hey, Mr. Baker. Do you think there's a place around here where we can have a little get-together for Manny and his buddies coming up from San Diego to be at the wedding?"

With a big grin, Mr. Baker said, "I have to confess that you Marines can usually teach us sailors a thing or two about marching and shooting. But there is nothing you can teach an old sailor about having a party."

Kenny smirked but didn't rise to the bait. Mr. Baker continued, "I already have the lodge locked in. There will be a keg and lots of good grub to eat, but Lori's mom found out about my plans and made me promise to not hire any strippers. But if you decide you want to invite a girl to dance for us, I will introduce you to my buddy, Herb. He has all the connections for any entertainment you may want."

Kenny shook his head in amazement. "You're okay, Mr. Baker."

The next day, the four of them went to the church so Lori could explain to Manny how it would be decorated. As she pointed to locations where different arrangements of flowers would be placed, Manny nodded. "That sounds nice, babe."

Lori stopped and dropped her head in disgust. A moment later she looked up at her cousin and said, "Daddy was right."

Suzy shot Manny and Kenny an appalled look. "I'm afraid so."

"What?" said Manny. He knew he was in trouble, but he wasn't sure why.

Finally, Lori said, "If I said we were having pasture clover here and lawn dandelions there, you would say, 'Fine.' Admit it: you don't care about the flowers."

Manny was confident that anything he said would be wrong.

Sensing his buddy's dilemma, Kenny said, "What did you mean when you said your daddy was right?"

"You men have no sense of making things as nice as they can be. This is a special moment in a girl's life, and she wants it to be just right. You just want to get it over with," scolded Suzy.

Before either man could respond, Lori burst out crying and sat on the floor.

"Now look what you've done," said Suzy.

In his defense, Manny said, "I didn't do anything."

"*Exactly!*" yelled Suzy. She stormed out of the church, and Kenny went after her.

As Lori sniffled on the floor, Manny lowered himself hesitantly beside her. After a few moments, he said, "Lori."

"It's okay, Manny. I understand. No, I don't understand, but I do accept it," she said without looking at him.

"Well, I have to say that if you are confused, that makes two of us," Manny told her in a low, somber voice.

"When I told my parents that I wanted to show you the plan for the church flowers to get your approval, my dad said that you wouldn't care. And he was right," she said.

"Aw, Lori. The only thing I really care about is the bottom line, and that is your happiness. If the flowers make you happy, they're great with me. Even if they really are dandelions," Manny replied.

With that lighthearted comment, Lori broke a little smile, and after a few more minutes and a little more discussion, she and Manny stood up.

"I love you so much, Lori."

"And I love you, Manny Smith, but I still owe you one for throwing me into the ocean."

"Threats are always a good way to start a marriage."

"I just want to be honest with you," she said primly.

Lori's parents were attending a New Year's Eve party, so she and Manny stayed home to relax and watch the New Year festivities on TV.

"I hope you don't mind staying home this evening?" Lori asked Manny.

"Words can't express how happy I am to be here with you. Heck, my best girl, good shows on the TV, and a fridge full of great food. It doesn't get any better than that," Manny replied.

"I'm very flattered to be listed ahead of the great food," Lori teased.

"Hey, I take enough grief from Suzy and Kenny about my refined palate," Manny stated. "Do I have to hear about it from you?"

"Refined palate. Oh boy, Kenny and Suzy are going to love hearing that," Lori said with a huge grin.

"Do I sense blackmail?" Manny asked.

"You are very perceptive, Lieutenant," Lori replied, pleased to have Manny on the defensive.

"Okay, what is the payoff to make your blackmail disappear?" Manny inquired, very much enjoying this game.

Lori relaxed her smile a little as she took Manny's hands and said, "Just promise me that you will always love me."

Manny's lower lip quivered as Lori wrapped her arms around him and pressed herself tightly against him.

"Lori Baker, in a few days we will become husband and wife. But even the formality of marriage won't make it possible for me to love you more than I already do."

"Oh, Manny. I love you so much."

Manny enthusiastically returned her kiss. Within seconds, his hands moved down Lori's back to press her hips tightly against his. Still kissing, he lifted her off her feet, and she wrapped her legs around him.

Manny suddenly realized what precious cargo he held in his arms and lowered her, allowing her feet to touch the floor.

Lori sought to ease Manny's concern over the baby. "It's okay, Manny. Holding me tightly is okay. Our baby is perfectly fine."

"You're sure?"

"I am very sure."

Manny was uncertain. Then Lori said very calmly, "I am so sure, in fact, that I'm going to my bedroom, and I sincerely hope you will join me."

He trusted Lori, but Manny was still very nervous and caught up in the moment as Lori sauntered away. After a few seconds, he followed her. By the time Manny got to the bottom of the stairway, Lori was at the top, and he heard her giggle as her blouse floated through the air over his head. Manny took the remainder of the steps two at a time.

The next day was relatively slow paced, considering there was to be a wedding in two days. The television was tuned to the football games—the typical calm before the storm.

January 2 started abruptly when Manny was roused from a deep sleep by Mr. Baker yelling, "Reveille, jarhead! We have a big day ahead of us, so let's get moving."

Lori shuffled by in her robe and said, "Suzy just called and said they were leaving Vista shortly."

Kenny and Suzy were coming to Anaheim, and then the boys were taking two cars to Los Angeles International to meet the plane from Denver with Dr. Wheeler, Kenny's mom, and the three Smiths.

The plane was on time, and it was an exciting meeting of the families as everybody looked forward to the joyous occasion with great anticipation. The boys greeted their mothers first but then almost pulled Dr. Wheeler's arm from his shoulder as they thanked him again for the dress blue uniforms.

"You are both more than welcome, but as I said on the telephone, I went to Pappy and he came up with the idea."

Turning to Pappy, Kenny said, "You're amazing, Pap."

"Yes, you are," added Manny. He grabbed his grandfather in a big hug.

"Hey, easy does it. All this hugging—you're both spending too much time in California," the grandfather stated.

"Pay no attention to him," Maria said to the boys. "He spends too much time breathing the exhaust fumes of that saw motor at the lumberyard."

All smiles, the group headed to the baggage claim area, then to the cars and on to Anaheim.

"Lori's mom said we have to bring you to the house for lunch first; then we'll take you to your hotel. You can see a lot of Disneyland from your rooms," Manny told the other three Smiths in the car.

"I've been to a lot of places in my life, but I have never been to Disneyland," Pappy said.

"I've never been there either. We should go the day after the wedding," Cindy hinted.

"Let's make sure Aunt Carmella and Uncle Manuel don't have other plans for us," Maria said.

"If you do go to Disneyland, Lori and I may see you there," said Manny.

"What do you mean?" Cindy asked.

"I'm taking Lori to Disneyland for our honeymoon," Manny stated.

"You're taking her to Disneyland? Why in the . . ." Cindy stopped quickly as she realized she was again the butt of her brother's teasing.

Maria asked, "Where are you going, Manny? Or don't you want to tell us?"

"Lori and I decided that we'll call from where we are, but we're not going to tell anybody beforehand," Manny said with a little grin of embarrassment.

"Oooh!" Cindy snickered.

There were only thirteen people eating lunch at the Baker house that day, but the Bakers had enough food for fifty.

When asked about all the food, Mr. Baker said, "I initially questioned the amount we were getting, but my wife is right. Anybody coming to town for our little girl's wedding is welcome to stop at our house to eat. That includes those gyrenes from Camp Pendleton or San Diego." Mr. Baker did not say that some of the food platters were going to the lodge that evening.

The pastor of the Bakers' church stopped by just as Manny and Kenny were about to take their families to their hotel. As they had previously discussed, the wedding would be very simple and traditional. However, the pastor was wondering about the phone call he received from some Marines asking if they could stop by around 1600 today to recon the church and conduct a rehearsal.

"The gentleman I spoke with was very polite, but I would feel better if one of you was there with me. And is the sword drill anything more than just the arch of swords?" asked the pastor.

Pappy started to laugh, but Kenny stepped forward to say, "Don't worry, sir. I will be there to greet them and oversee their rehearsal. It will be very short, I promise."

As the pastor drove away, the boys followed him out the driveway and headed to the hotel. On the way, Kathy asked, "How many Marines will be there, son?"

"There will be only eight in the sword detail, but a few more are coming for the wedding and party."

"What party?"

"Did I forget to mention Manny's bachelor party?"

"Kenny Reynolds, you promise me right now that you will not get your best friend drunk tonight."

"I promise, Mom, I promise."

"Well, I would certainly hope so."

"You'll be there, won't you, Dr. Wheeler?"

"You bet."

"You're a little old for bachelor parties," Kathy said doubtfully.

"I'm afraid not. Besides, it would be rude not to accept the invitation."

"Yeah, Mom, you know how you hate rudeness."

Kathy bit her tongue, determined not to nag.

That evening as the boys stopped by to pick up Pappy and Dr. Wheeler, Maria came out with Kathy and Cindy. "Please drop the three of us at the Bakers' house," Maria said. "We girls are going to have our own party so Kathy and I can tell stories to Lori and Suzy about you boys growing up."

"That will make for some interesting conversation in the years ahead," said Kenny.

"I'm sure it will," Manny sighed.

Later that evening at the lodge, the party started slowly, but Kenny took over and announced, "Listen up, men. I have a few words about the next casualty from the ranks of bachelorhood!"

Kenny went on to say a few nice things about his best friend, but the night was to be one of fun and laughter, so Kenny also told the story of Manny's first date in junior high when Manny was so nervous he forgot the girl's name. And the stories went downhill from there.

While Kenny dominated the floor, several Marines had stories about Manny. Some made Manny the humorous butt, but overall, the stories and comments reflected the high regard everyone had for the lieutenant.

At a short pause in the action, Kenny again took charge of the evening when he stepped forward, raised his glass in the air, and bellowed, "GENTLEMEN, TO A MARINE'S MARINE! TO MANNY SMITH!"

The resulting "TO MANNY SMITH!" rocked the room.

After they drank their toast, some slapped Manny on the back and shook his hand. After a minute or so, Manny raised his hand to signify he wished to speak.

"AT EASE!" someone yelled.

The room got quiet and Manny said, "I can't tell you how much this evening means to me. Thanks for being here to share it with me."

After a short rumble of concurrence, Manny went on. "I would like to make a toast, also, so please charge your glass." A few moments later, Manny continued, "It's important to have special people at a special night like this: my best friend, Kenny; Dr. Wheeler; and all my Marine Corps friends from the area. But there is someone here who is more special than any words can ever describe. And I would like you to join me in a toast to my grandfather, First Sergeant Roy Smith. GENTLEMEN, TO FIRST SERGEANT SMITH AND THE OLD CORPS!"

Some of them repeated the toast before they drank, but most of them unleashed a roar of motivation and dedication: "OOOOORAAAAAH!"

The shouts continued as Pappy and Manny moved toward each other, Marines slapping them on the backs while the two men hugged.

"I am so proud of you, hard charger," said the old man.

"Thanks, Pap. I love you," Manny returned.

Soon after, Manny ran into his future father-in-law in the crowd.

"Manny, I want you to know that I am really proud to have you as a son-in-law," Mr. Baker said.

"Thanks, Mr. Baker." Manny's face hurt from all the smiling; he was so full of joy that it was almost painful.

For the next hour the party revolved around a few more beers and the chow on the table. There were several beer-chugging races. Manny was tickled to see Lori's dad in competition with one of the Marines.

When the party came to an end because they had to leave the lodge, Kenny noticed a handful of men enter the room. Mr. Baker announced, "Fellows, no one should ever drive after he has been drinking. These men are fellow lodge members who are happy to drive you home tonight."

Kenny had to concede that the old sailor really did know how to party; having designated drivers was a class act.

Dr. Wheeler drove Manny, Kenny, Pappy back to the hotel. As they entered the lobby, Cindy motioned them to come into the lounge, where they found Kathy and Maria seated at a table.

"You men have probably had your share of alcohol tonight, but we want to have a toast before we turn in," Kathy said.

After the waitress brought them all a drink, Maria stood and said, "I hope you're happy to join me in a toast to all our blessings."

"Indeed we are, Maria. Please offer the toast," said Pappy.

After a moment of reflection, Maria said, "To all of the wonderful blessings the Lord has given us, and may we be worthy of such wonderful blessings in the future."

"Here, here," said the doctor. They all raised their glasses and drank.

The next morning, Manny awoke with a little headache, but it was nothing compared to the excitement he felt.

He found Kenny in the bathroom.

"Big day, eh, Manny?"

"You can say that again," Manny replied with a cheek-stretching smile.

Slipping on some casual clothes, they checked with the others before heading to get a bite of breakfast. After breakfast, Manny and Pappy went for a short walk and then proceeded to their rooms to get ready for the trip to the church.

"You've worn dress blues before, but this is my first time," Kenny said as he and Manny pulled the plastic hanger bag off their uniforms.

"I'll give you a hint," Manny offered.

"What would that be?"

"It's easier if you just put one leg in at a time," Manny offered seriously.

"You better watch dishing out smart remarks. I'm giving the toast at the reception," Kenny threatened.

"Well, then I give the toast at your wedding," Manny countered with a grin.

At the church, the pastor greeted the bridegroom and best man and escorted them to the choir room. "Try to make yourself comfortable, if that's possible," the pastor told them.

After the pastor walked out the door, Kenny peeked out. It was a sharply divided crowd. On the bride's side were mostly people Kenny did not know. And the groom's side was mostly Marines in uniform.

"Hey, Manny, there are more Marines here than were at the party last night," Kenny said.

Manny walked to the cracked door to satisfy his curiosity and was amazed to see some of those in attendance.

"Manny!" Kenny said suddenly. "There's Captain Tanner from Golf Battery, except he's now Major Tanner."

"Yes, I see him!" Manny replied excitedly.

The background music stopped, and the organist began a new tune. That was Kenny's cue to get Manny to the altar. Lori would soon be coming down the aisle.

As the two young men took their respective positions and turned to face the back of the church, Manny looked again at Major Tanner. The major smiled broadly and gave a slight nod. Manny returned the gesture, but then his attention was taken by the sudden increase in tempo and volume of the music.

As the wedding music played, Suzy walked down the aisle and took her place at her side of the altar. Then the wedding march began, and Lori and her father began moving down the aisle.

"Here we go, buddy," Kenny said in a low voice.

"Oorah," Manny softly replied.

From the back of the church, Lori's smile beamed as she moved forward. But as she got closer, Manny also saw tears in her eyes as Lori was unable to contain her happiness. He had to swallow hard and fight back his own tears of joy.

The pastor made the ceremony very easy as he spoke slowly, and in short phrases, throughout. Manny had been afraid he would be too nervous to repeat his vows properly, but he made it through with no problems.

Finally, the pastor said, "You may kiss the bride."

Manny pulled Lori close to him and said, "I love you, Mrs. Smith."

"I love you, Lieutenant Smith," she replied.

Manny wanted to kiss Lori longer, but he knew there would be more time later.

"Ladies and gentlemen, it gives me great pleasure to present to you Lieutenant and Mrs. Manny Smith."

Cheers and oorahs and clapping erupted from all the men wearing short hair and green uniforms.

"I hope the pastor doesn't mind all my rowdy friends," Manny whispered to Lori.

"It doesn't matter. I love enthusiasm," she responded.

After the noise faded, the pastor announced that the wedding reception would take place immediately in the church social hall next door. Manny and Lori walked back down the aisle and to the social hall where they waited to greet their guests. After everyone was greeted, seated, and getting their drinks and munchies, the wedding party went back to the church for a few quick pictures.

Upon their return to the reception, the buffet line was opened and the music began. Manny never considered himself a good dancer, but he was pleased by how well he moved to the music as he and Lori did their wedding dance.

Kenny approached Manny and Lori to ask, "Will you give me a heads-up a few minutes before you shove off? We need the detail to get their swords on."

"Now that Kenny brings it up, how long do we have to stay?" Manny asked Lori.

"Why do you ask? Is there someplace you want to go and something you want to do?" she asked in return.

"Maybe," he said, a twinkle in his eye. He spotted Major Tanner carrying a large envelope their way. Stopping in front of their table, the major said, "I've been holding this for almost two weeks so I could give it to you in person. Consider it a wedding present from the Marine Corps."

"Thank you, sir. Should I open it now?" asked Manny.

"Save it for later," he said. Then Major Tanner added, "And like so many times before, please accept my sincere congratulations."

Less than sixty minutes later Manny said to Kenny, "We're going to say goodbye and head out in a few minutes."

"Okay, we'll get ready. Do you think she suspects anything?" Kenny asked.

"No, but take it easy on her," Manny cautioned.

"Okay, okay," Kenny said, biting back his smile.

The word quickly spread that the bride and groom were preparing to leave. People surged outside ahead of them to see the sword arch, say goodbye, and pelt them with rice. In fact, Manny and Lori had to wait a minute to allow people to clear the door. While the newlyweds stood in the doorway of the social hall, Kenny and nine other Marines stood on the sidewalk Manny and Lori would take to their car. On Kenny's command, they raised their swords such that the five Marines on the right crossed their swords with the five Marines on the left, thereby creating the arch of swords that Manny and Lori were to walk through.

"I like this," Lori said to Manny.

"I hope you can say that later," replied Manny as they stepped down to the sidewalk and walked toward the first set of crossed swords.

"What do you mean?" Lori asked.

A sudden shower of rice gave Manny an excuse to not answer. Walking under the sets of crossed swords was uneventful, until they reached the fifth set of swords. Kenny and the other Marine in the final set lowered their swords to block Manny and Lori's path.

Kenny said, "A kiss for the Corps."

Guests cheered, and Lori happily kissed her new husband.

When they completed their kiss, the sword blockade was raised so the couple could continue.

Walking past him, Lori was pleased to hear Kenny say, "Welcome to the Marine Corps, Mrs. Smith."

Lori turned her head to say thank you and then felt a sharp sting on her butt as Kenny whacked her with his sword.

"Oww!" she said in surprise. She glared at Kenny, then saw the big grin on his face and glanced quickly at her new husband, who was unsuccessfully trying to hide his own smile.

"Like you said, it's very exciting."

"I owe you two," Lori replied.

After they climbed into the car, Lori rolled down the window. Seeing her cousin just a few feet away, Lori said, "I almost forgot, not that you need it." Then Lori threw Suzy her bridal bouquet.

Suzy caught the flowers and held them close to her chest as she waved goodbye.

After settling on the seat, she said to Manny, "Well, husband dear. Where are you taking me on our honeymoon?"

"I told you to trust me. Are you still worried?" Manny asked.

"I was not worried until Suzy told me I was crazy to let you surprise me with the location of our honeymoon," Lori said.

"Well, even though it is Southern California, the temperature is a little chilly this time of year. So, I thought we would head south," Manny answered.

"South to . . . ?"

"South to Acapulco," Manny answered.

"Oh, Manny, are you serious?" she asked.

"The only thing I ever said that was more serious was that I love you." He thought for a moment. "And 'I do.'"

Seconds later, Manny noticed the large envelope on the floor of the car and realized it was the envelope Major Tanner had given him. Overwhelmed by curiosity, Manny opened the large envelope and found another slightly smaller envelope inside. The second envelope was marked as official business for the Marine Corps. Manny realized he was holding his orders. These papers would direct him to his next assignment, wherever that might be.

Manny experienced a cold chill. Camp Pendleton was what he hoped for, and he knew that Lori hoped for the same.

"Open it, Manny. Whatever it says, it says," Lori told him.

Manny opened the envelope to read the contents; Lori found herself holding her breath.

"I can't believe it," Manny said.

"What is it? What does it say?" Lori asked.

Manny stared at her and said, "I'm being ordered to report for duty at MCRD, San Diego."

"Oh, Manny. This is wonderful," Lori said.

"I know. It's more than I could have ever hoped for," Manny replied.

"I hope you don't want to skip our honeymoon so you can check in to the depot as soon as possible," Lori told him with a grin.

"Heck no," Manny answered quickly. "I want to get to Acapulco and try out some of the great local Mexican cooking."

The weather in Acapulco was wonderful. Manny and Lori enjoyed lounging around the pool of their hotel and strolling on the beach. Lori was very self-conscious about her pregnant belly, but Manny assured her that he loved it. Their third day in Acapulco was a little cooler than the first two days, so the newlyweds put on their shopping clothes and headed for the local marketplace. Lori felt a little embarrassed when people commented about her pregnancy in Spanish, and she could not understand the comments Manny made in return. She was sure that it was one of Manny's typical jokes because the remark always made people laugh.

"I wish you would stop making fun of me to these people," Lori told him.

"What makes you think I'm making fun of you?" Manny replied.

Lori just pouted at him.

"Oh, lighten up, Lori. People are being very complimentary about what an attractive young mother you will be. I just remind them that I am responsible for the glow in your smile," Manny said.

CHAPTER TWELVE

SAN DIEGO STATE AND THE BASIC SCHOOL

San Diego

Manny and Lori liked the area in San Diego where Kenny used to live. They liked it so much that they decided to live in the same apartment complex Kenny lived in as a student at San Diego State. Aunt Carmella and Uncle Manuel were thrilled to have Manny and Lori close by.

"I cannot wait for the baby to be born," Aunt Carmella said as she helped Lori sort through some of the things she'd received at the baby shower Suzy had thrown the previous day.

"That makes three of us, Aunt Carmella," Lori responded, patting her stomach.

"You know I would never interfere, but I hope you will allow me to visit and babysit often," Carmella commented.

"Don't be silly. You're always welcome here, but how will Uncle Manuel manage the restaurant without you?" Lori asked.

After a moment of silence, Carmella responded, "We have talked of selling the restaurant."

At first Lori didn't know how to respond. "Does Manny know?"

"No, you are the first person to know besides Manuel and me," Carmella replied.

Sensing that Carmella felt a little awkward, Lori said, "Well, I think the two of you have worked long and hard and should retire and enjoy life."

"It's not that we don't enjoy the restaurant anymore, but it is a lot of work. And another family has expressed interest in buying it," Carmella explained. She added, "But now with you and Manny so close, we are reluctant to sell because we know how Manny loves to come there and eat."

"Aunt Carmella, Manny will want you to do what is best for you and Uncle Manuel."

"I know, but we love having you there, also."

"And we love being there."

Carmella nodded but said nothing. The decision to sell the restaurant would not be easy, but she'd known that it would happen one day. Lori was not surprised that others were interested; the restaurant was well known for good Mexican food and had an excellent location.

Carmella broke the silence. "When will Manny report to the recruit depot to learn what his new assignment will be?"

"He's going to check in tomorrow. He has some more leave, but he cannot wait to learn what he will do."

"And what about continuing his education?"

"We hope he can take a couple night classes when the second semester begins in two weeks, but only if the university lets him sign up for classes this late. And provided his new job allows him to go to school."

"And if they do not?"

"I don't know. I guess he'll wait for the summer semester."

"I hope they allow him to get started right away."

"That's what Manny and I want."

After Aunt Carmella returned to the restaurant, Lori sat at the table in their little kitchen. She felt the baby move on a regular basis these days but never failed to place her hand on her stomach and marvel as the baby did so.

"Hey, Tormentor, how's my girl and our baby?" Manny asked as he walked into the apartment.

The look on his face told Lori that something good happened at the university.

"Well, what did they say?"

"My first class is tomorrow night."

"Oh, Manny, that's wonderful news. We were so worried."

"I just hope my Marine Corps assignment doesn't interfere." Sitting at the table, Manny continued, "I had the best stroke of luck. On the way to the registrar's office, I ran into Dr. Stinter, one of my old professors. He asked what I was doing, and I told him I wanted to enroll in a couple evening classes. He insisted on going with me, and the next thing I know, I'm enrolled."

"That's terrific. You must have made a big impression on Dr. Stinter when you were in his class," Lori replied.

"I remember suspecting that he was a veteran. It turns out that he served in the Marine Corps in World War II and Korea," Manny stated.

"I take it you and the professor spent some time talking about the Marine Corps after he helped you register," Lori asked.

"You know how we Marines like to talk."

"Right, and eat and drink, and other things," Lori added, placing her hand on her stomach.

"Yeah," said Manny proudly.

"Now we just have to hope the Marine Corps cooperates," Lori added.

"I think they will, especially because I'm an officer," Manny said with slight hesitation.

"What's wrong?"

"I worry a little that I may lose my commission because I don't have my degree. That's why I'm so anxious to return to school," Manny confessed.

Later that afternoon, the phone rang.

Manny picked it up. "Kenny! How is The Basic School?"

When Manny entered the bedroom ten minutes later, Lori asked, "How is Kenny? What did he say?"

"He's fine. Says he misses me a lot, and misses Suzy a little too."

"Good thing I have my feet off the floor with all the BS you spread."

"Kenny said it's a little boring. They're doing a bunch of admin stuff right now, but the training schedule begins tomorrow, so it should get better."

"I am sure it will."

After a moment, Manny asked, "Do we want to eat here or go to the restaurant tonight?"

Lori said nothing as she gathered the courage to share Carmella's news.

"Well, any preference?"

"I want to tell you something, and then I want you to go for a run. We can talk about it when you return."

Manny quickly sat on the floor. "Let's hear it."

After taking a big breath, Lori sat up and said, "When Aunt Carmella was here today, she said that someone made them an offer to buy the restaurant."

"Did Aunt Carmella say anything else? Do they want to sell?" Manny asked.

"They don't want to sell because they think it will upset you. They know how much you love to go there, and they love to have you there."

When Manny said nothing, Lori suggested, "Instead of your Marine Corps run, how about an expecting mother's walk?"

"Good idea. Let's go," Manny responded.

Ambling around the block, neither of them said anything for a while. Then Manny said, "It will seem strange to not be able to visit them and eat at the restaurant, but at their age, it might be best if Aunt Carmella and Uncle Manuel sell."

"I think we all agree that it would be best for them in the long run." Lori added, "It will make it a lot easier if you tell them you support the idea of selling."

"I know, and that is what I will do," Manny replied.

The next morning as Manny headed off to work, Lori yelled, "Good luck! I love you."

Manny didn't hear her. His mind raced through the various duties he might be assigned when he reported to the depot. But no matter his assignment, it was good to be back.

Manny's orders were to report to the commanding general, Marine Corps Recruit Depot, San Diego, California. As Manny approached the front office to the depot headquarters, the door opened, and the commanding general himself emerged. Instinctively, Manny rendered a sharp salute and said, "Good morning, sir."

"Good morning, Lieutenant. Checking in?"

"Yes, sir."

"Welcome aboard. I am Major General Barlow."

"Pleased to meet you, sir. I'm Lieutenant Smith."

"Lieutenant Manny Smith, I assume," the general said, to Manny's surprise.

"Yes, sir, Manny Smith."

"Major Tanner did everything short of threatening me to get you as his deputy."

The general said something else, but Manny did not hear it clearly. He was stunned by the revelation. Suddenly, Manny was startled by a loud voice as the office door briefly popped open.

"Get in here and check in, Lieutenant. We have work to do!"

"I think that's my cue to leave," said General Barlow.

Manny snapped to attention and saluted. "Have a good day, sir."

"Thank you, Lieutenant Smith," the general replied as he returned the salute.

Manny headed into the building to see Major Tanner's extended hand. After a strong handshake, the two officers moved into the privacy of an office.

"Hope you don't mind being blindsided, Manny, but I want you to be my right-hand man at the DI School," the major stated.

"No, sir! I would love to work at the Drill Instructor School," Manny said.

"That's good, because we have some changes the general wants made," Major Tanner told him. Manny listened attentively to his former battery commander. "These changes are not that big, so I plan to have them implemented by June. After that I expect to lose you anyway."

Curious, Manny asked, "Sir?"

"I expect you to be accepted into the degree completion program by summer."

Manny did not know what to say.

The major continued, "You are a fine young Marine, Manny. The Marine Corps did well to make you an officer, but if you wish to stay an officer and have a career as an officer, you must get to school and get your degree."

"I've already looked into taking some classes at night, sir," Manny said.

"That's great. I expected you would. But one or two classes a semester is not good enough. You need to get to college full time, and the degree completion program will allow you to do that."

Manny stood and extended his right hand. As the two Marines shook hands again, Manny told his boss and mentor, "Thank you, sir. I will do my best."

"I know you will, Lieutenant. You always do," Tanner said.

That evening, Manny and Lori stopped by the restaurant on the premise of wanting to tell the Riveras the good news about Manny's assignment.

Manuel and Carmella were delighted that Manny's Marine Corps duties would allow him to be a student at the university.

"When I asked Major Tanner about going to school, he said I was going whether I wanted to or not," Manny told the Riveras.

After a little more discussion about Manny's assignment to the DI School, Uncle Manuel changed the topic. "Carmella told me that you know of the offer we received to sell the restaurant."

"That's right, Uncle Manuel. And if the price is right, Lori and I think you should accept," Manny answered.

"Actually, there has been no mention of a price at this time," Manuel stated.

Manny and Lori looked at each other with a little skepticism.

Manuel continued, "We really aren't sure what a fair price would be."

Lori spoke up immediately. "We should call my uncle. He'll be able to determine a fair price for a restaurant like this."

"I am confident you should get top dollar," Manny added.

"Do you think Mr. Miller would have time to help us?" Aunt Carmella asked.

"Aunt Carmella, he would love to help you," Lori responded.

Later, as Manny and Lori left the restaurant, Lori said, "I wonder if they realize what a prime piece of property the restaurant is."

"I was thinking the same thing."

Even with the unsettling news about the restaurant, Manny had other things on his mind.

"How do I look? Do I look like a college student?" Manny asked Lori as he prepared to go to his first class

"Manny, you and I both know you are not the average college student."

"I know, but I don't want to look too conspicuous."

"Just don't go grabbing anybody by the throat if they say something rude."

"If a cute college girl says something smart to me, can I grab her somewhere else?"

"Sure, and then you can get kicked out of college and the Marine Corps, not to mention getting kicked out of this apartment," Lori said in a tone that reflected her lack of appreciation for Manny's little joke.

"Geez, Kenny likes my jokes much better than you."

"Then tell them to Kenny."

"Hey, I'm sorry. What are you so upset about?"

Lori looked down at the floor for a second. "What you said is true."

"What's true?"

"There are going to be many cute girls in your classes and on the campus. And they will have cute figures, and here I am looking more like a whale every day."

"Lori?"

Lori didn't respond, but her eyes welled with tears.

"Aw, Lori, how can you think that any girl at the university could be appealing to me? You have to know how very much I love you."

After a few moments she said, "How much do you love me?"

"I love you more than all the barbequed ribs in the world," he told her.

"That much?"

"That much," he replied.

"Do you love me more than all the enchiladas in the world?"

"I'll have to think about that one," he answered with a grin.

Less than half an hour later, Manny was again grinning about Lori's outburst as he walked to his class and saw numerous pretty girls heading toward the same room. Manny quickly forgot about the girls as he took a seat and noticed the extensive reading list on the blackboard.

Arriving back at the apartment later that day, Manny was met at the door by his beautiful, pregnant wife. "Well, college boy, how did it go?" she asked.

"This first class is going to be a little rough."

"What's the problem?"

"The professor seems okay, but the reading list is a bear."

"Is that mean professor going to make you read?"

"It certainly looks that way."

Quantico

Kenny found himself caught up in the spirit and enthusiasm of the training at The Basic School. He already knew many of the other lieutenants in his company from OCS. The initial check-in procedures were time consuming and boring but necessary. The lieutenants received their weekly training schedule, and things would pick up as the week progressed.

Late in the afternoon of day three, Tom Mitter asked, "Hey, Ken, what do say we go down to the Hawk and drink a cold one?"

Kenny was writing a letter to Suzy and not really in the mood for drinking, but Tom seemed like a real nice guy. "I think I could force one down if you twist my arm."

The Hawk was the short name for the Hawkins Room, the bar/club of O'Bannon Hall, primary residence of Marine lieutenants attending The Basic School. Named for Lieutenant William Hawkins, recipient of the Congressional Medal of Honor for his heroic actions during the battle of Tarawa in World War II, the Hawk was a very popular place for lieutenants and TBS staff officers to relax and share a beer as they rehashed the day's training.

As they entered the glass doors to the Hawk, Tom said, "Why don't you grab that table and I'll get the first round."

Waiting for Tom, Kenny surveyed the room and the people in it. The Hawk had fifteen or so round tables to sit at while unwinding with a cold one. The atmosphere was relaxed, and Kenny was glad he'd accepted his roommate's invitation.

Tom handed Kenny a bottle. "Is this okay?"

"This is my favorite kind of beer," Kenny replied.

"Good, I like Devil Dog beer, too."

"I wasn't referring to the brand. My favorite is cold and free," Kenny said.

Tom chuckled. "I think I'm going to like rooming with you."

As Kenny sat talking with Tom, he felt a strong hand squeeze his shoulder.

"Lieutenant, why aren't you in your room studying?"

Looking up quickly, Kenny said, "Mark Richards, how are you doing?"

"Just fine, Ken. How was OCS?" Mark replied.

"OCS was just fine," Kenny told Mark. "Mark, this is my roommate, Tom Mitter."

"Hey, Tom, where you from?"

"Pennsylvania. Penn State, to be more specific."

"Geez, I'll bet I've met ten guys from Pennsylvania since I got here," Mark said.

"There must be a hatch going on," Tom said with a smile.

"What?" asked Kenny, puzzled.

"Never mind, it's an old fly-fishing joke," Tom said.

Mark sat down to join Kenny and Tom and said he was glad to hear about Manny.

"How did you know?" Kenny inquired.

"Word of what happened to Manny is all over Quantico, and probably all over the Marine Corps," Mark said.

Kenny figured he shouldn't be surprised.

"How long have you been here, Mark?" Tom asked.

"Almost four months. I'm getting short," he told them.

"What do we have to look forward to, old-timer?" Kenny asked with a grin.

"Lots of classwork and field time, lots of PT, and lots of beer in the Hawk," Mark told them. After a pause, Mark asked, "Who is your staff platoon commander?"

"Captain Wassel," Kenny answered.

Mark shook his head. "Captain Mark Wassel. Better known to lieutenants as 'Captain Dark Asshole.'"

Kenny and Tom looked at each other nervously.

"What's his problem?" Kenny asked.

"Who knows? He's just wound too tight."

"He sounds like he's really impressed with himself," Tom said.

"You hit the nail right on the head," Mark told them.

"Any advice?" Kenny asked.

"Yeah, just tolerate his shit and realize that all the staff around here are not like Wassel."

As Kenny reviewed a small handout in their room later that evening, he wondered how the studying was progressing for Manny in California.

San Diego

"I like the name Maria, but I am afraid it may hurt my mother's feelings," Lori told Manny.

"Lori, if you don't make a decision soon, they're going to refer to our baby girl as No-Name Smith."

"Manny, this is important. If we have a little girl, I want her to have a name she likes."

"I know, but there are so many pretty names. Can't you pick one and stick with it?"

"I will."

Manny just shook his head, and Lori stuck out her tongue at him.

"I hope your mom and Aunt Carmella are here a good bit as she grows up so our baby has some proper female adult behavior to follow."

"Oh boy! You're one to talk."

The phone rang and Manny said, "Saved by the bell."

It was Aunt Carmella making her daily phone call to learn how Lori was feeling. After a few minutes of assuring Aunt Carmella that she was fine, Lori indicated to Manny that he should talk to Carmella.

Walking back from the bathroom, Lori heard Manny say, "You must be patient and do as Mr. Miller tells you. People are going to try and buy the restaurant for much less than it's worth, and you must not let that happen."

After hanging up a couple minutes later, Manny just shook his head.

"Sounds like the wheeler dealers are still at it," Lori commented.

"Yes, they're still telling Uncle Manuel they have no money but will take good care of the restaurant and say many prayers for my aunt and uncle if they sell at a cheap price."

"I hope they can resist the come-on line those people are dishing out. I get the impression your aunt and uncle are getting a little anxious to sell now that they have decided to do so."

"My thoughts exactly," Manny said.

The next morning, Manny went into MCRD early to work out. He always found inspiration to run farther when on the grounds of the recruit depot. As he ran, he heard a car approaching from behind. The car came to a quick stop, and a sergeant jumped out.

"Lieutenant Smith, we just got a phone call that your wife is having the baby."

Manny dove into the car and was dropped off at his office where he grabbed his wallet and keys and headed home. He found his aunt and uncle ushering Lori out the door.

Seeing Manny approach, Lori said, "You were here to start this pregnancy. Glad you could make it for the finish."

"Always glad to do my part," Manny replied.

"Let's still go in our car," Aunt Carmella insisted.

"Okay," said Manny. "I have Lori. Get her suitcase from Aunt Carmella, Uncle Manuel."

"Oh my, this is so exciting," Carmella said as they drove to the hospital.

For the first thirty minutes in the waiting room, Carmella paced and talked and paced and talked.

"Carmella, come and sit down," Manuel told his wife.

She sat with her husband and great-nephew for a few minutes and then stood again, saying, "I cannot just sit here."

"Maybe you can call Maria. What do you think, Manny?" Uncle Manuel asked.

"If that will help, sure."

Carmella hurried away to find a phone.

A little later, Carmella returned to say that although no one was home at the Smith house in Lower Vale, she did get through to Lori's mother, and the Bakers would soon be on their way to San Diego.

A nurse approached about twenty minutes later. "Mr. Smith, your wife would like to see you."

"Is everything okay with Lori and the baby?" Carmella asked the nurse.

"They're fine. Her blood pressure was a little high at first, but now she and the baby are doing well," the nurse answered.

In Lori's room, Manny said, "Hey there, beautiful. Is everything okay and under control?"

"How should I know? I've never done this before," Lori answered.

"I hope you're better than Aunt Carmella. She's a nervous wreck," Manny said.

"I'm better now that you're here. I just wanted you to hold my hand and tell me you love me," Lori explained.

As Manny took her hand in his, Lori's face suddenly went tense with pain.

"Are you okay?" he asked.

"Contraction," she said. "You ought to try one sometime."

Within an hour, the contractions were closer and more severe, and Manny was told to return to the waiting room so they could take Lori to the delivery room. Manny found Mr. and Mrs. Baker waiting.

"How is she doing?" Mrs. Baker asked.

"They're moving her to the delivery room now, so it shouldn't be too much longer."

As the ladies fussed, Mr. Baker moved close to Manny. "How are you holding out?"

"I'm good."

"How is she?" came an unexpected voice.

"Suzy, how did you know?" asked Manny as Lori's cousin hugged her aunt and uncle and then turned to him.

"I called Lori, and when she didn't answer, I called the restaurant," Suzy said. Manny was grateful for her intuition.

Only twenty minutes later, another nurse came to them and said, "Mr. Smith, would you like to come see your wife your new baby boy?"

Cheers and emotions filled the room as Manny followed the nurse. There in the recovery room were Lori and their tiny new son.

"Come get a closer look at Charlie," Lori said as she turned the baby so Manny could get a better look.

Moving closer, Manny was speechless. He swallowed a lump in his throat that appeared the moment Lori said his father's name. He had experienced a wide range of emotions in his lifetime, but nothing was as wonderful as this. Manny kissed Lori and touched the baby's hand. "Hey, Charlie, how's my boy?" he asked as he thought of his mother and father and grandfather.

By midafternoon, every family member in California had seen Lori and the baby. Even Mr. and Mrs. Miller made it soon after the birth. As Lori and the baby rested at the hospital, the others went to the restaurant where a celebration dinner was held. Many of the Riveras' regular customers knew Manny and were also asked to participate.

But the highlight of the party was the phone call Manny made to Lower Vale. After a couple rings, Cindy answered the phone.

"Cindy—" was all Manny could get out before she cut him off.

"How is Lori?" Cindy demanded.

"She and the baby are fine," Manny told her with satisfaction.

"Eeeeee!" Cindy screamed. "Mom, Pappy! Lori had the baby."

"Cindy, can I speak to Mom?" asked Manny.

"Boy or girl? What did she have?" Cindy demanded.

"Wouldn't you like to know," Manny teased his little sister.

"*Manny Smith*! I will kill you," Cindy threatened.

"Manny, how are Lori and the baby?" asked Manny's mother after taking the phone from Cindy.

"Lori and Charlie are both doing fine," Manny said.

A swift intake of breath and silence answered him.

"Mom, are you okay?" Manny asked.

A moment later his grandfather said, "Manny, your mother is okay. Just a little overcome with emotion."

After talking to Pappy for a few seconds, Manny heard his mother again. She was thrilled that her grandson had been named after her late husband. For the next ten minutes Manny walked them through the day's events. Then Aunt Carmella took the phone and told Maria the same thing Manny had just said. He figured it must be more reassuring to hear it from another woman.

That evening, Manny tried to study but could not concentrate. He knew that Suzy would tell Kenny about the baby, but he decided to call his best friend anyway. After twenty minutes of unsuccessful attempts, the phone in his apartment rang.

"Where's my cigar?" demanded Kenny.

"Hey, amigo. What do you think?"

"I can't tell you how happy I am for you, Manny. It's just wonderful."

"Thanks for calling, Kenny. And hang in there."

"Pass on my best wishes to Lori."

Manny hung up and was walking to the refrigerator when the phone rang again. This time it was Mrs. Reynolds and Dr. Wheeler calling to offer their congratulations. After a short discussion about Lori and the baby, Mrs. Reynolds made a comment that seemed a little odd to Manny.

"Do you like living in California, Manny?"

He answered, "Sometimes I miss the Colorado mountains, but I have to say that I like it out here."

"I thought you did. The weather is certainly wonderful," Mrs. Reynolds said.

Things were very different around the apartment with a new baby, but Manny and Lori were as happy as they could be. By May, Manny considered himself to be an expert diaper changer. He had been certain he would hate changing messy diapers, but he did not mind it at all, and in fact took pride in how good he was.

As a young Marine recruit, he'd learned how to disassemble and reassemble his rifle blindfolded, so one day as Lori and Mrs. Baker were at the grocery store, Manny challenged himself.

"Okay, Dad," he said to Mr. Baker. "Time me while I change this diaper blindfolded. Then you can inspect to make sure I did a good job."

"You gotta be kidding me."

"No, I want to show you how good I am."

"You Marines are some weird sons'a bitches."

"Oorah," Manny replied.

San Diego

The phone rang as Manny was talking to Lori while she bathed the baby. He expected to hear the voice of Mrs. Baker, Aunt Carmella, or Suzy and was very pleased to hear his DI friend, Staff Sergeant Bass.

"Staff Sergeant Bass, it's good to hear from you. How's everything?" Manny asked.

"Our battalion commander is having a dining-in, and we wanted to invite you and your lady to attend."

A Marine Corps dining-in was a formal banquet where the Marines and their ladies assembled to share in the camaraderie of the Marine Corps.

"That sounds great. We would love to come. When is it?"

"June 15 at the MCRD Staff Club."

"This is exciting. Thank you very much."

"Is there a chance your grandfather could attend?"

"That's really nice of you to ask. He just might be able to since my family will be here in June for my best friend's wedding."

"I remember your friend. Would you like me to see if he can attend?" Bass asked.

"Thanks, but he'll be on his honeymoon."

"Okay, sir. We'll get out your invitation today, but mark your calendar now," Bass said.

"Consider it done, and thanks again."

It was a very hectic time for Manny. He was working hard at the DI School and still frequently getting up in the middle of the night to help Lori with the baby. He was also enrolled in two classes at the university. Aunt Carmella and Uncle Manuel visited often, and Carmella accompanied Lori to Vista a couple times a week as the final plans were made for Kenny and Suzy's wedding.

"I should be back from the airport in about an hour," Manny told Lori as he headed out to pick up his mother, sister, and grandfather.

"See you then. Bye, Daddy," Lori said, waving little Charlie's hand at Manny.

The plane from Denver was on time, and Manny beamed with joy as his family emerged into the arrival terminal at the San Diego airport.

"Manny, I miss you so much. It's so good to see you," said Maria.

"Hi, Mom. It's wonderful to see you too," he replied, embracing her.

"Good morning, Lieutenant," Pappy said with a proud smile and firm handshake.

"If it were any better, I couldn't stand it," Manny replied. He looked at his sister. "Hey, sis." Cindy gave her brother a warm embrace.

"Alright, the greetings are done. Let's go see that baby boy," Pappy said.

The trip back to the apartment was short, but on the way, Maria told Manny about Kathy Reynolds and Dr. Wheeler's planned arrival. Manny already knew the details, so he did not pay close attention to what his mother was saying. Instead he considered how he would tell his mother of the Riveras' plans to sell the restaurant.

After the initial fuss over seeing the baby for the first time, Manny decided to go ahead and tell his mother the news.

"Mom, I want to tell you something that will likely make you a little sad."

The room fell quiet.

"Some people have expressed an interest in buying the restaurant from Uncle Manuel and Aunt Carmella," Manny said in a subdued voice.

After another moment of silence, Maria asked, "Do they want to sell?"

"In a way they do, and in a way they don't," Manny replied.

Lori wanted to jump in and explain the different factors influencing the decision but figured she should leave this up to Manny.

Then wise old Pappy Smith said, "I have to admit that I wondered how long they would continue to run the restaurant."

Still Maria said nothing, deep in thought as she gently bounced her grandson.

"Lori and I have talked about it a lot, and they could make a bunch of money if they sold. It's a valuable piece of property, according to Mr. Miller," Manny added.

"I guess we like to think that some things will last forever, even though we know they really cannot," Maria finally commented.

Lori spoke up. "Aunt Carmella asked me to call them as soon as you arrived. Should I call them now?"

"Would it be okay if we went over there?" Maria asked the others.

"I have a strong suspicion that they would not mind if we stopped in for a surprise visit," Pappy said.

The visit to the Riveras was emotional. Maria cried in the arms of her aunt, which caused Aunt Carmella to cry also. For the next hour they talked of the baby and selling the restaurant and the wedding. Pappy sounded a little disappointed when Manny said that there would be no bachelor party.

"Hell, we have to do something."

"How about if we take Kenny to dinner? Just the men. I'm sure Uncle Manuel and my father-in-law and Mr. Miller and Dr. Wheeler would be happy to have a boys' night out."

Manuel nodded his concurrence.

"It won't be much of a party, but it's better than nothing," Pappy groused.

"Oh, Pappy. You boys can get loud and belch and act like idiots. I bet you'll have a good time," Lori said.

"You're darn right we will," Pappy said.

"But you will not get Kenny drunk for his wedding," insisted Maria.

"Don't worry, Mom. We'll have a doctor with us," Manny said with a smirk.

Before Maria could respond, the phone rang. After a few minutes, Manuel hung up and said, "That was Mr. Miller. He has something he wants to discuss with me, and when I invited him down, he said the three of them would be here in about an hour."

The news Mr. Miller delivered was not good. The offer for the restaurant was far below what the Riveras were told to expect. Mr. Miller was very apologetic, but everyone knew it was not his fault.

"Please don't be upset," Aunt Carmella told him. "We will just not sell the restaurant if we don't get a fair price. I would like to still own the restaurant when this little guy gets old enough for solid food."

Chuckles followed the remark.

Then Lori asked Suzy, "When does Kenny plan to get here?"

"The day after tomorrow," she replied with a wide smile.

"What about Mrs. Reynolds and Dr. Wheeler?" Carmella asked.

"They're not arriving until two days before the wedding because they're staying in California for several days afterward. Dr. Wheeler has some business here, and they're going to do some vacationing," Manny answered.

The next couple days flew by for Manny with his family there. When he arrived home for supper the night of Kenny's arrival, Lori said, "Kenny is at Suzy's house. They just called a half an hour ago."

"Can they come down?"

"Yes, but seeing you is third on Kenny's list of priorities."

"What do you mean?"

"Seeing Charlie is Kenny's first reason for coming to San Diego."

"What else is ahead of me?"

"Aunt Carmella's cooking. We're meeting and eating at the restaurant."

CHAPTER THIRTEEN

KENNY AND SUZY'S WEDDING

Vista

MANNY GAZED LOVINGLY AT his baby boy as they all waited at the restaurant. He was anxious for his best friend to arrive so Kenny could get his first look at Charles Kenneth Smith. Manny was fairly sure no one had yet told Kenny that the baby was his namesake too.

"They're here," Manny heard.

Lifting the baby out of the little bassinette, Manny moved toward the door to greet Kenny and Suzy.

"Hey, Manny!" Kenny yelled.

Holding Charlie in his left arm, Manny extended his right hand to Kenny and said, "What do you think?"

"You know what I think," Kenny replied as the two friends shook hands. Both peered closely at the baby boy, who drooled in greeting.

"May I hold him? I promise I won't drop him," Kenny said.

"Oh, it's okay. I drop him a couple times a day to toughen him up," Manny said.

"Manny," Lori warned.

"You are still the worst liar I ever hope to meet," said Suzy.

"I thought that a bride-to-be was supposed to be nice and sweet?" Manny lamented.

"Shows how stupid you are," Suzy shot back.

"Take my advice and run away, Kenny. Run fast and far while you still have time, old friend."

"That's enough, Manny. I don't know how you ever expect to coach high school kids when you act like one yourself," Lori told her husband.

Kenny looked at Manny with surprise. "What is this?"

"I just learned for sure yesterday. The local high school was going to cancel its wrestling program this fall because they couldn't find a wrestling coach. I asked them if I could help, and the principal said he would be pleased to have me," Manny answered.

"That's great!" Kenny said with much enthusiasm.

"Can you boys talk while you eat?" Aunt Carmella asked as she hugged Kenny.

"Of course, Aunt Carmella," Kenny replied.

After everybody was seated and the blessing was said, Lori asked Kenny, "Well, Lieutenant Reynolds, are you ready to get married now that your wedding has been all planned and prepared without you?"

"Hey, yell at the Marine Corps, not me," Kenny defended himself.

On the day of the wedding, the boys reminisced about growing up in Lower Vale as they drove north from San Diego to Vista. Arriving at the church, they were surprised to see so many people there ahead of time. But the biggest and best surprise was the appearance of Tarzan and Jane.

Manny welled up a little as he and Kenny took turns embracing their lifelong friends from home. As he hugged Sarah, Manny felt something familiar and looked down at her stomach. Sarah smiled and nodded to confirm.

"Yes!" he bellowed, causing Kenny and Tarzan to stare at him in surprise.

Manny hugged Tarzan again and said, "Congratulations, Dad. I'll give you some pointers on changing diapers with your eyes closed."

Kenny caught on and cheered loudly himself as he hugged Sarah again.

The four old friends were soon joined by the others from Lower Vale as Pappy and Maria and Cindy arrived with Manuel and Carmella. The highlight of the pre-wedding events was the arrival of Mr. and Mrs. Baker with little Charlie Smith.

"What do think of my boy, Sarah?" Manny asked.

"I'm glad to see he has his mother's good looks," she replied, smirking.

"And to think I tried to be polite and call you Sarah," Manny muttered.

After some more fussing over the baby, Kenny set himself up for abuse by protesting, "Hey, why is the baby getting all the attention? I'm the center attraction today."

"You wish, jarhead. Just hope you're the center attraction tonight," said Mr. Baker with a big grin. While everybody laughed, Pappy Smith reminded them that it was time to move into the church.

Kenny and Manny went around the side and entered through the pastor's entrance next to the parsonage. Although it seemed like an eternity to Kenny, just ten minutes later Manny peeked out the door and said, "I see them lining up to start down the aisle. It won't be long now."

When the wedding music began to play, the two friends stood before the altar and watched the wedding procession coming down the aisle. Kenny was pleasantly surprised at how calm he felt, but as the bridal march began and he saw Suzy, a mild case of jitters hit him.

Manny was standing slightly behind and to the side of Kenny, and best friends know when moral support is needed. "Hey, you can blame Mickey Mouse for all of this. If we hadn't gone to Disneyland to see that stupid mouse, we might not be here."

Suddenly, Kenny was back at Disneyland on that day he first laid eyes on Suzy. He was infatuated with her smile from the moment he saw her, and now she was walking toward him with that same beautiful smile to be his wife. Keeping his eyes on Suzy, Kenny said to his best man, "Remind me to write Mickey a thank-you letter."

The wedding went off without a hitch, except for a brief moment when Kenny's voice cracked during his wedding vows to Suzy. It was all Suzy could do to fight back her tears as she reached up and wiped Kenny's cheek. But when she looked past Kenny and saw Manny's tears, Suzy lost her composure and let hers flow.

The wedding was beautiful, but Kenny thought the photographer overdid it as they posed for pictures after the ceremony, taking multiple shots in every position. After the photo session, Kenny asked Manny, "Does your face hurt from smiling so much?"

"Yes, and I am glad I'm not paying for all these pictures. He must have taken ten rolls of film," Manny replied.

Moving to the adjacent church reception hall, Suzy commented to Manny, "You must be starving. It's been at least three hours since you've eaten."

"Hey, Fluzy, are you trying to be a little funny on your wedding day?" Manny asked.

"Sorry if you're so sensitive today," Suzy replied in jest.

Kenny cut in quickly. "You might want to be careful, Suzy. Manny will be at the end of the sword detail."

Manny and Lori laughed at the dumbfounded expression on Suzy's face.

"Go ahead, Suz. Continue to fight with me and see who gets it in the end," Manny told her with a big grin.

The introduction of the wedding party went well and set the tone for the rest of the reception.

About two hours into the reception, the band started to play "Can't Help Falling in Love," and Suzy told Kenny to ask his mother to dance.

Kathy Reynolds beamed with happiness as her son extended his hand. While they danced, Kenny asked his mother what she was thinking, and was surprised when she said, "Kenny, I don't know if this is a good time or a bad time, but I have something important to tell you."

"What is it, Mom?"

"I think everyone from Lower Vale and their families should hear the news together."

"Mom, you're scaring me. What is it?"

"No, we must all get together. Please help me gather our family and friends."

Minutes later, all those with a Lower Vale connection were gathered in a small side room off the large social hall. Manny shot Kenny a questioning look, but Kenny could only shrug.

Kathy went to the front of the room to speak. "I appreciate everyone keeping the news a secret from Kenny and Manny."

The two young men gawked at each other in disbelief.

"You see, boys, you two are the only people here that are still in the dark on developing family matters."

After a moment to let Manny and Kenny digest things, Kathy continued, "Dr. Wheeler has received a wonderful offer from a good friend from medical school to join a very successful medical practice in Carlsbad. He told me he would never leave Lower Vale unless I agreed to marry him and move to Carlsbad with him. I told him I would marry him and go to Carlsbad, but it would be very painful to leave behind my best friend and neighbor."

Kenny and Manny sat stunned. Everybody knew how close Kathy Reynolds and Maria Smith had become over the past twenty years, and their sons knew instantly how painful their separation would be. The normally jovial and loud young men listened quietly.

Kathy surprised them further by saying, "Boys, Maria will tell you the rest of the story."

After a deep breath to gather her thoughts and composure, Maria directed her gaze to Manny and Kenny. "When my dear friend Kathy told me that Dr. Wheeler proposed and wanted to take her to live in California, I was so happy for the two of them. I was also very happy for me. You see, that made up my mind on a deeply personal matter. I went directly to Pappy Smith, and we reached a decision."

If Manny and Kenny had looked around, they would have seen everybody else in the room with giant smiles on their faces, but the boys could only sit frozen in shock.

Maria continued, "Kathy's pending move to California convinced Pappy, Cindy, and me that we should move to San Diego to buy and take over the restaurant." She again looked directly at the boys as she said, "If anybody here does not think this is a good idea, speak now or forever hold your peace."

Maria smiled wide as she opened her arms to embrace the approaching Manny. Kenny picked up his own mother and whirled her in a circle. Within moments, everybody in the room was hugging everybody. It was a joyous occasion beyond description, and Aunt Carmella's tears were definitely tears of a dream come true.

Lori and Suzy were beside themselves as they celebrated the successful surprise. After the boys stepped away from their mothers, Lori and Suzi pounced on them and giggled loudly.

Then Suzi said, "In years to come, we can celebrate our anniversary on the same day we celebrate the greatest trick in the world."

The twinkle in Lori's eyes said it all. Manny hoped she'd finally gotten her revenge for being thrown into the ocean.

After the families returned to the reception, the news spread quickly. Manny and Kenny exchanged glances and ear-to-ear smiles several times.

Less than an hour later, Manny said to Kenny, "I hate to tell you this, but you crazy kids have a honeymoon waiting for you."

Manny motioned to another Marine to gather up the others in the sword detail. Then he picked up the microphone and announced to the reception that the bride and groom would be departing in about fifteen to twenty minutes.

Outside the reception hall, people watched with excitement as Manny and the other Marines marched out in two columns.

"Detail, halt. Center, face!" Lieutenant Smith commanded.

After a moment's pause, Manny instructed the Marines to draw swords. The Marines pulled their swords from their shiny silver scabbards and extended them high to create the traditional arch of swords.

When the doors to the reception hall opened and the newlyweds stood in the doorway, Manny again spoke: "Ladies and gentlemen, it is my honor to present Lieutenant and Mrs. Kenny Reynolds."

While people clapped and cheered, Kenny and Suzy moved through the sword arch only to be stopped at the end by the lowered swords of Manny and another Marine.

"A kiss for the Marine Corps," Manny demanded, just as Kenny had done to Manny and Lori about six months earlier.

It wasn't Suzy's best effort. Her mind was on Manny; she knew he would break his promise to not hit her hard after she and Kenny were allowed to move forward.

Speaking in a low voice, Suzy said, "I'm warning you, Smith."

Suzy was still watching Manny when the newlyweds stepped past, so the sharp swat on her backside was entirely unexpected. Jerking her head the other way, Suzy caught a glimpse of the other swordsman returning his sword to its original position.

To add insult to injury, Manny said, "Welcome to the Corps, Mrs. Reynolds."

While the swat on her butt was not too painful, Suzy grimaced at the smirk on Manny's face.

Lori yelled, "Welcome to the club," holding little Charlie as she waved and blew a kiss to her best friend and cousin. Suddenly, all was right with the world for Suzy.

"Are you ready to roll, Mrs. Reynolds?" Kenny asked his new wife.

"I am ready, Mr. Reynolds," Suzy replied.

Kenny looked at her and with a straight face said, "You seem to forget that I am Lieutenant Reynolds, or you can just call me *sir*."

Suzy didn't even blink at Kenny's comment. She was sure Manny had put her new husband up to it. Even married and living hundreds of miles apart, Suzy knew she would always live with the influence of Manny.

On the way back to San Diego, Lori had a wonderful time teasing Manny.

"You didn't have a clue. Admit it."

"I cannot believe that everyone in Lower Vale knew, and no one told Kenny or me."

"That's because everyone wanted to make you two wise guys look silly."

"Well, it worked, but I'll take that kind of embarrassment anytime to get the good news that came with it."

"It was terribly hard keeping it from you. But I promised your grandfather I wouldn't tell you."

"I knew it. I just knew that Pappy was involved somewhere near the center of it."

"I guess it runs in the family."

Manny knew he was in for a lot more teasing at Uncle Manuel and Aunt Carmella's house. But throughout the post-wedding celebration, Manny was anxious to hear more details about the move.

"Mr. Miller found us a great house just two blocks from the restaurant," Maria excitedly told her son. "I remember the neighborhood very well, Manny. Your father and I walked through the neighborhood often when he was courting me."

Pappy interjected, "Kenny's father-in-law said it was a fixer-upper, but your mother and sister and I think it's great."

Not to be outdone by the rest of the family, Cindy added, "While Mom and I are working at the restaurant, Pappy will be working at the house to modernize and other things."

Manny was at a loss for words—not a common feeling for him.

Maria and Lori smiled at each other, sharing the satisfaction of this tough Marine looking so helpless.

Kenny felt a little guilty as Suzy and her parents hugged and said a tearful goodbye. After the honeymoon in Las Vegas, the newlyweds would continue east toward Lawton, Oklahoma. Although a Marine officer, Kenny would be attending the US Army Field Artillery School at the Fort Sill Army Post. The Field Artillery Officer's Basic Course was only about three months in duration, but it would be the Millers' longest separation from their only child. So saying goodbye was difficult, and Kenny was very patient.

Mr. Miller stuck out his hand to Kenny and said, "I know you love her very much, but I have to remind you that we're counting on you to take good care of our little girl."

Kenny clutched Mr. Miller's extended hand. "I do love her, very, very much. And we will take care of each other."

Then Kenny hugged Mrs. Miller and Suzy hugged her dad again before the couple got into Kenny's car and pulled away. Suzy broke into tears as they drove down the street. Kenny said nothing but was startled when Suzy suddenly started laughing.

"I feel so foolish. I'm a grown woman, and here I am crying like a little girl because I'm leaving my mommy and daddy."

"I'd be surprised if we don't see your folks in a month or two. They say that Lawton isn't a very exciting place, but it is close to Dallas. If they come for a visit, we can go to Texas for shopping and dinner," Kenny told her.

"You won't mind if they visit us?" Suzy asked.

"Of course not. I just don't want them to visit us for the next few nights in Las Vegas," Kenny said, giving her a sly grin.

"Neither do I, sweetie. Or should I say, neither do I, sir," Suzy replied with her own impish smile.

After arriving at their room in the hotel, it soon became obvious to Suzy that someone had repacked her suitcase. "I am confident that Lori was in on this, but I strongly suspect this was Manny's idea."

With that, Suzy held up a set of completely sheer red lingerie.

"That's my amigo Manny. Always thinking of me." Kenny wore a giant grin.

Las Vegas was electrifying. They went to a different restaurant each night and saw several great shows. They also made a point to place a small wager at all the major casinos on the strip, and sometimes they even won the bet.

"We should have kept a diary of all our bets to see how much we end up losing," Suzy commented.

"Suzy, you're as cute as cute can be, but aren't you a little old to be keeping a diary?"

Suzy looked at Kenny as if he were crazy. "No."

"Okay, you call it a diary if you like, but it will still be a logbook to me," Kenny replied.

They could not believe the week had passed so quickly as they pulled away from their hotel. But orders were orders, and Kenny had to report to Fort Sill.

The drive was long. Suzy marveled at the desert scenery. "The desert is beautiful, but also very intimidating to me."

"That's how I felt about you when I first laid eyes on you at Disneyland five years ago."

Suzy wondered how she'd gotten so lucky.

Lawton

Arriving in Lawton, Oklahoma, Kenny followed the signs to Fort Sill. His first obligation was to check in with the Marine Corps office to stop his leave. The senior Marine at Fort Sill was a full colonel, and Kenny heard rumors that he expected the Marine lieutenants to all be at the top of their class.

"I shouldn't be long," Kenny told Suzy as he looked at himself in the car window one last time to make sure his uniform was squared away. He did not want to accidentally bump into Colonel Martin and make a bad first impression.

Entering the office in the long stone building, Kenny's eyes were still adjusting to the dim office when he heard, "Are you checking in, sir?"

"Yes, I am," Kenny replied. He focused on the Marine corporal standing behind the desk to his right.

Suddenly, a loud voice boomed, "Lieutenant! In my office, now!"

The corporal grinned and nodded toward the hallway leading to the back part of the building.

"Colonel Martin wants to see you, sir."

Kenny was not sure he wanted to see the colonel, but he took a deep breath and stepped off. Reverting to his Quantico days, he pounded on the open doorway and said, "Lieutenant Reynolds reporting as ordered, sir!"

"Get in here, Lieutenant Reynolds."

Kenny was relieved to see the tall senior Marine stand and extend his hand with a broad grin. "Welcome aboard," the colonel stated, giving him a crushing handshake.

"Thank you, sir."

"I see a wedding band, Lieutenant. Where is your wife at this time?"

"She's out in the car, sir."

"Well, that must be a lot of fun for her, don't you think?"

"Probably not."

"Definitely not!"

After a short, awkward moment for Kenny, the colonel said, "Lieutenant Reynolds, go get your wife and bring her in here and out of the sun and wind."

"Yes, sir."

Kenny thought he'd made it perfectly clear to Suzy that she was to accompany him to Colonel Martin's office, but her reply was simply "What?"

After reinforcing the fact that Colonel Martin wanted Kenny to bring her inside, Suzy reached for her pocketbook and took out her compact.

"Suzy, you don't keep a colonel waiting," Kenny said anxiously.

"Well, colonels shouldn't surprise a girl with an unexpected invitation," Suzy threw back.

After what seemed like an eternity to Kenny, Suzy nodded that she was ready to go inside. The corporal and a staff sergeant both stood when Kenny and Suzy entered the Marine liaison office. After a brief moment of silence, Kenny said, "I'm Lieutenant Reynolds, and this is my wife, Suzy."

As he shook hands with the staff sergeant, both men were startled by the colonel.

"Mrs. Reynolds, I am so pleased to meet you and welcome you to Fort Sill."

"It's nice to meet you, sir. Sorry we took so long to come inside."

"Nonsense, you were very quick to respond to my unanticipated invitation."

Looking at the enlisted Marines, Colonel Martin said, "Get Lieutenant Reynolds checked in while I talk with Mrs. Reynolds."

The colonel was very informative. He told Suzy that while Kenny might be very busy at times as an artillery student, there was no need for Suzy to sit around and be bored.

"My wife will hold a couple of social events to help you ladies get to know one another. After that you should all feel free to get together and do things on your own. And we will have a few more get-togethers in the next few months," Colonel Martin told her.

After completing the required paperwork, Kenny joined Suzy and the colonel.

"I will be seeing you both again in a few days. Good luck in finding an acceptable place to live," Colonel Martin said as Kenny and Suzy left the building.

"Why didn't he say a nice place to live?" Suzy asked nervously.

"I don't know, but I picked up on that too."

The rest of the day was spent looking for an apartment, but Suzy was not happy with anything she saw. Finally, they found a decent-looking apartment complex with one-bedroom apartments that had potential. As they walked back to their car and drove around the eight-building complex, Kenny stated, "It seems that about one in three cars has a blue officer sticker."

"Okay, let's take this apartment. It's only for three months," Suzy said with a little scowl.

Kenny felt bad that the apartment was not as nice as Suzy wanted it to be, but he had little control of the apartment situation in Lawton. After signing their lease, they were off to the supermarket for food and cleaning supplies. That evening was spent cleaning and getting things put away.

The next morning Kenny awoke to a large truck driving by their bedroom window. The next thing he heard was his new wife asking, "Kenny, what is a truck doing outside our apartment this early in the morning?"

"It's the garbage truck, Suzy. Not much we can do but go back to sleep," Kenny replied.

Suzy said nothing but put her pillow over her head as if that would fix things. Kenny's mind was not on going back to sleep. He thought ahead to the coming artillery education and training he would receive. After a few minutes, Kenny slipped out of the bed to put on his running outfit.

"What are you doing?"

"Just going for a little run."

While Kenny was leaning against his car, stretching his legs, another car stopped beside him.

"Hey, Reynolds. You here for arty school also?"

Kenny could not believe his eyes when he looked up and saw Durango, a crazy TBS buddy from Texas.

"Durango! You're here to attend artillery school?"

"Ken, I used to think that you were a smart guy. What else would I be doing in Lawton?"

Kenny rolled his eyes.

"I guess it's safe to assume that you and your new bride are living here also?"

"That's right. Isn't it a small world?"

"Small is good. Guess we can carpool and the wives can have a car to use during the day when we're in class."

"That will work out really well," Kenny replied.

On his run, Kenny wondered who else was assigned an artillery MOS from his TBS platoon and company. He was confident he would at least recognize any lieutenant from other platoons in the company.

Arriving back at their apartment after the first day of school, Kenny was greeted by Suzy's question: "So, how many Marines are in your class and how many do you know?"

"Of the fifteen Marines in our class, I know or at least recognize all but two," Kenny replied.

"You sound upbeat," Suzy said, smiling.

"I am. I think this school has potential to be a good three months," Kenny replied.

Kenny's prediction turned out to be accurate. Artillery school went well for Kenny, and married life was going well too. Sometimes Suzy wanted more of Kenny's time than he could give her when a big gunnery exam was pending, but for the most part, the time they spent in Oklahoma was very good.

Weekends were the highlight. Most of the married couples and a few bachelor lieutenants usually got together to socialize. Going to dinner or having a cookout became a regular weekend routine.

With only a couple weeks remaining before graduation, it seemed certain that Kenny would be the top graduate in his class.

When leaving Snow Hall the last Friday of class before graduation, one of the Marine captains on the instructor staff at Fort Sill called to Kenny.

"Lieutenant Reynolds, I need to speak with you for a second."

Approaching the captain, Kenny executed a sharp salute. "Yes, sir."

"I just came from Colonel Martin's office. He told me to let you know that he needs to see you today," the captain told Kenny.

"Yes, sir," Kenny replied. Then he added, "Any idea what the subject is, sir?"

"The colonel will fill you in, Lieutenant," the captain replied, turning abruptly and striding away before Kenny could salute.

Kenny had a bad feeling about the captain's disposition and was anxious to see the colonel. However, he had a weapons class right now, and the colonel was a stickler for students not missing any classes, so Kenny was off to weapons.

"Are you with us today or back in the sack with your wife?" Durango asked as they left the weapons building after class.

"I have to see Colonel Martin, and I have no idea what's wrong."

"What makes you think something is wrong?"

"I really can't put my finger on it, but I got a bad vibe from the captain who told me to see him."

Kenny's bad feeling was reinforced when he entered the Marine office and received somber looks from the enlisted Marines.

"I'll tell the colonel you're here, Lieutenant," the admin chief said.

Colonel Martin came out of his office before the staff sergeant took more than a few steps.

"Lieutenant Reynolds, please come on back."

The colonel instructed Kenny to have a seat and then said, "I know that you're doing very well academically, Lieutenant. And you are well respected professionally by your peers and instructors, but I want to know if you are enjoying OBC."

"Yes, sir, I am."

"What about your wife?"

"Yes, sir. Suzy has made some friends, and they do things together during the week, and we all get together and socialize most weekends."

"I assume that you've been to the Plantation?" the colonel asked, referring to an old restaurant outside of Lawton.

"Yes, sir. The Plantation is quite memorable; in fact, we're taking my wife's parents to dinner there this weekend."

"That's good. I suspect they will find it quite memorable also."

Kenny was now convinced that something was not good. Colonel Martin was making lighthearted small talk but never came close to cracking a smile.

"I'm sure you're wondering why I wanted to talk with you, Lieutenant Reynolds. The truth of the matter is that your orders to California have been changed. The 11th Marines needs good officers soon, and you are one of several officers who will be heading to Vietnam after Fort Sill and a couple weeks' leave," stated the elder Marine.

Kenny was flabbergasted. His thoughts immediately turned to Suzy and how upset she would be. Then he thought of his mother and the fear and worry she would experience.

Before Kenny could collect his thoughts and say anything, Colonel Martin continued, "I know this comes as a shock, Lieutenant Reynolds, and I know it will not be well received by your wife. However, the needs of the Marine Corps require that we augment our artillery units in Vietnam with some strong officers. That's why you were selected."

Kenny was pleased to be considered a strong officer, but his head spun.

It seemed that Colonel Martin was reading Kenny's mind. "Take some time to collect your thoughts and decide how you will break the news to your wife. This will be very difficult, but you had to know it was possible. Did you ever mention that possibility to her?"

"No, sir. I have to say that I never did," Kenny replied.

"There is no way to predict how she will take the news. Most likely there will be a lot of tears and anger. And resentment towards the Marine Corps is not unlikely. Let her vent her feelings, Lieutenant Reynolds. I know this doesn't help you and your situation, but I will tell you that I went through a similar situation almost twenty years ago."

Kenny was very glad that Durango had driven that day. While Kenny and his Texas buddy were riding home that afternoon, Kenny asked him how he thought the news should be broken to Suzy. But Kenny didn't even hear the advice his friend offered; he was busy wondering how Suzy's parents would react.

When they arrived at the apartment, Kenny decided there was no sense in delaying things. The situation was not likely to get any better.

Colonel Martin had been very accurate in his advice. Moments after Kenny informed Suzy of the change to his orders, she cried and cried as she hugged Kenny. Through her sobs, she added denial and stated that it wasn't fair.

"You've been to that godforsaken place. You were almost killed. You paid your dues. Why do you have to go back?" Suzy cried.

After a while, the tears stopped flowing, and as the colonel predicted, Suzy felt anger toward the Marine Corps. For a sweet young lady, Kenny was surprised at some of the language she used.

Kenny answered the phone when it rang. After a brief conversation he said, "Okay, buddy, thanks a lot. I'll tell her."

Suzy frowned, waiting for an explanation.

"Durango called me to say that Colleen wants to know if there's anything she can do," Kenny said.

"She can drive me over to see Colonel Martin so I can give him a piece of my mind," Suzy crossly stated.

"I know this doesn't help, Suz, but shooting the messenger isn't going to change anything."

The look Kenny received made him wish he hadn't said anything.

It was actually very good timing with the Millers arriving that weekend. Their two days in Lawton helped Suzy calm down considerably.

Two weeks later, as they prepared for Kenny's graduation, Suzy elected not to attend; she did not wish to see Colonel or Mrs. Martin. Kenny coaxed her for a little while but then decided to back off because he wanted to have a pleasant ride back to California where he would spend three weeks of leave prior to departing for Vietnam.

CHAPTER FOURTEEN

MANNY TO COLLEGE AND KENNY TO VIETNAM

San Diego

MANNY WAS NOT SURPRISED when Lori told him that Kenny was on the phone. The two friends talked frequently about Kenny's studies at Fort Sill and Manny's studies at San Diego State.

"Hey, amigo. How are things going as you prepare to leave Fort Sill?"

"You're not going to believe this, Manny, but my orders to Pendleton have been changed. I'm being sent to Vietnam."

Manny was speechless for a moment. Then he replied, "Holy crap, Kenny. When did you find out?"

"Actually, I've known about it for a couple of weeks, but we decided not to tell anyone so you wouldn't worry."

"How is Suzy taking it?"

"Not very well. She's really angry with the Marine Corps."

Lori was used to outbursts of laughter and loud, colorful language when her husband talked to Kenny, so she immediately picked up on the different tone of the conversation and moved to Manny's side. Manny covered the phone with his hand and whispered to Lori,

"Kenny is being sent to Vietnam."

Lori put her hands over her mouth to stifle her cry of disbelief.

"I guess Suzy's folks aren't very happy either," Manny said into the phone.

Little Charlie started to cry loudly, so Lori went to him. By the time she returned to Manny's side, he was asking, "What's your ETA here in Southern California?"

"Three days" was Kenny's reply.

Lori moved back away from Manny as the baby fussed a little more.

"Drive safely. We'll see you when you get to Vista," Manny said before hanging up.

Manny was so caught up in his thoughts that he didn't hear Lori approaching until she put her arms around his shoulders. "All we can do is pray that God will watch over him."

"I know, babe, but it still makes me worry."

"Charlie is sleeping again. Can I help you with your studies in any way?"

"Thanks, but I'm done for the night."

As they lay in bed, neither said anything, their thoughts dominated with worry for Kenny and Suzy and Kenny's mom. Lori decided not to tell Manny that she'd suspected something was wrong a week earlier when Suzy and she last spoke.

"Manny, you don't have class until ten tomorrow morning. Why don't you go to the depot and go for a run? That always cheers you up," Lori suggested.

"Good idea, Mrs. Smith," Manny said.

"Why, thank you, Mr. Smith," Lori replied. She quickly corrected herself. "Sorry about that, Lieutenant Smith."

At the high school the next day, Manny was asked by one of the boys, "Hey, Coach Smith, what was your wrestling record in high school?"

"If we wrestle hard and give it our best next week, I'll tell you."

"Sun Valley has a really good team every year, Coach. That will be a tough meet to win," a senior wrestler protested.

"I never said that we had to win. I want us to wrestle hard and do our best. If we do that, I will be happy to tell you my high school record."

"You won't teach us the move that got you pinned all the time, will you?"

Manny shook his head with a smile and simply basked in the glory of working with the boys. It was almost as good as working with privates as a drill instructor.

About thirty minutes later, it was time to call it quits.

"Okay, men, good effort today," Manny said later as the boys left the locker room. He always made a point of providing a word of encouragement after each practice. Then he added, "Don't forget to complete your studies tonight. If you are not mentally tough enough to do your studies, you will never be as physically tough as you can be."

That evening, like many other evenings, Manny drove to the restaurant to meet Lori and Charlie and the rest of his family. He wondered where Kenny and Suzy were at that moment.

The drive from Fort Sill to Vista was not going as badly as Kenny feared it would. Suzy was still upset about Kenny's orders to Vietnam, but she was also excited to be heading home.

"Kenny, should I live at home while you're away?" Suzy asked.

Kenny did not answer immediately, but he had been giving that very question some serious consideration for more than a week. On one hand, Suzy was a grown and married woman, and Kenny suspected that she would want to set up her own house. On the other hand, maybe she would like the comfort and moral support of living with her folks while he was in Vietnam.

Playing it safe, Kenny answered her question with "You should do whatever you feel comfortable with, Suz."

She did not let Kenny off the hook. "What do you feel comfortable with? Do you have a preference?"

Kenny decided to tell the truth. "I've been thinking about this, and I would really feel better if you lived at home. But if you want a place of your own, I hope it will be close to your folks."

"I think my preference is living close to my parents, not with them."

"Do you think your dad can help?"

"He doesn't normally deal with rentals, but I suspect that he knows someone who does. I'll call him tonight."

There was a long period where neither of them said anything as they drove through the desert.

Kenny broke the silence by asking, "After we spend some time with our families, is there anything special you want to do while we're home?"

"Anything we do is good with me, as long as we do it together. Do you have anything in mind?"

"Well, I was kind of thinking that we could spend a day with our old buddy Mickey."

Suzy burst out laughing.

"What's so funny?"

"Oh, sweetie. The combination of what you said and the look on your face and the tone of your voice is so precious. I would pay a million dollars to have that all on tape."

Manny, Lori, and Little Charlie were at the restaurant with the rest of the Smith clan when they were surprised by Suzy's parents, who walked in with Kenny's mom and Dr. Wheeler. After a round of smiles, hugs, and handshakes, Pat Miller broke the big news that Suzy and Kenny should be arriving at the restaurant in the early afternoon.

"They're anxious to see all of us, so we asked Manuel and Carmella if we could all meet here for a little homecoming get-together," Louise Miller stated.

The Smiths simultaneously looked at Manuel and Carmella, who stood together with big smiles on their faces.

Aunt Carmella broke the silence. "Come on, Manuel. Let's start getting some food prepared."

Dr. Wheeler said, "It was Carmella's idea not to tell you. I think Manny gets his mischievous nature from both sides of his family."

"Carmella! Way to go!" Pappy exclaimed.

"She is a wild one," Manuel added as he put his arm around his wife.

Less than thirty minutes later, Lori's parents also arrived, so the whole gang was there. Little Charlie was passed around like a football until Lori grabbed him away from her mother to feed him.

A little later Manny asked Lori, "Did he drink a lot?"

"Yes," Lori replied. "Why do you ask?"

"Kenny and Suzy will be here soon. And you can bet that Kenny will take Charlie and give him a little toss in the air. With a little luck, Charlie will throw up all over Kenny."

At Lori's befuddled stare, Manny demanded, "What?"

"Remind me to get you some therapy," Lori said.

Kenny and Suzy's arrival was just short of a mob scene; everybody wanted to hug them and shake hands. However, when Suzy took little Charlie from Lori, everybody backed off and gave her room.

"Oh, Lori, he is so beautiful," Suzy told her cousin. The room got quiet, and Suzy continued, "It's so nice that he doesn't look like his father."

With that unexpected shot at Manny, the room erupted in laughter. Manny laughed and started to say something back to Suzy, but caught himself and said nothing, letting her enjoy the moment.

After supper that evening, Manny announced to Kenny that their Marine Corps buddy Staff Sergeant Bass was a new father and had given Manny two cigars for himself and Kenny.

"Manny, I hope you're not planning to smoke that cigar around your baby," Maria said.

Kathy added, "I hope you're not going to smoke a cigar at all."

"Come on, Mom," Kenny replied. "It would be rude to not smoke this cigar after a fellow Marine gave it to me to celebrate the birth of his child."

The two best friends went outside and down the sidewalk.

"So, tell me, did Bass really have a baby? Or are these cigars a scheme to get us away from the families?" Kenny asked.

"Bass really did have a baby, and he really did give me these cigars, about two months ago. It was just recently that I realized I could use them to get us away from the crowd."

"Well, you are brilliant. There is no way we can talk about Vietnam with Suzy around," Kenny said.

The two friends walked and talked, mostly about Kenny's orders. After thirty minutes or so, the boys heard a familiar voice yell, "Hey, what are you doing besides thinking of ways to get into trouble?" Lori smirked as she and Suzy strolled toward the boys.

Suzy added, "We thought we better find you before you got into a fight with a motorcycle gang or something."

"Gee, Kenny. There were so many nice girls that wanted to marry you. How did you manage to pick this one?" Manny said.

"You better watch your lip, Smith, or you'll wish it was a motorcycle gang instead of me you were fighting."

Manny shot a pleading look at Kenny.

"Don't look at me, buddy. This is a one-on-one battle," Kenny told him.

Manny turned back to Suzy, stuck his thumbs in his ears, and wiggled his fingers while crossing his eyes and sticking out his tongue.

"My husband is so witty," Lori deadpanned to her cousin.

"I hate to interrupt the usual Suzy and Manny bonding session, but what brings you girls out here? Are you worried we might run off and join the Marine Corps?" Kenny asked.

Suzy replied, "No, smarty, we just thought we would make plans for the four of us to go visit your old buddy Mickey."

"All right! Now we're talking about important matters," Kenny exclaimed.

By the time the four of them arrived back at the restaurant, they had made their plans for Disneyland. It was very easy to do because only Manny had any obligations to meet in the next three weeks.

Unfortunately, the next three weeks passed like three days, and suddenly Kenny was packing to head for Vietnam.

Standing in the Millers' driveway, Suzy sobbed as she said, "I'm sorry, Kenny. I just cannot be there to see you fly away."

"I understand, sweetie. It's okay," Kenny said, trying to comfort his distraught wife.

Just a couple days earlier, Suzy had begun having doubts about watching Kenny's plane take off for Vietnam. The decision was finally made that Manny, Kenny's mom, and Dr. Wheeler would drive Kenny to the airport to see him off. It was going to be a tough trip, but all four of them were determined to make the best of it.

"I wonder if I'll see anything significantly different from what I remember."

"I would be surprised if you didn't," Manny replied somberly.

"We are getting out of that wretched place, so I hope it's done in a rapid but safe manner," Kathy commented.

The remainder of the trip to the airport consisted of occasional nervous comments. Upon arriving at the departure terminal, Manny dropped off the other three and went to park the car. When he entered the area of Kenny's departure gate, he had to stop and regain his composure at the sight of Kenny holding his mother as she cried. After a couple deep, calming breaths, Manny approached his best friend. Kenny stuck out his hand, but Manny moved past and gave Kenny a bear hug that would have stopped a grizzly.

"Take care, Kenny."

"I will."

"And be a little patient this time when the mail arrives."

"I will, Manny. I promise I will."

The drive back from the airport was a long, quiet trip. Kathy wept softly now and then, but that was not unexpected.

Everybody gathered at the Millers' house that evening. Things were going well for the most part until Suzy suddenly broke down and ran to her bedroom. Nobody followed her because there was nothing anybody could do. It would take time for her to handle the fact that Kenny was in Vietnam, and time could not be rushed.

Vietnam

Kenny's thoughts raced as they received word that the plane would touch down in Da Nang in less than an hour. He flashed back to the first time he went to Vietnam. As a young Marine, he did what he was told. This time, he would do the telling, and he was nervous about whether his decisions would be the right ones.

"How are we supposed to breathe?" asked one young Marine as they got off the plane.

Without giving much thought to it, Kenny replied, "Hang in there. You'll get used to it."

Like a herd of cattle, the Marines debarked the aircraft.

Kenny was pleased when he distinctly heard a voice yell, "11th Marines!"

"Are you going to the 11th Marines, Lieutenant?" the tall staff sergeant asked as Kenny approached.

"I am."

"Sir, make sure you get your paperwork stamped and then hang around here for a little while. Then we'll head to the six-by and get out to the regimental CP."

After checking in at the desk to verify he was there, Kenny rejoined the 11th Marines staff sergeant. Kenny told him, "If you show me the list of names you're expecting, I'll check them off as we identify them."

"I don't have no list, Lieutenant. That would make too much sense" was the reply.

Likely seeing Kenny's frustration, the staff sergeant added, "The master sergeant just told me to take a truck to the processing center and pick up anyone heading to the regiment."

"I understand," Kenny replied.

When they departed the processing center, Kenny and the Marine corporal driving the truck made small talk. The ride to the 11th Marines command post was less than fifteen minutes, and Kenny's time at the regimental HQ lasted only a few. By coincidence, Kenny's new battalion commander was at the regimental headquarters and offered the new lieutenant a ride to the 3rd Battalion command post. On the way, Kenny informed his new battalion commander that he had been a cannoneer in 3/11 a few years earlier as an enlisted Marine. Lieutenant Colonel Black asked several questions, and before long, Kenny had conveyed the whole story of his previous experience in Vietnam.

"Whatever happened to the girl whose letter was so important that you took shrapnel in your shoulder to get it?"

"I married her a few months ago."

"Glad to hear it, but I don't want you taking any more shrapnel for her letters in the future."

"Don't worry, sir. That won't happen."

"You know what, Lieutenant? It just occurred to me that we did not discuss what you would be doing in 3/11 this time."

"No, sir."

"You are going to Hotel Battery. Your battery commander, Captain George Smith, expects you to be his fire direction officer."

"That's great, sir. I'm pleased to be an FDO. I enjoyed gunnery very much, but to tell you the truth, I expected to become a forward observer."

"That was a consideration, but the company commanders are happy with their FOs and asked to keep them. Besides, we knew you were high in your gunnery classes at Ft. Sill, so making you the battery FDO was easy."

"Sounds good, sir," Kenny answered. He hoped it didn't sound like he was approving what the battalion commander told him, but the colonel seemed to give his choice of words no notice.

"I need to talk to the battalion staff for a couple minutes. Then I'll take you to Hotel Battery myself. It gives me an opportunity to visit the battery—not that Hotel Battery needs visiting. Captain Smith runs a tight ship. I suspect you will learn to appreciate and learn a lot from him."

When they pulled into the Hotel Battery position, Captain Smith approached.

"Smitty, this is your new FDO, Ken Reynolds."

"Welcome to the battery, Ken. We're glad to have you on board."

"Thank you, sir. I'm glad to be here," Kenny replied without thinking.

He turned bright red as the battalion and battery commanders looked at each other and chuckled.

"We'll give you a few weeks and then ask you the same question, just to compare answers."

Before Kenny could say anything, the two senior officers walked away. Soon he was approached by another Marine.

"Lieutenant Reynolds, sounds like the captain and the colonel had a good laugh at your expense. Was it about you still shittin' American chow?" the Marine asked.

"No, I inadvertently said I was glad to be here," Kenny replied.

The man smiled and shook his head as he extended his hand. "I'm Karch Davis, the battery XO."

Assuming that Davis was a first lieutenant, Kenny said, "I'm Ken Reynolds. Glad to meet you, sir."

"Between the two of us, it's Karch. In front of the men, call me XO, okay?"

After helping Kenny stow his gear and get a few things, the two walked the battery position. Kenny met a lot of Marines in the next thirty minutes but was unable to retain many names until the XO said, "Lieutenant Reynolds, this is Staff Sergeant Flatts, your fire direction chief."

"Welcome aboard, sir," stated Kenny's new right-hand man.

The staff sergeant was a short man with a small Hitler-type mustache and black military glasses, but the most notable feature was his ear-to-ear smile.

"Thank you, Staff Sergeant. I look forward to working with you," Kenny said.

After spending a little more time with Lieutenant Davis, Kenny wandered back to the fire direction center. He spent the next couple hours talking with Staff Sergeant Flatts and the Marines he would work with to compute firing data for the Marines on the gun line. According to Flatts, they had not fired many missions in recent weeks, but some reliable sources said that might soon change.

"What makes you think that?" Kenny asked.

"Well, Lieutenant, a buddy of mine knows a guy in the ammo business. This guy told my buddy that a whole shitload of arty ammo is inbound. Why would a bunch of ammo be coming if we weren't going to shoot it?"

"You make a good point. I wonder if there's a big push going on," Kenny replied as he looked outside the tent.

His thoughts were interrupted by Flatt's advice. "Sir, you better write your wife a letter to let her know you have arrived safely."

"Thanks. You're exactly right," Kenny replied.

San Diego

That night in San Diego, Manny was bursting with pride. His team had just defeated the wrestling team from Sun Valley High. The excitement in the eyes of his wrestlers was overwhelming. Manny also noticed the principal, Mr. White, yelling with his arms outstretched to the ceiling. Lori and other members of the family stood back as the team mobbed Manny and each other in celebration. Eventually Pappy made his way to his grandson and, with a huge smile, gave Manny a big hug.

"This was some night, don't you think, Pappy?"

"That's putting it mildly, hard charger!"

"Oh, Manny, we are so happy for you and your boys."

Manny spotted Mr. White approaching and introduced the principal to his mother and grandfather. Manny then waved for Lori and Charlie to come closer.

"Mr. White, this is my wife, Lori, and our son, Charlie."

"Lori, I have to tell you how grateful I am that you share Manny with us. He is the best thing to happen to this school since we got an automatic dishwasher!"

"Thank you for giving Manny the opportunity to coach, Mr. White. He just loves working with the kids."

After the crowd thinned out and his family departed, Manny headed to the locker room. Relishing the moment, he did not recognize that the locker room was strangely quiet. The quiet turned to bedlam as Manny turned the corner. It seemed that every wrestler on the team participated in grabbing their coach and hoisting him in the air to carry him toward the waiting shower. Manny's attempt to get loose was wasted, and he quickly accepted his fate.

The young men screamed with joy as they threw their coach under the cold spray. To make matters worse, as Manny scrambled to get out of the shower, his leather-soled shoes slipped, and he went down again. Manny was more careful when he got up the second time. Walking out of the shower area, he shook his fist at the boys, grinning at all the fun the wrestlers were enjoying.

At the restaurant later that evening, Lori shook her head in disappointment. "Those boys really upset me for doing that."

Her statement caught them all off guard because everyone seemed to think it was funny. Then Lori continued, "If they ever do something like that again, they better tell me ahead of time so I can be there to watch it!"

The restaurant was again in a mild uproar as all continued to enjoy the unexpected victory and the subsequent team celebration at Manny's expense.

Vietnam

Kenny had been with the battery for a little more than a week when Flatts pulled him aside and said, "Remember last week when we first talked, Lieutenant?"

"Of course, Staff Sergeant. Why do you ask?"

"My buddy learned the arty ammo is headed our way, so you know what that means," Flatts said excitedly.

Kenny did not know how to respond at first. "Let me see if the captain knows anything before we let this get out to the troops."

"My thoughts exactly, sir," the staff sergeant said.

Walking to the XO pit to talk with Karch, Ken suspected that Staff Sergeant Flatts was correct. The staff NCOs always had a good feel for what was going on in any unit.

"What's the good word, Ken?"

"I have a question to ask you."

"Ask away. I put on clean skivvies today, so I feel great."

"The staff NCOs are hearing rumors that a ton of ammo is headed our way."

"Very interesting," Karch replied.

Kenny was hoping for a better answer. "Very interesting. What kind of answer is that?"

Suddenly Karch lost his smile and said, "Let's go talk to the boss."

When they approached their battery commander, Karch surprised Kenny by yelling out, "Skipper, Reynolds doesn't believe that I have a naked picture of his wife."

Kenny rolled his eyes skyward in disbelief, and the captain laughed at Kenny's reaction.

"In case this is your first exposure to Lieutenant Krotch Deviant's dark side, I can assure you that it will not be your last."

"Sir, rumor is that we have a shitload of ammo headed our way.

Do you have anything you can share with us?"

"It's more than a rumor. I suspect I will have plenty to tell you when I return from my meeting at battalion tomorrow morning."

Kenny thought he was over the jet lag, but he couldn't sleep that night. His mind raced through different scenarios requiring a large amount of artillery support. He'd thought the war was winding down, but what if a new offensive was about to begin? Would this extend his tour in Vietnam? Plus, there was no doubt that the public would learn of a new offensive; Suzy and his mom would be sick with worry.

"What do you think, Karch?" Kenny asked the XO as Captain Smith departed for his meeting with the battalion commander.

"Beats me, Ken. I thought things were winding down, but now I'm not so sure," Karch replied.

A couple hours later, Captain Smith returned to the battery position. Getting out of his jeep, he yelled, "Gunny, get the battery to a schoolhouse circle around the XO pit. Everybody except security personnel at the perimeter."

While the senior enlisted Marines followed the CO's command, Karch and Kenny approached the battery commander.

"Anybody who thought he was going to have a cakewalk out of Vietnam is in for a big surprise. It looks like we're going out with a bang—a big bang!" Smith said.

After the men settled in around their battery commander at the battery XO pit, Captain Smith addressed his Marines. "Gentlemen, any rumors you have heard are true. Within a few days, we're going to shoot like few of us have ever shot before. We'll be airlifted to a remote firebase, and from there we'll blast the hell out of Charlie. Men, this is why we became United States Marines!"

The responding roar was motivating. Kenny could not help but get caught up the excitement of Captain Smith's message. They were trained to fight, and fight they would.

Later that day Kenny overheard some of his fire direction men discussing a fire support base, so he decided to share some of his experiences, although he would not admit how he was wounded.

"I'm not sure exactly what we'll do this time, but my previous unit was also lifted by helicopters to a remote fire support base. At this position we were in the middle of nowhere and could only be resupplied by helo. When we are located at a fire support base out in the boonies, we have to shoot our big guns, and we have to provide our own local security. On the bright side, the other batteries in our battalion will all be in support of us."

The next few days were hectic as the battery made preparations to move. The helo-support Marines arrived to attach the airlift slings, and the men made sure they had their personal gear in order. At the distant firebase they would live in shelter halves and eat C rations. It seemed that the mission would not be an extended one.

When the day arrived to move to their new position, the Marines were ready. Kenny made one last check of his fire direction gear. He wanted to be sure they were ready to compute firing data as soon as the guns were laid. Standing with the Marines and preparing to fly to their new position, Kenny wondered if his men sensed that he was very nervous.

He glanced toward the Marines riding with Staff Sergeant Flatts. They were laughing as Flatts yelled something and made an obscene gesture. Suddenly Kenny felt a lot more relaxed. He studied the men he was standing with just outside the landing zone. One of the young Marines had his eyes closed and head bowed as he prayed. When the young man opened his eyes and glanced up, he saw Kenny with his thumb up and a confident look on his face. The young Marine smiled and returned the thumbs-up.

Then the wind started to blow and swirl like crazy as the CH-46 Marine helicopters set down to be boarded by the waiting Marines.

Five minutes into the flight, Kenny could not help but think of Manny being shot down in a similar situation. He was very subdued until one of the Marines behind him yelled, "All right, something stinks here. Which one of you pussies shit yourself?"

The laughter put Kenny at ease.

The journey felt like an hour, but fifteen minutes later, the helos started their descent. The men scurried off the CH-46 and followed the lead Marine out of the landing zone. Kenny saw Karch moving toward him.

"Kenny, take these men and establish a defensive line along the edge of the flat area over there," the XO instructed.

"Okay, let's go," Kenny yelled, starting in the direction Karch had pointed.

Just as Kenny had the men positioned where they could see all avenues of approach to their position, the battery gunny headed his way.

"Lieutenant Reynolds, the XO says when you see the guns setting down you should send every other cannon cocker to help lay them," the gunny yelled.

"Check," Kenny replied.

Only a few minutes later, the helicopters with the howitzers began arriving. Kenny marveled at the speed with which the young Marines attacked the howitzers to get them adjusted and ready to fire.

Flatts waved his arm, motioning Kenny his way. Heading toward the staff sergeant, Kenny saw a tarp lift into the air and realized that would be their makeshift fire direction center.

"Take that thing down. Many more choppers will be coming in and out of here before the day is over," Flatts yelled at his men as Kenny approached.

Kenny was impressed with the efficiency of the battery. Within an hour, the guns were laid and had ammo, and the FDC was ready to compute firing data. If someone called in a fire mission, the battery was prepared to shoot.

"Lieutenant, it looks like the captain wants to talk to you," a Marine told Kenny.

Kenny and the battery XO converged on the battery commander.

"What's going on, Skipper?" Karch asked.

To their surprise, the captain already had a preplanned list of targets they would shoot at during the next several days. A target of opportunity received from a forward observer would trump any pre-planned target, but that was not very likely.

"I don't understand, sir," Kenny replied.

"We're going to shoot the shit out of the jungle to make it look like the grunts are attacking. However, what we're really doing is attempting to cover their withdrawal back to Da Nang," the captain explained.

"Well, I'll be damned," Karch exclaimed. They were finally leaving Vietnam.

The captain handed Kenny and Karch a duplicate list of the target locations and the times each target would be fired on.

Captain Smith then asked, "Any questions?"

"How long do they expect we will be here, Captain?" Karch inquired.

"I don't think it will be very long, but I can't say for sure."

Upon arriving at the makeshift FDC, Kenny informed his Marines of what he had just learned. Staff Sergeant Flatts took the target list and began delegating instructions as the Marines set to computing firing data for the howitzers.

The next day at the newly occupied fire support base, Hotel Battery went hot. At least twice an hour, the guns fired on targets somewhere in the distant hills and valleys. Around suppertime that day, they were resupplied with many pallets of ammo.

"Looks like we have a lot more shooting to do," Kenny stated to his men.

Just a few seconds later, one of the Marines put down his headset and told Kenny, "Sir, the captain wants to talk to you at the XO pit."

"Thanks, Bevins."

Crossing the uneven terrain, Kenny could still hear the sound of the last ammo bird flying away. Suddenly the helicopter rotors were drowned out by a loud rushing sound overhead. Then, to his right and down the mountain, there were two loud explosions. Kenny wheeled around and dashed back to his men at the FDC. The battery was under attack, and they all needed to take cover.

The next moment was surreal. Kenny received the force of a tremendous blast from his left. The concussive force picked him up and threw him back to the ground with great pain. Then there was nothing.

CHAPTER FIFTEEN

WOUNDED IN ACTION AND RETIRED

Vietnam

KENNY DID NOT KNOW how long he had been unconscious but quickly recognized the presence of the Navy corpsman attending to him.

"Take it easy, Lieutenant. You're going to be okay," the seaman assured him. Kenny heard the high pitch of turning helicopter rotors.

"What's going on? What happened?" asked Kenny. He began to recognize his current surroundings and realized he was being medivacked. He felt a sharp pain as he tried to raise his head to look around the helicopter. It was then that Kenny realized there were three other Marines on stretchers and being evacuated. He also discovered he was able to see from only one eye. Kenny raised his hand to his face and felt a large gauze bandage. Instinctively, Kenny lifted the bandage and was relieved that he could see from the covered eye.

"Try to be still, Lieutenant. You have a nasty head wound, and moving your head will aggravate it. We have the bleeding stopped but it's necessary for you to not move," the corpsman told Kenny.

Vista

Like every person who had a loved one in Vietnam, Suzy worried about Kenny all the time and wrote letters to him daily. She'd heard others' stories, like her good friend Maria Smith who had twice received a visit from a casualty assistance call officer. But the terror she experienced that morning when the green sedan stopped in front of her parents' house was too much. She fainted on the walkway to the front porch.

"Suzy, Suzy darling. Can you hear me?" her mother pleaded.

Everything was a blur to Suzy as she responded to the smelling salts and found herself on the living room sofa. Suddenly, she grabbed her mother.

"Kenny, Kenny, oh God, *nooo!*"

Her mother said in a loud, firm voice, "Suzy, Kenny is alive. He was wounded, but he is alive and will be coming home to you."

Suzy was stunned and speechless. She sat up on the sofa, trying to make sense of what her mother just told her. It conflicted with the terrible shock from assuming the worst.

Mr. Miller got down on one knee beside his wife and daughter. Suzy grabbed her father and sobbed, still trying to register the information.

"I don't understand. What happened to Kenny? What happened to my husband?"

Mr. Miller quickly said, "This Marine officer came by to inform you that Kenny has been wounded and is currently in a hospital in Vietnam. He will likely be flown to the United States in the next few days."

"How bad is he wounded? How was he wounded and where is the wound?"

"I'm sorry, ma'am. I cannot tell you any additional details because I don't know them," replied the Marine lieutenant.

"Lieutenant, do you have any idea when we may learn more about

Kenny's injury, or when he may come home?" Mr. Miller asked.

Before the lieutenant could respond, Suzy's mother suddenly gasped, "Oh God! Does Kathy know yet? Lieutenant, does his mother know? She lives in Carlsbad."

The lieutenant was upset with the whole situation. He almost lost his composure as he apologized again and said, "I'm very sorry, but I don't know whether or not Lieutenant Reynolds's mother has been notified. I was assigned to notify his wife, and that is why I'm here. I am very sorry."

Suzy and her parents all shared the same thought as they frantically worried how to best handle the terrible task of notifying Kathy that her son was currently in a hospital in Vietnam.

Suzy spoke first. "We have to tell Manny as soon as possible."

After a couple minutes of agonizing over Kenny's situation, the Millers and Suzy agreed that using Dr. Wheeler to notify Kathy and using Pappy to notify Manny was their best course of action. While her father dialed Dr. Wheeler, Suzy and her mother held each other. It was obvious from the one-sided conversation the ladies heard that Dr. Wheeler was asking more questions than Mr. Miller could answer.

Suzy's father told Dr. Wheeler, "We're going to call First Sergeant Smith to notify Manny."

When Mr. Miller finally hung up, Suzy thought her dad was about to break down and cry. Louise immediately went to hold him.

"Oh my," he said with a drained voice. "I feel like we need to be with the Wheelers. I can't imagine what Kathy is going through with her son wounded and thousands of miles away from her embrace."

"I understand, Dad, but we have to tell Pappy Smith. Even without the horrible task of telling Manny, this is going to be very hard on Pappy. He helped Kathy raise him." Suzy announced, "I'll call Pappy Smith."

"Oh, Suzy. Are you sure? It will be extremely difficult, and we don't know how Manny's grandfather will react."

"I know it will be hard, but I want to tell Pappy. And I want us to do it in person."

"Okay, let's get ready to go," said her dad.

"Should we stop by to see Kathy on the way to San Diego?" asked Suzy's mother.

"I understand your intentions, dear, but I think our priority is to inform Manny and his family in San Diego. Maybe we can stop in Carlsbad on our way back," replied Mr. Miller.

"Dad's right, Mom. Let's go."

Suzy was surprised that she was so composed as the three of them drove south on the interstate. She was very anxious to learn more about Kenny's injury and when he would get back to the United States. She tried to put it out of her mind but couldn't avoid remembering the horror of the moment she'd seen the casualty officer get out the car. From there her thoughts went to Maria Smith and the fact that her husband was killed in action and would never come home to see his wife or children again.

"Suzy, are you okay?" her mother asked as she saw the tears on Suzy's cheeks.

"I'm okay, Mom. This all seems like such a terrible dream."

Arriving at the Riveras' restaurant, Mr. Miller dropped his wife and daughter near the front entrance and went to park the car. Lori and Maria spotted the two ladies through the window and emerged to greet them.

"Hey, what a great surprise," Lori exclaimed.

But all the smiles and excitement turned to silence when Lori and her mother-in-law saw Suzy's expression.

"Oh, God!" cried Lori.

Maria could say nothing. She covered her mouth as tears formed in her eyes.

Lori and Suzy embraced as Suzy told her cousin that Kenny was alive but hospitalized with an unknown injury, and that they were still waiting to learn more details.

Pappy and Uncle Manuel were still inside, but the actions and expressions of the four ladies outside said it all. Within a few seconds,

Mr. Miller joined the ladies, and they all went inside. As the seven of them sat to talk and console each other, the conversation naturally focused on Manny and Kathy. Suzy did her best to inform everybody at the restaurant of what had transpired up to that moment, but even after intense discussion, it seemed that nothing was resolved except that Pappy would greet Manny when he arrived home from school. And Uncle Manuel would naturally tell Aunt Carmella.

No one paid attention to the phone ringing until one of the waiters picked it up and moments later said in an elevated voice, "First Sergeant, this is Dr. Wheeler on the phone. He says he is sure you will want to speak with him."

"Dr. Wheeler, how is Kathy? How are you?"

All eyes were on Pappy as he spoke on the phone. The tension was almost unbearable. Pappy showed very little emotion and asked only a few questions, nodding and looking up at the others every once in a while.

Finally, Pappy informed Dr. Wheeler, "We expect Manny to arrive home in thirty minutes or less. We'll all be here for him and break the news. In the meantime, please give our love to Kathy and assure her that she is in our thoughts and prayers. And we will keep you informed the minute we learn anything more."

After Pappy hung up, he told everyone, "As we expected, Kathy took the news very badly. Dr. Wheeler has canceled all his appointments and will be home with her as long as needed. They're in the same situation we are. What we don't know is so difficult to handle."

As she sat between her mother and her cousin, Suzy broke down and cried a little. Uncle Manuel rose and lingered for a few seconds before leaving the group. He still had the difficult task of telling his wife the terrible news. Pappy wandered outside. He sought to be alone and to intercept his grandson before Manny entered the restaurant.

Looking down the street, Pappy realized he had already been spotted. Manny's arm was in the air, waving at his grandfather. When Pappy did not respond with his typical enthusiasm, an uncomfortable feeling came over Manny, reinforced when he drew close enough to see the look on his grandfather's face.

"Pappy, what's wrong?"

"Kenny has been wounded. We don't yet know the extent of his injury, only that he's in a military hospital over there."

The two men hugged to support each other.

"He's going to be all right, Pappy. He's going to be all right."

Vietnam

"Lieutenant Reynolds, take your time in responding. If you can hear me, I would like you to wave your hand," said a person Kenny could not see.

Kenny waved his hand. Only a second later the same voice said, "Lieutenant, try to not be scared that you cannot see. We have bandages covering both your eyes as a precaution."

"Am I allowed to speak?"

"By all means, if you are comfortable speaking, please do," answered the voice.

"How long will I need to keep the blindfold on my eyes?"

"Let's take them off in a little while. If things go well and you see fairly well, we may leave them off," Kenny was told.

"I can go a little longer without seeing, Doctor, but if you want me to heal properly, I really need to call California and speak to my wife. Can someone take me to a phone where I can call California?"

The doctor realized no medicine or treatment would help Kenny more than the phone call he was requesting, so he instructed the attending corpsman to take Kenny to the hospital phone room.

Unable to get Suzy in Vista, Kenny decided to call his mother.

As luck would have it, his mom answered the phone on the first ring with a quick "Hello."

"Mom, it's me."

Unfortunately, Kenny was not able to speak with his mother; she broke down crying at the sound of his voice.

"Mom, Mom, can you hear me?"

A few seconds later he heard on the phone, "Kenny, it's Dr. Wheeler. Your mom is okay, just very much overcome with emotion."

"I understand, sir. Please assure everybody that I'm okay."

Dr. Wheeler said he would gladly do so and then told Kenny, "Here is you mother. She says she can talk now."

"Oh, Kenny, we are so worried. The young Marine really didn't know much. How are you, dear?"

"I'm okay, Mom. Try to not worry."

After a short talk with his mother, Kenny asked, "Mom, I tried to call Suzy, but there was no answer at the Millers' house. Do you know where she is and how she is?"

"Like the rest of us, Suzy is worried sick about you. Right now she's heading home from the restaurant where they broke the news to Manny and Pappy and all the family there."

"Okay, Mom. Thanks. I'll call again soon."

After hanging up, Kenny decided to call Manny, but as crazy luck would have it, he accidentally called Suzy's number again, and the call was answered after the first ring.

"Hello, Miller residence."

Kenny couldn't believe it as he struggled to say, "Suzy, it's me."

"Oh, Kenny, I love you and miss you so much. I was so terrified I'd lost you."

During the remaining minutes they had on the phone, Kenny couldn't answer many of her questions.

"I'm sorry, Lieutenant, but we have to end this call soon," the operator cut in.

"I'll try to call tomorrow, Suzy. Do me a favor and tell Manny I said 'Oorah.'"

"Okay, I prefer to avoid talking to him, but I will because you asked."

Kenny was thrilled with Suzy's response. The fact that she was slamming Manny told Kenny that she would be okay.

"That's my girl. Love you."

"How was the call with your wife, Lieutenant Reynolds?" asked the corpsman after Kenny returned to his bed.

"It was so good to hear her voice."

"Glad to hear it," the corpsman replied with a smile and a nod.

The next day Kenny inquired, "What's the main reason I'm here, sir?"

"Oh, I think a four-inch gash across the back of your head is reason enough," said the doctor. "How do you feel?"

"Now and then I have a small headache, but I'm feeling pretty well."

"That's good to hear, but we will continue to watch you closely. Head injuries can flare up and cause problems later, so you are not out of the woods yet," the doctor warned Kenny.

"Sir, I have to ask about the other men from my battery. There were several men on the bird I was on. Can you tell me anything?"

After a moment the doctor said, "I really don't have many details, but I learned the attack was short and vicious. They hit the battery with a good many rockets and small arms, then fled into the jungle."

"What about injuries? How many and how bad?"

"I heard there were several killed and seven or eight wounded."

After a short period of silence, a corpsman said, "Doctor, we're ready to change the dressing on the lieutenant's wound."

"Good, let's get to it. Lieutenant, please sit here so I can undo the bandages and have a look at your head."

Kenny did not feel anything as the process began, but as the bandages attached to dried blood began to separate from Kenny's scalp, it hurt a little. Then the doctor placed his hands on Kenny's head, and there was a painful sensation. After the doctor moved back around to stand in front of him, Kenny cautiously opened his eyes.

"Doctor, my vision is a little fuzzy."

"I'm not surprised. I thought you might experience serious vision problems, but your wound seems to not affect your eyes too much," the doc stated.

"That's good, right?" Kenny asked.

"Of course that's good, and the stitches look very tight with very little seepage from the slice in the back of your head."

"Just across the flesh, and not my skull?"

"You are extremely lucky. The shrapnel grazed the back of your skull just a little bit. Another inch or so, and there would have been much more serious consequences," the doctor said. "We still want to watch you very closely. We don't yet know what, if any, effect there is to your brain and your cognitive processes."

To Kenny's great surprise, two days later he was informed he had a seat scheduled on the medivac aircraft heading to San Diego the next day. He was going back to the world.

Coronado

"I am confident I can handle debarking from the aircraft by myself," Kenny told the corpsman.

"You probably can, sir, but our orders are to assist everyone," replied the corpsman.

Five or six ambulances were staged outside the aircraft, but Kenny and many others were given the opportunity to walk the short distance to the terminal. As they entered the terminal door, a chorus of cheers and greetings met them.

Kenny quickly spotted Suzy and the others there for him. "Hey, babe!" he yelled.

Tears and cries of happiness abounded as people greeted and hugged their loved ones.

"I love you so much, Kenny!"

Kenny soon noticed that everyone was hugging only his torso. Even without the very obvious bandage around his head, everyone was well aware of his wound and careful to not touch his neck or head.

The hardest part of the reunion for Kenny was seeing his mother cry.

"It's okay, Mom. I'm going to be okay."

The welcome event in the terminal continued for less than thirty minutes before the announcement was made that family and other visitors should begin to depart and service members should board the large bus on the aircraft tarmac.

Kenny spoke to everyone as a group. "I'll call Suzy as soon as I learn where I'll be and what my daily schedule is. She will call all of you to let you know."

Naval Hospital

"You know you don't get a discount for multiple visits to this place," the nurse said as she entered Kenny's room.

Caught off guard, Kenny could only respond with "What?"

"I don't expect you to remember me, Lieutenant, but I remember you from your time here several years ago."

"I'm very sorry, but I must confess I don't remember you."

"My name is Jean Horner, and you have no reason to be sorry. I remember you very well because you went on to play football at SDSU. My husband and I are SDSU football fans," the nurse explained.

As they discussed SDSU football, Kenny and Nurse Horner were startled by a deep voice.

"I hope you realize, Lieutenant Reynolds, that your football days are gone forever."

The originator of the surprise comment walked into Kenny's room and added, "My name is Dr. Diego. I'm on the hospital neurology staff. Also a fan of San Diego State football. And I'm your doctor, Lieutenant. Get yourself situated, and as soon as possible I want a current set of

X-rays of the back of your head."

"Yes, sir."

"I remember one of your visitors. He was here almost every day, as I recall. Frequently in his Marine uniform," stated Jean.

"That's correct, and you can expect to see Manny here frequently during this stay."

"Lieutenant, if you have nothing else for me, I should be going. We'll have plenty of time to talk in the weeks ahead."

"To be honest, I've been feeling really good and my head doesn't hurt. I'm hoping I won't be here very long. When will I learn my daily schedule?"

"I'm afraid I can't answer at this time, but I suspect you will learn tomorrow," Jean replied.

"That's great."

"See you tomorrow, Lieutenant. You really should try to get some sleep and start getting back on San Diego time," Jean said as she left the room.

The only problem with Jean's well-intended advice was that Kenny wasn't at all sleepy. Later that evening, Kenny was deep in thought and never heard the door open and close, allowing someone to slip in and stand quietly in the room with a big smile on her face.

When Kenny finally turned, he was momentarily speechless, then blurted out, "Suzy!"

"Quiet," Suzy said quickly, putting her finger to her lips.

"How did you get here?"

"In case you've forgotten, this is not the first time I've visited you in this hospital, and I still know my way around."

"I'm so glad to see you. I've missed you so much," Kenny said. He wrapped his arms around his beautiful wife and held her close. Suzy returned the embrace as they kissed passionately.

"I love you, and I need to make love to you."

"But your injury won't let us," she protested.

"My injury is not as bad as they're saying. I don't have any headaches, and my vision is perfect."

"Oh, Kenny. I thought of it as I was walking here. But I could not live with myself if anything happened to you."

"I know how I feel, and I feel good. All the examinations and X-rays have good results. They are being overly cautious, and I appreciate it. But I am really feeling good."

"I hate that I can't control myself around you."

"That's how I feel as well."

After a short period of silence, Suzy sighed and said, "We have to be gentle to avoid any movement of your head and neck. And we have to be quiet, and we have to lock the door."

Kenny nodded slightly in agreement and moved to lock the door. Then he turned back to see Suzy pull down the bedspread and top sheet of his bed. While Kenny stood mesmerized by Suzy's presence, she reached under her skirt and removed the black panties she was wearing.

"Come here and lie down on your back."

"I can't believe you're here. This is a dream come true," Kenny whispered as he got into the bed and rolled onto his back.

"Aren't you the Marine who often told me that if you want something very much, you have to make it happen?"

There was no more conversation, but the smiles they exchanged said it all.

A short time later, after she unlocked the door, Suzy told Kenny, "Now do you believe that I missed you more than words could describe?"

"We have a lot of wonderful memories, but this has to be the new leading memory," Kenny replied as he kissed his wife.

The young couple spent several more hours that evening talking and reminiscing and enjoying being together. When Kenny could not suppress a big yawn, Suzy took it as her cue that it was time to leave.

In another part of San Diego, Manny was on Cloud Nine. "Hey, buckaroo!" he said to little Charlie as he picked up his baby boy and spun around in a circle.

"As I expected, someone is happy to have his best friend safely home."

"I can't describe how great it felt to see Kenny and Suzy hug. However, I have to confess that the memories it dredged up were uncomfortable."

Lori moved to Manny and put her arms around him. "Oh, Manny, we are so lucky to have our love and little boy and family and friends."

After a minute or two of holding each other, Manny told Lori, "I have some reading to do for class tomorrow."

"Speaking of school, when are they going to make you decide on your major? It seems to me you're heading for a degree in education just like Kenny, but then, why should I expect anything else?"

"Honestly, being at the high school and working with the boys on the wrestling team has got me thinking about a second career as a teacher and coach after retiring from the Marines."

"Really, Manny! What a big surprise and total shock that is! I would never have guessed in a million years that you are considering teaching and coaching," Lori cried out with her best melodramatic voice and gestures as she rolled her eyes. "It's been very obvious how miserable you are as you tolerate those terrible kids. I'm just amazed you've survived the situation. I've thought about having you placed on suicide watch because those boys make you so miserable."

Manny just stood there and grinned at Lori's teasing, but when she stopped he went into attack mode. "Why, Lori, I am offended by your harassment, and I do believe you are sassing me. We all know your mother recommends that I paddle your cute little bottom when you get sassy with me."

As Manny moved toward Lori, she raised her fists toward him and said, "You can forget what you're thinking, because it ain't gonna happen!"

In a flash, Lori snatched up little Charlie, ran to the bedroom, and closed the door. Then she said through the door, "Let me alone, bully. There will be no paddling today, and that's just as well because you have reading to do for school tomorrow, so why don't you go to the restaurant or the library and do your reading?"

"Aw, come on, sweetie. I was just kidding. Why don't you come out and give me a goodbye kiss."

"Forget it, weirdo. Go do your reading, and I'll see you later!"

"Manny, to what do we owe the pleasure of your visit?" Aunt Carmella asked as he entered the restaurant.

Hearing Manny's name, his mother came out from the office area to greet her son and ask her favorite question: "How is my grandson today?"

"I'm fine, Mom. It's good of you to be concerned for me and ask how I'm doing."

"I know you're good. I see you standing here in front of me. But I don't see that precious little baby boy, so I am asking about him."

"Charlie was just a little bit fussy, and I need some peace and quiet to study, so I came here."

"Next time have Lori bring Charlie here, and you stay home to study," Uncle Manuel said with a big smirk.

"Did I miss the announcement of the daily comedy hour?"

"I think I'll call Lori to see if she needs anything for Charlie," Maria said, picking up the telephone behind the counter.

For a brief moment Manny panicked as he envisioned Lori answering the phone and telling Maria that little Charlie wasn't fussy. Without hesitating, Manny said, "If Charlie is sleeping, you may wake him."

"Yes, you are correct. I won't call now."

Manny breathed a quick sigh of relief, but he knew his mother would ask Lori about the matter sooner or later.

Back at their apartment that evening, Manny told Lori, "You know, babe, I don't know why I haven't discussed where I'm going with my studies. I feel terribly guilty about it. You are my wife, the mother of my child, and I want to share the rest of my life with you. Please forgive me."

Seeing that Manny was genuinely upset, Lori moved to her tough Marine husband and put her arms around him. "It hasn't been a real big problem with me, babe. I have been very content to see you enjoying school, so I'm not really worried about the details."

"I have a number of years remaining in the Marine Corps after I get my degree, but it certainly wouldn't be a bad idea to consider some long-term planning."

"Why don't you get an appointment to speak with your academic advisor?"

"I will—and we'll speak to him together!"

"You want me to go with you?"

"Of course. I want you to hear any guidance I am given. You are the smartest person I've ever known."

"So, you're finally admitting that I'm smart."

"Lori, I've always known you are very intelligent. You married me, didn't you?"

She tried to not laugh, but it was a wasted effort. Then she retorted, "It's obvious you also think of yourself as very clever."

"Like Kenny and I always say, 'We're Ed Sullivan material.'"

"You guys are straitjacket material in my book."

"Again, I must remind you that you married me."

As they embraced in laughter, Manny stated, "I think it's about time to hit the hay. I have a busy day of classes, and then I'm going to visit Kenny."

"I agree it's time for bed, especially since I'm in a sassy mood."

"I love you!"

Venting his frustration more than a month later, Kenny told his best friend, "I've been feeling really good, and I keep telling the doctors that, but no one seems to want to discuss allowing me to go home."

"I'm not sure what to tell you, Ken. Have you requested permission to go on convalescent leave? Because you'll be living so close, you can assure the doctors you'll come in frequently. Heck, you could really make it in here daily if that's what they want."

Kenny added, "I asked the doctor if I can drive as soon as I'm released, and he said it may be possible because my test results have been good."

"Even if you can't drive, Suzy or I or others can transport you to and from the hospital."

"Heck yeah. Tomorrow I'm going to press the issue with the doctor."

"Good luck, buddy. But I also had another serious topic I want to discuss while the two of us are alone," Manny told Kenny.

"Let's hear it."

"After Lori and I talked, we decided I should have a meeting with my academic advisor. So, I contacted him, and he said he was planning to call me in to discuss things."

"That's great, Manny. When do you see him?"

"Lori and I have a meeting with him tomorrow afternoon."

"Lori is going with you? Great thinking."

"After we see my advisor, we want to come here to see you and grab some chow."

"That's outstanding! I'm excited to see Lori, but dinner in the hospital cafeteria doesn't count as taking her out to a romantic dinner."

"Yeah, she's already reminded me of that," Manny said with a grin.

"Listen, stop by to see me, and then you two go to the waterfront for dinner."

"I think that's an outstanding idea."

Manny stood to depart. Nurse Horner entered with her usual pleasant greeting, then moved close to the boys and said in a soft voice, "Lieutenant Reynolds, I can't give you any details because I don't know any; however, I think a decision has been made on your health and rehabilitation situation. I think they may talk to you as early as tomorrow."

Manny and Kenny looked at each other with victorious fists and big smiles. Then Kenny picked up his nurse and hugged her. Two seconds after Kenny put her down, Manny picked her up for a second hug.

When Manny released Nurse Horner, she said with a big smile, "I can't wait to get home to tell my husband about the two men flirting with me today."

Then Kenny planted a big kiss on Jean's cheek and said, "Are you going to tell him about the kissing that went on today?"

"Let's just keep that little secret between the three of us," Jean replied.

After the nurse left, Manny stated, "I thought I was having a big day tomorrow, but now I'm much more excited about your meeting."

"I almost wish she hadn't said anything. It's going to be really difficult sleeping tonight."

"Try to hang in there."

"I will, and good luck with your advisor."

"See you tomorrow."

The next day, Manny and Lori were excited to get to the hospital to see Kenny. They had a very positive meeting with Manny's advisor and were anxious to share the news. More importantly, they wanted to find out if Kenny had learned anything about the status of his rehab and how much longer he would have to stay at the hospital.

Upon entering Kenny's room, Manny and Lori were delighted to see Suzy sitting in one of the chairs. But the look on Suzy's face was not her usual beautiful smile. Manny and Lori looked at Kenny, and it was easy to see that he was forcing his smile.

While the two cousins hugged, Manny and Kenny shook hands, and Manny broke the awkward silence. "What did they tell you, Ken?"

"The good news is that I'm leaving the hospital, and the bad news is that I am leaving the Marine Corps."

Suzy began to cry, and Kenny kneeled down to comfort her.

"Everyone who knows you and everyone who has served with you knows your discharge will be a big loss for the Corps. But we knew it was a possibility from the beginning," Manny said sympathetically.

"I told Suzy it could happen, but I never discussed it with her because it was not something we wanted to happen."

Suzy surprised the other three by saying, "The great news is he won't ever have to go back to Vietnam. The bad news is that Kenny will no longer be Lieutenant Reynolds, United States Marine Corps."

"That's not correct, Suzy. You've heard us say it before. 'Once a Marine, always a Marine,' and legally Kenny will always have the title 'Lieutenant Reynolds, United States Marine Corps, Retired.'"

"So, the Marine Corps is making you retire?" Lori asked.

Kenny explained that according to the officer who talked with him earlier that afternoon, a medical board determined that the wound to the back of Kenny's head made him vulnerable to further injuries that could have more serious consequences. Therefore, it was the board's recommendation that Kenny be medically retired with the rank of first lieutenant.

Suzy started to sniffle again, but this time she caught herself and said, "I'm sorry to be crying, but the whole situation is so overwhelming."

"Do your folks know, and how about Kathy and Dr. Wheeler?" Lori asked Suzy.

"No, just the four of us know," Kenny answered.

"Maybe we can talk about it over dinner?" Suzy suggested.

"I agree; where do we want to eat?" asked Lori.

"How about the corn dog stand at Disneyland?" Manny said slyly.

"That's got my vote!" Kenny quickly added.

The two girls just looked at each other, smiled, and shook their heads.

"Hey, we have more to talk about than Kenny's discharge," Suzy stated.

"Yeah, how was your meeting with your school advisor?" asked Kenny.

"We have a ton of things to talk about, but let's get to a good place to eat first. Lori is starving," Manny told the others.

"Remind me again why you married such a big fat liar?" said Suzy.

Lori smirked and then said, "It's been a while since we ate at Dave's. Is everybody okay with Dave's?"

"We'll see you there in thirty minutes," Kenny replied.

"Check," Manny responded.

At the restaurant, Lori was the first to broach the subject. "Do you have a plan to notify your folks about the latest development?"

"To be honest, we both think it won't be a big deal. Kenny and I are confident that our folks will be very happy to learn that Kenny is leaving active duty," Suzy quickly responded.

The waiter handed out menus and filled their water glasses as he told them the daily specials.

Manny advised the others, "I haven't eaten here many times, but the few meals I had were all very good."

"What meal have you ever eaten that was not very good?" Suzy challenged.

"I think I'm going to have the stuffed pork chops," Manny said, ignoring her.

After they gave the waiter their orders, the discussion quickly returned to informing family about the big news. It was not a joyful topic, but the four friends considered some of the different career options ahead of Kenny.

When no one had spoken for about thirty seconds, Kenny declared, "That is enough about me. Suzy and I want to hear about the college boy in our presence. What did your advisor tell you? Do you have a target graduation date? Come on, what's going on?"

Manny and Lori looked at each other for a second before Manny spoke. "As you know, in the degree completion program, I am required to carry a full load of classes every semester in the school year, and by doing that I should graduate in eighteen months."

The four friends spontaneously cheered the good news. Most of the restaurant glanced their way, including the manager.

Approaching their table, the manager asked, "Can you share the good news with us?"

"It appears our Lieutenant Smith is on track to graduate from SDSU," Kenny said.

"Oorah," the manager said with a smile. He waved over their waiter, whispered something in his ear, then bid the table a good day.

Less than a minute later, the waiter came to their table and presented the four friends with a bottle of wine, saying, "Compliments of Dave's!"

Two more servers approached with their food.

As the four dug into their food, they returned to the subject at hand.

"Everybody thinks of our guys as Mutt and Jeff or Tom and Jerry or Heckle and Jeckle. So, I'm confident people won't even raise an eyebrow in the future when they learn Kenny and Manny go by the titles of Coach Reynolds and Coach Smith," Lori said.

"You think you're so smart, Lori, but I'm not sure what career path I will pursue now that I'm joining the 1st Civ Div," Kenny replied.

"I was just kidding, Kenny. You'll likely end up pushing papers, talking on the phone, and sitting in an office all day" was Lori's quick response.

"Yeah, that's the way I see it," Manny added.

"You have some say in Kenny's career, Suzy. Don't you agree with Manny and me?" Lori said to her cousin.

Suzy looked at Lori first, then at Manny. When she looked at Kenny, she lost her composure and started to laugh. "Kenny, do you really think you can fool Manny and Lori? They know you as well as you know yourself." After hesitating for a moment, Suzy continued, "Sweetie, even before today, we talked of you being a teacher and coach like your dad."

The mention of Kenny's dad created a short period of silence.

Kenny broke it. "Okay, okay! What if I am easier to read that a third-grade library book? I just wanted to throw smarty-pants Lori off track for just a moment."

"Not even for a moment," said Lori with a smarty-pants grin on her face.

"Manny, you haven't added much to the conversation. What are you thinking?" Suzy asked.

"I'm thinking these pork chops are almost as good as your dad's ribs. I wonder if they have any more in the kitchen?" Manny said with a straight face.

The other three smiled.

"There was never any doubt in my mind that one day my best friend and brother would be an outstanding coach and teacher," Manny said pointedly. "I hope that one day, whenever I join the USMC retired list, he will take me under his wing and be my mentor as I pursue a career in teaching and coaching."

It was like the two Marines were on the drill field as they simultaneously stood and hugged for a few moments, followed by a hearty slap on the back. Lori and Suzy got a little teary eyed as their husbands sat down again.

"That was a very poignant segue into our other topic of discussion," Suzy stated.

"Why dive into the pool when you can make a bigger splash with a cannonball!" Manny said.

"My sentiments exactly, sir," said Kenny.

"Why thank you, sir," responded Manny.

The cousins glanced at each other and shook their heads.

"I have no doubt you will also be an outstanding teacher and coach one day, Manny. But for some reason, I've never thought of you as being anything but a Marine," Suzy stated.

"Thank you, Suzy. I accept that as a big compliment, and while I will always be a Marine in my heart, the fact remains that one day I too must pursue another career," Manny replied.

"Today at the advisor's office, Manny declared himself to be an education major like Kenny was at SDSU. I've suspected for a while that my guy would enjoy teaching. Heaven knows he enjoys working those boys on the wrestling team," Lori declared.

"I do enjoy my time with those young hard chargers."

"You know, I think most people will agree that discussions are more interesting when there is an occasional element of surprise," Suzy stated. She wore a small, enigmatic smile.

"Are you saying the four of us are boring?" challenged Lori.

"Hey, if the shoe fits . . ." Kenny said.

"I say we go out and get into a fight with the local motorcycle gang," Lori said.

Manny chuckled. "I told you not to give my wife that second glass of wine."

Standing by their vehicles in the parking lot, Lori declared, "We used to laugh and have so much fun at the beach and Disneyland. But now, I'm afraid we may indeed be a little boring. Next time, we must have a third bottle of wine and renew our old verbal abuse."

After a moment of silence, Suzy spoke with a little more excitement and volume. "I always look forward to us getting together, even if my husband thinks we're boring. But is now a good time to ask him if he thinks being a daddy will be boring?"

"Yes, yes, yes!" screamed Lori as she wrapped her arms around her cousin and squealed with delight.

Manny gaped at Kenny. "Why didn't you say something?"

Kenny shot Suzy a sour look for spilling the beans.

"Sorry, sweetheart. I had to say something tonight to break the boredom."

"Cousin, you are the queen of breaking the boredom," Lori said.

"It seems to me you two didn't waste any time," Manny observed.

"Actually, the timing was perfect," Suzy added. "And no matter if the baby is a boy or a girl, we are considering 'Hospital' for a middle name."

"I don't believe it! You two made a baby in Kenny's hospital room!" Manny shouted.

"Turn down the volume, buddy. This is kind of private information," Kenny said.

"Am I correct in assuming your mom knows?" asked Lori.

"Yes, she took me to the doctor," Suzy replied.

Manny cleared his throat before declaring, "Earlier today, I thought this was a big day for me. But you two Reynolds kids had a day that makes me want to fall asleep thinking about my news."

"Isn't that the truth," added Lori.

"So, let's get back to the subject of the hospital," Manny said.

Suzy quickly replied, "Forget it, Smith. You will never learn all the horny details you are so anxiously inquiring about."

Kenny lost his composure and started laughing at the dumbfounded look on Manny's face. That set Lori and Suzy off, and moments later the four old friends were all hooting with laughter.

Lori regained her composure first. "Well, if this is a boring evening, what will happen when we do have a crazy evening?"

"I can't wait to find out," replied Kenny.

CHAPTER SIXTEEN

MANNY'S GRADUATION

San Diego

MORE OFTEN THAN HE liked to admit, Manny found himself reminiscing about the past. He knew some people referred to it as daydreaming and a waste of time, but Manny didn't consider it to be unhealthy. Although he didn't make it to church every Sunday, Manny never failed to thank God each night for all his blessings, and he truly felt he led a blessed life. Yes, events were set in motion in the worst way when Manny's father was killed. But after Pappy Smith entered Manny's life and Kenny became his best friend, things went well in so many ways. When he joined the Marine Corps, Manny fulfilled his life's goal of being a United States Marine, just like his father and grandfather. He still got goose bumps when he heard the Marine Corps hymn. However, the greatest blessings of his life were Lori and young Charlie, and the new baby Lori was now carrying.

"Lieutenant Manny Smith" sounded from the public address system.

Suddenly, Manny was terrified, unsure if he'd missed hearing his name a first time. He started across the stage to receive his baccalaureate degree from SDSU. Clutching the hardback folder securely in his left hand and shaking hands with the dean, Manny continued across the stage and waved to his family. Lori was waving both fists in the air. On Lori's right were Mr. and Mrs. Baker, and to Lori's left were Manny's mother and Pappy.

Even with hundreds of people clapping and cheering, Manny heard his grandfather shouting, "WAY TO GO, HARD CHARGER!" The final family member in that row was Cindy. In the row immediately behind sat Kenny and Suzy, beside Kathy and Dr. Wheeler. Aunt Carmella and Uncle Manuel had young Charlie and young Teddy back at the restaurant where preparations were underway for the graduation party.

Manny was only able to get a limited number of tickets to the graduation ceremony, but there was no limit to the people welcome to the graduation party. Maria, Lori, and Carmella conspired to keep all the congratulations cards from Manny until the party, so a large pile of envelopes and several boxes waited on a table at one of the eating booths.

It was very obvious that Manny had many Marine Corps friends in attendance at the party. They may have been wearing civilian attire, but a quick glance at their haircuts was a dead giveaway. That was especially true of the Marines from the recruit depot where a "high and tight" haircut was the norm.

Because he was attending a civilian school in civilian clothes, Manny's hair was very obviously not the DI haircut he previously wore, and more than one Marine enjoyed asking Manny about it. Several of them offered to buy him a Marine Corps haircut, and many smiles were shared on that topic. There were also a few Marines at the party from Camp Pendleton.

Just about everyone who knew Manny also knew Pappy, and the old first sergeant received plenty of well wishes at the party. Marines unfailingly respected the experience of those Marines who went before them and created the legacy of the Marine Corps.

Without Manny's knowledge, his family and friends had agreed that Kenny should give a speech and lead a toast to celebrate the day. Everyone was startled when First Sergeant Smith bellowed, "AT EASE, PEOPLE, AT EASE!"

As the once noisy crowd became very quiet, Kenny stepped up onto a makeshift platform and stated, "Ladies and gentlemen." With all eyes on Kenny, he said to the crowd, "We are all pleased to be here to celebrate the college graduation of our good friend, Lieutenant Manny Smith, United States Marine Corps!"

The room erupted in thunderous cheers from the civilians and "oorah" grunts from the Marines in attendance.

It took almost a minute for the crowd to quiet down, and Kenny continued, "I have to tell you that while a few family members have known Manny longer than me, no one knows him better. And that includes you, Lori."

Lori raised her hands and shook her head in agreement as much of the crowd laughed.

After making eye contact with Manny, Kenny told the crowd, "Like it was yesterday, I remember shooting baskets in my driveway in Lower Vale. I looked up and saw Manny walking my way. We casually talked and shot a few baskets before the neighborhood bully rode up on his bike. I was terrified when he started to pick on me. I was sure things were not going to end well, when suddenly Manny flashed by me and knocked the bully to the ground. He then proceeded to pounce on him and smacked him a few times before the crying bully got to his feet and quickly rode away."

The guests at the party roared their approval, and Kenny had to wait another minute to continue.

"After that day in Lower Vale, I should not have been surprised thirteen years later when he chose to fight an Oceanside motorcycle gang!" Kenny said with a louder and upbeat tone.

The crowd went wild, and Manny was mobbed by all who stood relatively nearby. Wisely keeping their distance from Manny, Lori and Suzy were laughing like crazy. Nobody at the party was enjoying Kenny's comments more than the two cousins, who had insisted that

Kenny mention the motorcycle gang fight in his remarks.

Kenny continued with some lighthearted stories about high school and Manny's preferred route of travel past the post office so he could see the Marine Corps recruiting poster in front. The guests at the party, especially the Marines, got a good chuckle from the story of the four-holer in Vietnam. However, Kenny's tone became more somber and the crowd quieter as Kenny said, "Many of us have seen Manny in uniform, and we know he wears the Bronze Star for valor. For anyone who may not know, I would very likely not be here today if Manny had not risked his life to pull my wounded body from an intense enemy mortar barrage."

The restaurant fell completely silent as Kenny swallowed back an unexpected wave of emotion. "Lieutenant Smith is without a doubt what we often refer to as a 'Marine's Marine.'"

The crowd quickly came back to life, and more "oorahs" filled the room.

"As long as I have known Manny, he has wanted to be a Marine. Anyone who has served with Lieutenant Smith knows he is an outstanding one. But I cannot speak of him without also emphasizing how much Manny loves his family and friends, and I thank the Lord that I am blessed to be a friend of Manny Smith."

Like the Red Sea, the crowd at the graduation party separated as Kenny and Manny walked toward each other. No one in attendance said a word; everyone there understood the friendship the two best friends shared. They hugged and slapped each other on the back. Lori and Suzy wiped their eyes, and Maria cried softly as she hugged Pappy Smith.

Kenny stepped away, leaving Manny by himself yet surrounded by all in attendance. Again, the room fell very quiet as everybody waited for Manny to speak.

It took a few seconds and several deep breaths, but as he controlled his composure, Manny said to his family and friends, "I am confident everyone knows my father was killed in Korea when I was very young, and that was the saddest moment of my life. But another very sad moment in my life was the day I disappointed my mother when I dropped out of college."

Manny paused before stating, "Many of my friends in the Marine Corps have encouraged me and supported my effort to get my college degree because it would be good for my career, and if my degree is good for my career, so be it. But I want to make clear to everyone in this restaurant today that the driving force for me to get my college degree was my mother."

Manny saw his mother approach him with tears streaming down her face, and the tough Marine could not fight the tears forming in his own eyes. Embracing his mother as she reached him, Manny said softly, "I love you, Mom."

The silence at that moment was deafening. Many of the "high and tight" attendees were fighting to maintain their stoicism. Pappy and Cindy joined the family hug, and people began to clap. Moments later, Lori, carrying little Charlie, approached with Uncle Manuel and Aunt Carmella in tow. Everybody in the restaurant appreciated the special moment Manny and his family were having. When the family hug ended, Manny found himself alone again. Additional words were expected from the man of the hour.

Manny continued, "It should be obvious to all that I have truly been blessed with a wonderful family. And while he avoided the family hug, my brother, Kenny Reynolds, is a special part of my family and my life. Kenny made it obvious that we share a special bond that started when we were young boys. And we know that we will maintain that special bond until we are both no longer on this earth.

"However, at this very moment I want you all to know that Kenny Reynolds is terrified. He is worried that I will get my payback and tell a few stories about him."

Manny's threat was well received by the crowd, but they were disappointed because Manny had only the best of stories about his friend and soul mate—a couple about growing up and going to school in Lower Vale, along with a story or two about the Marine

Corps, and finally the story of the two best friends meeting their wives at Disneyland.

After a brief silence, Manny said, "I owe so much to my mother and my grandfather. Their influence on my life has been so positive that it is difficult to describe. But describing my best friend's influence is simple: Ken Reynolds has been nothing less than a central part of my life since the day we met shooting baskets and getting into a fight."

The two best friends again hugged but said nothing. Nothing needed to be said.

CPSIA information can be obtained
at www.ICGtesting.com
Printed in the USA
LVHW100552240622
722033LV00003B/60